UP JUMPS THE DEVIL

UP JUMPS THE DEVIL

MICHAEL POORE

ecco

An Imprint of HarperCollins*Publishers*

HarperCollins books may be purchased for educational, business, or sales promotional use. For information, please write: Special Markets Department, HarperCollins Publishers, 10 East 53rd Street, New York, NY 10022.

FIRST EDITION

Designed by Suet Yee Chong

Library of Congress Cataloging-in-Publication Data has been applied for.

ISBN 978-0-06-206441-7

12 13 14 15 16 OV/RRD 10 9 8 7 6 5 4 3 2 1

for Mom and Bill

UP JUMPS THE DEVIL

1. The Wonderful, Terrible Show

Dayton, Ohio, 2005

JOHN SCRATCH LOOKED LIKE the Devil.

His fans said so. The All-Celebrity News Channel said so, too.

He climbed from his limo, zipping his pants.

Just as the door closed, cameras flashed on a pair of long, naked legs on leather upholstery.

Cameras swarmed John Scratch as he crossed a street in a low-rent suburb, walked across an unmowed yard to a house with peeling paint, and rang the doorbell.

Cameras rolled while he waited, black ponytail shining.

SIXTY MILLION PEOPLE watched John Scratch ring the doorbell a second time. While they waited, between snacks, they repeated what they'd read on the celebrity blogs.

"If the Devil's here on Earth, you know this show's exactly what he'd be doing."

"But he seems nice."

"Are you high? You couldn't be nice and do this show."

"He looks Italian."

"He looks like he's from Argentina."

"Like you know what someone from Argentina looks like. Besides, he's an American."

"How do you know that?"

Shrug. "Everyone knows the Devil's an American."

The door opened, and there stood tonight's guests.

The guests were always different, and always kind of the same. They might be rich or poor. They were always surprised by the lights and cameras. They always seemed a little scared of John Scratch, whom they recognized because, like everyone, they had seen his show. His wonderful, terrible show.

Tonight's guests were a husband and wife in their thirties. The man wore a tank top and had eyes like knives. He wore the tired, peevish look of a man who had peaked early, maybe in high school. The woman wore a Tweety Bird sweatshirt and a pound of eye makeup. She looked like the kind of woman who enjoyed talking about people behind their backs.

They were in love, though. The TV audience could see it in the way they answered the door like one person with two heads, leaning on each other a little.

John Scratch had come to make them an offer. That's what his TV show was for.

He offered them five million dollars to move far away and never see each other again.

They laughed, at first.

Then they both got the same exact haunted look.

"I wouldn't do it," said some of the sixty million viewers.

"I would," said others.

"Then something's *wrong* with you!"

"Something's wrong with *you*!"

That's how people watched the show.

On-screen, the man and woman talked. Together, first, then one at a time.

They fought, shouting, together.

She agreed to the offer.

He did not. Red-faced, he seized her by the elbow and said something the microphones couldn't catch. When she twisted away, stumbling, he lunged for John Scratch and had to be restrained.

The airwaves smash-cut to a commercial, and the crew retreated across the street.

JOHN SCRATCH WAS almost to the limo when the live audience around him began to shout and boil. At first it seemed as if they were excited about something.

No. Their voices were fearful.

Someone was pushing his way toward him. Bodyguards and cameras staggered and went down.

It was a mountain in a ski mask and gloves, holding a pistol in both hands.

John Scratch didn't look at the pistol; he looked at the big man's eyes. They were angry, but they were mostly frightened. They were complicated eyes. Like the eyes of the couple John Scratch had just destroyed, they were haunted.

They were also familiar.

John Scratch appeared to relax.

He looked up at the man the way you look up at a friend, and said, "It's going to be okay."

The man aimed his pistol and shot John Scratch six times.

BANG BANG BANG BANG BANG BANG!

On camera, it looked so cool, the way the limo door opened right behind John Scratch, and swallowed him up.

No one saw what became of the big man in the mask.

The limo raced for the hospital.

"Jesus, Johnny!" said his backseat companion, former child-star-turned-bad-girl recording artist Jenna Steele.

"Hand me those napkins," he said, coughing blood. "I'm trying not to bleed on the leather."

He'd been shot before. In fact, there were very few things that had not happened to him, because John Scratch really *was* the Devil.

The actual Devil. In a limo with Jenna Steele, a bag of Mexican weed, and six bullets in him.

He was an American, too. The fans and blogs were right about that.

He had been an American for a very long time.

2. The Village

Providence Bay, 1623

THE DEVIL HADN'T WANTED to be an American, at first.

Not the new kind, anyway. The white kind, with their ships and Bibles, who called themselves "English."

He much preferred the forest dwellers. He had lived among the Yellow Earth People, hunted with the Big Belly People, and farmed with the Corn People. He had traded with the Big Voice People, and with the Yellow Earth People after they were driven off by the Corn People and became the People Who Wander.

He had been happiest among the Falling Water People, in the South. It was easy to grow sleepy and content in their world, with its endless woods and great rivers. More like Eden than Eden had been.

Then the big wooden ships appeared, like houses on the water. White men stomped ashore, and built a fort they called Jamestown. The Devil moved north to get away from them, joining the Morning People, who lived near the sea where the sun first touched the land. But the big ships came there, too. Before he could say "Hell" they had popped ashore and made a fort. And then a village.

The Devil watched them from the forest, smoking mice in his corncob pipe, scratching his wooden head.

If the white people had a plan, he observed over time, it was this: Come ashore, build a fort, and starve to death in it.

"People like this can't amount to much," muttered the Devil.

The Jamestown whites had been stupid, too. They had dug for gold instead of planting food.

"Stupid," observed the warriors among the Morning People, who attacked the fort and came back all shot up, "but with fabulous weapons!"

"They'll have to go," said the Devil.

THE ENGLISH WHO landed in the North called themselves "Pilgrims." They learned faster than the Jamestown bunch. By the third spring, they learned how to plant food and store it so it didn't run out in winter, and how to cut back the woods to give them room to shoot at the Indians.

The Jamestown bunch had been allergic to work.

Thinking about Jamestown, the Devil couldn't help thinking about Pocahontas.

He tried *not* to think about Pocahontas.

ONE NIGHT, THE Devil smudged himself with black war paint, and snuck out of the woods, uphill, across the cow pasture, glistening with midnight dew, until he stood among the sleeping cows.

He awakened them with a soft, seductive "Moo."

"Moo," answered the cows, and trudged over to have their backs scratched.

Animals either loved or hated the Devil, just as they loved or hated other animals. Cows loved him.

Loved him, as it happened, to a degree the Pilgrims would have found shocking. One by one they turned their hind parts to him, and the Devil satisfied them, one by one.

The Devil was—always had been—a generous and undiscriminating lover. The old bull, Palestine, came thundering up to protest, stopped when he recognized the Devil, and thundered off again lest the Devil mistake him for something he wasn't.

× × ×

IN THE MORNING, the cows wandered in and were milked behind the pasture shed. Pilgrim women and children, dressed in black, crouched beside them like crows. The milk filled wooden buckets, steaming in the morning chill, and the buckets were carried indoors.

The Devil, like the Pilgrims, became crowlike. He roosted in the thatch atop the blacksmith's forge, and cast a dark eye all around. He tried not to think about Pocahontas. She wouldn't have understood.

The Pilgrims did as they were used to doing. Some of them shouldered their blunderbuss guns and took to the woods a-hunting. Others tended gardens. Their leaders gathered by the creek, arguing about whether to build a mill and a waterwheel, and about whether it was a sin to put berries in porridge.

"*Everything* can't be a sin, Elder Mather," said one.

"Life itself is a sin, Miles," said Elder Mather, the minister. "Original sin."

And someone else said, "Balls!" and another someone said, "Language, John," and Miles said they needed to strengthen the fort before they thought about luxuries like waterwheels. To which John replied that if a wheel and mill were a luxury, then eating must be a luxury, to which Miles replied that not getting eaten by Indians would be a luxury, too, if they didn't watch out.

Meanwhile, from the houses round about came a general mutter of discontent, and by and by the wives came out into the little lane between their homes.

William, Miles, John, and the other notables marched over to see what was the matter.

"The butter won't come," said the minister's wife, Jenny Mather.

The other wives echoed this complaint. It didn't matter how they knocked about with the paddle, neither butter nor buttermilk would form.

"You're stirring too fast," suggested John.

John's wife suggested that she had been churning butter for thirty years and knew how fast to stir.

"It's too warm," said Miles, and was ignored.

"Something frightened the cows, perhaps," said Elder Mather.

"The wind!" someone suggested.

"Wolves!" said another.

The wives sighed and went about other chores.

"Frightened, indeed," muttered Jenny Mather, who had green eyes like a cat. She gave the pasture and the woods a long, hard look, and headed home to do the spinning.

THE NEXT DAY and the next, no butter came.

It was a hard thing, for these new Americans. Butter was one of their few comforts.

The Devil put on his best gopher-skin leggings and went to trade furs inside the fort. The Pilgrims preferred to trade with Indians who had been baptized. They called them "Praying Indians." So a lot of the Morning People, including the Devil, got baptized in order to do business.

"Who's there?" asked the guard at the gate.

"A brother in Christ," said the Devil, and the gate opened.

Between transactions, he played softly upon his fiddle, Old Ripsaw, and surveyed the village with a secret eye. The Pilgrims seemed glum, distracted, like a holiday turned inside out.

Good.

The blacksmith, who came to trade a hatchet for a sack of fox hides, was a quiet man to begin with, and practically mute today. His thoughts were elsewhere, and the Devil easily cheated him two whole furs.

"What's wrong?" he asked Giles Dorrit, a fisherman. "Bad weather coming?"

"The butter won't come," growled Giles. "This beaver fur has a hole in it."

The Devil explained that beavers had holes for breathing underwater. Giles shrugged, and paid full price in dried mackerel.

It wasn't so much that there was no butter to eat, the Devil understood. Religion and superstition were much the same, and cows that gave no butter meant evil was afoot.

A few months of this might see them on their way, the Devil thought, kneeling to gather his stock and profits.

But a shadow fell over him, and he looked up into Jenny Mather's cat-green eyes.

"The butter," said Jenny Mather, "would come again soon enough if you left the cows alone."

It was an inconvenient fact that some folks had eyes to see strange things, and the Devil was sometimes recognized.

"You wouldn't need to worry about me *or* the cows," he answered, rising, "if you were to load them on ships and sail back to England."

Jenny Mather was a handsome woman. The Devil looked at her down the length of his wooden nose and felt a powerful twitching all over his skin, and when Jenny Mather said, "If you leave the cows alone, I'll kiss you," he found himself saying, "Deal."

They slipped into the curing shed, where fifteen hams and a steer hung from the beams, and Jenny kissed the Devil deep and slow.

The Devil, gambling that a bargain for a kiss might go further, once begun, was breathless and disappointed when she pulled away and was gone without so much as a squeeze.

Still.

The Devil could cheat and the Devil could lie, but a deal was a deal.

He'd miss the cows.

The butter came back, and the glumness and the superstition faded, and things were much as they had been. The Devil watched it all from an apple tree, disappointed with himself and smoking baby birds like crazy.

SPRING TURNED TO summer. The fort grew. The trees retreated before the Pilgrims' axes, and the hunters foraged deeper than ever into the woods.

The Pilgrims had brought disease with them, and Indians died. Lots of them.

The Devil resolved once again to be rid of the English.

This time his eye fell on the children.

He entered the children's dreams one night and whispered to them, then crouched behind the henhouse to await morning.

At dawn, the hunters went a-hunting. The notables gathered by the well, arguing about whether to send to England for a gunsmith.

"There's Indian sign on the deer trails," said John, who knew a man who knew a man who'd been skinned alive in Virginia.

"The Indians are dead," spat Miles. "Mostly."

"But the ones who are not," said Elder Mather, "are desperate and afraid, and may pool their numbers to attack. I think we'll always have Indians, in great numbers or not, which begs the question of the gunsmith."

Indians prowled their dreams. They were in the closets and under the beds. Indians were blamed for everything from dull razors to spiders in the firewood.

Down in the lane between houses, a column of children appeared.

The arguing notables fell silent all at once, and stared.

Not a passel of children or a mob, but a column, as if they were soldiers. Ten children? Thirty? It looked like all the children in the village, from Molly Fellberry (young for thirteen) to tiny Abigail Fetters, less than two.

There was something disquietingly unchildlike about them. The men discerned an unnatural wisdom about their eyes, something otherworldly in the way they marched without making a sound.

This strange column turned left at the stockade gate, and filed in silence out of the fort.

The notables, followed by a number of wives and some fishermen, found the children stopped in two neat rows, like a choir, just this side of the pasture fence, staring at the woods below the hill. The adults looked at the children, then looked at one another. They were reaching for the children when the children began, all at once, to speak.

The children described the future as if it were something that had visited them in their sleep. They pointed at the woods as they spoke, because the woods were west, and the future was west.

They said that the Indians would die of mumps and pox and tooth decay, and other white diseases.

They told how the new country, starting right here in their churchy little village, would grow up rooted in blood and gold and slavery.

There would be a race of retarded people called Rednecks, kept like a national pet. There would be schools like factories, factories like prisons, and prisons like cities. There would be a machine like an eye, which would talk to people and show them pictures, and people would do whatever the eye said. That was as far as the children could see.

And then the children looked at their mothers and fathers, and said a thing or two about how some people today, right here at home, seemed to spend time in sheds and barns with people who weren't their husbands or wives—and you never saw a bunch of grown-ups move so fast; they snatched up their little ones, and bore them away to confinement.

FROM HIS WIGWAM at the edge of the forest, the Devil watched the village retreat into itself. He hoped the Pilgrims were thinking about sailing back to England if the children didn't shut up.

At twilight, Jenny Mather crossed the pasture to stand at his door.

For a moment, her shadow and shape were enough like Pocahontas to make his heart ache.

Jenny untied her bonnet and shook loose her long dark hair, and offered to screw him inside out if he would lift whatever spell he'd laid on the children. The Devil heard himself agreeing. He couldn't help it.

THE DEVIL AND Jenny Mather did things under the sun, and then the moon, which embarrassed the natural creatures all around.

After she staggered off home, the Devil fished around among his few things—furs and bones, arrowheads and seeds and his pipe—until his wooden fingers closed around a glass ball the size of his fist.

He stared into it. The glass ball was clear as a raindrop. Wasn't it? Or were there shadows and clouds inside? The more he stared, the more the ball changed. It showed the Devil the same future it had shown the children.

"Why does the future always look so hard?" he wondered aloud.

He put the ball away. It didn't do to see things he didn't understand yet.

AUTUMN CAME, AND the Hunter's Moon. Crisp winds changed direction; the sea and sky turned gray. The Devil lost himself on the deer trails, lost himself in the harvest feasts of the Morning People and the Fish People and the Big Voice People. He lost himself in thinking about *her.*

He was going to have to stop that. Time moved forward. No one knew that better than he.

The villages of the forest people were smaller than before. Fewer.

"Watani-ay tougash misoughioughi," one sachem told him. "It is the coughing sickness."

"Ni quoi quoi ai watha," said another. "The old ones shit themselves to death."

These were strong people, and they were dying of children's diseases.

The Devil remembered to be angry with the Pilgrims. When they died, more Pilgrims appeared from over the sea. When forest people died, perhaps children would be born to replace them, but the children died, too.

When winter came, sure enough, the Pilgrims shut themselves indoors and began to freeze and starve and die. The cemetery bulged. Even the cows died, which saddened the Devil.

These people were not fit to build a nation.

There would have to be fighting. The Falling Water People had fought, at Jamestown. The Devil winced. Pocahontas had hated the fighting.

Still, he went to the forest villages and said, "You should do something about these clowns while you still have some warriors left," and they agreed.

THE PILGRIM FATHERS were gathered in the meetinghouse, in retreat from a screaming arctic gale, telling scary stories.

"At Jamestown"—John coughed—"they starved so badly they began to dig up the dead."

"Bosh!" sniffled Miles. "It was only the *fresh* dead that were eaten."

Elder Mather tried to add something, but it was lost in a great sneeze, and before he quite recovered, they were interrupted by the watchtower bell, its alarm riding the howl of the wind.

"Indians!" They all coughed, and ran outside to see.

Indians, indeed! They seemed to be part of the storm itself, pouring out of the dark, loosing arrows or throwing hatchets, then vanishing again. It was hard to know what to shoot at.

BOOM! BOOM! Musket and blunderbuss flared on the stockade wall, followed by wheezing and feverish moans.

One Pilgrim fell outside the wall with an arrow in his throat. Another died of the flu while loading the swivel gun.

In the lane by the well, Jenny Mather raised a lantern for the wives and children, who followed her to the meetinghouse, where they coughed and shivered and prayed.

Outside, they heard the wind, and fewer gunshots. More and more, there was the wind and Indian war cries.

"We're lost." Teenage Molly Fellberry sneezed.

The younger children began to bicker about whether 'twas a sin to want to be buried wearing ribbons.

THE DEVIL WAS among the first warriors over the wall.

He set fire to the potato barn and was just about to piss in the well when a dark figure emerged from the driving snow, green eyes inside a woolen hood, reflecting the Devil's torch.

Jenny Mather looked frightened, but she had come to do something that needed doing. She offered to give the Devil her soul if he would let them live.

The Devil was a sucker for souls.

He said yes before giving it any thought, reached into her hood, and squeezed her jaw until her mouth opened.

Something like a mockingbird fluttered out, and roosted on the Devil's finger.

He admired its feathers and the sharpness of its eyes, then allowed it to hop back down Jenny's throat.

"Deal," he said, baring his long white teeth.

The warriors climbed back over the wall, melting into the storm and the winter woods, and the Devil turned himself into a handsome red fox and ran off smoking his pipe.

HE STOPPED FIGHTING the Pilgrims, after that.

They had a certain practicality of spirit, if Jenny Mather was any indication. He decided to see what they did with it. More ships came and more forts went up along the shore. They built a road, and another village appeared in the woods, some miles from the sea. Then another and another. Winter came and they died, but there were always more.

Some of the seaside Pilgrims even moved away, after a time, to one of the new villages. John and his wife, and Miles, and others, with their children and their things piled aboard oxcarts, made their way around the pasture and down the road to New Coventry and New Lincoln and New Stafford-upon-Welpole and other American places. Sometimes they passed empty Indian villages, but they passed without noticing.

They also failed to notice, in the gathering dark, an extra Pilgrim walking among them. He might have been a farmer or a trader, or both. He smoked a foul-smelling pipe, and you wouldn't know, unless you touched him, that he was made out of wood.

He walked slowly, letting the Pilgrims pass by, until he came to the tail flap of the hindmost wagon, where two children sat arguing over which of them was most likely to catch sick and die.

They shut up when the stranger smiled at them, then laughed as he reached out and pulled coins from their ears.

"Shiny!" gasped the children.

"That's gold." The Devil winked. "Put it in your pockets. Guard it with your lives. Get some more, if you can. Good boy. Good girl."

He handed them the coins like a farmer planting a seed.

3.

The Death of Dan Paul Overfield

Kansas, 1969

THE KANSAS SKY HAD seen the buffalo roam, and watched them die. It had rained on the horse cultures and the covered wagons crossing oceans of prairie grass, until they were gone. It had hovered over the Depression, with its dust and its hollow men, until those passed away, too.

Now highways rolled between power lines and radio towers, and beside one of those highways, three Volkswagen Microbuses were parked, painted like cars in a circus train. One red and one green, with psychedelic designs, and the third like a picture of outer space. Around the buses, a village of tents and lanterns and campfires had spilled out. At the center of this village, the World's Grooviest Guitar Player lay dying.

ROLLING STONE HAD called him that, back in San Francisco. His name was Dan Paul Overfield, and the people of the tent village were his roadies and the kids in his band. They were still young enough, these kids, to think Peace and Love would see them through.

Dan Paul Overfield lay flat on his back in a tent. He refused to go to the hospital and it scared the kids. They didn't know what to do, but whatever needed doing, they wanted to do it right. After all, *Rolling Stone* would probably do a tribute piece, and they all wanted to come off as strong and soulful cats.

The huge, twinkling sky was no comfort. It reminded them how far they were from home, home being as many different places as there were constellations.

Memory, the singer, was beautiful and tall. She was called Memory because she had amnesia, and could remember nothing of her childhood or teen years. She guessed she might be around twenty. Doctors would have studied her, if she let them.

Mark Fish, the drummer, came from California. His eyes seemed somehow dishonest. He knew this, and wore sunglasses around the clock.

Zachary Bull Horse, the bass player, from Arizona, was nine-tenths Apache. Zachary was a big fellow, and you could tell he was going to be fat when he got older.

These three sat crowded around Dan Paul, who looked like God might have looked when He was thirty. He lay with his shirt torn open, half asleep.

Things would have been great for him and his band (the Dan Paul Overfield Band), except his heart was weak.

"It might stop any day," he had told them a year ago when they first started playing for money. "Any second."

They believed him, but it hadn't seemed real until today, when they had pulled over to camp in Kansas. Dan Paul, as usual, made a fire and started cooking. And he fell over. He was lucky he didn't fall straight into the fire.

"Put him in the red bus!" Memory had cried. "The one that hasn't broken down yet. Where was that last town we passed through? Is it closer than the next one?"

"Fuck me," growled Fish. "Who's got a map?"

Zachary, the giant, lifted Dan Paul in his arms, and started for the red Microbus.

"Just put me in my tent," said Dan Paul.

SO ZACHARY LAID Dan Paul in his tent, and they gathered around him. Memory ripped his shirt open because it seemed the thing to do.

She sat cross-legged now, with Dan Paul's head in her lap, rubbing his temples, and humming.

Zachary hulked over his left side like an Apache Buddha.

Fish burst head and shoulders into the tent, and hovered there over Dan Paul's ankles.

"Why don't you want to go to the hospital?" he demanded.

Dan Paul whispered something in a weak voice.

"He says it's too late," said Memory.

Dan Paul whispered something else.

He wanted them to sing.

"Jesus," said Fish.

Memory tried to think of just the right song.

All their songs had been written by Dan Paul. Back in San Francisco, *Rolling Stone* had asked him what his songs were about.

He said he had a happy outlook on life, but his ticker might stop any second. "So," he explained, "I write campfire songs about death."

It was true. Their songs, even the sad ones, had a lighthearted sound. They were easy to sing. Easy to memorize. You could dance to them. And they were about death, every one. The radio and the record stores ate it up. In less than a year, the band had campfire-sung and groovy-guitared their way to the edge of fame.

Before they sang, Fish produced a big fat joint and they passed it around, just like they did before concerts.

Then Memory started a song called "Down in the Hole."

Zachary and Fish joined in. Dan Paul had made them practice harmony until it was second nature, and they sounded all right, now, even with their voices cracking and sad.

There's a hole in Russell's farm
Bigger than a baby or a lucky charm
Smaller than a granny in a rocking chair
Everything he loses ends up down there

Russell lost his cow
He took more milk than the cow allowed
How much does it take to fill a bottomless bowl?
The cow jumped the moon and came down in the hole

Russell lost his barn
Crows built a nest in the fire alarm
Ashes, ashes, all fall down
Ashes in the hole, but the smoke made town

Russell lost his wife
Sixteen beers and a sugarcane knife
Red is the color of his true love's hair
Look down the hole and see her slumbering there

Russell lost his way
Between the state pen and his gettin'-out day
Between the moon and the night and the rain and the wind
Can a man down a hole find his way up again?

In a perfect world, they would have looked down then to find that Dan Paul had slipped peacefully away while they sang.

What happened instead was that a roadie named Osgood came crawling into the tent just then, without really looking where he was going, to announce that some of the crew had gone off to hide in the woods in case the cops came.

Dan Paul groaned. "Ozzy, bro, you're on my leg."

Those were his last words.

× × ×

QUIETLY, THE NEWS PASSED from tent to tent, to the woods, to the cook fire, to the Microbuses and back.

Some of the roadies searched the galaxy with stoned eyes, looking for signs of the groovy soul departing.

"Now what?" Fish sulked. "We're the Dan Paul Overfield Band without Dan Paul. It's not fair."

He kicked at the weeds outside the tent.

Zachary started to say something about how Fish ought to be thinking about Dan Paul instead of himself. But Fish had only said what was on everyone's mind.

The three of them talked for a while about Dan Paul and how much they would miss him. How much they had loved singing and playing his songs.

When it seemed okay to do so, they talked about what to do about Dan Paul's body.

"He would want to be buried right here," said Zachary. "Under the stars, with a few words."

"We can't," said Memory. "It'll seem suspicious."

Some of the roadies were supposed to be in Vietnam. They couldn't afford suspicion.

It was decided that they would drive Dan Paul into the next town and see what the funeral home had to say. They weren't broke, exactly. They could afford something cheap and legal.

Memory wandered down the highway a hundred yards while Zachary wrapped Dan Paul in a sheet. She sat down on a guardrail over a starlit creek.

Fish was right. Bubble Records was recording their songs and getting them on the radio. Bubble Records was spotting them three used Microbuses and gas money. They had just been invited to play a huge outdoor rock festival on some guy's farm in New York. They had been within an inch of getting everything they ever wanted.

For the first time, Memory felt how badly she wanted what she wanted.

Which was what? Fame?

Yes.

But didn't everyone want to be famous, at least some of the time?

Sure. But this felt different. It wasn't *want.* It was a *need* with deep, hungry roots.

Was it some psychological shit, like thinking you wanted fame, but really your imaginary fans were a substitute for sex or love or being popular in high school? Maybe, for *her,* fame was a substitute for remembering. Maybe fame was her way of making sure the rest of her didn't disappear.

What difference did it make? Dan Paul was dead. Her magic beanstalk had fallen.

She felt fame fading out of her future, and the rest of her fading along with it.

"Fuck," she sang, one sad note.

IT WAS ZACHARY who brought up the Devil.

They had gone through several phases in the hours since Dan Paul had died. Eating supper. Going around in a big circle with the rest of the camp, saying nice things about Dan Paul. Then everyone doing their own thing for a while.

It was after midnight.

It was the time of night best suited for talking about strange things. A quiet and mysterious time. They might never have even talked about the Devil if the crew had been dancing and singing, or trading stories again, or if the noise of people fucking had gotten loud enough to invite applause, or if it had rained.

But it was this, instead: Clouds sailed in, with clear stars behind, as if the sky had split into different rooms. Joints and cigarettes glowed here and there, some by the fire, some by the road, some by the woods.

Zachary and Memory were sharing a plate of cold beans when Fish sat down across from them. He didn't say anything.

It was necessary that no one speak for a while, to clear the way for strange ideas.

Finally, Zachary said, "You know what they say about Robert Johnson."

"Uh-huh," said Fish.

"What do they say?" asked Memory.

"They say he met the Devil at the crossroads and sold his soul to be a big star."

Then it was necessary that there be a second chapter of the silence, which there was.

"You think we oughta go down to the crossroads," said Memory, laughing.

Zachary shrugged.

Memory looked from Fish to Zach and back again.

"Bullshit," said Fish. "That's just part of how the producers sell records. Every time somebody great comes along, especially if he plays the guitar, there's got to be some story that says he sold his soul or has a guitar made in the Underworld. They say Howlin' Wolf went to the cemetery and got his guitar tuned by a dead man, right? Remember what they said about Dan Paul?"

Memory looked puzzled.

"It was before your time," Zachary told her.

"Dan Paul used to be just another folkie," said Fish, "traveling around and playing bars. He heard about this other guitar player named Two-John Spode who supposedly had won a guitar duel with the Devil and trapped his own death inside his guitar. So Dan Paul went down to Louisiana and found him back in the swamp, and tried to get him to help start a band. Way back before he found us. They had a guitar contest between the two of them, the idea being that if Dan Paul won, Two-John would come with him, and if Two-John won, he got to keep Dan Paul's guitar. And Two-John did win, but he was so impressed that he let Dan Paul keep his guitar. Not only that, and this is the important part, he put his death in Dan Paul's guitar, which is how Dan Paul was able to play the way he did, sounding like two or three guitar players, because Two-John's death was plucking the strings from the other side."

Zachary cleared his throat.

"I vote we bury it with him," he said.

No argument.

"Your point?" said Memory to Fish.

"Record-industry fairy tales," he replied. "That's all it is."

"You ever see him take the strings off his guitar?" asked Zachary.

An owl hooted, and they all shivered.

They didn't talk about the record industry, or the Devil, any more that night. They went off to their tents and blankets and slept, except Fish. A groupie who dug him crept under his blankets and they stayed awake all night long.

4.

The Devil's Unusual Constitution

Dayton, Ohio, 2005

THE HOSPITAL PEOPLE HAD to keep reminding John Scratch that he'd been shot.

He had lost consciousness in the limo on the way to the hospital, and when the orderlies reached in to grab him, he woke up.

"What?" he asked, disoriented.

"You've been shot, Mr. Scratch," they told him. "Let us slide you out of there and help you. Sir?"

He was out again.

Next, he woke up on a gurney. Doctors and nurses were rushing him down a bright hallway. Someone had stuck tubes in him. They all looked worried.

Jenna Steele was not among them. She had gone to have her hair done before appearing on camera.

They passed by a waiting area with a wall-mounted TV set, and he saw himself on the screen. Saw himself on a gurney. Twisting his head, peering behind him, he saw—upside down—a techie with a TV camera, following.

"What's going on?" he asked.

"What's going on?" asked his image on the TV.

"You've been shot," someone told him, echoed on-screen.

He faded to black.

HE WOKE UP during surgery (the Devil had an unusual constitution, and was a light sleeper besides).

"Jesus!" cried one of the surgeons. "What's with this guy?"

One of the nurses asked, "Don't you know who this is? It's that guy from that TV show where they make you an offer, like—"

"I know who he is. Somebody juice him again."

TV cameras poked over shoulders, under elbows. The surgery had gone out on pay-per-view at fifty bucks a pop.

Instinctively, the Devil smiled for the cameras, and fell back asleep.

Viewer surveys soared when they found the first two bullets in John Scratch's liver. The rate went up to sixty bucks and kept climbing. It would probably level out, unless it looked like he was going to die. Then the whole thing would spike.

The ratings, however, did spike, five minutes later, when Jenna Steele, hair perfect, burst in, wearing go-go boots and chewing bubble gum.

The cameras left John on the table, fighting for his life, and buzzed like a hive around Jenna.

She looked like she might be a little drunk. She often was. Her music was a billion-dollar teen-pop industry all its own, though. No matter what she did. Last month at the zoo, she had opened her blouse in public, on camera, and pretended to breast-feed John Scratch. The outraged public paid ten million dollars to watch.

The ratings bounced again, just a little, when John's health insurance agent came charging through, gloved and gowned in his company's trademark blue.

"Take your hands off that," the agent commanded. "He's not covered for that."

"That's his liver," said the doc.

"You'll have to sign for it, then," said the agent, and they had a five-minute paperwork break, during which the Devil woke up, moaned in pain, and gasped.

"What—?"

"You've been shot, babe," crooned Jenna Steele.

The Devil gave her a funny look.

"What are you doing here?" he asked.

He'd been meaning to break up with her. Now suddenly seemed like a good time to do it. But before he could say anything, sleep tackled him again.

Jenna Steele tried to blow a bubble and accidentally spit her gum into a nurse's hair. The gum sat there like a tiny pink topknot.

The cameras ate it up.

"Cute," said millions of viewers.

5.

Soulful Cats at the Crossroads

Kansas, 1969

GETTING DAN PAUL BURIED was easier than expected. The morning after he died, the band caravanned into the next Kansas town on the map, arranged for a cheap casket with no embalming, and sang songs around his fresh grave. Fish stopped at the post office on their way out of town and sent telegrams to the studio, and to the booking agents who'd hired them for various gigs.

"We're sticking with our schedule," said the telegrams, more or less, "Dan Paul or no Dan Paul."

Then they climbed into their spacey, swirly Microbuses and headed east, leaving the World's Grooviest Guitar Player to decompose among strangers.

DRIVING THROUGH THE night, listening to the radio, the three musicians heard themselves on the airwaves, singing "Down in the Hole."

The deejay read a news bulletin about how Dan Paul Overfield, who might have been the greatest guitar hero ever, had died on the road, and how sad that was. He said nothing about the surviving band, on its way to upstate New York.

Memory, tired but not sleepy, watched the highway roll at them out of the night and thought about the difference a day made.

One very heavy day. For the first time in her brief set of memories, something seemed like a long time ago, and it made her sad. She thought about the crowds they had played for, the crowds they were *going* to play for: crowds in front of stages, in city clubs, adoring her on the radio, maybe television, too.

It occurred to her that famous people probably weren't superior to other kinds of people. They were maybe a little inferior, because they had a hole in them so vast that only the attention of thousands—millions—could fill it. Memory wanted thousands of people to think about her, to keep her in their mind's eye so she wouldn't just evaporate like her past.

She was fighting tears when the bus—the red bus, the one that hadn't broken down yet—lurched beneath her. Something creaked like an old door.

"Transmission," groaned Zachary, behind the wheel.

"Suspension," argued one of the roadies, eating beef jerky in the back.

The creaking faded, and the Microbus, for the moment, rolled on.

"She needs new shocks," the roadie elaborated, "or one of these days we're going to hit a bump and go scraping down the highway on our ass."

"She needs all kinds of shit," snapped Fish, yawning and sitting up. "None of which we can afford."

"Call the studio," suggested Zachary.

"*You* call 'em," said Fish, kicking the back of Zachary's seat. "They're probably going crazy trying to get ahold of us anyway, so they can tell us to tear up our contract and come home."

"Stop kicking," said Zachary.

"Shit," said Fish, folding his arms and crossing his legs until he became a petulant, sleep-deprived ball. "Maybe we *should* call 'em. Get it over with."

"You don't know—" began Zachary.

"Like hell I don't! Who's going to honor a contract with a band whose one big-name musician is fucking dead? We should have finished having this conversation last night, but we're too scared to face facts. It's over. You know it and I know it. So why are we still burning gas we can't afford?"

Something in the engine gave a knock.

"Vapor," said Zachary.

"Vapor," agreed the roadie. "Are we going to get paid?"

"Yes," said Memory. "One way or another."

"With what?" asked Fish. "Weed? After the studio tells us to bring their buses back and sign over the rest of our gas money?"

Memory said nothing.

Neither did Zachary. He was too busy wondering what lay ahead for him if the band folded. Instead of being famous and influential and maybe having a chance to change the world, maybe he could get a job as a bouncer. A lot of big Apaches were bouncers. Just what he'd always dreamed of . . . a glorious life of drunks and blood and bad vibes.

Fish, simmering, thought similar things. It had looked as if they might make a ton of money, given another year. So much for that. It pissed him off. He liked money. People treated you differently if you had it. Money was a girl magnet. Money was a magnet for more money.

Memory looked out the window and thought about all the years she couldn't remember. Like thinking about the time before you were born. One of the nice things about singing to crowds was that someone, at any moment, might recognize her, shout her name, introduce her to herself.

Without memory, what was a person, really? Without it, all you had was *now,* that patch of black ice between the past and future.

The ache became too painful to bear in silence.

"We can't just let this end," she said, voice cracking.

It would have been hard to find any three people, anywhere, who felt more cheated, more frustrated, more like screaming, than these three. Because they missed Dan Paul, and what Dan Paul had made of them. Because nothing crushes the heart faster than touching something bright and rare and wonderful and then having it snatched away before you can grasp it.

"Memory—" Zachary started, but just watched her reflection in the windshield instead, not sure how to comfort her. The shocks creaked.

Fish leaned forward. He pulled a half-burned joint from his shirt pocket and lit up. He inhaled deeply and passed the joint to Zachary. Zachary took a short hit and said, "We're not stoned enough to be having this conversation," and inhaled again, "but I say we go to the crossroads."

"You gotta be joking," said Memory, waving the joint away. "I mean, how do you go about, I mean, what do you even do?"

"The crossroads," said Zachary. "Every story I've ever heard about the Devil—"

"Then what?" asked Fish. "Is there some magic Apache dance or you cast a spell or do the evil eye or what?"

"I think you just *go* there. Finding him isn't supposed to be the hard part."

Memory threw up her hands. Fish took another hit. Zachary chewed on his lip. In the silence that followed, they decided to actually do it.

"When?" asked Memory.

Zachary shrugged his mighty shoulders.

"Now," he said.

Memory changed her mind about the joint.

THE DEVIL IS usually nearby when you want him.

Not this time, though. He was on vacation.

He'd had a good year. A good decade. He had pushed his pet nation hard, and the ball was rolling.

They were stuck in a nasty jungle war, in Vietnam. War meant new discoveries and money. There was also a war being waged at home, by people demanding justice and equality.

They had just walked on the moon! Now whenever anyone, anywhere in the world, looked at the moon in the sky, they would know it was an American moon.

And there was a revolution, of a kind. Young people called hippies who insisted on "Being Themselves."

Yes, America was boiling. People down here on Earth were *evolving*, and when people could think for themselves and fly to the moon, what did they need God for anyway?

The Devil stood in the middle of the Magic Kingdom, at Disneyland, dressed in Bermudas, a straw hat, and a plaid shirt. He looked like an insurance salesman. All American men looked like that on vacation.

When Americans were working, thought the Devil, adjusting his sunglasses, they built cars and roads. On vacation, though, they came to silly places like this, where they paid too much for everything and stood in long lines.

In four hundred years, he still hadn't figured Americans out.

Minnie Mouse and Goofy came lolloping his way from opposite directions. He dropped a fifty-dollar bill on the ground and sat on a nearby bench, hoping they'd fight over it.

They didn't. Goofy picked it up and turned it in at the Lost and Found.

The Devil got a snow cone and headed for the parking lot.

Found his car, a midnight-blue Lincoln.

Sometimes people stared at the Devil's car, wondering why it looked familiar. Those who thought about it long enough, or searched their memories hard enough, were usually horrified. Sometimes they took pictures.

The Devil always smiled for the pictures. He was proud of his car.

× × ×

IT TOOK HIM two hours to leave the L.A. traffic behind. He turned east, toward the Mojave and Death Valley, and turned on the radio. His straw hat almost blew away as he gathered speed off the Barstow exit. He caught it with a long, nimble claw, laid it on the passenger seat, and settled in for a long ride. Maybe all night.

The roads the Devil traveled were not always on the map. Strange forces and realities attended him. Sometimes, on the Devil's road, it was day when it should have been night. Quite often, the sun and moon shared the sky and eclipsed each other.

Something like a campfire song was playing on the radio. Catchy! The Devil turned it up. It was a cheerful number called "Cruel April," about people who had been executed in the springtime.

The guitar player could make the guitar talk. Made it sound like three guitars, at least, having a conversation. The singer's voice seemed to echo, faintly, as if accompanied by its own ghost:

Clark Freeman, gas chamber! Such a pretty day!
Winter's dyin'! Dandelion! Cyanide spray!

It was the Devil's kind of song. He tapped his long nails on the steering wheel and left the highway. Ahead, two roads crossed between cornfields. Mist poured through the corn, washing over the road. A swirly-painted Microbus sat parked on the shoulder, to his right. In front of the Microbus, three hippies sat holding hands in a circle. Two boys and a girl.

The Devil parked his car on the opposite shoulder and climbed out. He didn't look like a tourist anymore. He looked like an old hippie: long-haired and tan, with a Fu Manchu beard, Lennon glasses, shirt completely open, boots and jeans.

These kids would expect horns, so he had horns.

"I like that gas-chamber song," he said, crossing the road, pocketing his keys.

Three pairs of eyes goggled at him.

They were petrified. He had known they would be.

"Let me know when you're ready to talk," he said. Then he stepped into the middle of the crossroads, stirred up a campfire out of nowhere, and began roasting a marshmallow.

Dammit. They always caught on fire, no matter how careful he was.

He peeled the black skin and captured it with a long, prehensile tongue, careful not to get it in his beard.

"Hey," said the girl, beside him.

"Hey back," he said.

"Is this for real?" she asked.

"You came to the crossroads at midnight. What did you think was going to happen?"

"I don't think we thought anything was going to happen, really. I don't think any of us really believe in the Devil."

"Do you believe now?"

"I don't know. Do we believe now, Zachary?"

One of the boys, an Indian with the body and face of a cliff, had joined them.

Before Zachary could answer, the other boy stopped beside the Devil's car.

"Hey!" he bellowed. "Far out! This is the Kennedy limo, isn't it? From Dallas! Holy shit!"

The Devil nodded proudly, and Fish joined them at the fire.

"He made a fire out of nowhere," Zachary told Fish.

"I think I'm scared," said the girl.

"Let's go for a ride," said the Devil.

He opened the shotgun door for Memory. Zachary sat on a jump seat, behind the Devil. Fish sat all the way in back.

"This is right where *he* sat," bubbled Fish. "This is where Kennedy fucking *died,* man."

They rolled off into the mist.

Fields and trees flashed by. The wind tossed their hair. Mist soaked their clothes.

"What do you want?" asked the Devil.

In the back, Fish started to say something, but the Devil interrupted.

"Think about it. Even if you already have. Think about it some more. Then tell me."

"All of us?" asked the girl. "Or each of us, personally?"

"That's up to you," he answered. "But be careful."

They were all quiet for a while.

They passed through a town with a mighty limestone courthouse. The courthouse dome held a giant clock, lit from inside. Beside the courthouse, railroad tracks.

The Devil stopped at the tracks. Moments later, the gates lowered, flashing and dinging, and a train rumbled out of the dark.

The Devil liked trains.

The gates went up. They cruised out of town, past a Purina grain elevator and a dead tree.

"I want to be famous," said the girl. "It's what I started out wanting. And we were almost there. I guess I mean I want to be famous without Dan Paul. Do you know what I'm talking about? It's like—"

The Devil raised a hand, silencing her. "A little talk goes a long way," he said.

The limo caught a cloud of fireflies unawares. They struck the windshield and splattered into green luminescence.

Fish spoke up.

"I want money," he said. "I've thought about it hard. When I get right down to it, that's why I practiced so hard to do this music shit. When I think about records and playing gigs, that's the thing I think about."

"I get it," said the Devil.

They passed a Greyhound bus.

Zachary didn't say anything at all until they got back to the crossroads, and then he said, "I want to change the world."

"We all change the world," said the Devil.

"I mean in a big, huge, amazing way."

"You sure?"

Zachary was sure.

"Far out," said the Devil.

THEY TOASTED WIENERS around the campfire, and the Devil explained how the deal worked.

"I'm like the landlord of your soul from now on," he told them. "It belongs to me, and it does what I want it to do. It'll change you. Maybe a little, maybe a lot. Everyone's different. But don't be surprised if you feel a little crazy from now on. More impulsive, more hungry—"

"More like you," said Fish.

The Devil nodded.

"And we get—?" asked Memory.

"You'll also be smarter. Quicker. More talented. Luckier, if you believe in luck. And I provide services, like any good landlord. I'll open doors. I'll tip things in your favor. I'll make sure you get what you asked for. Along the way, you'll be making the world faster and leaner."

The Devil's voice rose as he spoke. His eyes burned. Sharp teeth reflected starlight. He looked Memory up and down in a way that was, somehow, both gentlemanly and *not* gentlemanly.

"Sexier, too," he said.

"And when we die," said Zachary. "What happens then? We go to Hell?"

"There's no Hell," scoffed the Devil. "Why would there be? God's not a monster; He's just selfish. When you die, you and I stop being of use to each other. Your soul will do what everyone else's soul does."

"Which is what?" asked Memory, eyes wide.

The Devil shrugged.

"Maybe go to Heaven, for one."

"There's no Hell," said Fish, "but there's a Heaven?" He sounded doubtful.

"Heaven makes sense," admitted the Devil. "Heaven is like the engine of the universe. It's God and God's angels and light and energy and time and all that crap. Living souls are part of it. It pulls them like gravity. You could even think of Heaven and God as the laws of Nature, except that Heaven is awake and thinks it's *better* than Nature. Which is dumb, and snobbish, and . . ."

His voice began to rise again, and his eyes to burn, and the kids looked at him in a worried kind of way. The Devil took a deep breath.

"Anyway, suffering for eternity makes no sense. It would serve no purpose. So maybe you go to Heaven. Maybe you stick around and get reborn. Maybe you dissolve into the atmosphere and turn into plant food. Everyone's different. Your soul will do what you expect it to do."

"So if you expect it to suffer," said Fish, "it would suffer."

The Devil gave Fish a narrow-eyed look.

"You're kind of an asshole, aren't you?" he asked. "I'll tell you one thing. All of you. As far as I'm concerned, you're here to make the world a smarter, shinier, braver place. If you start making the world a dumb, frightened place, I will end your contract and burn you up like a fucking marshmallow, body and soul both. So watch your ass, you hear me?"

They heard him. They nodded, swallowing hard.

"That's the deal," said the Devil.

A silence passed over them.

"So," said Memory, clearing her throat. "Do we sign in blood, or dance naked around your campfire, there, or—"

"Do you want to?" asked the Devil. He wouldn't mind seeing Memory naked.

"I'm kinda tired," she said.

The Devil shook his head.

"It's already done," he said. "If you want out, say so now. It's the only chance you'll get."

The kids fidgeted nervously, but no one said a word.

He let them see their souls, which was a treat.

Memory's was a butterfly.

Zachary's soul was a stone, but a wonderful stone, gleaming and translucent and shaped like a perfect egg.

Fish's soul was a fish. It popped its head out between his lips, gulped once, and retreated. He didn't really get to look at it. He didn't care.

"You'll get what you asked for," the Devil told them. "You might get more, but you won't get less. Now back that Microbus over in front of my car."

The kids looked puzzled, but Zachary went to do as he said.

The Devil retrieved an armload of tools from the limo.

"Towing kit," he explained.

Zachary drove up, and the Devil got down on his back in the gravel, cursing and banging things around.

"You're coming with us?" said Memory.

"That a problem?"

She chewed her lip. *Was* it a problem?

"No," she said. "It's just that—"

"You're not sure where you're going, or what to expect when you get there."

"Right. Plus what am I going to tell our crew, waiting for us at the Howard Johnson's back in Springfield?"

"Tell them I'm the fucking Devil, I don't care."

"You don't have to be rude."

He sighed.

"Sorry. I banged my thumb, and it hurts. On top of which, it's been a long day, and Disneyland wasn't relaxing."

Oh.

"You need anything?" she asked.

"No, hon. Thanks. Be just a minute, here."

AN HOUR LATER, they pulled into the Howard Johnson's parking lot. Zachary flashed his lights, and the crew gathered around as he parked.

Memory slid the side door open and spoke to the whole assembly.

"Democracy!" she shouted. "Who votes we stop for the night?"

A few hands.

The Devil peeked out, over her shoulder.

"Who votes we move on, switching drivers, until we get to our next gig, two states away, and have a whole day off when we get there?"

More hands, and a cheer. The crew dug democracy.

Memory reached for the door, but the crew had questions.

"Who's the new cat?" someone asked.

"That's the Devil," said Memory.

Another question. Someone pointed at the Lincoln.

"Isn't that the JFK death car?"

"Yes," she answered. "Anything else?"

No. They were a mellow crew. They hit the road.

6.

Wildness, Kindness, and War

Upstate New York, 1969

FOR A WEEK OR so, the Devil drove the space bus. He drank a lot of coffee.

He drove the band to a gig in Virginia. When the producers wanted to cancel ("Dan Paul is *dead,* man!"), the Devil spoke softly to them.

The band played. They were loved. Memory's voice, soft and windy, seemed to grow into the space left by Dan Paul's guitar. It was a new sound, both wilder and more poetic, and the crowd was into it.

In Wilmington and Philadelphia, too, the Devil spoke softly, and the band was allowed to play. Now they were on their way to Newark. The Devil lit a cigarette and thought about Elvis.

Just fourteen years ago. Was that all?

He couldn't have invented Elvis if he'd tried. And Elvis had *known* he was special. His mama had taught him that.

"Come give mama a kissy-wissy," she would tell him. Always with those two, it was baby talk.

"Yes, Mama, widdle Elvis give his mama a kissy-wissy," the boy would answer.

And he was religious. Hardly anybody in the world knew how fucking religious that boy was, now that he was famous for shaking his pelvis.

"Elvis give Jesus a kissy-wissy," said the Devil aloud, crossing the Delaware.

Elvis hadn't come to the crossroads. No way.

His father had, though. Old Vernon Presley, half drunk, had found the crossroads somehow.

"Got me a boy thinks he can sing," Vernon Presley had said to the Devil.

"Can he?" the Devil had asked.

"I reckon he can. I'll sell you his soul if you'll make him rich and famous."

"You can't sell someone else's soul, Vernon. Shame on you."

Vernon spat in the dirt, looking lost. And finally he said to the Devil, "Well, how about if I sell you mine?"

The Devil thought Vernon Presley's soul was worth exactly shit. But when a man offered his own soul to lift up his son, that soul gained weight.

"It won't guarantee anything," the Devil told Vernon.

Vernon said he'd take his chances, and the deal was done. Vernon Presley's soul was a cloud of cigarette smoke.

That mama's boy had gone and put the Devil's Music on the charts. Music that put the whole country in touch with its wild side. Exactly the kind of go-juice this new age needed.

They didn't talk anymore, he and Elvis. Their work was done.

The Devil looked over his shoulder at the sleeping stars of the Dan Paul Overfield Band, and tried to get excited about them.

There was the girl, Memory. He was a little excited about her. Less excited about the guys.

Memory reminded him of someone. A long time ago.

"Kissy-wissy," he said, speeding up, forcing the rest of the caravan to follow him into the fast lane.

× × ×

THAT NIGHT, THEY rocked Newark, and rolled north toward the music festival they had their hearts set on.

"They *will* let us go on," said Zachary, riding up front with the Devil. "Right?"

From a pay phone at a Holiday Inn, the Devil called the festival promoter, a very cool, very smart hippy king named Michael. Softly, he told Michael that if the Dan Paul Overfield Band were allowed to play, he could make sure lots of people came to the show.

"That would be far out," said Michael. "We'll see you when you get here."

ON THE FESTIVAL'S opening day, the Dan Paul Overfield Band ran into traffic. Cars jammed the road for miles.

"They got a whole lot more people than they was expecting," a cop told them. "Nearest best place to park is probably back past Bethel, and walk back in."

They drove back to Bethel, slowly, between meadows full of parked cars. Finding nothing in Bethel, they drove past White Lake, until finally they stopped at a farmhouse and called Michael.

"We can't get there from here," the Devil explained.

"No one can," Michael replied. "Most of the performers are staying at the Holiday Inn in Monticello."

"Now you tell us," said the Devil.

"Yeah," said Michael. "It's just that there's a lot of people, you know?"

"As promised," said the Devil.

So they wound up at the Holiday Inn, where they lounged around, digging the air-conditioning and watching TV, and waiting for the phone to ring and tell them what was going on. Sometimes a helicopter landed in the parking lot, collecting other musicians and taking them to the festival.

The news broke in, announcing that the concert site had been declared a disaster area. But the fans they interviewed were happy. They said it wasn't just about music anymore. They said it was about people being beautiful.

The TV showed the road through Bethel, choked with people. A great tribe, it seemed, washed through the farmland toward the stage at its heart.

"Far out," breathed Zachary.

"It *will* be," said Fish, "if we get to play."

"Stop worrying," said Memory.

"Stop worrying," echoed the Devil.

They had originally been scheduled to play late Saturday morning. Three times the phone rang, telling them they'd been bumped back to Saturday evening. Later Saturday evening. Maybe really, really, late Saturday night.

Night fell. Morning came. No one could sleep.

The Devil watched the TV with silent intensity.

People dancing, some of them naked. Wildness and kindness, mixed together.

The wildness and the kindness and the faraway war all worked together. In the end, they were part of the same thing. He had planted seeds. The harvest was groovy.

Most important, it made good television.

THE PHONE RANG, and suddenly there was chaos. The organizers wanted to change the order again, but now they were being bumped up. They would play this afternoon, in a few short hours.

The musicians met their helicopter, carrying what little equipment they needed. A second helicopter scooped up the crew. The Holiday Inn dropped away beneath them. Green fields and woods and summer haze passed below, and in minutes they passed high over the outskirts of the festival, over more people than the eye could handle, and landed behind the stage.

Stagehands and managers hustled them up a wooden ramp, past stacks of equipment, past trucks and litter. The roadies, marshaled by Osgood, began hauling sound equipment off the second helicopter.

The Devil lifted his face into the noontime air, and felt mist and electricity. Was it raining? Hard to tell. The sky had a nasty, ragged look he didn't like. But he liked the electricity, because it came from the crowd happening out there.

They had an hour until showtime. He left the band in the hands of the organizers and wandered off on his own. He hiked over mud and electric cables and pools of standing water, climbed a wooden fence, and let himself be swallowed up by a half million of the nicest people he'd ever met.

"Hey," they said to him as he passed, and he smiled and said "Hey" back.

A short hike brought him to one of the lighting towers. Looking up, up, up, the Devil had a moment of vertigo as the peak of the tower seemed to fall backward against the rolling clouds. He reached out to steady himself on the shoulder of a heavyweight hippie with a long black beard.

The heavyweight smiled and said, "Hey."

The tower was crawling with people. Mostly young men, some of them naked, hanging casually among the steel bars, not far off the ground. Others climbed higher, as if they meant to escape the Earth or at least say "Hey" to the spotlight operators.

Through the crowd, through families with nursing infants, past couples doing whatever under blankets, he moved on. Past people sharing water and food and cigarettes, uphill forever and ever, until the people gave way to green grass and stood in lines to use portable toilets. There was a security headquarters made of psychedelic buses.

He watched a man and woman undress and make love in a meadow. He waded in a pond where young men shaved and shouted and paddled around in canoes. He joined a half circle of stoned people doing yoga.

"Breathe in," said the yoga master. "Find your root chakra."

"Hey," said the stoned people, breathing.

The Devil was making his way back, emerging from the woods, when a guttural, animal sound ripped along the hillside, echoing among the trees. A motorcycle passed on the Devil's left, bearing a wild-haired man in a hand-tooled vest and a pretty woman in a loose cotton dress.

The wild-haired man glanced the Devil's way and he knew this was Michael, the one who'd brought this mad, giant, peaceful thing together.

The motorcycle rumbled toward him, and paused a yard or two away.

"Hey," said the Devil.

"Hey," said Michael.

In billions of years, you were bound to meet some people—people with unusual power or vision—who changed the world.

The motorcycle tore off through the grass, Michael saying something that made the woman laugh, and the Devil laughed, too.

THE DAN PAUL Overfield Band, meantime, was herded up a ramp, between walls of unpainted plywood. Here and there, a famous face looked their way.

One famous face, framed in sunglasses, a groovy headband, and a huge, natural Afro, shined a smile at Memory and said, "Welcome to Mars."

They were welcome here. They *belonged* here. This was who they were now.

For an instant, with a knifelike pain, she wished Dan Paul were there.

She and Fish and Zachary made small talk, having a tablet of this, a drink of that, and eating pills like Alice in Wonderland. Time was a purple whirlpool.

Then the whirlpool steadied, and they were being herded again, onto the stage at Woodstock.

× × ×

IT WAS LIKE being in a Bible story.

An ocean of people. They might have been on their way to the Red Sea or Jordan.

Zachary put on his stone face, and hit them with a slow, snaky bass. Followed by Fish, with a jungle beat. Memory waved her arms over her head, pretending to be tossed by drums and wind.

And the wind *was* rising, pushed from behind by dark clouds.

Memory's voice rode electric currents and flowed out over them all with its soft, impossible echo.

"Like she's accompanied by a ghost," some whispered, up high on the towers and down below on blankets. They fell in love.

Her head rolled lazily, and her shoulders rolled slowly, and her thin body grooved to one side and the other as if she were a thread weaving through time and the day, and if you were having a good trip on good acid—not the brown stuff—you saw her weaving at the center of bright flashes as if the universe were snapping Kodak pictures; you saw her soul and your soul and everyone's soul together, all part of the same Bible story, and you looked at her and loved her, even though you started feeling real wind toss your freak-flag hair and looked over your shoulder at the clouds racing in, because those clouds looked like a Bible story, too.

IT *WAS* A Bible story!

That's just what the Devil was thinking, offstage, watching the band and the clouds, but mostly watching the vast, multicolored multitude. Pocahontas would have loved this, he thought, before he could remember not to think about her. The Pilgrims, who talked about peace but prepared for war, wouldn't have understood. These people had outgrown their ancestors. A new world would come out of it, before everything was said and done.

It didn't hurt that there were lots of free drugs, and people humping in the bushes.

× × ×

THE DAN PAUL OVERFIELD BAND played only one song at Woodstock.

Melody sang three verses before the clouds began to spit, and some guy with a beard walked out and covered the mike with his hand and said into her ear, "You guys, wow, I'm so sorry, it's about to piss down rain and we have to get the equip—"

"Sure," said Memory, nodding. "Yeah."

"You'll be the first back on when . . . you know . . . whenever. You know?"

Then he spoke to the crowd. He told them to cover up and be patient and please get the fuck down off the towers.

NO ONE TOLD the band what to do, so they found their way down a ramp at the back of the stage complex, and stood in muddy gravel behind a crane, trading dumb looks.

"This bites," said Fish.

"That was wonderful," said Zachary.

Memory's mind reeled, still high from being onstage. In a minute, she would have shaken it off, but the wind grabbed a canvas sail tied atop some scaffolding, and pulled a tower over right on top of them.

USUALLY WHEN SOMETHING like that falls on people, the people are killed.

None of the Dan Paul Overfield Band were killed.

There was a rush of things crashing around them: wood splintering, gravel flying, steel pipes and clamps shivering and bending, shrieking.

All around them, voices shouted and cursed. Boots and sandals and bare feet ran toward them, climbed down to them.

"Get someone from the hospital tent!"

Memory was unhurt. Two stories of the scaffold had slammed down around her like a squirrel trap, driving steel into wet gravel.

Fish thought he was unhurt until he saw his thumb lying in the gravel. He felt sleepy and dizzy all of a sudden.

Zachary was knocked into a deep rain puddle, where he lay on his back, stunned. Two seconds later, a high-voltage winch splashed into the water beside him.

A FLASH, like a giant welding torch.

A SNAP like a cracking whip.

Zachary came to his feet like a zombie in convulsions, and stood there, staring at nothing, drooling and jerking.

Memory climbed out of the wreckage, shaking. When she spied Zachary, her stomach lurched.

"Zach?"

No response. A tiny stream of Fish's blood swirled past Zachary's left foot.

Help arrived. They dragged Fish loose, and wrapped his hand in a T-shirt.

"Get my fucking thumb," said Fish, and someone did.

Others gathered in a loose circle around Zachary. Someone said, "This cat's been electrocuted."

They wrapped him in blankets as the helicopter came thundering down.

Memory had a sudden mental picture of her future. It was empty, like her past, like amnesia in reverse.

7.

The Excellent Mr. Scratch, a Patron of Science

Philadelphia, 1750

BENJAMIN FRANKLIN WAS UP past midnight, giving himself electric shocks in the name of science.

He took a copper cylinder filled with lemon marmalade, and lowered it into a zinc cylinder filled with vinegar. He clipped copper leads onto each cylinder, then crossed the leads to see what would happen.

ZZZZZT!

Marmalade, he wrote in a leather-bound journal, *can hold a charge.*

He sat for a bit with his hand in his chin, pleased with himself, as he often was.

THE DEVIL SAT on a shelf in the corner of Franklin's laboratory, perched excitedly between a pair of encyclopedias.

Franklin—America!—was about to capture lightning—God's own superpower!—and tame it like a dog. For the first time in hundreds of years, the Devil began to hope again that Earth might surpass Heaven after all.

"Comfortable?" asked Franklin.

The Devil wondered who Franklin was addressing.

"I don't mind the intrusion so much," said Franklin, tinkering with the marmalade coil, "as the not introducing oneself. It's poor manners."

It dawned upon the Devil that Franklin was one of those rare, wise souls who could see him when he made himself invisible. Nevertheless, he was taken by surprise when the scientist turned and flung an old wheel of cheese at him.

"Well?" said Franklin, regarding him over the rims of his spectacles.

The Devil, knocked from his perch, stood and offered a courtly bow. "I hope," he said, dusting himself off, "that you will take my intrusion as a compliment. You have become a gifted and important man of science."

"Rubbish!" boomed Franklin, but he blushed.

The Devil asked, then, if he might be permitted to continue observing, or even to assist in, Franklin's lab work.

"Why didn't you just ask, before?" Franklin inquired.

"You seemed religious."

Franklin's belly shook with glee. "I very much *mean* to seem religious," he said. "Quite right! You may call again at noon tomorrow. Good day!"

The Devil bowed again, and vanished up the chimney.

LATE THE NEXT MORNING, Franklin bumbled about the lab, preparing a demonstration not only for the Devil, but for other guests as well. While he worked, he addressed his dog, a great black Newfoundland bitch named Queen, who had been driven from the house by Mrs. Franklin.

"All things hover between the province of Heaven and the Devil," Franklin told his dog. "A shade of gray, as it were, between ideas of pure form."

Queen seemed neither to agree nor disagree.

The lab hosted a library of jars and bones, volumes of law, a stuffed otter, a stuffed cat—strangely featured, from the Orient—and an unopened box of cotton kneesocks.

A clock, hidden away on the shelves, chimed noon just then, and three gentlemen let themselves in at the door. These were the Devil and two Presbyterian strangers he had encountered upon the walk: two fat, dwarfish men in black frock coats.

Franklin introduced them as "the reverend brothers Poole: Jacob and Bosley."

Indicating the Devil, he said, "Your Eminences, such as you are, may I present the Excellent Mr. Scratch, a patron of Science."

There were pleasantries and Madeira wine. Franklin disappeared through a rear door and staggered back in, wrestling an enormous, warlike turkey.

Feathers scattered. A jar shattered. Franklin plunged the turkey into a wooden cage and locked it up tight.

"Much has been made," he declared, holding aloft a pair of wire leads, "of electricity's seemingly contradictory power to create or destroy. On the one hand, we have lightning, which burns houses. On the other, properly shepherded—"

"All *I've* seen it do," barked Bosley, "is cause a woman's hair to frizz and rise round about her head."

"Or to make tin glow in a Leyden jar!" added Jacob.

"Properly controlled," Franklin argued, "electricity can kill."

"Lightning kills," said Bosley. "That's no surprise."

"Man cannot control lightning," answered Franklin. He indicated cylinders attached to the leads. "He *can* control *this*."

Soberly, Franklin knelt before the cage and hobbled the turkey with a pair of copper manacles.

"With apologies to this fine bird," he said, "I offer you gentlemen the advent of electricity as a weapon both terrible and—"

Franklin twisted a wire.

SNAP! FLASH!

A thousand suns! Followed by thick smoke and the stench of overcooking.

The smoke sank to reveal a recumbent Franklin, rising like an island in a receding tide. He seemed to be asleep. One of his hands was burned. Indeed, it still smoked.

The turkey was on fire, and also somewhat inside out. At the front of the cage, the copper manacles and their wiring lay melted.

The ministers Poole hovered over Franklin from a distance.

"Is he—?" said Bosley, coughing.

"Has he—?" said Jacob, trembling.

The Devil observed that Franklin was breathing evenly.

"The good doctor will live to strike another day," he assured the Presbyterians, ushering them toward the door. "Let us consider our adventures complete for the day."

"But—" began Bosley, indicating the blazing turkey.

"See here—!" barked Jacob, indicating the battery, which had begun to glow and spit marmalade.

The Devil drew himself up, dark and tall.

"Good day," he bid them, in a certain voice he had.

The ministers made their goodbyes. The Devil bolted both doors and closed the windows. With a wave of one wooden hand, he extinguished the battery and the turkey. He located a roll of clean linen and a jar of ointment, and sat down to tend Franklin's hand.

"Wake up," he told the scientist.

Franklin's eyes shot open. He spied the Devil leaning over him and smelled smoke.

"If this is Hell," he grouched, "it's a disappointment."

"You're not dead," the Devil told him. "Only foolish. Now sit up."

Franklin sat up, peering into the turkey cage.

"Piddle," he said.

"Hmm?"

The Devil released Franklin's hand, neatly bandaged.

"The poor creature was in a state, naturally," explained Franklin. "Its bladder emptied on the floor of the cage, the leads crossed amid the moisture, completing the circuit ahead of its time, unleashing . . . Well, you were there. You saw."

"It wasn't grounded," said the Devil, in a patient tone.

"That's right," said Franklin, eyeing him with surprise.

"You need help," declared the Devil. Inspired, he reached into the cage, tugged loose the two smoking, thoroughly cooked legs, and scraped them clean with a pocketknife. He offered one leg to Franklin, who accepted, and took a bite from the other. They chewed a while in silence.

"You mean *your* help," said Franklin. "I'd rather not."

"Listen, friend," said the Devil, "let me tell you something of your future, and then decide what help you need."

Franklin was suspicious, but he said, "Go on."

"Without my help," said the Devil, "you will be held to scorn in the British courts. You and your son will find yourselves on opposite sides in a bloody war, and history will say you were a buffoon who chased after women young enough to be your granddaughter."

"Twaddle!"

"*With* my help, the ages will remember you as the greatest scientist of your time, and as a father of a nation of free men."

"History will say what it will," said Franklin, tossing aside his turkey bone. "Besides, nothing is without its price. Least of all, as I understand it, your help. I'll take my chances, and keep my soul."

"It's of no use to you," the Devil said.

"You seem to think yourself awfully clever," said Franklin, cleaning his spectacles with a handkerchief. "If I were to depend upon you for my success and reputation, it would behoove me to determine just how clever a fellow you really are."

"What is it you suggest?"

"Nothing much." Franklin turned away, unearthed a pen and an inkwell on his workbench, and began to write something on the flyleaf of a book. "I will ask you a riddle. If, at the end of a week's time, you can answer the riddle, I will forfeit my soul on terms agreeable to us both. If you fail, then the terms will be reversed."

The Devil bit his bottom lip. Franklin was a prize like no other.

If any mortal could help Earth surpass Heaven, it was Franklin, and the country he would help to hatch.

If Franklin did everything just so. Which he wouldn't, the Devil didn't think, without his influence.

"Very well," said the Devil, reaching into his pocket. "But I should like to add something into the bargain."

He produced a glass ball, which he placed on the workbench.

"This crystal ball will show you anything you like of the past, present, or future," he said.

Franklin's pen quivered.

"I will leave it on the workbench for the space of one week. In that time, you must never look into it. If you do, then your soul is mine regardless of my success with your riddle."

"Done," said Franklin. He finished writing on the flyleaf, tore the page loose, and handed it to the Devil.

The Devil read, frowned, and reread, aloud: "'How far can a dog run into the woods?'"

"Your riddle," Franklin said. "Till next week, then?"

The Devil turned toward the door, hesitated, and faced Franklin again.

"What's wrong?"

"Nothing," said the Devil. "Except I wonder if you might be so good as to let me borrow your dog?"

THE DEVIL WAS DEVOTED to Science. He was methodical.

He hired a carriage to take himself and Franklin's great Newfoundland out of the city, and leave them at the edge of the woods.

"I suppose," said the Devil, "that this is the sort of woods he meant."

Queen gave him a sideways look and licked his hand.

"Fine, then," barked the Devil, speaking Queen's own native tongue. "Off you go!"

And off she went, running. It was important, he had told her, that she run. The riddle, after all, did not ask how far a dog could stroll into the woods, or saunter, gallop, dance, or trot. Queen, trained to obedience, ran all the way through the woods, stopping on the other side, where the Devil contrived, by unholy means, to be waiting for her.

He had purchased a notebook, in which he now scrawled, *All the way through the woods.* He noted that it had taken her about two minutes, and that the effort had caused her to slobber.

A good scientist, in the Devil's opinion, was to observe and record everything. Later, he would be better able to judge what was and was not important. It was often said that the Devil was in the details, and he knew this to be true.

They were at the woods an entire afternoon. The Devil had Queen run through the woods in the opposite direction (two minutes, ten seconds). Had her make an effort to avoid obstacles (three minutes, fourteen seconds), and to travel in a straight line regardless of dead trees, gopher holes, and a briar patch (nine minutes precisely, mostly due to the briar patch). He had her run backward. He had her run as if hunting, and then as if being hunted. He had her enter the woods at different points. He made notes about the position of the sun, the position of the moon (which rose at half past, nearly full, but quite pale), and the temperament of the weather, which he recorded as *Uneasy.*

That night, feeling that both he and the beast had earned a reward, he registered them at a respected inn and ordered an entire roasted lamb, which they split.

"This isn't going to be easy," he remarked to Queen.

Queen didn't care.

COOL AS HE HAD BEEN with the Devil near at hand, once left alone with the crystal ball, Franklin found its mere presence a challenge.

He didn't look into it.

"Only God may know the future," he muttered, drafting designs for a lightning rod.

His own future concerned him, certainly. And there was the future of the country, of course. He caught himself straining out of the corner of his eye—

"Dash!" he bellowed, throwing a shop rag over the thing.

A minute later, having returned to the problem of the lightning rod, he stole a look sideways, and discovered that the shop rag had fallen aside.

The ball gleamed at him.

"Get thee behind me!" Franklin hissed, and struggled to concentrate.

WHEN THE WEEK WAS PAST, Franklin descended to his workshop to find his dog and the Devil waiting. Queen was glad to see him. With a bearlike bound, she cast herself full length upon her master.

"Bosh!" cried Franklin, scratching her behind the ears.

"Good morning," said the Devil.

"Good morning, indeed!" boomed the scientist. "There's the week, then, and not a tot have I looked in your damned glass. Won't say I wasn't sore tempted—"

"You are a man of uncommon virtue," said the Devil. So saying, he extended his hand; the ball leaped into his palm and was hidden away in a pocket.

"Thank you," said Franklin.

"Unfortunately for both your soul and your virtue, however, I have solved your riddle."

"Ah." Franklin's stomach turned.

The Devil stood looking down his nose. He didn't always look wicked, but he looked wicked now.

The Devil cleared his throat and said, "A dog will run into the woods . . . as far as she wishes. No more, no less."

To which Franklin, with great false modesty, replied that this was not the answer.

The Devil seemed disappointed, but not surprised.

"A dog may run only *halfway* into the woods," declared Franklin, eyes alight, "because after that, you see, she is running *out*!"

The Devil moaned in despair. Franklin, triumphant, stamped his foot. The Devil—being an angelic creature, by origin, and thus composed entirely of soul-stuff—shrank into the form of something like a black orangutan. Thus reduced, this thing tried to crawl into a woodpile near the stove, but Queen surrounded it with paws and teeth until it leaped with a horrid cry into a butter churn.

Franklin wasted no time in fastening the lid and pounding it snug with a mallet.

The Devil's soul howled within, quite trapped, Franklin's property, fairly won.

FRANKLIN STOOD several doors down the street, before a looming Presbyterian church. He had with him an astonishingly long ladder—tapered at the end, as if for apple picking—with which he wrestled, trying to bring it to rest against the steeple. At his feet, wrapped in burlap, lay the finished lightning rod, attached to a coil of steel cable.

It was his intention to fasten the lightning rod to the steeple, and this intention had seemed uncomplicated, in the safety of his laboratory. On the street, however, facing the steeple's considerable altitude, he found himself apprehensive.

Dark clouds threatened. A sharp wind swooped upon the street.

Against this wind, Franklin staggered to and fro.

While he was thus engaged, his butter churn came down the street, sort of knocking and kicking as if animated by a spell.

"Let me out!" croaked the butter churn.

Franklin raised his eyebrows and said, "Why would I want to do that?"

The wind and the ladder tugged him down the street a yard or so.

The butter churn followed . . . *hop, knock, hop.*

"Listen," it said to Franklin, "I was only trying to be of assistance. And your winning our little wager has merely served to prove my point."

"Which was—?"

"Your own cleverness. The shrewdness and spirit of your countryfolk, by extension. It gladdens me to admit I have underestimated both."

"Still," grunted Franklin, "'that which is fairly won—'"

"I'll let you look in the ball," said the butter churn.

Franklin appeared to consider, sidestepping the butter churn as the wind bore him in the other direction, quite missing the steeple.

"And I'll assist with your ladder, there, as well."

"Done," said Franklin, passing by once again.

"Done!" cried the Devil, springing like a jack-in-the-box from the churn. In a trice, the wind came about and planted the ladder squarely around the steeple tip, and the Devil sat on a rung maybe thirty feet up, tipping his hat.

"Have some respect!" gruffed Franklin. "That's a church."

Thunder rumbled. The few Philadelphians about the streets clutched their hats and rushed for home. The Devil dug in his pockets, produced the glass ball, and tossed it down. Franklin caught it neatly with one hand, and looked.

Gazing, he saw armies and fields afire. He saw great arguments and new ideas. New machines. He saw his death, and carried what he saw with him all his days. The knowledge, though it saddened him, made him fearless. He stared into the ball for a good five minutes, then pitched the ball back to the Devil, who slipped it into his pocket.

Lightning flashed and thunder cracked at nearly the same time.

Franklin unwrapped his lightning rod and regarded it with trepidation.

"I don't suppose," he said to the Devil, now sliding down the ladder toward him, "you'd like to take *this*"—he indicated the lightning rod—"and attach it to *that*"—he pointed at the steeple tip—"in the name of science and municipal safety?"

"No," said the Devil, reaching the street and pulling his collar high.

"Whyever not?"

"It's your big idea. You do it."

"It is mine, sir, to take notes and make observations. Never underestimate the value of good notes."

"I won't. And I'll wish you the best of everything, and be going."

Franklin held the ladder in place with his shoe and wiped his spectacles on his coattails.

"As you will," he said to the Devil. "I wonder, then, if you're not awfully busy, if you wouldn't mind stopping at the house, on your way, and asking *Mrs.* Franklin to step out and lend a hand?"

8. Favorite Foods and Good and Evil

Various highways, 1969

SO MUCH FOR THE Dan Paul Overfield Band, thought Memory.

It had been a day and a night since the tower had fallen on them. Fish and Zachary had been admitted to a New York City hospital, where doctors would try to restore Fish's thumb and would test Zachary for brain damage.

"We won't know much for a few weeks," they told Memory, regarding Zachary. "There's no point in waiting around . . ."

She visited Fish, who lay with his arm in a fat white cast. Doped up on painkillers, he was alert enough to blame Memory for making them play Woodstock, and tell her to fuck off.

"Whatever," she said.

It didn't much matter what Fish, or anyone else, had to say. A numbness had come over her, as if amnesia were spreading from her mind to her body. She left the hospital in a fog and sat down at a bus stop a block down the street. She watched the pigeons and blinked once in a while.

It was over. The big dream had died with Dan Paul, come back to life briefly and wonderfully with the Devil, and now it was dead again. It was too much.

The Devil was conspicuously absent.

So that's the kind of friend he is, she thought. Shouldn't be surprised.

People gathered to wait for the bus. The bus arrived and departed, and Memory barely even noticed. She sat there for an hour. More people gathered. Buses took them away. Memory stayed, like a stone in a flowing stream. She had no plans to move. No plans of any kind.

A bus pulled up. Not a city bus this time, but a Microbus.

The space bus, towing the death limo, both splashed with upstate mud. The Devil rolled down the window and whistled at her.

"Want some candy, little girl?" he called, winking.

Memory didn't move. She wasn't sure she remembered how.

The Devil climbed out of the Microbus, scooped Memory off her bench, installed her gently in the passenger seat, and got back behind the wheel. A wave of his hand, and they skated easily through midday traffic.

"Where have you been?" Memory asked, stirring herself with some effort.

"Paying off your crew and driving this piece of shit to the city," he answered.

Whatever.

"Why are you still here?" she asked as they crossed the George Washington Bridge into New Jersey. "And where are we going?"

The city dropped away behind them. The Devil lit a cigarette.

"I thought you wanted to be famous," he said.

"I did," said Memory, propping her bare feet on the dashboard. "I do."

It was true, she realized. More than ever. Her numbness receded.

"We're headed south," said the Devil. "You need new musicians."

"Why do we have to go south to find—"

"Just trust me."

"Trust you? Are you kidding? I *did* trust you, until—"

"Things don't always happen the way you want," said the Devil. "It doesn't mean they won't happen. And haven't I held up my end as far as you're concerned? You want to be famous. I'd say you *are* pretty much famous, after yesterday."

"I want it to last."

"All right."

She punched him in the arm. The Microbus swerved.

"No matter what I say," complained the Devil, "it's the wrong goddamn thing!"

He stomped on the brakes and wrestled the Microbus to a stop, half on, half off the shoulder.

"Tell me what's the matter," said the Devil, "and I promise I'll give you straight answers."

Memory exploded.

"Is this all some kind of game to you? Two weeks ago you made a deal with all of us, and we forked over what you wanted, and all we've gotten since is—"

"You sang for a half-million people."

"Is there going to be more? And what about the guys?"

"They'll be all right."

"That's not an answer!" screamed Memory. "Fuck you, man!"

She kicked her door open and stormed into the tall weeds along the shoulder. Face flushed blood red, she howled, "You said they'd have doors open for them, and where are they? Zachary's drooling down his chin and Fish will never play again! You have our *souls,* and you . . . do you even *have* a soul?"

"That's a complicated—"

"Shut up! Everything you say is either a lie or just *useless*! Why couldn't I have met you in the part of my life I can't remember?"

She stomped off down the highway, as if making war on the asphalt.

The Microbus crept up alongside her.

"Hi," said the Devil.

She ignored him.

"You're not done being famous," said the Devil. "It's your time. It'll get better."

He stopped the van and hopped out as he spoke, approaching Memory with his hands in his pockets.

Memory jumped across the ditch and plunged through a narrow stretch of woods, emerging at the edge of a wheat field. The Devil followed, fiddling with his sunglasses.

"Why haven't you asked for your memory back?" he called after her.

Memory faced him.

"Maybe I don't want it back."

"I think you do."

Memory folded her arms across her chest.

"I don't think you *can* give it back to me. Maybe I'm wrong."

The Devil grinned a sharp-toothed grin, and fished a long-stemmed clay pipe from his shirt pocket.

"No. You're right; I actually *tried* to wake up your memory one night, but I couldn't. Couldn't even find it."

"You tried to bring back my memory without asking me?"

"I thought it would be a nice surprise."

He packed the pipe, lit it with a fiery forefinger, and passed it to her.

She took it and inhaled.

"Since when does the Devil do nice surprises?" she croaked, passing the pipe back.

"People think they know me," muttered the Devil, smoking. "I can do nice things like anyone else."

She turned and looked at him. He must be impossibly old, she knew, and if you looked closely, you could see it. In his tanned face were traces of furrows and scars, like a battlefield healed and grown over. Beneath it all, she sensed hidden rumblings and vibrations. He was like a storm that hadn't happened yet, a thought you weren't quite thinking.

A memory you didn't have.

"You said I reminded you of someone," she said.

The Devil tucked the pipe away in his shirt pocket.

"Yeah," he said. "It's partly the way you sing. Maybe I'll tell you about it if you'll quit being mad and come back to the van."

Memory waited a minute just so he wouldn't find her too easy, then followed him through the trees, back to the road.

THEY TALKED ABOUT lots of things, the next few hours. Like favorite foods and Good and Evil.

They talked about practical things as well.

"How much did you get for the other vans?" asked Memory.

"Thousand each."

She wrote this down on a notepad. They only had so much money left.

"And I paid off the crew with the last of your studio cash."

"Cool. Why are we going south?"

"I asked you to trust me."

"And I told you no."

He didn't answer.

"Answer me."

"When I feel like it. Jump out if you don't like it."

She didn't like it, but she didn't jump out.

The morning became afternoon, then evening, and they stopped at a Holiday Inn. The Devil signed them in as Mr. and Mrs. John Scratch, and the clerk asked no awkward questions.

FARTHER SOUTH, the next day.

In the Smoky Mountains, they parked the Microbus on the shoulder of a National Park Service road, and Memory followed the Devil through a silent forest until he stopped at an old, dead tree.

He stuck long claws down inside, and pulled out something wrapped in leather. He didn't speak, and she followed him back to the road, where he undid the leather and drew out a fiddle and a bow.

A fiddle, which might have been wood or solid gold, depending on the light, and a bow made from the same wood or the same gold, strung with what might have been horsehair, but wasn't.

"Haven't needed Ol' Ripsaw here for a while," he said, looking the fiddle over from every angle.

"What do you need him now for?" asked Memory, even though she thought she knew.

"*You* need him," said the Devil. "Because you need a guitar player."

He drew the bow across the strings, and Old Ripsaw groaned like an old, sleepy soul.

"Please tell me where we're going," she asked.

"Louisiana," he said, drawing sparks with his bow. "To see if old Two-John Spode has been practicing."

THE SECOND THEY CROSSED into Louisiana, the radiator blew.

Memory woke up, saying, "What happened?"

"This thing's not even supposed to *have* a radiator!" complained the Devil, pulling over. "Air-cooled German technology! Who the hell customized this thing?"

"The studio bought it for us," said Memory, yawning. "It was cheap."

"Well," said the Devil, "go find us some cheap water to keep it running."

"Why don't you just magically make the radiator not leak? Else what's the point in being the Devil?"

"It's hard to explain."

"Try."

The Devil walked around behind the bus, and opened the rear doors to hunt for something like a bucket.

"It would get boring," said the Devil, overturning blankets, old food wrappers, and an amplifier. "You'd be surprised how much of your happiness has to do with little problems. Like having to go get toilet paper or having to fetch some water. If you just sat around and 'magicked' everything, then you'd wind up just . . . sitting around."

"Why don't we drive the limo and tow the bus?"

The Devil looked offended.

"That car," he said, "is not a tow truck."

"How come I'm the one who's got to get the water?"

"What's the point of being the Devil if I can't make people bring me water?"

He appeared at her window with a bucket.

There was water in the ditch. She fetched three buckets of ditch water, the Devil plugged the radiator with a piece of black-cherry bubble gum, and they went another fifty miles.

SWAMP TREES AND KUDZU framed the road at first, then gave way to flat country and fields of green sugarcane.

The horizon piled high with clouds. Thunder spoke, far away.

The second time they needed water, they happened on a gas station. After they had filled the radiator, Memory climbed behind the wheel.

"What are you doing?" asked the Devil.

"Driving. If I gotta fetch the water, I should at least get to drive some."

"Do you have a license?"

"I don't know."

But she didn't move, except to turn the key and start the engine.

The Devil walked around to the passenger side, and they rolled on south. Before long, the cane fields gave way to swamp forest again, and not long after that, it came down raining.

MEMORY TRIED TO get the Devil to tell her what was so special about Two-John Spode.

"You heard what the boys said," he reminded her.

"They made him sound about half real."

"He's real."

"Then—"

"Watch the road."

Rain slathered the windshield. Not far ahead, red taillights glowed, and Memory slowed to follow an old farm truck.

"Why wouldn't you tell me where we were going when I asked?"

"You wouldn't have come. I had to wait till we were too far down the road."

He closed his eyes and tried to catch some sleep.

"That's some devious shit," said Memory, "for somebody who wants to be trusted."

"I suppose it is," said the Devil, without opening his eyes.

The rain made a fog, which crept and rose. Everything beyond the windshield might have been a trick of the eye, except for the red lights of the farm truck, which sped up, and then slowed again.

"It's like driving between worlds," Memory told the Devil.

The Devil had fallen asleep.

"Yep," he said, nonetheless.

9.

How God Stole the Devil's Girlfriend

Heaven and Earth, the Age of Creation

THE DEVIL DREAMED.

When most people dream, it's a casserole of wishes and fears. Being several billion years old, the Devil had a lot of memory backed up—and you can wind up with issues if you don't sort through it all somehow. So when the Devil dreamed, he *remembered.* It kept him from talking to himself more than he did.

Dreaming in the passenger seat, he remembered the very oldest things of all. Before he was the Devil. When he was Lucifer, in Heaven.

Back before Heaven and Earth were separated, because there was no Earth. There was hardly much of anything except God and the angels, surrounded by something called "the Face of the Deep," and something called "the Waters."

"The Waters" were a kind of flood, about six inches deep, and quite calm. You could either walk around in it all the time, or sprout wings. The angels sprouted wings.

No one knew what the Face of the Deep was, except that it was deep and surrounded the Waters.

"What *is* it?" the angels sometimes asked, but God only answered with a proud, inscrutable silence.

A lot of angels thought God was kind of self-absorbed and crazy right from the Beginning, and would have left Him more or less alone if He hadn't insisted they sing to Him around the clock.

This wasn't as awful as it might sound. There was something bright and correct about God, plus it gave the angels the idea of Competition. In this scramble for excellence and holy favor, Lucifer emerged as God's undisputed Golden Child, shining over them all like a cherry atop a sundae.

ONE DAY, out of nowhere, God said, "Let there be light."

Something like a nuclear FLASH tore across the Deep, causing the singing to falter into blindness and screaming.

When his eyes cleared, Lucifer approached God and asked what *that* was all about.

"I'm not sure," He said. "But look!" He waved at the Deep with an expression of dumb wonder.

Stars and galaxies exploded all over the place.

The angels staggered around God in their ranks and millions, and sang to Him in shaking voices.

God was impressed with Himself, of course, but at the same time, Lucifer could tell He was troubled.

"I didn't know it was going to do that," He told Lucifer, indicating the expanding universe overhead.

They splashed through the Waters, side by side.

Lucifer shrugged and said it was a nice surprise.

"Surprise." It was a new idea.

"It was an impulse," God complained. "I won't fly off blind like that again. There should be an order to things." He looked over his shoulder at the neat, concentric choirs of angels.

Lucifer asked if God planned to create more things, besides just light.

"I do," answered God.

"Like what?"

And God answered.

The Plan (as He called it) would take effect over billions of years. Step-by-step, God would fill Heaven with living wonders—and he had it all figured out in advance this time. Oceans and streams of water and air, rich with new forms and structures.

But as he watched the universe spreading out like so much radioactive spaghetti sauce, it seemed to Lucifer that this creation had a wild seed in it. He wondered if the Plan was going to proceed with the order God intended. While ideas like "surprise" and "wild" were fascinating to Lucifer, he suspected God would be less than overjoyed with their effects.

The beginnings of the Plan were cause for celebration: The sun and moon were greeted with symphonies. The angels sang like never before.

Lucifer made note of the angels' joy, which frothed and bubbled. He made note that God didn't share in this. God was *pleased,* but He never frothed or bubbled. Lucifer realized then how distant God must be, how different from them all in ways they could never understand.

The Plan continued.

The angels went bananas when the dry land appeared. That was their favorite. Everyone came in for a landing, then took off again, because the dry land was hot. But they sang while rubbing their feet.

"This is Good," said God, more pleased than ever.

It was a strange idea, "Good."

Lucifer frowned. If this or that, from now on, was "Good," then by implication there were things that were not.

"Life" was the most complicated part of the Plan.

"What is it?" asked Lucifer, touring the first sandy beaches with God.

God didn't quite know.

"It's sort of like what *we* have, you and Me and the angels. It's got question marks all over it, but it will grow in good order, I think."

"What if it grows in some way you don't expect?"

"I'm okay with . . . what did you call them? Surprises? I'm willing to be surprised, within reason."

"Within whose idea of reason?"

God faced Lucifer, and gave him a very direct, very final kind of look.

"Mine," he said.

Lucifer stood biting his lip. "Maybe it will *choose* to grow in good order," he said.

God's brow furrowed. "Choice" was another new and uncomfortable idea.

LIGHTNING STROKED the sea.

A few proteins woke up and started putting themselves together like puzzles.

The puzzles were symmetrical, like God and His angels. This pleased God, and He said it was Good.

The puzzles became complicated, and soaked up chemicals from the sea. They turned green, and ate up light as if it were food.

"I didn't see that coming," said God, "but I like it. That's Good."

The green spread out all over the place.

Some of the protein complexes grew arms and legs like God and the angels ("Good!"). These things crawled up onto the dry land and started eating plants. ("That's Good, I suppose," said God. "They've got to eat something.").

One day, God and Lucifer were patrolling the fringes of a hot, misty jungle when they happened upon a small creature eating weeds. There was something calm and satisfying about this little scene, and they paused for a moment to watch.

The moment was broken by another creature, larger and more pointy than the first, which lunged up out of the water, grabbed the herbivore around the middle in a flash of fangs and gore, and dragged it screaming beneath the water.

God shuddered. He put His hands over His face and said emphatically that this wasn't Good at all.

"Maybe 'Good' has nothing to do with it," said Lucifer. "Maybe it's just a way of doing things. Maybe Life won't necessarily do things the way *You'd* do things."

Maybe he let impatience creep into his voice. *Something* in what he said or how he said it got God's attention. God lifted His face out of His hands and met Lucifer's eyes. When Lucifer saw God's face, he stifled a cry, took wing, and fled.

If it was possible to not be God and somehow understand what being God was like, Lucifer understood it, however dimly, in that moment. He hadn't expected the deep, awful loneliness in those eyes. When You had created everything, and everything was a part of You, then no matter how much You filled up the universe, You were still alone. And when the universe began making its own choices and doing its own thing, everything it did made You feel left out, just a little. There was infinite greatness in being God, of course. But Lucifer saw that there were horror and isolation, too, and that these, too, were infinite.

THE CARNIVORES DIDN'T FAZE Lucifer; he couldn't get enough of Nature. He wandered the planet night and day, watching the growth and the changes. Particularly, he found himself hypnotized by sex.

Reproduction wasn't what captivated him; it was the weird business of coupling. Two creatures came together and basically became one, for a time. And you couldn't watch it happening all over the place without sort of wanting to do it. It looked like fun.

This, of course, was where the real trouble started.

There was this other angel, see.

The other angel wasn't male or female, because angels hadn't had those ideas yet.

The angel's name was Arden, and Arden was Lucifer's friend. A close friend.

They wandered together and sang together, shared misgivings about "Good" together, and together they watched animals coupling and were equally spellbound.

One day in a forest of lowland cherry blossoms, an awkward suggestion arose.

"You know . . ." said Lucifer.

"Mmm?" said Arden.

"Nothing."

"Something, obviously."

Lucifer pursed his lips, and they went back to watching male squirrels chase female squirrels.

"We could try that," he said, after a while.

Arden nodded thoughtfully, and said, "I don't see how."

Lucifer said that, obviously, some changes would have to be made.

Arden said, "You mean like this?," and when he looked, Arden had become beautifully, hauntingly, nakedly "female."

Lucifer made some changes of his own, was flooded with new sensations.

He knew right away that these were animal feelings. Dark, earthy feelings, like hunger. Like pride in his own strength and beauty. Like wanting to love and be close to other creatures, and also, paradoxically, wanting to hurt them.

"Oh," whispered Arden, eyes wild.

"Oh," growled Lucifer, eyes burning.

And they came together and were overwhelmed by each other.

IT QUICKLY BECAME the thing to do, among the angels who walked the Earth.

God didn't like it, of course. Lucifer guessed that sex, more than anything else, made God lonely.

"You have *got* to be kidding," He said, when He saw what was going on.

He turned away. He shook with wrath. These angels were quite obviously more interested in one another than in Him. This was something new.

"It's unholy!" He roared, shaking Heaven and Earth. "Everybody up here on the double!" And He waited with His galactic arms crossed, glaring.

"Unholy," said Lucifer, "I take it, is the opposite of 'Good.'"

"Lots of things are the opposite of 'Good,'" answered God. "Shut up."

They all stood together in the Waters, in a mass of concentric circles, God and Lucifer in the middle like two sixth graders on a playground.

"Clean it up down there," God demanded.

"What do you mean, 'clean it up'?"

"You know damn well what 'clean it up' means."

Lucifer told God something He'd never heard before.

He said, "No."

Part of him was scared when he said it, but part of him was angry and hungry and earthy, too, and his eyes glowed red for the very first time. God took a step back when He saw that. Lucifer showed his teeth. He wanted them to be sharp, so they were sharp.

Some of the angels, the ones who hadn't discovered fucking, wrung their hands and moaned. Why was this happening?

Lucifer felt their sadness and frustration, but how could he explain that the more earthy angels paid more attention to one another than to God because a lot of them had fallen in love? Would they—would God—understand that kind of love? It was something that happened in the soul and blood of natural creatures, or divine creatures who had sampled natural ways. It was a different kind of love than the love they had for God. You had to earn the love of a natural creature, whereas God-love had been sort of automatically installed—by God.

The more he thought about that, the more Lucifer found God's complaints selfish and puerile, and was damned if he'd explain himself to this crowd of sterile, bootlicking fruitcakes.

So he kept a rebellious silence.

And then God said, "Fine. Wallow in it. It's all yours. Just get out of here and don't come back."

He clenched His fists, and just like that Earth stopped being part of Heaven. It fell away into empty space, dragging Lucifer and Arden and their friends with it.

They fell through space and air, crashing down all over the place in deserts and rivers and oceans and wide, grassy places.

Lucifer stood, raising a defiant fist to the sky.

Then: "Where were we?" he asked Arden, who had fallen to Earth nearby, and they came together, biting sweetly.

SOME OF THE FALLEN ANGELS plunged right in, ruling the Earth with tooth and claw. They took a special interest in the two-legged monkeys that had recently appeared, helping the monkeys plant crops and build cities. The monkeys, in turn, worshipped the Fallen as gods, and it would have been the best of times if most of the Fallen hadn't had second thoughts.

"We're not animals," they told Lucifer. "We want to go home, if God will have us."

Arden, Lucifer was panicked to discover, was one of these.

"You can't be serious," he said to her.

They lay naked beside a river.

"I don't like feeling this way," she admitted. "But I'm serious, yes. And I'm frightened."

"Of what?"

And Arden nodded at the flowing water and said, "Of that."

"That" was a female hippopotamus, giving birth.

They watched the whole thing from messy, churning, bloody beginning to bloody end, with a tiny new hippo swimming around in its own slime, gasping for air.

"It's messy," agreed Lucifer, "but—"

"It's not just that," Arden interrupted. "Watch."

The mother and baby swam around nuzzling each other for a while, and then another hippo came charging through the tall grass in the shallows, roaring and showing its teeth.

The baby's daddy.

The daddy hippo shoved the mother aside, and killed the baby with a snap of its mighty jaws.

Arden drew up her legs and buried her face behind her knees.

"What do you expect?" asked Lucifer. "The baby would have grown up to be competition."

"I get it," snapped Arden. "But I don't like it, and I don't think I can stand it."

Lucifer understood her horror. Living things survived by devouring other living things. A little horror was fine with him, but Arden and many others preferred to endure it from a distance, in a cool and stately Heaven.

Across the red water, Lucifer spied a caravan of warriors on their way to kill people. He was frightened, suddenly. Frightened in a deep, helpless, hollow way.

"I'm leaving," Arden told him.

She said it softly, like trying to hit someone softly with a stick.

UP THEY FLEW, more than half of the Fallen. The sky opened up with a golden sunburst and took them right in.

Swallowed them, more like it, thought Lucifer, raging.

God had kicked him out of Heaven. That hurt, but he could handle it.

But now God had stolen his girlfriend.

He roared at Heaven.

He stood there by the river, knee-deep in hippo blood, raging and crying and becoming the world's first broken-heart story.

10.

Bluesmen

Louisiana, 1969

THE MICROBUS BEGAN to lose speed.

The engine rattled and coughed.

"I'm pulling over," said Memory.

"Yep," said the Devil, shaking off sleep.

They pulled onto the gravel shoulder and rolled to a halt. Ahead, taillights dimmed out of sight as the farm truck left them behind.

"It wouldn't kill you, you know," said Memory, "with a wave of your hand, just once—"

"Not necessary," said the Devil.

Memory looked, and saw taillights. The farm truck was backing down the shoulder toward them.

The truck stopped. A door slammed. A watery figure appeared, shrugging its way into a poncho.

Memory and the Devil got out, shoulders hunched against the rain.

The driver of the farm truck had green eyes like searchlights, and a deeply grooved face. The kind of features that can look either friendly or mean as all hell, depending on the person who wears them. These features were friendly.

"Thought you might be having engine trouble," he said. "Else you'da passed me a long time back. Richard Yeager."

"John Scratch," said the Devil, shaking hands.

Memory said, "Memory."

"Ma'am. Listen, I got some cable in here, and a towing hitch. I can tow you on into St. Judy. Might be like driving a train, since you already got a car in tow, but we'll take it slow. They'll fix you up proper if we can make it there."

"All right," said Memory, and they got busy doing what needed to be done.

"YOU'LL HAVE TO KEEP IT in neutral," Yeager told the Devil, when the chains were in place. "And—"

"Tell the driver," said the Devil, nodding at Memory.

Yeager gave some instructions about watching his taillights and leaving the steering wheel alone.

"That way, we'll all get into St. Judy in one piece."

Before Yeager could climb back in his truck, the Devil said, "We've come looking for a fellow called Two-John Spode."

Yeager's eyes darkened.

"Never heard of him, brother," he said.

FLASH! Lightning, then thunder, close enough to rattle teeth.

"That's all right," said the Devil, turning back to the Microbus.

"HE'S LYING," said Memory, smoothing wet hair out of her face. "Why would he lie?"

"Why does anybody lie?"

"Because they're scared."

"There you are. He'll change his mind before we get to St. Judy."

Ahead, the farm truck eased away. The chains caught with a jerk, and they were on the highway again.

HOURS LATER, when rain-dark had yielded to night, Yeager towed them off the road, into a wide gravel lot.

A hundred colored lightbulbs hung between utility poles. The lot served as parking for a gas station, a diner, a motel, and a bait shop. Beyond this roadside oasis, swamp jungle towered, wild with Spanish moss.

Yeager got out and knelt between the vehicles, pulling at the chain.

The Devil joined him. He leaned over Yeager with one boot on the Microbus bumper.

Yeager looked uneasy.

"When you asked about Two-John," he said, "I shouldn'ta said I never heard of him."

The Devil pulled an apple out of nowhere, polished it on his sleeve, and began to peel it with a rusty pocketknife.

"Maybe I'm superstitious," said Yeager. "People don't like to talk about Two-John, same way some people don't like to talk about the dead. Down here ain't like the rest of the country, you know."

"I know," said the Devil.

"They say there's people in New Orleans can raise the dead. I don't go to New Orleans."

The Devil took a bite out of his apple.

"There used to be a roadhouse here," said Yeager. "It burned down a couple years ago. Two-John played there sometimes. I never saw him, but they said he was good. He was pretty famous all around here, but he never made a record. Some people say he's dead, some people say he's got him a place back in that swamp there. That's all I got for you. That, and the garage over there opens in the morning. I guess they can put you up at the motel until then. I hope you get back on the road all right."

The Devil shook Yeager's hand, and Yeager got in his farm truck and drove away.

THE DEVIL RETRIEVED his fiddle, still wrapped in leather, from the back of the Microbus, and walked toward the bait shop, where a light burned in one window.

His stride was long; Memory hurried to keep up.

"Where are you going?" she asked. "Aren't we going to wait for the garage to open?"

"Nope."

"I thought we could at least get a room at the motel there, you know? Dry off and clean up?"

"Why clean up to go out in the swamp?"

"We're going in the swamp?"

The Devil shot her a wink, and together they mounted two rickety steps to the bait-shop door.

Knock-knock.

A fantastically old woman opened the door. One of her eyes was gone, stitched shut. The other wallowed in a sea of cataracts, turquoise blue all over. Blind as night, the woman still managed to look right where the Devil was standing. Looked him right in the eye.

She raised a crippled hand, and backed away.

"Je savais que c'était vous!" she whispered. "The Devil! I knew it!"

And the Devil said, *"Je suis pas ici pour vous, grand-mère.* I'm not here for you, Grandmother."

The old woman calmed down enough to beckon them inside.

The Devil started to say something.

"Je connais quoi faire t'es icitte," said the old woman. "I know why you're here."

She led them through the shop, and out through a back door, onto a half-rotten dock that creaked under their feet. Black water flowed beneath.

An ancient pirogue, motor bolted to the stern, floated at the end of the dock.

"We're going out in *that*?" whispered Memory. "At night?"

She heard the old woman chuckle under her breath.

"Can't get there in the Microbus," said the Devil.

He helped her down onto a tiny bench in the prow. In the dark to her left, something belched and went *plop* in the water.

Before the Devil could sit down and take the tiller, the old woman gestured at him, holding out her palm.

The Devil passed her a five-dollar bill.

"Bonne chance, Grandmother," he whispered.

The old woman limped off back to the bait shop.

The Devil yanked the engine to life. The pirogue lifted a little under Memory, the prow rising over smooth water and lily pads, and they moved off into the dark.

Night noises rose around them. Who could tell what made such noises? Nameless things sang and grumbled, buzzed and sawed. Shadows moved between shadows.

The Devil said, *"Allume-toi!"* and a tiki torch burned at the very stem of the boat.

"If you can do *that,*" said Memory, "then how come—"

"Because," rumbled the Devil. "Quiet, now."

LIGHT MADE THINGS WORSE.

In the dark, there was only the dark, but the torch cast a wizard-space around the pirogue, as if they were motoring through a cave made of fire. Around this cave, things moved. Great wings in the air. Great swellings in the water. The whole night seemed to crawl.

Memory realized that she didn't feel safe, even though her travel mate was the Devil. Something uneasy haunted his eyes. He didn't appear frightened, exactly, but *something* was there.

"What is it about this man," she asked, "this Two-John? I asked, but you never said."

"Quiet, now."

"No. You tell me."

The tiki torch darkened. So did the Devil's eyes. He looked different by firelight. His teeth longer, his hair longer, his eyes coal black.

The Devil told Memory how there were no more angels on the Earth, but sometimes there were people who looked like them a little. Maybe even made music like them, in their own way, and were dangerous.

Memory pretended to understand.

She watched the torch and the dark beyond, and she *did* understand, now, the Devil's expression as he steered. It wasn't fear; it was respect.

The difference didn't make her feel better.

Just then, Memory became aware of a rushing noise. Near or far, it was hard to tell. A world of sound, a roar like a cheering crowd.

The Devil cursed.

"Is it wind?" she called out.

"It's water!" shouted the Devil. "All that rain. Grab onto something!"

The universe of noise became a wall of water. It hit them like a train, lifting them up, smashing them down, and dragging them under.

"I SHOULD HAVE known better," said the Devil, hours later, at the edge of dawn.

They crouched in the pirogue, braced against a cypress deadfall, bailing muddy water.

All around them, mist. The sun had risen, lending the mist a white glow. It was like floating inside a lightbulb.

"Now what?" asked Memory. "Where are we going?" She pulled her hair back, and wrung it like a rag.

The Devil pointed with a long, witchy finger.

Memory looked, and beheld a house on stilts in the middle of the water, anchored by a great, mossy chain.

"We're here," he said.

THEY DRIFTED UP to what might have been the front of the house. There was a door, a half-rotten porch, and a ladder descending to the water.

The Devil caught hold of the ladder, and gave a tug that rocked the pirogue a little, but rocked the house, too, and he said in a big voice:

"Come out, come out, Two-John Spode!"

The things that were said and the things that began happening, then, felt to Memory like the way things might feel inside a story. As if they had already been told and could not happen any other way.

From behind a rusted screen door, a crackly voice yelled: *"Va-t'en, Diable!* Go away, Devil!"

And the Devil said, "Two-John! Come make a bet with me."

Something like a scarecrow appeared on the porch. A tall scarecrow with a red waterfall for a beard, and round glasses for eyes, and hair as long as the Devil's. The rest of him was hidden away in flannel, denim, and a monstrous pair of green rubber boots.

"Two times I bet you," said Two-John, "and two times I win. What reason I got to bet you again? You bet me for my soul I could not charm the 1963 Sugarcane Queen into my bed, and I did, me, and her sister, too, and you had to bring me pirate gold! I hate to make you poor and broke, Devil."

"He tricked you?" Memory asked the Devil.

"He gave me wine," he explained. "*Good* wine."

"A second time, for my soul," Two-John continued, "you bet me I could not trap death in my guitar, and when I did you gave me three years' good luck. I fear you will run out of magic."

"Death?" said Memory, in a small voice.

"Wine," explained the Devil.

He addressed Two-John again: "I don't come for your soul! It's *you* I want, Two-John. Want you to play your guitar and be famous. Want you and this one"—he indicated Memory—"to be the most famous band there ever was."

"I told you once, me," said Two-John, "I have all the fame and gold I wish."

The pirogue had drifted away from the ladder somewhat, and passed beneath the anchor chain. The Devil gave the chain a healthy yank, and the house shook. Two-John looked uncomfortable.

"Go get your guitar," said the Devil, "and I'll tune my fiddle, and you and me will play. If I play better, then you'll leave the swamp and give back my gold and play music with this pretty one, *la jolie blonde.* And if you play better, then you can have my fiddle for your own."

The Devil reached into the bottom of the pirogue and unwrapped Old Ripsaw. Holding it high in the strange white mist, he let it glow bloody colors, casting red on the water.

"Foolishness," said Two-John, but his eyes followed the fiddle as if hypnotized. After a while, he said, "It don't hurt me, Devil, to take your luck and money. But I will take your bet only if you will take a jar of wine, else they will say Two-John is a poor host."

The Devil reached up and accepted a great glass jar, and set it down in the bottom of the pirogue.

Two-John ducked inside to fetch his guitar.

"Don't drink that," warned the Devil.

"Don't *you,*" said Memory, tucking the jar away under her seat.

There was a sharp, bloody flash, and the Devil's fiddle became a fine red guitar.

The Devil plunked the strings the way you plunk a shot glass on a bar.

TWO-JOHN RETURNED with his own guitar in his hand. It was the color of an old, forgotten barn. It was worn away in places, where the pick had struck or fingers pressed. It looked experienced and alive the way some people look.

Two-John sat down at the top of the ladder and hit one string with his thumb, so softly it could have been an accident. A note like a ghost. It made Memory shiver.

The Devil played a chord so hollow it seemed to come from far away.

Two-John flexed his shoulders and cracked his red knuckles. The mist moved around him like a soul.

A frog jumped up on the porch beside him. Behind the house, a Lord God bird took the air like a cloud.

Two-John grinned his foxy grin, and said, "I will play the blues, Devil, and then *you* play the blues, and we'll see who will take what."

"Deal," said the Devil.

TWO-JOHN SHAPED HIMSELF about his guitar, as if the guitar were a bed he meant to sleep in. His beard and hands and everything about him gained an air of unutterable sadness, and when he played his first note it went out and hung itself by the neck.

For the longest time it was the only note Two-John played.

Then another note came along, drunk and bleeding and shoeless, and another like a well. The notes came faster and began to fall like tears.

They were heavy notes. The kind of notes that sound like empty rooms and twist you up inside.

He didn't show off and try to play what Regret sounded like, or make them hear what Heartbreak sounded like, because the blues is not about those things, if you let the blues be what they are. And you could tell Two-John knew it, and let it be what it was, which is the smallest and most lonely of moments and the most distant of sounds, the loneliness and sadness that are there for no reason at all, which maybe only an old man can know, or a man who knows witchcraft, and his blues were so perfect that no one even knew when the song ended and Two-John stopped playing. They might have sat there all day, knowing the strange things the song made them know and remembering the small things it made them remember, gazing dumb-eyed into the fog on the water, if the Lord God bird hadn't returned, a passing shadow, awakening them with a cry.

WHEN THE DEVIL started playing, it sounded like a choo-choo train.

It was so simple, compared to the salt-mine-of-the-soul Two-John had played, that it sounded like a cartoon. Memory thought it was a joke, at first.

But the chord grew.

It wasn't sad. Not all blues songs moan. Sometimes they HOWL.

Like an old, bent dog, the Devil crashed against his guitar.

The song was like a car wreck, but with rhythm.

It was like being stabbed, with rhythm.

It was razors cutting, with rhythm like a hundred trains, and it sounded like a hundred guitars. The harder the Devil played, the more like the Devil he seemed to become. In all the white mist in the white world of the swamp, his eyes were the only color, shining red like something living kicked apart.

The Devil understood the secret of the blues, too, and he knew that the blues are about the bluesman. These blues weren't loneliness or the smallest of empty moments. These blues didn't leave them staring into space, feeling sullen and empty. This blues had enough problems without people feeling sorry for it. This blues wanted them scared to death, because somebody was going to PAY, goddammit! The Devil had been kicked out of HEAVEN! and had his true love stolen by GOD! and his true love had left him four different times and he hadn't seen her for three hundred YEARS! and when he played the guitar it was like strangling Creation because no one *ever, EVER* had the blues like the Devil had the blues, and even if they *thought* they had the blues anywhere near as bad, when the Devil finally burned to a stop, covered in sweat and tears and Spanish moss, they were way too scared to say so.

TWO-JOHN LEFT THE PORCH and went inside. He emerged with a duffel bag over one shoulder, and his guitar in a burlap sack under one arm. Before, he had looked as if he belonged in another world. Now he seemed to be collecting himself in this one.

He climbed down the ladder, into the mist and the water, and waded over to the pirogue.

"I don't think she'll hold three of us, John," said the Devil, standing in the stern, looking for something to put in his pipe.

But Two-John just tossed in his guitar and duffel bag, and said, "I ain't getting in. You're getting out." He grabbed the boat and gave it a wobble, and the Devil pitched over backward into the swamp.

Memory didn't fall. She had the sense, in a narrow boat, to stay seated.

The Devil came up sputtering and steaming, eyes glowing.

"Calm down," said Two John. "I need you to help me with something."

They had a short, quiet conversation, then dove under the water and didn't come up for a while.

× × ×

THE HOUSE LEANED a particular way, stilts cracking.

The anchor chain went slack.

Then Two-John and the Devil, draped in swamp muck, rose up beside the pirogue, bearing a muddy, moss-covered, but nonetheless solid gold anchor as big as a man.

"You can't put that in the boat," said Memory. "I'll meet you on the shore."

She crawled across the pirogue, over the Devil's guitar—a fiddle again, wrapped in leather—and gave the motor a pull.

"How far is the shore?" asked the Devil, hoisting his end of the anchor and trudging after the pirogue.

"It changes," said Two-John.

Memory nudged the tiller, aiming between trees. She picked up the jar from between her feet, and drank a little of Two-John's wine.

"By the way," said the Devil to Two-John, "I brought you something."

He jerked his chin at the pirogue, and Two-John craned his neck to peer over the gunnel.

In the bottom of the boat lay a beaten old guitar case. It hadn't been there a minute ago, Memory was sure.

"That's Dan Paul's guitar," she said, sipping at the wine.

"His guitar," said Two-John, stumbling a little under the weight of the anchor, "but what's in it belongs to me. Ain't sure I'm happy it come back."

"You're gonna need it," said the Devil.

Inside the case, something moved and scratched.

"There's something in there," Memory observed.

"Pas de bêtise," said Two-John. "No shit."

Behind them, the house surrendered to the floodwaters and drifted off into the fog. All around, the vines hung low, the moss hung low, and the river ran through it all like coffee.

× × ×

THE MICROBUS STARTED just fine, despite spending the night tire-deep in floodwater. The engine was cool, at least. That much Memory absorbed before the wine she had tasted put her to sleep.

Two-John and the Devil drove fifty miles, slowly, down the flooded northbound highway, until the rear shocks cracked into pieces under the weight of the solid gold anchor and the Microbus fishtailed, hurling the Kennedy limo into a ditch, where it tipped up and sank like a rock.

Memory woke up with a headache like a mad dog.

"Told you," said Two-John. "It's too heavy."

"Shut up," said the Devil.

"'That anchor needs a dump truck or a train to carry it,' I said. Didn't I say that, me?"

"He doesn't listen," said Memory, trying to get her eyes to focus.

"I *listen,*" complained the Devil.

"You couldn't just snap your fingers—" said Two-John.

"He doesn't do that," Memory told him.

"Fine!" said the Devil. Half turning in the driver's seat, he offered Memory a courtly, if sarcastic, bow. He climbed out of the Microbus, straightened his hat, and snapped his fingers.

The limo hauled itself out of the ditch.

The bus roared to life, good as new, or better, and bounced on perfect shocks.

The solid gold anchor flew out the back doors, and lay across the limo's backseat.

The Lincoln sagged, but the Devil snapped his fingers and the car steadied itself. He climbed in behind the dripping wheel, raced the engine, and waved goodbye.

"See you soon," he called, passing on the shoulder and accelerating north, leaving a muddy wake behind.

"Which way is civilization?" Memory asked Two-John.

"That way," he answered, pointing south. "New Orleans."

× × ×

BY THE TIME they crossed Lake Pontchartrain and rolled down the city streets, Memory felt more or less herself, except for an uneasy stomach. She looked for a pay phone to call Bubble Records in California.

They were halfway down Bourbon Street when a tavern manager gave a yelp, leaped tables, and went down before her on one knee, kissing her hand.

Two-John shuffled beside her. He didn't feel clear yet about his role, where Memory was concerned. Was he supposed to protect her? Romance her? Treat her like a sister, what?

He decided the tavern manager wasn't a threat, which he wasn't.

He was a fan.

He babbled that he'd seen her on television, on the news, that people were still talking about the Woodstock concert and everyone who'd played there, including the mystery band who'd played part of one song and then vanished during the rainstorm.

Memory was the Amelia Earhart of rock 'n' roll.

Would she sing with his musicians in the tavern that night? He'd give her all the receipts just to be able to say she had sung at his little dive.

Memory said she would. Then she asked to use the phone, and he tugged her indoors.

Two-John bought himself a Miller beer and sat at a nearby table, watching Memory through his long hair.

Memory got through to California. Dan Paul's old studio boss wasn't in the office, but the office went nuts and patched her through to his home in Malibu.

She told him Hello when he answered, and then sat and listened while he talked—yelled, really—for almost an hour.

Her eyes got bigger and bigger.

Two-John drank his beer and gave his guitar case the evil eye. Something inside plucked a low note.

"Frème ta djeule," growled Two-John. "Quiet, you."

11.

Homes and Gardens in Egypt

The Northbound Highway, 1969,
and then Egypt, 2500 BC

THE DEVIL DROVE NORTH with the top down. The humid southern air turned his hair into a long, wet whip. He drove the Natchez Trace amid the ghosts of thieves and madmen. He drove by roads that were strange and half real, and near Memphis he stopped for chili. Near Franklin he stopped at a Holiday Inn, where he toweled his hair dry and stared out the window, watching taillights on the highway.

Then he cranked the air conditioner, smoked half a cigarette, and fell asleep dreaming a memory of long ago, when he had won back his true love in Egypt.

HE REMEMBERED walking like a giant among the Earth's first kingdoms.

The Fallen who stayed behind were kings in those days. They rutted and mated and made children who were gods and monsters.

As the centuries passed, though, the Devil met fewer of the Fallen. Earth wore at them in a way Heaven had not, and one by one they were claimed by a bottomless sleep. He sometimes felt this great sleep grasping at him, but he was stronger than the others, and the pain of his broken heart sustained him. He missed Arden until finally he thought his loneliness must rival God's. That was the day he lay down in the desert and slept for hundreds of years.

HE MIGHT HAVE TURNED to dust and blown away if the desert hadn't started to move over his head.

He sat up to see what was happening.

People were building mighty cities on the Nile River.

The Devil, coughing sand, blinked in amazement.

These were a new kind of people. Enterprising, and busy with impressive work. They knew mathematics and astronomy and architecture. They built pyramids, temples, and whole cities of painted stone. They called their nation "Egypt."

People like this, thought the Devil, might someday make Earth the envy of Heaven.

The idea took his breath away.

In a single moment, purpose rushed back into his life.

Arden might be able to stomach the world the Egyptians were making. There were scholars among them, and artists, and poets! Perhaps she would come to Earth and be his again.

He got up out of the dust and marched into Egypt, determined to win his girlfriend back, and raise the civilizations of Earth until they looked down on Heaven.

HE WHISPERED IN the ears of Egypt's mathematicians. He labored among her masons. For a time, he wore Pharaoh's double crown.

He urged them. Forced them.

They were an ancient and religious people, though. They depended to a large degree on fear and mystery, so he put on the body of a lion and the head of a man, and crouched by the roadside, asking riddles. They called him Sphinx, and honored and dreaded him.

The mission of the Sphinx was to help make Egypt wise by eating dumb people.

He would ask travelers, "Who is wiser: a wise man or a fish?"

If the traveler did not answer "a wise man," maybe because he wished to seem clever, or because he suspected a hidden meaning, the Sphinx would eat him. In this way, he culled the stupid and the pretentious, and improved the Egyptian gene pool.

ONE DAY, the Sphinx crouched by the roadside, and a traveler came by, cloaked and hooded.

"Which is wiser," asked the Sphinx, "a wise man or a fish?"

"It is a trick question," said the traveler. "The answer is 'a wise *woman,*' the wisest of all wise things."

The traveler's voice was familiar.

She shed hood and cloak, revealing wings and a body of shining light.

Arden.

And they fell, coupling, right in the middle of the road.

THEY WERE HAPPY for a time.

The Devil had been right: the pyramids and the calendars impressed her. They took a modest apartment. Domestic life was something new for them both. With only each other to entertain, they sat together in gardens, or walked in the bazaars.

"This," she observed, "must be the way lives are supposed to fit together."

They lay together in bed in the late morning, listening to boats and voices on the canal outside the window. The Devil was happier than he'd ever been.

If you had told him, at that particular moment, that she would be leaving again, he would have just laughed.

Practically every night, he would sit up late, talking with neighbors over the kitchen table, over mugs of beer, and platters of bread and oil. It was difficult for Arden at first, but she got used to chatting sociably and eating little finger sandwiches.

She became close with a woman named Nabiri, a young newlywed. Nabiri's husband, Apoo, had a good job with the priests, predicting the moods of the Nile. Arden and Nabiri started a kind of neighborhood women's orchestra. There were a couple of widows with panpipes, Nabiri played the oboe, and Arden sang. Every Tuesday night they practiced, and boatmen would linger on the canal beneath the windows.

The Devil became friends with Apoo, and taught the Egyptian what the stars really were, and Apoo started work on a calendar. The Devil taught him weather, and he drew tables matching rainfall to the way the river ran. When they'd been at this for more than a year, Apoo made a prediction.

"There is going to be a terrible flood," he said.

The Devil agreed.

Apoo gathered the tables and charts, and rushed off to warn the priests, who would warn Pharaoh and the people. But he was back a short time later, looking tired and stunned.

"They didn't believe it," he told the Devil. "I showed them the charts and explained the numbers and the weather. But they dismissed me. My assistance is no longer required at the temple."

Apoo collapsed into a chair.

The Devil's eyes darkened.

"It's about money," he told Apoo.

"What is?"

"You just told a group of priests—*rich* priests—that this year's crop—this year's *money*—is going to be wiped out by the weather."

"I didn't just tell them. I showed them numbers."

The Devil spread his arms wide, then let them fall in frustration.

"I've always kind of assumed," he said, "that people would thirst for knowledge and understanding. But they don't. They thirst to know things that support what they already believe. They especially like to hide from anything that looks like it might cost them money."

"But that's insane!" cried Apoo, stomping his feet like a child. "Ignoring it doesn't stop it from happening! And if they acted, they could build dams and levees! They could dig ditches to redirect accumulated rain, and save it in reservoirs! They could build terraces in the hills, and farm away from the floodplain! We'd have to find a way to get water to higher elevations, but how hard can it be? Do you have a stylus? I need something to draw on . . ."

This, thought the Devil, with fire in his eyes, was what humans were supposed to sound like!

"I think we could build some kind of wheel that would carry water," said Apoo, "and—"

"Who's going to build all this?" asked the Devil. "You just got fired."

Apoo struggled for a response. Instead, crushed, he gathered his charts and slunk out the door.

"YOU COULD HELP THEM," said Arden, later that night. They lay side by side in bed, arms crossed on the windowsill, gazing over the moonlit canal.

"What?" asked the Devil. "Snap my fingers and change the weather?"

"Why not?"

The Devil caressed her arm, thinking.

"You used to build or destroy whole kingdoms. Your sword was heavy with blood. Anyone who wouldn't listen, you sliced them up."

"I know better now," he answered. "You can't *make* people see reason. I think they have to suffer. They don't learn something until it hurts them."

"They're not stupid, though," said Arden. "They're complicated, but bad at dealing with complicated things. They like to simplify problems but don't see that you have to *understand* complexity before you can simplify it."

The Devil looked at her in amazement. Already, *he* was learning from *her*. It gave him an erection.

"The flood will be like a teacher," he said.

Arden began to protest, but the Devil silenced her with a kiss. Embracing her, he brushed her neck and shoulders with soft lips and sharp teeth, and didn't hear her when she gasped, "Don't count on it."

THE FLOOD CAME down from Upper Egypt like a wall. Fat and dark, the river rolled over the plain, washing everything away, until it smashed at the walls of Memphis, and roared through its streets and temples.

The fields and canals were erased. Even Pharaoh was inconvenienced. Leaving the palace at the last moment, the royal barge nearly capsized in heavy water, and a nephew of some sort was snatched away by a crocodile.

Arden and the Devil watched the flood from atop the highest of the pyramids.

When they came back into the city, they found that the priests had lashed Apoo to tide stakes, in the mud that had been his own patio. Calling him a witch, they had blamed him for the flood. How else could he have known, how else could he have told them the strange things he had told them?

The rising water had drowned him.

Nabiri sat above the waterline, on a ledge beneath their bedroom window. She hugged her knees and stared down at Apoo, who had begun to swell and draw flies. Arden hugged her close, but Nabiri didn't even know she was there.

The Devil waded in knee-deep water, gnashing his teeth.

"Animals," he said aloud, kicking at a chair as it floated by, "can at least face facts."

Leaving Arden with Nabiri, he went to sort through the dreck and wreckage of his own home. Arden came home just as he finished burning their wrecked furniture, and they went to sleep on the floor.

After midnight, Arden woke him up. She stood over him, glowing. Her wings folded like a hood over her head.

"I'm going back," she said.

He was too sleepy, at first, to panic. He just said, "Why?"

"Because nothing has changed."

"But people *have* grown. They'll grow more. It's a process."

"I can't wait here while that happens. The world is still terrible. It's like the Earth and everything on it was made to tear itself to pieces."

She ached to recoil from everything around her—he could sense it, smell the fear on her. She loved him—he could smell that, too—but revulsion overwhelmed her.

The Devil spread his own wings, which had become leathery in all these years on Earth. He tried to soothe her, as a lizard might soothe a dove, and she screamed at his touch. With a look of bottomless agony, she flashed like the sun and was gone.

THE NEXT DAY, too numb to feel angry, the Devil became the Sphinx and sat along the northern highway, beyond the reach of the floodwaters.

Eventually, a Nubian traveler came down the road.

"Which is wiser," the Devil asked him, "a river or a stone?"

The traveler started to answer, but the Devil was feeling rejected and mean. He ate the poor fellow up before he could say anything at all.

HE AWOKE with a start.

It took the Devil a minute to remember where he was. The rattling air conditioner. The soapy smell of the Holiday Inn.

The dream faded slowly. His waking self, his waking heart, straddled centuries.

He made a choking noise, drawing a deep breath.

He held his head between sharp, crooked fingers, too lost to cry.

12.

Fish at the Helen of Troy

Troy, Ohio
Christmas Eve, 1969

THEY WOULDN'T LOOK for him here, thought Fish.

He stood outside a Greyhound station in Troy, Ohio, ankle-deep in snow, in the clothes he'd been wearing for two days. There hadn't been time for luggage. He'd been lucky to escape Buffalo with his life.

Luck.

In Buffalo, he had run into the bus station, just when there was no line at the window he wanted. Got a ticket for a bus scheduled to leave in five seconds, and pulled out just as Jimmy and Bigfoot Terwilliger ran onto the platform, looking this way and that, with twenty buses to choose from. Fish had slid down low in his seat, ball cap over his face, and stayed that way until he estimated the bus had gone forty miles.

Out of the frying pan, for now. Other problems presented themselves.

Like avoiding freezing to death. Troy, Ohio, swirled with snow, all closed down for the night. Fish aimed himself in a downtownish direction, and found that if he walked hard and kept his left hand in his pocket, he warmed up.

His right hand wouldn't fit in a pocket, because it was still in a cast. Pins kept his reattached thumb from twisting off. That hand had felt cold since Woodstock.

It was warmer than Buffalo, at least. Jesus, that place!

He had fled his apartment without a coat, but at least was layered in T-shirts, a flannel waffle shirt, flannel outer shirt, and flannel quilted shirt. Heavy socks, too. His shoes were impractical. Some kind of leather zip-up boots. They'd seemed hip, two months ago, just out of the hospital, back in New York.

There was downtown, a few blocks away. A town square, with Christmas lights. Would he find a motel? How would he pay for it if he did? Could he get someone to put him up and give him time to make some phone calls, have some money wired?

Shit. Call who? Money wired from where?

He might have to sleep in a shelter, some church basement. But he realized, as he plodded on around the square, that the churches of Troy, Ohio, probably didn't have shelters, didn't need them. This wasn't Buffalo. Here, the churches were for church people.

Once in a while, a family car hushed down the street, on its way to Christmas Eve services. Midnight church, with candles and Christmas carols. They passed him by. They sometimes waved.

He stopped.

Christmas Eve services! Eureka! Every town had them! Every church, maybe. He'd get to huddle inside and warm up awhile. Maybe get a bite to eat, if there was a coffee hour afterward. The idea cheered him.

He was just beginning to hum "Midnight Clear" when the cops pulled over to wish him a merry Christmas.

The cops weren't necessarily looking for someone to hassle, Fish told himself. They just saw somebody having a rough time in dumb shoes on Christmas Eve.

"Merry Christmas," said the driver, rolling down his window and extending a hand in a way, Fish knew, that meant "Hello" but also "Stop."

He stopped. He said "Merry Christmas" back, and shuffled over to the cruiser.

"Can we give you a lift somewhere?"

Fish decided to almost be truthful with them.

“I was trying to get to Miami by bus,” he said. “Ran out of money. Now I’m just trying to find someplace warm till I can call a friend or two, have them wire me something. I’d be willing to work for a room and a sandwich. I don’t want trouble.”

“What a coincidence!” The driver grinned. “Neither do we!”

They invited him to ride in the back while they drove him up Main Street to a place called the Helen of Troy, a local motel and restaurant beside the interstate. They didn’t embarrass him by escorting him to the front desk. Instead, the driver managed to call the desk on his radio.

Specifically, he called “Deb,” who was on duty, and whom he seemed to know.

He asked if they’d put Fish up overnight, or until the banks opened after the holiday.

And Deb said, “Sure, Ricky. It’s Christmas, ain’t it?”

The cops didn’t even stay to watch and make sure he was nice to Deb. They backed out, leaving black tire tracks in fresh snow, and rolled off downtown again, toward the square and the Christmas tree.

Two minutes later, Fish was in his room, which smelled like cigarettes and shampoo, and had a color TV. He took off his ball cap, and ran his fingers through long, greasy hair.

It occurred to him that he could take a shower. Hell, he could probably find a way to wash some clothes, at least his underwear.

He ran the water hot. Decided on a bath, instead. The room steamed like Niagara Falls.

Fish sank in and let the heat sting him. Let it run through him and clear him out, loosen him up. He found himself making plans.

The plans included work. Fish didn’t like work, but had no choice.

Maybe they would have enough Ohio goodwill to set him up for a few days washing dishes or pushing a broom. Enough to get him bus and lunch money to Miami. Then . . .

He fell asleep in the tub.

When he woke up, the water was lukewarm, and all he could think of was getting between a set of those crisp Helen of Troy sheets. He dried himself halfheartedly, stumbled naked into the relative chill of the bedroom, lit now only by the blue glow of the color TV, where the Devil sat at the little round table by the window, crushing out a cigarette in a big glass ashtray.

Fish clapped his hand over his mouth and won a quick struggle for control.

The Devil got up and flicked the TV off. "We need to have a conversation," he said, "you and me."

"How the fuck did you get in here?"

"Does it matter? Get dressed," said the Devil. "We need coffee."

IT TURNED OUT you could get breakfast in the middle of the night at the Helen of Troy. So the Devil bought steak and eggs for himself and an omelet for Fish.

The Devil stared at Fish while he ate. He wore a brace of heavy rings, and kept his nails long. It was like being stared at by someone who owned a pawnshop.

"How'd you come to be almost freezing to death in Ohio?" asked the Devil.

"Don't you know?"

"Humor me. And watch the attitude."

"I got out of the hospital after they rebuilt my hand," Fish said, "and they had me on painkillers. I had just a little bit of cash saved back from what they paid us up front on our record deal, and—"

"The short version."

"I was in a bar having some drinks, and I met a guy named Fong, a bail bondsman. I shared some of my painkillers with him, and we cooked up this idea for selling prepaid bail bonds."

"Sounds like a great idea on booze and pills."

"Why have to wait around in jail when you fuck up, if you were the kind of person who was likely to fuck up, when you could just have bail waiting for you like an insurance policy? We'd use my money for capital, and Fong would be the people person, the bond expert, because he already knew the clientele. The plan was geared toward certain kinds of people, see—"

"People like Jimmy and Bigfoot Terwilliger," said the Devil.

"You *do* know," said Fish.

The waitress came. She poured coffee. She left.

"So where have you been," said Fish, "if you knew I was in trouble?"

"No, keep going," said the Devil. "Your stupidity amuses me."

"I was on painkillers," Fish reminded him. "So, yeah. Bigfoot and Jimmy are these guys who like to strong-arm the taxi companies for protection money, and they found us a convenient way to store and launder stolen cash."

"Let me guess," said the Devil. "One day they wanted to take their money back out, and you didn't have it."

"It was busy," said Fish. "The money was busy making money. A business has to invest."

"Did you explain that to Jimmy and Bigfoot?"

"I didn't get a chance. I went down to the store and Fong was sitting there with a hole between his eyes. I barely got out of Buffalo."

The restaurant had emptied, and was silent. The waitress eyed them from the cash register.

"Listen," said the Devil. "I know you think you're some kind of superpractical hard-ass, but you're not. You're a lazy, deluded candy-ass, and if you keep fucking around in the underworld, the real hard-asses are going to eat your face. You don't need to do anything illegal to take other people's money. So don't."

"Okay. So what do I do? You have my soul, you know. Isn't it all just supposed to fall out of the sky, more or less?"

The Devil sipped his coffee and looked disgusted.

"You haven't figured out yet," he said, "that if you want to get money and keep money, you have to work a little. Money is like a fast car or a woman. If you ignore it, it will fall apart or leave you."

"Thanks for the advice. But—"

"Here's some more advice. Watch out, over by the door."

"Door?"

"You have company," said the Devil, pointing.

Fish was startled to discover Jimmy Terwilliger advancing across the restaurant. A tall man in a fake leather, full-length coat. Fur collar. Fur hat. Dressed for winter in Buffalo. One hand inside the coat, gripping something.

How—?

Adrenaline and fear took over. Fish threw a chair, and bolted past Jimmy into the lobby.

There was cursing behind him, but Fish didn't look to see if Jimmy was following. In the lobby, he got down on his hands and knees, out of sight, until he reached the stairway, then flew upstairs to his room and locked the door. All without blinking or taking a breath. Now he sank, panting, onto the floor, back to the door.

The Devil was watching *It's a Wonderful Life* in black and white on the color TV.

"How in the hell did you get—!" began Fish, shaking and near tears, but the Devil shushed him until the movie was over.

"WHAT HAPPENED?" Fish blurted, the moment credits rolled. "How'd he find me?"

"Imagination, kid."

"When he missed me at the bus station, he bribed or threatened the desk clerk to tell him what bus I took and how far I was going?"

"Was that so hard?"

"No. Except where's Bigfoot? How come it's just Jimmy?"

The Devil threw up his hands. "Does it matter?" he barked. "We've got work to do. You need to understand money a little, if you're going to be rich like you want."

Outside the door, someone coughed. Keys jangled. A door slammed.

Fish jumped a mile at every sound.

"Can we do this fast?" he asked. "It would solve a lot of problems if I were rich right this exact second."

"Listen," said the Devil.

Fish was a jumble of nervous energy. He lit a cigarette. He put it out. He turned the TV off.

"I'm listening," he told the Devil.

"There's no such thing as money," the Devil began.

Fish didn't argue. The Devil could have said President Nixon was a psychologically accelerated house cat, and Fish would have agreed.

"Money represents something called *value,* which occurs in something called a *market.* It works like this:

"If someone wants something, its value is whatever they are willing to give up so they can have it. A man might repair a doorknob in exchange for a loaf of bread. In that case, the value of the loaf of bread is exactly the time and effort taken to fix the doorknob. The same is true if he exchanges a ten-dollar bill for a nice dinner, or six pigs for a horse.

"Now, the market won't work for long if exchanges don't make sense. Big things are traded for big things, small things for small things. You can't trade an apple for a horse, because only a fool would trade a horse for an apple. That's the first lesson."

"I get it," said Fish. "That was easy."

"They're all easy. The second lesson is: So what if you *could* trade an apple for a horse?"

"You'd get insanely rich," said Fish, getting up to turn the TV on again.

As he passed the window, a gun in a leather-clad fist shattered the glass.

Jimmy Terwilliger was back.

Fish peed his pants and screamed like a little girl.

His nerves were shot, but this was a good thing. When your nerves are shot, you become one big reflex. Fish's big reflex made him grab the leather-clad arm and pull it with him to the floor. Jimmy Terwilliger burst through the window, and the two of them collapsed in a heap.

It looked as if there might be wrestling and shooting. Desperate, Fish snatched a heavy ashtray off the top of the minibar and, using both hands, smashed Jimmy's head until it caved like a cantaloupe.

Snow drifted through the broken window.

Fish sat staring at the bloody ashtray lodged in Jimmy's temple.

The Devil looked at Fish in wonder. He produced a rum fizz out of thin air and said, "Here, man. Drink this."

Fish drank.

He could feel his brain trying to have a breakdown. All men wonder if they could kill someone if they had to. Most never find out. Now Fish was left with the murkier question of whether he could manage not to get caught. He finished the rum fizz, and took a critical look at the ashtray.

"Can you bring me a towel to put under his head?"

The Devil grinned approval.

"I'll go you one better," he said, and snapped his fingers.

Jimmy Terwilliger was gone. The ashtray, clean and emptied, sat atop the minibar again. The window was whole. The rum fizz refilled itself.

"I didn't think you did stuff like that," said Fish.

"You earned it."

"Thanks. Where is he? Jimmy?"

"What the fuck do you care?"

"I don't."

"Then Merry Christmas."

"Okay."

ON THE BED, Fish made a little fort out of pillows and buried himself in it. His brain was sort of giddy. The fort was a psychological fort. "So," said Fish. "How can you get people to trade horses for apples?"

The Devil stood at the window, watching the morning sun on new snow in the Helen of Troy parking lot. "Well," he said, "what if the value of a thing is fuzzy?"

"Fuzzy value? Like what?"

"Life."

Fish retreated into the fort, but remained visible.

"You mean—"

"I mean your living life force. Beating heart, thinking brain, blood in your veins. What do you think it's worth?"

"It's not like that. It's priceless."

The Devil leaned over the fort in a way Fish didn't like at all. "How much did Jimmy Terwilliger think your life was worth?"

Fish made a humming noise.

"Point being: Your life is valuable to *you*. To everyone else, it's worthless."

"Bullshit! My mother—!"

"If you fell over dead, your mother would get over it faster than you think."

"Are we still talking about money?"

"We're talking about life insurance. Money people pay to insure their lives. They trade you a horse, over the course of many years, and when they die, you trade them back an apple."

"That's sick!"

The Devil shrugged. "People love it," he said. "They like that the insurance company thinks they have value."

"You want me to go into *insurance*?"

"You want money, right? Well, you don't like to work and you don't have any special talent, so taking advantage of people looks like a fit for you."

"Fuck you, man," said Fish. But he said it in kind of a whisper. He was already thinking it over. It was already making sense to him.

"I gotta go down to my car for something," said the Devil. "We're almost in business, except you're going to have to study for a licensing exam."

The fort sagged.

"Money," said Fish. "I don't have money to pay for this room, let alone start-up cash!"

"Have faith," said the Devil, and shut the door behind him.

He returned shortly, dragging an enormous gold anchor.

"Here's your money," he grunted, heaving it onto the bed, which collapsed.

"Okay," said Fish, standing at the door, eyes wide.

Something was bothering Fish. He was forgetting something.

"All right," said the Devil, shaking his hand. "See you when I see you."

Fish frowned.

Forgetting something.

The Devil was gone.

He was back a minute later, though, knocking at the door. Maybe he had remembered the thing Fish was forgetting, thought Fish.

It wasn't the Devil, though.

"Merry Christmas, shithead," said Bigfoot Terwilliger, seven feet tall, grabbing Fish by the arm and forcing him back into the room.

"Ah," said Fish.

This was the thing he'd forgotten.

Bigfoot drew a gun from his pocket.

Pulled back the hammer.

And caught a glimpse of the anchor.

"Whuzza . . . ?" he began to say, but just then the Devil walked in through the door, saying he *knew* he'd forgotten something. He waggled his rings and fingers at Bigfoot, and Bigfoot vanished, screaming, in a sheet of hot blue flame.

Bits of his clothing survived, and a handful of twenty-dollar bills.

"Pocket money," said the Devil. "I meant to leave you some pocket money."

"What was *that*?" wheezed Fish, waving at the space where Bigfoot and the blue flame and the gun had been.

"We had a contract," said the Devil.

"That's what happens when a contract is over?"

"That's what happens when *his* contract is over. He was an asshole."

Fish collected the twenties off the floor.

The Devil paused on his way out the door.

"Don't be an asshole," he warned, and left.

13.

The Problem with Freezing People

Apache Junction, Arizona, 1969

THE DEVIL LEFT TROY and turned onto I-75. The road took him south to Dayton and west to Arizona. He turned left at the Superstition Mountains, cruised into Apache Junction, spent the night in a motel room Elvis had slept in, and in the morning he went to see Zachary, the electrocuted bass player, who had moved back in with his parents.

At the door, the Devil was very pleasant to Zachary's mother, who led him to her son.

Zachary was sitting like a sack of dirt on the living room couch, watching television. His mother brought them lemonade. An artificial Christmas tree sparkled in one corner.

The television was between programs. There was a news break, and at the end of the news break there was a show where you could win a new car. Then there was another news break about a concert in Houston that had been raided for drugs. The concert featured a new band, Purple Airplane. Purple Airplane starred Memory Jones, the chick who had disappeared after Woodstock.

"*Jones*?" said the Devil. "What, she get her memory back? Her name's Jones?"

"Studio clowns hung it on her, I'll bet," said Zachary.

The band also featured a Cajun phenomenon named Two-John, who played an acoustic guitar as if something dark were trying to get out of it.

"I kinda thought that guy was a myth," said Zachary.

The Devil shrugged. "Who says he's not? It's working, whatever they're doing. I can't turn on the radio without hearing psychedelic this-and-that."

"Did Mom offer you something to drink?"

The Devil rattled the ice in his glass.

"You miss it?" he asked Zachary. "The music thing?"

Zachary shrugged. "Never had it," he said, "except for two minutes at Woodstock."

"A heavy two minutes," said the Devil.

Zachary slumped again. He seemed to wind down as fast as he wound up.

"I'm different from Memory," he said. "That two minutes was all I ever wanted from that bass guitar. It was great, and it was enough, you know?"

Listlessly, he pointed at the TV. "She needs it, like, her whole life long. Maybe Fish, too, I don't know. But I don't. You seen Fish?"

"Yeah."

"How's he doing? Getting what he wanted?"

"Yeah."

Zachary watched a pain-pill commercial, drooling again.

"I'm sorry," he mumbled. "I slip back and forth. That's why it's just as well I don't feel like I have to play bass and be famous and all that."

"You can't play?" asked the Devil.

"It's like my brain doesn't talk to certain parts of me anymore, or only talks when it wants to."

His leg, as if to illustrate, gave a jerk.

Zachary raised his hands like he meant to say something else, but then he just froze that way.

Watched almost a whole game show that way, until his mother padded in and gently pushed his arms down, placed his hands on his knees.

She offered the Devil more lemonade, and he accepted.

"Sometimes," she said, nodding at Zachary, "you'd swear he wasn't even in there at all. Then he'll wake up and quote that whole stupid show back to you, word for word."

She looked like she was about to cry.

She went to get the lemonade.

"LISTEN," SAID THE DEVIL, leaning forward, tapping Zachary on the knee. "I can help, you know. Your nerves are scarred. I can change that."

"No," said Zachary. His eyes focused, and he gave the Devil a no-nonsense look. "I'm serious," he said. "Don't go doing it when I'm not looking, either. I may look half asleep, but I'm watching you."

The Devil pinched the bridge of his nose. Chinese monks had told him this could stop a headache. Sometimes it worked.

"It's up to you," he said, puzzled. "You were going to change the world, remember? And I don't do refunds."

"It's not that."

"Tell you what," said the Devil. "Let me show you something." The Devil waved his hand, and everything around them vanished.

THEY STOOD ON A ROCK the size of a capitol dome, with wind-swept trees growing from cracks and fissures. It was the kind of rock you climbed because you could see forever.

There were other domes and cliffs, visible far away, with gulfs of space between, and wind. It was one of the world's giant places. You could feel the earth turn.

On the dome's highest cap stood an Indian, weathered like a stick. In his arms he held a little girl, wrapped in a yellow blanket.

Beside the Devil, Zachary made a painful noise.

The old Indian laid the girl down on the rock, and began to sing. He wrapped the girl's head in his hands and just sat there, staring across the great world space. The Earth turned. The wind blew.

It was a scene from ten years ago.

This was Zachary's grandfather, Walter Bull Horse, and the girl in the blanket was Zachary's sister, Nita, who had polio and couldn't breathe well on her own anymore.

Walter Bull Horse picked up his granddaughter, and drove her home.

Home was an Indian movie village on the other side of downtown Sedona, tucked among red rocks and spruce trees, so movie crews could film the village and pretend it was a hundred years ago.

A movie crew was in the village now, in fact, cameras rolling, as Walter Bull Horse returned with his granddaughter. Walter didn't give a damn if they were filming or not. He carried Nita right through the middle of the scene, to the fake trading post that doubled as the Bull Horse family home, and let the door slam behind him.

Outside, the director threw a tantrum.

Walter heard his son, Proud Henry, apologizing. Proud Henry had built the movie village, and liked to keep the movie crews happy.

Walter placed his granddaughter in her iron lung, and waited while her breathing steadied.

Back outside, among the spectators, the Devil drew Zachary's attention to a particular, dark-eyed teenage boy. Zachary himself, on his fifteenth birthday. The boy watched his father apologizing to the director, and looked troubled.

"Aw, shit," said Zachary.

"I wonder what he's thinking," said the Devil.

"You know goddamn well what he's thinking."

Young Zachary was wishing he were wise enough to know who was right, his father or his grandfather. He was thinking that his sister wasn't old enough to die.

It would have surprised the Bull Horse family to learn that young Zachary considered himself unwise. He had been known since birth, after all, for deep and considered thought.

"It's not that I don't like traditional Indian clothing," he had told his grandfather when he was eight, "or that I like white clothes better. I have no preference. If there's a place in my Apache mind where such preferences live, that place is a void." And he made a sort of circle in the air with both hands, describing the void.

His grandfather had taught him meditation. Walter Bull Horse was a medicine man, or at least he said so. "Medicine men invented meditation," he told them. "We're the ones who sold it to the Japs. Chinese. Whatever Buddhists are."

"That boy has lightning in his head," was Walter's opinion.

"You're boring," his sister told him, because he meditated so much.

Zachary wasn't like his grandfather. He cared what people thought. So he taught Nita to meditate, and she changed her mind.

Nita, before she got sick, looked like she might grow up to be a warrior. She had clear, liquid eyes and a soft voice, but she was tall for her age, and had square shoulders. When she was six, her legs were long and strong enough to grip and ride a horse.

She allowed Zachary to teach her to meditate. Other than that, she preferred to be outdoors and moving, *doing* something, like her father.

Zachary wasn't like his mother either. She brought people things. Drinks. Mail. Old photos. Articles in the newspaper. It was a job certain people seemed to have. They were Thing-Bringers.

"HOW DO YOU KNOW you're meditating right?" Nita asked him one day. They sat facing each other in one of Proud Henry's movie tepees.

"If you say you're meditating," he told her, "then you are. There's no right and wrong way."

"I'm meditating," she said, and sat with her eyes closed for ten minutes until she slipped sideways and curled up on antelope fur, on the floor, asleep.

By the time she turned nine and he was fifteen, they could both get to a point where their bodies seemed to peel away, where they couldn't feel the floor beneath them or the clothes on their backs. Sometimes, afterward, they talked about what they saw in their minds (stars, rabbits, water, the color blue), or drew pictures.

Proud Henry affected to understand them.

"I've been meditating, too," he told them all, over dinner. "I need a solution to the shotgun problem."

The shotgun problem was a recent development in the world of movie stunts. Proud Henry, in his youth, had been a respected stuntman. He was even vaguely legendary for falling off a railroad water tower in *Riders of the Purple Sage.* Now, apparently, stunt purists were complaining that a man shot off the back of a horse by a pistol or a rifle should look different from a man shot off a horse by a shotgun. Proud Henry was on the job.

They found him meditating at a table in the front window of the trading post one morning, a cup of warm coffee cooling between his hands. His head was down, his hair hanging. He snored.

"Sleeping," observed Nita.

Zachary shrugged. "If he says it's meditating—" he began, but Nita shook her head.

"Sometimes it's just sleeping," she insisted.

BUT PROUD HENRY had instincts; you had to give him that. He came home on Zachary's sixteenth birthday with a locally made guitar, a masterpiece. Depending on how you strung it, you could play bass or regular guitar. It would accommodate six or twelve strings. The body was shallow, like a Les Paul, and polished a deep nut brown.

It didn't take long for Zachary to confirm his father's hunch: He had guitar music inside him, just like Proud Henry had stunts. Despite the guitar's many possibilities, he soon found he preferred it strung like a bass. Preferred the bottomless vibrations. The way bass notes sounded like a voice.

Before long, he was improvising whole bass concerts, sitting opposite his meditating sister.

"It helps," she said.

Walter Bull Horse agreed. Sometimes he meditated with them.

"It's like a drum," he muttered, and he would chant so softly he might have been humming, until, like Proud Henry, he began to snore.

One day when she was ten, Nita let go a long breath, emerging from trance or sleep, and stood to leave. She fell over sideways, one long, muscular leg gone wobbly underneath her.

Zachary thumbed a sort of falling-down zither on his bass.

"All right?" he asked.

"Leg fell asleep," Nita answered. And she made it on the second try.

That same night, Proud Henry dislocated his shoulder trying to solve the shotgun problem with a backflip off the rear of a horse. He spent four days with his arm in a sling, popping pain pills.

Zachary wondered afterward if anything would have been different if someone had noticed that Nita's leg seemed to have a hard time staying awake, more and more.

They did notice, the day she fell and stayed down.

"It won't work," she hissed, pounding her leg and crying.

So there were doctors, and the doctors in those days saw right away what the leg's problem was. They saw a lot of legs and children like that. Nita had polio.

"Sanitation isn't what it should be on the reservations." Her doctor frowned.

"We don't live on the reservation," Proud Henry was quick to inform him. "We own a movie ranch outside Sedona."

And the doctor looked at Proud Henry for few seconds. "*Riders of the Purple Sage!* You were the Indian they shot off the water tank!"

× × ×

MOVIE PEOPLE HAVE unusual powers, and as word of Proud Henry's sick daughter went out over this and that telephone line, those powers flexed.

A certain movie star got black-market medicine delivered to the ranch, and to Nita's doctor. Experimental medicine. Serious, desperate, hard-to-get medicine. But it didn't work.

The polio germs inside Nita attacked a lot harder than polio germs were supposed to. Most children lost the use of a leg, and wore braces. Nita lost control of both legs. Day by day, she shrank in front of them until her shoulders lost their bigness. She no longer looked like a warrior or a hunter, or even a young girl. Then came a numbness about her abdomen, so that Mother, who brought things, began to specialize in bringing Nita to the bathroom. Nita and Mother became a society of two.

THE DOCTOR WHO recognized Proud Henry from *Riders of the Purple Sage* authorized them to keep a shiny, state-of-the-art iron lung at home, in the trading post. He made certain the right wiring was present, the right outlets installed.

The arrival of the iron lung, which seemed to Zachary a kind of casket shaped like a roll of quarters, knocked the wind out of them all. People who went into iron lungs did not get better.

Zachary played the bass for her. Nita whispered that she had a hard time getting to sleep without it.

She slept more and more.

"Meditating," she insisted.

Zachary asked "What do you see?"

She shrugged. Her shoulders and the gesture were lost behind her neck gasket.

"I don't think I see anything. I just feel calmer when I'm done."

"Me, too. But I see things. Eagles. Water. Two suns in the same sky."

"I want to be outside when I die," she told him.

Zachary didn't know what to say to that. It was the kind of thing she was supposed to say to Mother.

× × ×

PROUD HENRY WOKE UP inspired one day, having dozed off in front of their twelve-inch TV.

"Rope!" he cried, startling his father, dozing in an adjacent chair.

"Pillows!" he cried, bolting out of the trading post, waking up Nita in the iron lung. Then he vanished onto the back lot, into the toolsheds. They heard him out there, banging around and whistling. It was a good day when he had a new solution for the shotgun problem.

When Nita had a good day, she could breathe on her own for an hour or more. Walter Bull Horse began wrapping her in a yellow blanket and driving her out by the airport, where the red rock dome overlooked the whole world. Where the wind came straight from the sky, blue and raw. Walter kept an eye on his watch, and was careful to bring her back before she began to struggle.

When Mother had a good day, lemonade or clean laundry might appear out of nowhere.

For Zachary, a good day was when he had an idea, like the melody of a song or a fast way to solve a math problem.

Proud Henry stuffed some throw pillows under his belt line, and tied a lasso around his waist. He lashed the other end around a totem pole. Then he climbed aboard a painted horse, and took off galloping.

He had sprayed a red *X* on the ground. This was supposed to be where a shotgun was fired. When the horse galloped past the *X*, the rope went tight.

Zachary was watching. It looked good. It looked exactly as if his father had been blasted from the saddle by bad guys.

Proud Henry landed sideways in a cloud of red dust and dislocated his hip.

Zachary loped over, concerned.

Walter Bull Horse had been pretending not to watch from the trading-post window. Now he jogged out, too, cursing.

He cut the lasso with a pocketknife, and the two of them walked Henry to the trading post.

In the front room, Mother was right in the middle of draping the yellow blanket over her daughter and her daughter's machine.

The blanket floated in the air, filled like a cloud, and settled without a wrinkle.

Mother didn't say anything. She took off her glasses, then put them on again.

"She wanted to be outside," Zachary started to say, but his voice stuck.

Proud Henry put his weight on his good hip. The pain made him pale, but he bore it. One injury at a time.

Zachary stared into the air, meditating with his eyes open.

THEN ZACHARY and the Devil were back in the living room.

Ten years had passed, and Walter Bull Horse had passed, too.

"So," said Zachary. "What was I supposed to see? My sister dying of a stupid virus they found a cure for less than a year later? I've seen that before. It was nice seeing Granddad again, though. Thanks."

"That wasn't the point," said the Devil, toying with a herald angel on the Christmas tree. "The point," he said "was to get you thinking about how things might be different if science had moved faster. And yet here you sit, with your partially electrocuted brain, and won't let me fix—"

"I have my reasons," Zachary snapped

"The point I see," he told the Devil, "is that sometimes death is a matter of scheduling. Her being dead when they beat the polio virus was like missing an appointment. What if she could have just been put on hold? What if people all over the place could be put on hold, if needed? People who need a few extra hours to get to a special hospital on the other side of the country? People who will be all right if they can just get a transfusion for a rare blood type, or hang on until the right kidney donor dies?"

The Devil didn't like the sound of this.

"What," he said, "exactly *is* it that you propose to do, Mr. Make the World a Better Place?"

"Invent a way to freeze people so they can be brought back and cured. Give them the time they need."

"That's not a new idea."

"I know."

"Most scientists say it can't be done."

"They're doing it wrong." Zachary leaned forward. "I'm not talking about curing death," he said. "Just stopping the clock. Like a time-out in football, you know? Listen: You said, 'What if the polio researchers had been able to move faster, think faster?' Well, what if that's already happened? What if my brain already *does* move faster?"

The Devil frowned. "Go on," he said.

Zachary came to his feet, energized. "Ask me a math problem. Something crazy."

"Seven thousand eight hundred forty-three times sixteen," said the Devil.

"One hundred twenty-five thousand four hundred eighty-eight," answered Zachary. "More."

"Nine trillion times pi."

"Twenty-eight trillion two hundred sixty billion."

"That's it? No decimals? Pi contains an infinite number of decimal places."

Zachary shrugged. "I used two decimal places, just like on math homework. But the answer I gave you is right. It's a whole number."

"Could you do this before?" asked the Devil. "You were smart before."

"Not this smart. Before, maybe I could have figured out a way to freeze people in a way that they could be brought back, and maybe not. Now I'm *sure* I can do it. Right now, out there somewhere, is some little kid with cancer or a bad liver, who just needs someone to push a pause button long enough for circumstances to change. And I'm going to make sure that pause button is there."

He blinked purposefully at the Devil.

"It's not," said the Devil, "that it doesn't make sense. It's just that I've seen the future, and it's not what you're supposed to do. You sold me your soul in exchange for a *destiny*, and freezing people is not it."

"How do you know? You got a crystal ball?"

The Devil fished his crystal ball from his pocket and waved it in the air. "If that's what it takes. Look!"

"No," said Zachary. "Let *me* show *you* something! Should have shown you right away. Follow me."

And he led the Devil through the utility room to the garage, to a workbench cluttered with plastic bottles and something like a chemistry set.

"The trouble with freezing people," he said, "or animals or anything, is that ice expands. Since our cells are all made of water, mostly, freezing them makes them explode. That's why lettuce gets mushy when you freeze it. So I need to invent a liquid that won't expand when it freezes. And we pump the bodies full of that when they die. Then we freeze them."

He was trying to make an intravenous freezing solution using everyday household products.

"Over here," said Zachary, pulling the Devil by the arm.

At the front of the garage, lined up on a strip of greasy carpet, were five old-fashioned milk jugs: metal jars about three feet tall.

Zachary pulled on goggles and gloves.

"You might want to keep back," he told the Devil.

"I'll be all right."

Zachary unscrewed the first milk jug, and heavy vapor poured loose, covering the floor. Zachary pulled something free, something wrapped in plastic.

He stood there holding it, looking around.

"Shit," he said. "I forgot to get out that ironing board, first."

The Devil fetched an ironing board from a Peg-Board rack, and opened it.

"You forgot," said the Devil. "But you don't want me to fix your brain."

Zachary laid the plastic wrapping on the ironing board, and stepped back.

"What's all the fog?"

"Dry ice. I fill them with my solution, to keep the cells from exploding, then immerse them in dry ice."

"Immerse who?"

Zachary pulled the plastic apart with leaf-shaped salad tongs, and there lay a coyote.

It didn't look particularly dead. A little brittle, maybe, especially about the eyes.

The Devil frowned. The longer he looked at the thing, the more it *did* look dead, and not brittle at all. Then he realized that it was changing right in front of him.

"Fucksticks," said Zachary.

The coyote liquefied in less than a minute. Even parts of the skeleton and teeth dissolved into gray pools, dripping away into the crawling mist.

Zachary took off his goggles.

"Needs less Clorox," he muttered. "Or more underarm deodorant."

Sensing opportunity, the Devil waved his crystal ball under Zachary's nose.

"Look here! It's not that you're failing in your experiment," said the Devil. "It's the wrong experiment for *you,* is all! Now look. *Look!*"

At first, there was only a sort of swirling, like the vapor on the garage floor. Then Zachary saw himself hunched over a cluttered worktable, elbow-deep in wires and circuit boards.

"*This* is you changing the world," whispered the Devil. "This is what your destiny looks like!"

"Of course!" Zachary bellowed. "That's me working on instrumentation! These things are going to need monitors that can tell when they're getting too cold or getting too warm!"

The Devil couldn't believe it. Four thousand years after Egypt, you still couldn't get people to see what was right before their eyes, not if they didn't *want* to see it.

"That's as far as your imagination goes?" said the Devil, his voice rising. "Building a better thermometer? If you can build instrumentation to do that, you can build an instrument to do *anything*! Why settle for just freezing dead people? It's like inventing the airplane and saying it's just for delivering the mail."

"It depends," said Zachary, "whether the inventor is interested in the airplane or the mail. In this analogy, I'm a mailman. Let someone else invent the airplane."

"Let someone else change the world."

"Mail can change the world."

"This is a stupid analogy."

"Look," said Zachary, already at work mixing Clorox and carpet cleaner, "you bought my soul with promises of support. If you're not going to help, give me my soul back and get out of the way."

The Devil sighed. Some people had to learn the hard way.

"What do you want from me?" he asked.

A smile crossed Zachary's big face. He drooled a little.

"Investors," he said.

SO THE DEVIL placed ads in the paper.

The ads basically said a small scientific organization was close to figuring out how to freeze people so they could live forever, and they needed money. Anyone who contributed a certain amount of money would be guaranteed frozen storage when they died. Anyone who wanted to know more could come to a special meeting.

The meeting took place in Zachary's parents' living room. It drew thirty people, including his parents, most of them over seventy years old. Zachary wore a business suit and only drooled a little bit. He explained a thing or two about freezing and unfreezing things. He was careful to point out that this was all one big experiment, but every day of research and every dollar invested made success more likely. The Devil had printed up some posters with illustrations and columns of numbers, which made it all sound terribly scientific.

And the old folks were convinced. They contributed with zeal.

When the house emptied and Zachary's mother and father had gone to bed, Zachary and the Devil sat down at the kitchen table and counted.

They counted twice. They couldn't believe it.

"Forty-three dollars and ten cents," said Zachary.

"It's an old-people thing," said the Devil. "People in their seventies in 1969 wouldn't have been the shaped-by-the-Depression generation. They don't tip well either."

Zachary shook his head.

"This is enough for eighteen bottles of Clorox," he said.

"Get your mom to iron that suit," said the Devil. "Tomorrow we'll hit the bank."

THE BANKERS WERE ARMED with calculators—enormous things, like typewriters—and amused themselves for almost twenty minutes getting Zachary to spin calculations into the billions, to six decimal places. They enjoyed the lunch the Devil uncovered in their boardroom, and the tea laced with trace amounts of local Indian whiskey. They enjoyed the pictures he painted of the future, drawing with words and with elegant fingers. Appealing to their "obvious good taste" and "preternatural sense of things to come," he made them feel good. Even generous, almost.

Almost. They said no.

"SHIT," SAID THE DEVIL.

They sat on a curb in downtown Apache Junction, eating sub sandwiches wrapped in newspaper. It bothered the Devil that he had failed to convince a boardroom full of bankers to shell out half a million bucks.

It's a difficult age, he reflected. The people with the money and the people with the vision aren't the same people.

A van full of movie cameras and sound equipment rolled through town, followed by trailers and a police escort.

Zachary thought he'd find out where they were filming. His dad would want to go watch. Maybe someone would recognize him from *Riders of the Purple Sage.* Every once in a while, someone did. It thrilled the hell out of the old man when that happened.

"Keep working that Clorox and Pine-Sol," said the Devil, rising. He walked off toward the Kennedy limo. "Someday soon, we'll talk to your buddy Fish."

"Why?" called Zachary.

The Devil started the Lincoln, and performed a squealing U-turn across the street.

"He's got an insurance company!" shouted the Devil.

Zachary waved faintly and watched the limo shimmer east past the Superstitions.

14.

Jenna Steele's Public Bad-Girl Avatar

Dayton, Ohio, 2005

JOHN SCRATCH WOKE UP in the middle of the night, and, as sometimes happened, couldn't recall where he was.

Then he smelled disinfectant atop disease, and remembered.

In a hospital. In Dayton, Ohio. He'd been shot.

He should have healed by now, but he hadn't. Not the way he used to, the way he should.

His night-ready eyes discovered Jenna Steele asleep across two chairs, nearby. Moonlight fell across her shoulders and chest, and he saw that she had made herself comfortable under a thin blanket. Shirt unbuttoned, bra hanging from an IV pole.

The Devil looked at her with an affectionate glow in his eye. The public rarely saw her like this. They wanted her badly behaved, mean, and selfish, and that's what the cameras fed them. The public didn't need to know that in her tiny private life, she was . . . nice. Something between a lover and a big sister.

They didn't understand her, he thought, any better than they understood him.

Most people speculated that Jenna Steele and John Scratch were just pretending to be in love. A media affair, cooked up in committee and scripted by writers. These people were right about the committee and the writers, but they were wrong about Jenna Steele. Jenna loved John for real. She dreaded the day the studio would suggest it was time for them to break up, which they would, if people stopped following them online and on the news.

John Scratch did *not* love Jenna Steele.

When the Devil felt love, he felt it the way the winter woods feels summer coming. After ages of moving among these small, short-lived creatures, he still couldn't focus on them with a full heart. They weren't substantial enough. And they didn't last.

They weren't Arden.

The best he could manage, the closest he could come to really loving a mortal, was an inflated puppy love, a quick-burning affection.

The Devil enjoyed the schizophrenic mix of Jenna's secret, gentle side and her public bad-girl avatar. He liked the way she turned to butter whenever he growled deep in his chest. His affection for her was very real.

Which made what he had to do more painful.

JENNA STEELE AWAKENED on her makeshift bed. She saw the Devil sitting up, looking at her.

"Listen," he said.

"You should go to sleep," she said.

"We can't see each other anymore."

"Shhhhhhh," she began, stroking his arm, then snatched her hand away.

"What?"

He gave her a long, sympathetic look. He began to hope she would take it well, behave with dignity.

He decided to just sit quietly and wait. He wouldn't tell her he was in love with someone else.

Jenna's eyes flashed. She lurched forward with a sob and yanked all the tubes out of his arm.

"Son of a bitch!" she rasped.

Her hand darted under the sheets and ripped out his catheter.

The Devil's eyes bulged.

She seemed to remember something. Yanked her phone out of her hip pocket, keyed "video," and set it on the counter, facing the bed.

Then she did something guaranteed to keep fans glued to her Web site.

She took a little handgun out of her purse and shot him—*BANG!*—in the belly.

It was awful, but a lot of multimedia fans said it was awful in a *beautiful* way.

The video was fuzzy and dark, but that only made it more dramatic. The phone rested on its side, so Jenna Steele (fashionably edgy in a tiny black skirt, black athletic leggings, and schoolgirl shoes, blouse unbuttoned, bra abandoned) seemed to defy gravity as she fled the room, swallowed by the bright square of the door.

Then came the unsettling last minute of the clip, where the camera autofocused until the figure on the bed became visible.

John Scratch, with his glowing eyes.

They watched him spit blood and chuckle, and then make a pained face.

They read his lips when he shouted "Nurse!" and almost exploded with coughing.

They could *not* read his mind, which was thinking that when girls who are mean in public are privately, secretly *nice,* the nice part is secretly bullshit.

15.
American Werewolf

New Jersey, 1777

THE WAR WOULD BE OVER by midnight.

America would be over. The British were coming, and they would crush her. The Devil didn't see any way around it.

The wind came howling up the Assunpink Creek. It moaned like a ghost through the streets of Trenton, and burst across the Continental troops so hard they couldn't help but take it personally.

The Devil pulled his cloak up higher.

They had crossed the Delaware and taken Trenton. Huzzah!

They were heroes. Huzzah!

They were going to be the shortest-lived heroes in history.

Because they hadn't fought the whole British army, here, the day after Christmas. They'd only captured a lot of badly surprised Hessians. Now the main force was coming. They would come through Trenton and across the creek, and drive them into the river.

The moon, nearly full, cast a blue halo. That meant ice in the air. The muddy roads would freeze. They could move up more cannon then, but they'd have to move fast.

The Devil turned, and trudged up the street toward General Washington's headquarters.

× × ×

THEY HAD MET just weeks earlier, in Pennsylvania. There was this rebellious new country being formed, and so much of it seemed to depend on this one man.

Washington.

It was like Roman times, with Julius or Augustus or Constantine, guys with heroic faces who said heroic things, and inspired others to do the same. Washington would have made a fantastic Roman.

Except he was getting his ass kicked, retreating from Long Island, White Plains, and Fort Washington. Congress and the country began to wonder if their general wasn't too timid. The Devil wondered, too. He had followed the Continental Army when it fled New York, and eventually caught up with the general in the woods.

Washington dismounted to have a pee on the western flank of an oak, and the Devil leaned against the opposite side.

"You need help," said the Devil.

Washington peered around the tree.

"Knew you'd show up sooner or later," he said. "Begone!"

"A little help," said the Devil, "wouldn't necessarily cost you your soul."

"It's the Nation's soul I'm concerned with," said Washington, "and in whose name I decline."

The Devil waited. Washington was a practical man with a large bladder. A little time to think served him well.

"Of course," he said, appearing around the tree, buttoning up, "if the Nation is smashed between here and Princeton, the condition of its soul will be moot."

"Great things grow from imperfect roots," said the Devil.

Washington rode thoughtfully back to camp, doing what he did best: looking great on his horse.

THE DEVIL KNOCKED at Washington's door, and stepped inside, out of the wind.

Washington looked over his shoulder. Just a flash of his cobalt eyes.

"Glass of Madeira?" he asked.

The Devil nodded, and Washington poured.

"I haven't decided," said the general.

"Be more aggressive. We look weak."

"We *are* weak. Half of our army is in prison ships. "

"Use what you have, attack like a wild animal," advised the Devil.

"No. I shall employ strategy."

The Devil almost hit him with a chair.

DOWN BY THE CREEK, the army huddled, and watched the dark. Watched the empty streets, and listened for boots, for hooves. At headquarters, reports came galloping in: American troops had traded shots with the British, not far up the road. American snipers had fired into the British as they marched in columns, but the British fired back and kept coming. As many as the stars.

With the British less than a mile out, Washington was still frowning over his maps.

"The troops will fall back through Trenton," he explained.

No shit, thought the Devil. They were already doing that. They could hear the first shots popping between houses.

"They'll fall back across the Assunpink Bridge," said Washington, "and form up on this side."

"And then what?"

"We'll let them have it."

But his eyes and voice were tired. The Devil sensed him wondering what the British would do with him, when he was captured. Hang him, most likely.

Fuck, thought the Devil. Without waiting to be dismissed, he turned and stomped out into the cold. He found his horse and raced toward the creek.

The clouds were low, and lit from behind by the gibbous moon. Muzzle flashes reflected against the clouds and windows. Cannon fire echoed against shops and garden walls.

The British weren't coming. They were here.

× × ×

THE DEVIL RODE through waves of fleeing townspeople, and reached the creek just as the fighting began.

American soldiers came tumbling back across the bridge, struggling across the creek. The bridge became a deadly bottleneck, full of screaming and panic.

The Devil dismounted, meaning to shout those men into good order, but suddenly they shaped up. Formed ranks. Quit pushing, even though they were being shot at from behind.

Washington had arrived.

He sat his horse to one side of the bridge, aloof and regal. The Devil saw the effort each man made to touch Washington's boot, or saddle, or horse.

That, the Devil knew, was why the birth of the new Nation depended so much on this man. Now that they had seen him, had touched him, the Americans would fight better.

The British marched out of the dark, poured out of the Trenton streets.

Bayonets flashed.

Drums pounded, lively.

There were so many!

Even the Devil felt sick.

A few patriots were caught on the far side of the creek. They gave up trying to reach the bridge, and turned to face the enemy. They fired and vanished, swallowed by the red tide. Great sheets of bullets poured across the bridge in all directions and suddenly there was no safe place anywhere. The ground underfoot became slippery with blood.

BATTLE CHANGED the Devil.

He would not remember scrambling and slipping down to the creek, or fighting his way up the opposite bank, or seizing a cannon at the foot of the bridge. He wouldn't remember coming back across the bridge on all fours, torn and bleeding.

He would vaguely recall seeing Washington on his horse, still just sitting there, as if wanting America to end with dignity, if not victory.

So the Devil fought his way to Washington, that timid bastard, and bit him on the leg.

Washington swore and gave him a kick. The Devil hit the ground, found a musket, and turned his attention elsewhere, sensing, in his battle-fogged brain, that he had accomplished something wonderful and necessary.

THE RED UNIFORMS began to charge across the bridge.

They were coming across, and no one could stop them.

Still, the patriots stayed in place, shooting, and getting shot. Their eyes witnessed things they would try to forget, if they weren't killed. The moon cast a cold and morbid light on it all, and made it worse, if that were possible. Still they stayed. America might die that night, but it would die fighting.

And then something changed.

"Washington!" the men began to shout, elbowing one another.

Something had gotten into the general.

He surged on his horse to the nearest cannon, and made them point it straight down into the creek, straight down at the struggling red faces of the enemy. And made them fire.

Made other cannon fire, just the same. The commands he gave came in a strained and angry voice, as if it were all he could do not to hurl his very important self down upon the redcoats.

"Give them canister!" he howled.

Canister meant firing a can full of tiny metal balls. It turned the cannon into a giant shotgun. Firing canister was a really nasty thing to do, even in battle. Not a gentlemanly order. But they didn't dare refuse him.

He moved them forward. He made them crowd the upper bank and fire volley after volley, until the creek choked on the dead. The bridge piled high. The battle became a horror show.

But it was an American horror show.

× × ×

AFTER A TIME the fire thinned.

The British stopped coming. They had seen battles before, most of them. But they'd never seen men do to other men what those Americans had done to them.

The Devil wouldn't remember anything but flashes and echoes, faint and dreamy.

When soldiers remembered, they would groan in their sleep.

You couldn't blame any of them for wanting to forget the Second Battle of Trenton. Even history would tuck that one away in the attic.

AFTER TRENTON, Washington was a more complicated figure to his nation, both fatherly and fearsome. In time, he became their president.

The Devil watched from the crowd as President Washington, in his Freemason's apron, laid the cornerstone of the mighty Capitol Building.

When he dropped by the president's hotel in Alexandria that night, hoping for nostalgic conversation and a glass of Madeira, he found Washington not in.

"Hang it," he said. He had plans to stir up Indian trouble in the territories, and wanted to get started. Maybe he'd find a good tavern on the road out of town. He struck off down the highway, and woods rose up on either side as he left the new capital behind. He was thinking of mutton and rum, grateful for the light of the full moon, when a dark shape came hurtling out of the night.

Glimpsing wet fangs and razor claws, the Devil drew his knife, but the shadow stopped in the underbrush on four legs, ragged breath steaming from its awful snout.

Then the creature stood up like a man. It looked at the Devil with strangely intelligent eyes.

It said, "You!"

The Devil, at a loss, said nothing.

Then the figure before him melted and changed, becoming a naked man of noble bearing and honorable years.

"Washington!" gasped the Devil.

"You bit me," said Washington, wiping—*blood?*—from his lips.

"We were losing," explained the Devil.

He offered Washington his coat, and the president accepted without remark.

"You have your nation," observed the Devil.

He thought about people he had bitten, down through the ages, and how his bite had transformed them. Here, at last, this dark gift had been put to good use.

"Mankind has its nation," argued Washington.

"Would you like to see it?" asked the Devil, producing his clear glass ball.

They hiked up to a low, treeless summit overlooking the mess that would become America's capital. Here and there, derricks rose, and scaffolding, amid mountains of lumber, marble, and brick.

They held the ball between them.

In the future, they saw a great green mall, a wide lawn broad enough to hold entire towns, framed by great white colonnades. A mile away sat a temple of alabaster stone and soaring columns, in which sat a stone god neither of them recognized.

Washington scanned the marble city in awe.

"It's Rome," whispered Washington.

"And Egypt," added the Devil, for in the middle of it all a white obelisk reached for Heaven itself.

"That's for you," said the Devil.

"It's a fang," said Washington, a nocturnal light in his eyes. "That's as it should be."

"Good work," said the Devil.

They shook hands.

Then Washington, still wearing the Devil's coat, headed downhill toward his hotel, his clothes, and, presumably, a good hard scrubbing.

16.

The Chicago Office

Chicago, 1970

THE LOGO OF ASSURANCE Mutual Life Insurance was a golden anchor.

In the field offices, the young guns in their first good suits whispered that the golden anchor was real. That Mark Fish had stolen a golden anchor from the Devil, and hocked it for cash to start the company.

"He's still got it," some said, over the watercooler. "It's in Chicago, in the company vault."

In Chicago, at the home office, they were careful about what they said, because Fish cruised those very halls.

Fish hadn't stolen shit from the Devil, some argued, hush-hush, whether they worked in Chicago or not. He had a *deal* with the Devil. How else did a guy twenty-five years old own the fastest-growing life insurance confederacy in the Midwest?

"It's just the Midwest," said some.

"Yeah, but the Midwest is like the New York of insurance. Besides, he was an extraordinary young blade even before. He played at Woodstock, man."

Late at night, they whispered that Fish had once killed a man.

"With what? Why?"

"With an ashtray. For wearing shitty cologne. How would I know?"

× × ×

IT WASN'T EASY being a top dog at Assurance Mutual. Because you could get conflicting orders sometimes, and your job might hang on which conflicting order you followed.

"It's more like conflicting philosophies," some said.

The more challenging philosophy did not come from the legendary Fish, but from a mysterious lieutenant of his: Mr. Scratch. No one seemed to know exactly what this lieutenant's title was or where, exactly, he fit among the cogs and wheels of the Assurance Mutual machine. People did observe that he had enough juice to contradict Fish and not get his ass handed to him. Beyond that, he seemed attended by the same sort of half myths and superstitions that attended the boss himself. He was sometimes found sitting in rooms he had not been seen to enter, and had a hand made of wood. Those who professed to know what kind of car he drove said he had either the balls or the explosive bad taste to drive an exact replica of the JFK death car, and there were others who whispered it wasn't a replica.

Mr. Scratch was known, one way or another, to campaign quietly —he was always quiet—for actuarial science.

Scratch somehow had lifestyle and mortality statistics going back three thousand years, and he'd made up tables based on those statistics.

The tables were scary.

"Scratch made a prediction one time," they whispered. "There was a car salesman in Lexington with three kids, on his second marriage, looked healthy, and exercised. Took maybe five drinks a week, and didn't smoke. But Scratch factored in stress from his divorce and some great-granddad of his who had a stroke, like, back before the Civil War, multiplied it by where he lived and divided it by his shoe size, and predicted this guy was going to kick on his forty-first birthday. Talked him into one huge down payment for a policy with a lot of fine print, and saved a hundred grand when the guy kicked exactly when he said he would. Scratch called it to the day."

Mr. Scratch's science was one philosophy. New men who had graduated from heavy eastern colleges tended to go with it.

The other philosophy, pushed loudly by Fish, was never to pay anybody any money if they could help it. "Deny all claims" was the first thing adjusters and investigators learned. Anytime someone asked to collect, you said "No." If they asked again, you gave them as little as you could get away with. You made them beg for every little penny. A lot of people, it turned out, didn't ask twice, and were too proud to beg.

Between these two philosophies, a lot of good people got ground up, and a lot of money got made.

ASSURANCE MUTUAL occupied most of a Chicago high-rise. Fish insisted on decorating all the offices and halls in polished mahogany, and framed pictures with scenes from history. Like George Washington crossing the Delaware, and Daniel Boone leading settlers into Kentucky.

The largest of these was a painting of Pocahontas saving John Smith from having his head smashed on a rock. It hung beside the elevator for one day before Mr. Scratch happened to see it.

"Take that down," he told the custodian in an odd, sad kind of tone.

The custodian said, "Well, now, Mr. Fish said for me to put it up there."

Mr. Scratch gave the custodian a certain look, and the painting was taken down.

The custodian was one of those people who got ground up.

THE WORKER BEES at Assurance Mutual knew very little about the private lives of their superiors.

They didn't know that the reason they saw more of Fish in the morning and less of him in the afternoon was that he was often drunk after lunch.

They didn't know that Scratch was the Devil. They didn't know he'd had a broken heart since the beginning of time. Or that he loved—*loved!*—the movie *Mary Poppins.*

SCRATCH TOOK FISH to a party for his twenty-sixth birthday. They chartered a private jet and flew south, drinking mai tais all the way.

"Enjoy," Scratch told Fish, raising his glass.

Fish enjoyed.

The jet flew south of the border, and landed on a grassy airstrip in the middle of nowhere.

The airstrip was attached to a sprawling, mazelike house, hidden among orchards and hills and man-made lakes, and in this astonishing house was a party that had been going on for a hundred years.

New people came and went, but the party itself was immortal. There was beer and wine and girls and opium. And boys. And acid and smack and cocaine. There was a Great Dane named Fidel, who wandered the party wearing a gold chain collar, and after two drinks he might talk to you.

SCRATCH WAS DRUNK. He was sitting at one end of a steaming hot tub, in the middle of a fake indoor rain forest. He felt good.

They had accomplished something, he and Fish. Built something. Betcher ass God had never built an insurance company!

And the company, the money, was only the start. He hoped.

Money ruined some people, but he had a hunch that Fish could be tempered by its touch. He would grow, become a person of value. He might become what the Devil thought of as the perfect human: someone who had power *and* vision. Who would focus his strength on making the world better, faster, and stronger. The kind of people the Devil needed on his planet, and who had yet to be born in any significant numbers.

Maybe such paragons weren't born. Maybe, like Fish, like an ugly duckling, they had to grow into it. And money would be their teacher, the mountain they measured themselves against. It had to be, because money was the fiery engine of civilization. Money itself was neither good nor evil. What a childish idea! Fish would master the fiery engine. The evil he did would be necessary, and bear fruit.

"We're on our way," said the Devil. "We've got our own building, for crying out loud."

"We?" said Fish, at the other end of the hot tub, nearly obscured by steam.

A toucan flew between them.

"You," said Scratch. "You know what I mean. Don't be an asshole."

He also *liked* Fish. The kid was pure devil. He had yanked a man through a window and killed him with an ashtray.

For that same reason, he often *dis*liked Fish.

He was insolent. He was proud. He was ambitious. That was pure devil, too, except rebellion was only great if *you* were the proud rebel. When someone else turned that shit on you, forget it.

Fish needed a lesson. A reminder. A growing pain.

"I want to show you something," said Scratch. "See that guy over there by the pool? The fat fucker in the black trunks, talking loud, obviously thinks he's a big deal?"

"No," answered Fish. "It's too steamy."

"Well, he's there. Let me tell you about him."

And he told Fish that this fat fucker had made himself president of a Caribbean island nation when he was only thirty years old, promising the military some nice things, promising the CIA some nice things, and then gaining the support of the people by promising *them* nice things. But then he didn't deliver. He got full of himself, and got very rich, and turned his island into a massive drug factory (which was the nice thing he'd promised the CIA). But you could only go so far like that before all you had around you were a bunch of disappointed, coked-up generals and a starving population.

"Sounds like a bonehead," said Fish.

The giant dog Fidel wandered by, ponderously sniffing the fake rain-forest soil, following the edge of the tub.

"Buenas noches, Fidel," called the Devil. Fidel loped away without answering.

Seconds later the Caribbean president ducked through the fake trees and slid his bulk into the hot tub, an oversize Japanese beer bottle in hand.

"Qué tal?" he boomed, saluting Scratch. Sensing someone hidden in the steam, he raised his bottle in that direction, too.

"Salud," said the Devil, sipping his mai tai.

The Caribbean president looked suddenly uneasy, as if he recognized Scratch's voice, but couldn't see Scratch quite well enough yet to place him.

"Dígame," began the president. *"Sois ustedes los—"*

"You quit answering your phone, Chico," said Scratch, eyes glowing. "The special red phone I gave you? Bad manners, amigo. Very rude."

The president dropped his beer and tried to scramble out of the tub, but he didn't get far. Scratch waved his drink, and President Chico became a screaming torch of blue flame. Eyes popping, fat boiling, he writhed and bled for a moment before the flames shrank to a point and vanished, taking him with them.

"Jesus *Christ,* dude!" gasped Fish. "What was the point of *that*?"

The Devil climbed out, jumped into his Bermudas, and headed for the cabana.

"You figure it out," he said. "Happy birthday."

FOR A FEW WEEKS after Fish's birthday, the high rollers at the Chicago office noticed a change. Fish was seen studying actuarial tables. He even held a daylong meeting about statistics, and produced a startling example of an account he, himself, had handled.

"There was a guy in Cleveland," he told them all, including Mr. Scratch, sitting in the back, wearing sunglasses, "who smoked and drank like there was no tomorrow, ate nothing but red meat, and had spinal meningitis as a child. But I added in his hat size and divided by the width of his wife's ass and multiplied the quotient by the kind of car he drives, and figured out that this guy was going to live to be ninety-eight fucking years old. We would have taken a bath. So I denied him coverage. We saved a quarter of a million projected, and didn't cost this fellow a dime either. Saving money is making money in this business, and no one got hurt. That's the kind of people we are, guys."

Applause.

Even the mysterious Mr. Scratch, in the back, was seen to nod approval (and he *did* approve! He was surprised and pleased. Fish was growing! What he had done wasn't nice, it wasn't visionary, but at least it was intelligent, something that had been missing thus far).

It didn't last. A month later, Fish called a meeting to discuss a new idea.

"Bill everybody twice," he commanded. "Some of those rubes will pay twice."

Mr. Scratch shook his head.

Fish was observed to strut back to his office and pour himself a strong one, and toast himself in a great big mirror.

17. Down the Rabbit Hole

Various cities, stages, highways, drug-fueled parties, and one very cool tree house, 1971

AFTER THE SOLD-OUT St. Louis show, the fans started out far away, across the parking lot, restrained by cops and wooden barriers. Memory waved at them. William Tell, the drummer, tried to show them his dick, but one of the bodyguards got to him in time.

Purple Airplane's bodyguards—Jerry, Gus, and Pig—were three jolly monsters whose job was to keep the band out of trouble. They could drink, snort, and smoke more than the band members, so that even when the good times got crazy, the bodyguards were always clearheaded enough to make decisions. They could also become sickeningly violent, if they felt the band was threatened. Pig, the largest, had once thrown an overenthusiastic fan off a roof, then run for a waiting helicopter with Memory under one arm and Jason Livingston, the bass player, under the other.

When the St. Louis crowd broke loose and overran the cops, the bodyguards adopted a siege mentality.

"Form the 'Turtle'!" roared Pig, wrapping his wallet chain around his fist.

They squeezed Memory, Two-John, William Tell, and Jason into a kind of rock-band sandwich, and raced for the buses.

Pig bit someone. Gus used his keys to rip open scalps.

For Memory, the experience quickly became frightening. She had gotten into the habit of dropping acid before big shows, and the crowd all had witch faces.

William Tell had an open bottle of whiskey, which he passed to Two-John.

"Jesus Christ," was all they said, smiling, sweaty but cool in their shades. Jason Livingston looked disgusted.

Gus and Pig went down. They came up together, bleeding, but not before two young girls, half dressed and wobbly-eyed, tackled William Tell and ripped his shirt loose.

"Goddammit!" spat Pig.

He reached for the twin Glock pistols in his waistband.

Suddenly a peculiar silence slammed down over everything, as if a magical bell jar of safety had descended from the sky. A tall figure took Memory by the arm. A tall figure who looked at once like a rock star and a rock, like a prince and a plumber, with eyes ten thousand years deep. Did he really look like that, or was it the acid?

The tall figure flashed a smile at Two-John and said, "How we doin'?" and Two-John handed him the whiskey bottle and said, "It's crowded."

The Devil.

The bodyguards, who no longer needed to club and smash, were like pleasant, edgy clowns. They smiled and suggested, moving the crowd with words. Then they were all on the bus, laughing. Except for Pig, who sat looking like he might throw up.

"I was about to pull my guns," he said.

He looked so pitiful. They laughed at him until he started laughing, too.

They formed an urgent line for the tiny bathroom, with the exception of William Tell, who just went outside and peed on the front bumper. The press took pictures, and Gus got blamed.

× × ×

AFTER THEY CHECKED into the hotel, they piled into the Kennedy limo, and went right back out into the night. Over two bridges, into the hills, to the home of a famous black comedian. A house with an impossible number of rooms, and both indoor and outdoor swimming pools. The comedian wore a woolly robe over a wet swimsuit. He smoked a cigar. At his party, he was too cool to be funny.

He tried, quite earnestly, to get Memory's memory to come back. He removed his sunglasses, revealing great, round, wonderful eyes. The acid in Memory's blood made them the eyes of God.

"You don't remember crying about something," said the famous black comedian, "when you were a kid, maybe? Crying so hard it made your head hurt? You know what I mean. The kind of crying where you don't even want to feel better, you just want to keep on crying like that for the rest of your life, you're so mad and so sad, all at once?"

Memory said "No." And she told him it was nice of him to try. She told him he was a Shiny Person.

She woke up in the pool the next morning, wearing someone else's fur coat.

The Devil sat on the diving board, watching her with bloodshot eyes. On the wall behind him was a sign: SWIMMING OOL. NOTICE THERE IS NO *P* IN OUR POOL. PLEASE KEEP IT THAT WAY.

Memory scrunched her eyes closed. It hurt to read.

She opened the fur coat, confirming that she wore nothing else.

"So," she said to the Devil. "You're back."

"For now," he said.

She wanted to get out, go find her clothes and a bathroom and some breakfast, but the water was warm, and her body felt heavy.

She went ahead and peed right where she was.

DAYS AND WEEKS blended. There were hotels filled with famous people and parties. Girls went wild for Two-John and William Tell. William Tell liked to make forts out of naked girls, and hide in them until they collapsed.

Girls liked Jason Livingston, too, when they caught a glimpse of him. He was the shy one. Freakishly tall and thin, with long blond hair and eyes that always looked as if he'd just stopped crying.

On the highway, people followed them. Kids mostly, in VW buses or whatever they could get to run. They weren't the kids from the concerts, necessarily. Just people who saw the bright, shining bus from miles away, read PURPLE AIRPLANE on the side, and fell in behind. Sometimes they rode alongside, waving. If somebody waved back, the fans would shriek and make peace signs. Sometimes they even rode alongside the tech bus, and waved at the roadies. Whatever the roadies did or said, it scared most fans away.

THE RELEASE OF *DOROTHY*, their first album, had carried them straight into the stratosphere of fame, where it seemed their slightest breath brought attention or sowed rumors. Like the rumor that Two-John was some kind of low-ranking East European prince, who kept a stable of rabbits for food. Like the rumor that Jason Livingston took pills by sticking them up his ass, or that Memory was called Memory because she actually had amnesia.

Through all the travel and the fame and the music, the Devil struggled to keep his own head in balance. He wasn't here to enjoy himself. Memory and her band had a purpose to serve, and he meant to see it was served right.

The music of Purple Airplane was like a magic carpet ride. It was a journey you went on; everyone said so. Maybe you danced to it. Maybe you stared into space, drugged by Memory's voice or Two-John's haunted guitar. But you went somewhere, something happened to you. Afterward, you felt like you knew a secret. Everyone said so, and the Devil thought, This is it! It's happening! The locked door at the center of everyday human life was finally opening, and they'd find some kind of wild garden inside where they'd grow into the beings he'd always known they could be.

And maybe they did, here and there, for a little while. Hard to say. If people felt the door open, they still got up the next day and answered the ordinary roll call of their lives.

Music journalists had a hard time explaining how the magic carpet worked. The Airplane's music spread in many directions, which was the same as no direction, and when one writer asked Memory what the band's direction *was,* she just stared right through him in the nicest way.

The Devil heard the question, though, and tossed it around in his head.

Being lost was a kind of direction, wasn't it? People talked about losing themselves in thought, in love, in conversation, or a TV show. You had to get lost to find the heart of anything, didn't you?

William Tell just snarled that if people needed directions they should ask a fucking cop.

IT WASN'T AN ordinary life, by any means.

Unless you had nothing to compare it to, which Memory didn't.

The funny thing about living and remembering, she had discovered, was that it added up so fast. You spent all week looking forward to something—maybe a show, or time alone to take a bubble bath and drink a bottle of wine—and before you knew it the thing was happening, and then it was past. A week past, or a month. And before she knew it, she was a year older and had a million memories.

It was better than it had been, right? When it was just her and the moment and a black, silent, twenty-year hole?

She sat in a bubble bath in a Miami hotel, drinking a bottle of wine, watching the steam rise, trying to catalog what she *did* remember.

The catalog began on a hot dirt road with Queen Anne's lace and summer moths fluttering around, and woods on both sides. Every now and then the buzz of cicadas would rise around her like an invisible storm, then subside, and then rise again, and she walked down the shoulder with no shoes on in a simple white dress, and didn't even know she didn't know anything, not even her own name, until a woman pulled over in a pickup truck and asked her where she was going, and she didn't know.

"Town," she had said. So the woman drove her to town.

The whole way Memory hid a rising panic, reaching out thought-fingers to find a complete and terrifying emptiness. The town turned out to be a college town, where another woman, a wonderful, knowing young woman named Dawn, discovered her in front of a Mexican restaurant, crying, and took her home to where she lived with a bunch of hippies. They named Memory "Memory" and helped her explore things like Being Useful—to clean things and wash clothes and cook a little—and important cautions like Don't Burn Yourself and Don't Walk in the Street. She learned things she Liked, like music, and Didn't Like, like coconut and yellow cheeses. This guy with a beard taught her to strum a guitar well enough that the people in the house encouraged her to play, until the day someone got her to sing, and she cast a spell on them. Her voice haunted itself from far away. And the bearded guy taught her that she liked making love, too, and dancing. She didn't like weeding Dawn's vegetable garden, particularly, but they all took turns. She learned about Helping and Work and Doing Your Share.

One day Dawn took her to the hospital to see if there was something they could do about her memory, but the doctors wanted to keep her under observation behind locked doors, and the two women barely escaped the hospital without getting snatched. Later that same week, some loud, happy men and women in a rusty Microbus stayed at the house for a couple of nights on their way to San Francisco, and when they left, Memory went with them. She watched the country unroll beyond the windshield until it frightened her, then made herself watch until it didn't.

San Francisco was like a fair for people like Memory, living in the present, unfettered by their past. One day she was singing along with a street band, and some older cat with a beard and sunglasses turned around and listened, and talked to her when she was done, and that cat was Dan Paul Overfield.

There was a year where they traveled and recorded songs, and, between Dan Paul and Memory, their band started getting famous. And it wasn't long before the band and the singing were all she knew, and she found herself wishing hard for real fame to come, because it might fill that twenty-year hole.

Now, of course, fame had risen like a spinning sun. But it did nothing to fill the hole, because you can't feed a soul-hunger. Feeding it just makes it hungrier. You have to feed whatever causes the hunger, and of course she couldn't.

"I can't!" she gurgled, opening her throat like Pig had taught her so the wine would just pour straight down.

The door opened. Cool air rolled in, making whirlpools in the steam. Pig peered at her (the band was cool with nudity. They didn't really have a choice).

"You all right?" he gruffed.

The tenderness in his voice—it was there, if you knew Pig—was the only real thing in her world, for just a second. It almost made her cry.

"Yeah, Pig," she said. "Piggy Pig."

The door closed.

The mist swirled and settled.

Fame was a surprising thing. It was and was not what she'd expected.

On one hand, it held her like a pink cloud. If she closed her eyes now, in the warm water and bubbles and steam, with blue pills and wine softening everything, she could feel them out there. A sea of blurred faces, listening, loving her. Floating her up. Filling her blank spaces. Sometimes, just for a moment, like right now, it was enough. It was like the music itself, and she was happy without having to think about it.

But it never lasted.

Because fame was like an animal, too. It was like having a lion on a silver chain. It impressed people that you had it. It brought you good things, but it made demands, too. It had to be fed. It was phones that never stopped ringing. It was deadlines and miles to be traveled and hard work to be done. It didn't float around like a happy cloud. It stared at you with green animal eyes, and roared questions at you, and interrupted your sleep and made you over in its own image until it seemed the You that was famous hardly resembled the You that was You. It was something most people would never understand or believe: being famous was hard work, and it was scary. It could swallow you. Or, worst of all, it could just walk away.

Memory opened her eyes, breathing hard.

Damn. One second she'd been so happy. The next, full of fear. That's what she got for stopping to think.

Little girl lost, she thought, and threw up in the bathwater.

Her discomfort and revulsion were momentary. She hadn't eaten all day. It was just wine.

"Bathing in my own wine . . . !" she sang.

The echo seemed to last forever. Like a studio reverb.

She fell asleep listening to it.

SOMETIMES, when he had inhaled a great deal of coke, the Devil found himself blurting that he loved her.

Not to Memory herself.

"I love her," he would slur to Two-John, Pig, or some stranger.

But no one heard or else forgot, and the Devil himself forgot the second the slightest distraction came along, like having to pee or realizing he had peed himself.

Falling momentarily in love and peeing yourself were common hazards of this fast, weird life, he realized. So were music and good times and the sense that a whole new world was opening.

"Let there be light," said the Devil, sprawled between naked women in a candlelit hotel room, stinking of pot and urine.

PURPLE AIRPLANE PLAYED Madison Square Garden, and stayed at the Chelsea Hotel.

Jason Livingston loved the Chelsea. He was a worshipper on a pilgrimage.

"The fucking Chelsea!" he gushed, slowly turning in the lobby, gazing at the upstairs balcony, watery eyes almost brimming over. This was where Dylan Thomas and Bob Dylan had lived, he told the rest of them, and Arthur Miller until not too long ago, and William Tell brushed past him and said he'd told them already, a hundred fucking times. Two-John paused long enough to agree it was "Nice." Then he ashed on the carpet and headed for the bar.

An Austrian circus was staying at the Chelsea, too. The musicians and roadies of Purple Airplane and the circus performers kept passing one another in the lobby all afternoon. Memory got in the elevator once, and found it occupied by a clown and a dancing bear on a leash.

"Don't be afraid," said the clown, in an Austrian accent. "She can smell fear."

The circus people were unusually beautiful. Every single one, it seemed. All during rehearsal at Madison Square Garden, they talked about how beautiful the circus people were.

After the show, they stayed up all night. The Devil drove them around in the Kennedy limo with a case of champagne, and they didn't get back to the Chelsea until after sunrise.

Everyone slouched off to bed except Pig, who announced that he was going to keep right on drinking, and vanished into the bar. Memory fell asleep on a chair in her bathroom.

She awoke to the phone ringing, and someone telling her that the dancing bear had mauled its owner and was wandering the halls. The manager and his crew were feverishly dialing each room, one by one, telling the guests to stay behind doors.

Outside Memory's door, something shuffled down the hall, and she croaked, "Oh, wow."

It took forever for the cops and paramedics to arrive. In the meantime, the bear wobbled into the bar and stuck its nose in Pig's drink.

Pig and the bartender gave the bear blank looks.

Then Pig slipped off his stool, took the bear's leash in hand, and led her back upstairs to her cage.

× × ×

PEOPLE DISCOVER NEW DRUGS and new lovers in the least likely of places.

Memory didn't know she was discovering heroin. She was going on *The Dick Cavett Show.*

There were to be two guests; the studio made sure Memory was introduced second. She walked onstage in platform shoes, to wild applause, and Dick Cavett introduced her to Eliot Crump, the Rock Star of American Bird-Watching.

Dick Cavett asked her some smart questions about psychedelic music, and she gave some smart answers, but mostly her attention was drawn to Eliot.

He was a handsome fellow in his thirties, but man, was he shaggy! He had an unmanaged mop of heavy black curls, five o'clock shadow all over his face, and a mustache like a great black jungle caterpillar. He looked at her across Dick Cavett, and his eyes drowned her. Never had she seen such lucid eyes. If a rainstorm was a pair of eyes, it would be these eyes. Later, when she understood more about heroin, she would understand why his eyes looked like that. But here, in front of a studio audience, taping for a million viewers, she just thought he looked relaxed.

Dick Cavett asked Memory about her amnesia—part of the reason she had agreed to do the show was a hope that someone might recognize her. After eight million album covers, no one had come forward yet.

"I think I'm kind of relieved," she said. "On one hand, it would be like a dream if some guy came out of nowhere one day and turned out to be my husband or something, but on the other hand, it would be more like a nightmare, you know?"

Dick Cavett sympathized, in a crisp kind of way.

He had already interviewed the Rock Star of American Bird-Watching, but he turned to Eliot again as they closed, saying, "What kind . . . Eliot, what kind of, ah, what kind of bird would you say Memory looked like?"

Apparently one of the cool things about Eliot was that he could instantly pair any human on Earth with whatever bird they most resembled, and his answers were always right on the money.

"An ibis, Dick," said Eliot. No hesitation.

The audience gasped and applauded. An assistant somehow flashed a picture of an ibis on the studio wall, and the taping ended in a swell of smiling and clapping.

Then the Rock Star of American Bird-Watching asked Memory if he could take her someplace for a drink, and she said "Yes."

And he said, "I'm your long-lost husband, by the way."

They became friends very quickly.

He drove her to a bar way down in Brooklyn.

He had his own car, a red LeMans, which he had driven in from Vermont. It was the first time in a while that Memory had ridden in something that wasn't a limo or a tour bus. She made the most of it, rolling down the window and turning up the radio.

"This is a treat," she sighed, propping her bare feet up on the dashboard.

Eliot didn't say anything. He just drove and listened to the music and looked relaxed.

MEMORY FOUND OUT why Eliot Crump was such a great bird-watcher.

Heroin.

The day after *The Dick Cavett Show,* he drove Memory up to his cabin in the Adirondacks, and the first thing he did was split a chocolate bar with Memory, and start smoothing out the foil with a wad of toilet paper.

"What the hell?" Memory wanted to know.

He asked if she'd ever chased the dragon.

"Is that a kind of bird?" she asked. When he laughed, his heavy black hair shook all over.

"Chasing the dragon is when you smoke smack instead of shooting up. It's healthier."

He explained that when you shot up, anything the heroin was cut with went straight into your bloodstream. If you smoked, the impurities burned away.

He made the foil perfectly flat, and dissolved a tiny caplet of Turkish smack in lemon juice. It turned almost instantly to liquid, rolling like oil around the foil.

Memory held a match beneath the foil, and Eliot inhaled through the glass tube.

White smoke spiraled up inside the pipe.

With one puff, his eyes got that bottomless depth. Another, and he switched with her, lighting a new match.

It was like nothing else she'd ever done. With one puff, it hit her like a golden train.

"Golden train," she said, rolling her head around.

"Yeah," said Eliot Crump, and they went out to his tree house.

At first, Memory couldn't handle how the mountains seemed far away, and then close enough to hold in her hand. The tree-house ladder stretched away through green branches and vines, but the climb was over in a second. Then there was a hollow dark all around, and they were in the tree house Eliot had built. It was a wooden deck cantilevered out over the floor of a mountain valley.

The valley was golden. The sky turned.

Everything she focused on made Memory know things she hadn't known before. She felt her lost memory hovering just beyond reach.

They sat in perfect calm and stillness this way.

Every once in a while, the Rock Star of American Bird-Watching would say, "There's a Halberd's speckled grackle," (or something) and take notes, and take pictures.

And every once in a while, Memory would say "There's a crow" or "There's a robin," and he dutifully took pictures and notes.

"Tomorrow," he told her, "we'll drive over to Fulker's Hollow and have a look for the bird of paradise."

"There's no birds of paradise in Vermont," Memory argued. She knew *that* much. "They're tropical."

Eliot nodded. "Except this one. It was a pet or something, and someone let it go. Did you know the bird of paradise is a perfect mimic?"

"Like a mockingbird?"

"Better. A mockingbird just imitates other birds. The bird of paradise can repeat any sound it hears. Even nonorganic sounds. This one must have lived in the city before it escaped; people will be out in the woods and all of a sudden they'll hear a train up in the branches, or a garbage truck backing up. It would be far out if I could get a picture. It would be the only temperate bird of paradise on record."

"You're fucking with me," she accused.

He shook his head. His hair bounced. Sparks of sunset flew.

"No," he said. "But since you mention it . . ."

He gave her a golden look. The shadows in the trees grew long.

They undressed each other with long pauses and long, fascinated looks. Sometimes they forgot what they were doing.

It took five and a half hours.

WHEN THE TOUR ENDED and the band started writing new songs full-time at Bubble Records' San Francisco studio or at Memory's beach house, Memory found herself preoccupied. She started spending a lot of money chasing Eliot Crump's golden dragon. She spent a lot of money, too, flying east to see the Rock Star himself.

The Devil didn't go with her. He had a good thing going with acid and cocaine, and preferred to spend his days wandering the beach. The beach near Memory's house was a rocky, misty strand, with pounding breakers and cold spray. He, and he alone, dared to swim its terrible rips, piercing the surf and floating way out to sea. He kept Memory in his mind's eye, lazily watching over her as if through a kaleidoscope a thousand miles long. She seemed okay. She was doing what she was meant to do. Things were good.

In Vermont, Memory and Eliot hiked Fulker's Hollow, all aglow and relaxed. They were watchers of atoms and molecules. No way a bird of paradise was getting past them.

They were deep in the woods. Eliot carried a tent on his back.

They spent the night, and through the mist the next morning, hiking between cliffs of moss and granite, green and gray, vibrating with the dragon in their veins, they heard a jackhammer.

"Jackhammer," said Memory. "Far out."

Eliot knew better. Quietly they climbed a hill of bald stone, where they relaxed and waited. It was Memory who saw it: bright plumage in a green Adirondack tree, nesting high above a forest floor of red pine needles. Feathered spikes crowned its head. Raising its wings like a cape, the creature shook its throat.

ACK-ACKA-DRRRRRRRRRRRRRRRR!

Pure jackhammer tones rang in the ancient valley.

Eliot let her take the photograph, and write down the notes, the day, the hour.

Temperate bird of paradise, she scrawled. The paper shined at her. *Fulker's Hollow, Green Mountains, Vermont. Nine o'clock in the morning,* AD.

It was the happiest moment of her life.

Everybody has one. It's a good thing they don't know it when it happens.

THE SECOND ALBUM would be called *Oolong.*

San Francisco, again. Working at Memory's beach house, they wrote lyrics during the afternoon, tapping out music on a rented upright with half-melted candles all over it.

There were half-melted candles everywhere these days. The Devil, usually dressed in sunglasses and a silk bathrobe, seemed to have put himself in charge of making sure they had twenty-four-hour candlelight. It was nice and mellow, but left everything, including musical instruments, dripping with wax stalagmites. Finally, Two-John stole a spatula from a waterfront tortilla vendor and presented it to the Devil with a bow tied around it, saying he was now also in charge of scraping up all the wax.

The Devil complied. He made himself useful in other ways, too.

Cooking, sometimes. Putting out kitchen fires. Repairing things in the kitchen. Common work, sure. But work, like drugs, was good for the soul, and it allowed him to keep an eye on the band, the project he had assigned himself for this particular and important stretch of history.

At sunset, the musicians and their bodyguards walked the rocky beach. They were recognized, but Frisco beach crowds were cool. They didn't want a pound of flesh, the way crowds in other places seemed to. They just sometimes waved Hi. Until Two-John borrowed a guitar and they gathered around a bonfire. Someone boiled shrimp, nearby.

It was just the guitar, at first. But then someone brought William Tell a set of bongos.

They were a little high, except Memory and Two-John, who were very high indeed. Memory had taught Two-John how to chase the dragon, because he was better at getting Gus, Jerry, and Pig to talk to dealers. The two of them wore sunglasses.

Two-John played some massive, heavy chords.

Memory sang Indian chants. Her voice seemed to go out and come back, and come from different places around the fire, different parts of the crowd.

Jason Livingston, stuck without a bass, stood nodding his head in rhythm.

The crowd played its part on old bottles and cans and shells.

The fire brightened like a sun.

Everything was gold and night, except Memory felt a little sick, and her heart fluttered. Some anonymous beach hippie kept her from falling into the fire.

Frisco beach crowds are cool, except this one wanted to take Memory to the hospital.

"No way," said Two-John, who carried her back to the hotel and kept her up all night, shuffling around and drinking water so her heart wouldn't stop.

Two-John was afraid, and trying not to show it. They had both smoked an awful lot of Turkish.

He glared at the Devil, busy washing dishes in sunglasses and harem pants, a silver syringe stuck behind his ear like a pencil. He had discovered smack, and wasn't so much washing dishes as admiring them.

"This isn't what you promised her," Two-John growled at the Devil.

"She's famous, isn't she?"

"You know what I mean."

The Devil didn't want to talk about it. He cast a spell that made Two-John forget he was there.

Rolling Stone gave the beach concert five inches in the April issue.

Some of the mainstream newspapers mentioned Memory's collapse.

The papers were not as nice as the beach crowds.

ELIOT CRUMP, THE bastard, ran off with some teenager to watch birds in India. Memory read about it in the tabloids.

Hurt more than she would have thought possible, Memory started shooting smack instead of chasing the dragon. It was stronger, that way. And she *wanted* stronger.

The house where she overdosed became a stop on Hollywood tour.

It was a nice party. It was golden water in an indoor swimming pool. So warm.

Some parties had more than their share of naked people, and this was one of them. Memory wasn't one of the naked people, though. She never was.

She wore fur, with nothing underneath, if she meant to swim. And she always swam.

This time the gold formed a tunnel, and the tunnel called to her.

It sounded like a jackhammer, like a socket wrench. Like a helicopter. And like music, of course, and shovels digging the earth.

Breathe, said the gold. So she breathed.

The pool, underwater, was like a blue sky, like air.

The gold became a hammer, crushing her chest from the inside.

It was one of those things you know and don't know, when you are becoming clinically dead. She knew, and did not know, that she had joyfully inhaled a double lungful of pool water.

She remembered thinking, sinking in her fur coat, And God knows what else; with all these naked people, there's gotta be more than *P* in this *ool*.

The Devil might have been inspired to snap his fingers and intervene, but he had gotten left behind in Atlanta and was throwing up behind a Piggly Wiggly there.

Things fall apart.

Memory vanished into a hospital. Then she just vanished.

Jason Livingston joined a European band within the week. The European band did an American tour wearing jack-in-the-boxes on their heads.

William Tell went solo with no trouble at all.

Two-John vanished back into the swamp. The rumor mill said he had bricked his guitar up in a New Orleans crypt, so whatever was in it couldn't get out.

The Devil went off to take care of other business.

He had to, with three or four expensive drug habits to support. Like a lot of people in those days, the Devil had discovered escape. Like a lot of people, he felt the world had become the kind of place that needed escaping from.

He wondered if the new world, the new awareness he had wanted for people, was still out there waiting to happen. It felt like a train he had missed, and sometimes, through the fog, this made him sad.

Sometimes, though, he thought they hadn't really missed the train. The train was just different, that was all. It wasn't a world thing. It was personal. It was internal. The new awareness was a wonderful and intoxicating isolation.

And being the Devil on drugs opened up all kinds of possibilities. He could be in Heaven again, if he wanted. He could sleep. He could burst like the sun, or hide and watch it all go by. Like Memory and

Purple Airplane, he could blaze like a meteor and fly apart in glory. If he tried hard enough, he could feel a mirage in his heart that was almost like love.

On the outside, he lost his sunglasses and his harem pants started falling apart. His hair grew stringy. He smelled.

On the inside, he burned. Sometimes he was fire, sometimes ashes.

Like the band, like Memory, he started the process of becoming a ghost.

18.

Dreams of Fire and Blood

Virginia, 1831

WHITE MEN COULDN'T HELP being cruel, thought Nat Turner.

It was like a curse God had laid on them. Maybe it was supposed to teach them something.

Nat had been taught to read as a child. He knew the Bible inside and out, and had read more books than most white men. He had a way of talking about things, and people called him "Preacher," whatever color they were.

White men were cruel because they weren't quite men. They were like children inside. That's what the curse had done to them, he thought.

Nat had a higher standard for black men, free or not. Black men were men, or Jesus would never have given them so much to bear. Now they had to find a way to be free, without losing their lives or their souls.

And when he thought these things, a wind blew inside him, and the voice of Jesus was on that wind, and he would know he was right.

Which is how he knew, the day he followed a noise down an alley in Jerusalem, Virginia, to find seven slaves at liberty and two free black men taking turns at Beulah Carter, the Carters' retarded house girl, he knew God meant for him to say something.

He flung them aside, and preached at them, "How you ever going to be men, when you act just like the animals the masters say you are? A man's got something extra in him, supposed to make him different from a pig."

He felt lifted up as he talked, light as a feather with Jesus on the wind inside him.

They listened to him. Ashamed, they turned away and went home.

NOT ONLY WAS Nat well read, not only did he have a way about him and the Jesus-wind inside him, he had visions, too. Nat thought of himself as a peaceful man, but the visions were not peaceful. They were fiery, bloody, and left him writhing as though his head would crack. Lately, terrible dreams had left him shaken and red-eyed.

The Devil, who had a nose for extraordinary people, sometimes turned himself into a bird and watched Nat from trees. He thought Nat might be useful to him, the way Washington had been useful.

The day Nat stopped the men from raping Beulah Carter, the Devil decided to talk to him.

When the preacher stopped on his way home to eat some corn bread and pray, the Devil made himself look like a proper angel, and perched on a nearby log.

Nat was too busy praying, at first, to notice.

"I'm a man of Peace, sweet Jesus," he was praying. "So how come you send me these dreams of tribulation?"

While he listened for an answer—for it seemed, sometimes, that God *did* answer—the Devil spoke up, and drew his attention.

"Maybe Peace isn't part of God's plan for you, Nat Turner."

Nat looked a little surprised to find an angel addressing him, but only a little.

"Peace," he answered, removing his hat, "is what's in my *heart,* angel, sir."

"God made your heart, Nat Turner. Do you know your heart better than God?"

"No, sir."

"Why do you think God gave you those great big hands?"

"I don't know, angel. To work, I suppose."

"No. For killing white people, is why."

The preacher's eyes narrowed. Slowly, he put on his hat, turned his back on the angel, and started down the road again, toward home.

The angel fished a pipe from its pocket, and lit up a bowlful of earthworms.

NAT FOUND WHAT the angel had said a trifle suspicious. Not only that, but the angel had a mark on its forehead that troubled him sorely.

All God's creatures bore a sign on their forehead, and Nat could read these signs. There were people marked Confusion, or Weak, or Hard, or Hungry. He knew a horse with a sign on its forehead, saying THIS HORSE MIGHT KICK YOU, and the horse kicked a man and broke his leg. Another time there were twin girls, and they both had a mark that was like a heart, except one of them had it stronger than the other, and the other had it like a bruise that was fading, and when it was gone, she died.

The angel wore a devil sign on his forehead, plain as day.

AFTER HE FINISHED his pipe, the Devil thought about making himself invisible and following Nat home, but he was tired. The kind of tired that comes after you've been angry about something all day long.

The Devil was angry with Americans for being hypocrites. They were so proud of their freedom and their talk of freedom, but so many of the big talkers owned slaves.

America—Earth!—didn't stand a chance with raw evil at its heart, and the Devil thought the solution was plain. The slaves must *seize* freedom, the way America herself had seized it. The way he, Lucifer, had seized it. It was how freedom was won.

It had never been difficult to get men to wage war, but in this case, the Devil had met resistance. Yes, there were voices among the enslaved that urged revolt, but these voices were either silenced by their masters or ignored by the majority, who thought revolt was suicide.

The Devil knew, though, that you didn't have to destroy an enemy to make him change his ways. You only had to destroy him enough to make him afraid. If the right leader could make white Americans *fear* slaves, then a new idea would dawn. Because all you had to do to keep slaves from being scary was give them their freedom. Rebellion could work, if the enemy didn't fight back too hard. And most Americans disliked slavery already. The nation just needed a push.

The Devil thought Nat Turner was the man to do the pushing. And they would listen to him, blacks and whites alike, *because* he had always talked peace.

THE NEXT DAY, mending a pair of iron shears in the garden shed, the preacher thought about his awful dreams, and about the peaceful wind inside him. He was confused and frustrated, and asked God for help.

He closed his eyes until he felt the Jesus-wind rise inside him, and said, "God, if You want me to go and work vengeance, You will have to give me a sign. In Your own good time, Lord, give me a sign."

But the Devil was listening in from behind the sugaring shed, and damned if the sun didn't turn lime green right then and there.

ON SUNDAYS, slaves and free black people from miles around came to the woods near the farm where Nat lived, to hear him preach, and eat supper with him.

Nat would read the Bible to them, and say wise and peaceful things. He would say how they must never hate, no matter how they were tested. Because hate destroyed a man. Hate and destruction were indivisible.

He told them common wisdom, too. He told the men that when

they sparked a woman, they should wrap their pecker in a rhubarb leaf until they were sure it was love they sparked, not just an animal passion.

He told the women they must keep their hair tied up and their clothing modest, not to tempt the childish white masters.

He told the children among them that they must guard their hearts so that hate would not take root.

The Sunday after the sun turned green, he read all the things he always read and taught the wisdom he always taught, but when it came time to tell them about peace, his mouth slammed closed and the words wouldn't come. For the first time he went straight home and didn't stay for the supper.

THERE WERE MORE SIGNS, one atop another, until one day in the woods, a bird called out, "Kill the white people!" as clear as could be, and Nat couldn't take it anymore.

He packed up a napkin with bread and cheese and dried meat, and sneaked away after the North Star.

But it wasn't that easy.

The first night, he saw a rabbit with two heads. The next night he crossed a river, and when he was halfway across, the river stopped flowing and then went to flowing the opposite way. (This was like a reprimand from God to him, but also a sign he was near the sea.)

It was like God was chasing him. The signs were clear.

He thought of Jonah, in the Bible, and how he ran from God and what God wanted him to do.

So, on the third morning, when he woke up and saw the angel with the devil sign sitting over him, saying, "Where do you think you're going, Nat Turner?" he answered, in a voice so tired, that he guessed he was going back home, and the angel said, "That's good."

WHEN NAT RETURNED, his master made him work field labor for a week, plus sleep outside chained to the water pump.

But Nat was too smart, in the master's estimation, to be used that way for long. So when the week was over, he was given a barn to build. It was the kind of thing that lifted Nat's mind and soul! Something to draw and imagine and make whole from the ground up, with God's help. He prayed a wind prayer, for Jesus, and a wood prayer, too, because the barn would be made of wood.

HIS WORK WOULD have been happier if the angel hadn't sat around bothering him every second.

"You have to *take* freedom," said the angel. "You have to—"

"Leave me alone, Devil," said the preacher, shaving boards in the woodshop. "I got work to do."

"How'd you know I was the Devil?"

"Sign on your forehead. It puzzled me, till I thought how there's one angel who *would* have a sign like that."

"Devil. Angel. There's not really a difference, you know."

"I suppose you're going to tell me war and peace are two parts of the same thing, too."

"You choose Peace," said the Devil.

"I do," answered Nat, still shaving boards.

"You, a slave?"

Nat lowered his head, squinting one eye to see where the wood was smooth.

"I am a man, sir. Slavery is a circumstance I find myself in. A man can be stronger than his circumstances."

The Devil was taken aback. Was this a new idea? He had met others, across the years, who would have liked the idea very much.

"What are you thinking of, Devil?" asked Nat.

The Devil almost said he was thinking of Pocahontas, but instead he said, "You put me in mind of someone, Nat Turner, with how much you love Peace and how much you're not going to get it. The only people who can really choose Peace are those who can also make War. Otherwise it's not a choice. It's like saying a rabbit chooses Peace because it doesn't fight the wolf. The wolf loves it when the rabbit chooses Peace."

“Thou Shalt Not Kill,” said Nat.

“Death is just a door,” said the Devil. “What does it matter if someone goes through the door because of you or because of old age?”

Nat flung a vise handle into the rafters.

The Devil vanished in a puff of smoke.

THE LAST SIGN was a total eclipse of the sun.

Nat was preaching a sermon when it happened. But by then he knew the signs had the Devil’s hand on them, so it wasn’t the eclipse that changed his mind.

It was thinking about what he, himself, had said. About man and circumstance. And for the first time, he wasn’t sure what God wanted. He just knew what he felt was right, and sometimes what was right was also wrong. Sometimes doing wrong was a burden you had to shoulder, to make room for something right.

In the woods on Sunday, the sun turned black and terrible overhead and the forest darkened around Nat and his congregation. The preacher saw how the light surrendered to the dark, as if trusting it for a time. And when the sun began to come back, he saw how the sun’s trust was rewarded. How it seemed to shine brighter than before.

He felt ashamed, then, for second-guessing God and His signs, even though what needed doing was so bad that God had sent the Devil to get it done.

When he opened his mouth to preach, Nat Turner had a dark light in his eye.

He told them their mission. He said he knew what an awful thing it was, but they had to do it. To everything there was a season, even a season to kill.

They listened, and they believed him. They had always believed him.

It scared him, the way they believed, almost as if they were half asleep, or some part of them were missing. Truth be told, he, too, felt as if he were half asleep or half real.

And they agreed when to meet, and spread the word, and when they went home after sundown, they sharpened axes and made horses ready.

WHEN IT CAME TIME to ride out and do the killing, it was mostly others who did it. Raiding parties rode here and there, hacking and burning, and Nat rode behind them, grim and stone-faced. Sometimes he found himself in the middle of things, though, and when that happened, he did his duty. He closed his heart and cut. He ignored screams. He closed whole rooms inside himself, and burned and killed until he was sore with it.

The sign on his brow was an ax, now.

He looked at himself in a dead farmer's bedroom mirror, and saw his sign fading to yellow, like a bruise.

When he stepped outside again, a new horseman had joined his raiders. Someone in a new linen shirt, never worked in yet, his skin as black as the bottom of the sea.

Nat mounted his own horse and rode quietly up to the stranger.

"Devil," he said.

The Devil nodded. His horse snorted.

"I hear they've got the army up after us," said Nat.

The Devil shrugged.

"That doesn't sound," said Nat, "like an enemy who's scared. It doesn't sound like an enemy ready to set his slaves free."

"After this," said the Devil, in a soft, even voice, "they'll have to sleep with one eye open."

"What they'll do," said Nat, "I think, is get just scared enough to kill any black man that looks at them twice. Free or not, won't make any difference. That's what I think."

"You regret this?" asked the Devil.

Nat shrugged. "Sometimes a man does right; sometimes he does what he has to. I hope good comes of it."

Night noises. Woodsy sounds. Down the road, new screams choked off.

"Come on, then!" grunted Nat, spurring his horse onto the road. "You brought us hate, now be a man and hate with us!"

"You *need* Hate," said the Devil. "You know what this world does to the gentle."

Nat tossed the Devil an ax.

"All right," said the Devil.

He walked into the farmhouse behind the barn, where a white family knelt in a circle, bawling and begging in their nightclothes. A tall, tan, bullish-looking man, a fat woman with black hair, and four boys, the youngest maybe three years old.

One of the boys had a bad-boy look to him, and he spat at the Devil.

So the Devil took him first.

It was only death.

HE FLUNG THE AX from halfway across the yard, and Nat had to duck to keep from being twins. Flecks of blood sprayed his shirt. Nat's stony eyes faltered, then, and for a second or two, his face was a mask of horror.

"Death is a door," said the Devil. "That's all."

"What have we brought ourselves to?"

"Do you doubt this?" said the Devil. "Nothing wrong with doubt. Jesus doubted. But what you've done is behaved as if you *mattered.* You've lifted your hand and said you refuse to be worthless, refuse to be what someone else thinks you are. You've behaved like a man."

Nat gave the Devil a blank look, and then he surprised both the Devil and himself by spurring his horse close, eyes blazing in the moonlight. His voice was raw, almost choking. A knife flashed in his hand, pressed against the Devil's throat.

"What do you know," he hissed, "about being a man?"

The Devil was inexplicably calm. He returned Nat's stare with eyes that were full of yearning for this world that could be so much except that it understood so little, and it was all that he had left.

They were eyes that wanted to be trusted, but they were angry eyes, and spiteful, too.

"You're a child, is all you are!" bellowed the preacher. "What have you ever done that wasn't for yourself?"

They froze that way, glaring fire, and it was the Devil who broke away first, launching his horse with a dreadful cry, and thundering into the woods.

NOT LONG AFTER, the Virginia militia came after them with muskets and hunting dogs. And some of the black men who had followed Nat Turner had signs on their foreheads too faint to see, and these died with the THUMP of a ball hitting flesh and bone, like someone getting hit with a gravy spoon. And they all ran, different ways.

Nat hid himself in a pile of sticks, and prayed. He felt around inside himself for the peace and the winds and the knowing that had always been there—and it was all there, but with its eyes closed like something that has done what it was made for.

Footsteps approached. "Who's there?" called a soldier.

"Me and the Devil," called Nat.

Then he looked around, twigs in his hair, and laughed.

"No," he called again. "It's just me."

THE DEVIL APPEARED while Nat waited in jail to be hanged.

He sat in the straw with the preacher and began to preach himself.

"You do not fit in your own time, Nat Turner, the way a dream doesn't fit daylight. But this had to be fought for. Even if it was only going to end like this. Because people will talk about this fight, and the reasons for this fight, and it will become a story."

Nat grabbed the Devil's wrists with impossible speed.

"Look at me, Devil. What do you see?"

The Devil looked the preacher in the eye, and didn't see a thing. Nat was a hollow man.

He meant to go down into the grave that way, Nat did. Silent. Hollow. Nothing happening to nothing.

But at the last minute, with the noose around him, bare feet splintering on the scaffold, someone called out to him "What color is God, you reckon, Turner?"

In the years to follow, he knew. And people would expect the story to say certain things and behave a certain way. So he scraped up what little simple joy remained inside him, and answered in a cracking voice, "I don't know any better than you do, you white turkey. Want to come with me and see?"

19.

O Pioneers!

Chicago, 1974

"I DON'T *FEEL* RICH," Fish complained to the Devil.

The Devil shrugged. A fistful of high-end cocaine was skinny-dipping in his bloodstream, and an unholy peace reigned over him.

"Maybe you never *will* feel rich," he told Fish. "I've heard about that. People who get their money all at once, or in strange ways, always feel like it's about to fall apart."

They were drinking twelve-year-old Scotch in Fish's Gold Coast apartment, celebrating. That afternoon, a customer named Charlie P. Scott had died at the age of ninety-two. His life insurance policy had paid out ten thousand dollars. Over the thirty years since launching the policy, they had made a quarter of a million off ol' Charlie.

"Here's to Charlie," said Fish, raising his Scotch, leaning against the kitchen bar.

He wore a gold ring, a thin black turtleneck, and lines on his face that most men didn't have at the age of twenty-six.

"So," the Devil asked Fish, "are you bored?"

Fish shook his head, sucking an ice cube.

"Not yet. Why? You got your eye on something?"

"I do."

"Something fun?"

"It's Zachary," said the Devil. "He's working on a project. Could pay off big. But he needs an investor."

"Zachary?"

"You're such an asshole," said the Devil. "Zachary! From the band!"

Fish rolled his eyes.

"The one who was going to change the world."

"He will, but he needs your help."

"What about *your* help? He sold his soul to you, dude, not me."

Sometimes the Devil wanted to end Fish's contract on the spot. Smoke him right there on his eighty-grand natural-fibers designer carpet.

Fish misread the silence.

"Cat got your tongue?"

The Devil vaulted into the kitchen, black-eyed, smashed his Scotch tumbler on the counter, and—*snicker-snack!*—sawed off Fish's left little finger with broken glass.

He did it because it needed doing, not out of anger. The Devil wasn't angry. The coke wouldn't allow it.

Fish opened his mouth as if to scream, but instead stood there, staring and unbelieving until belief and pain took hold.

He still didn't scream. He understood the lesson enough not to get mad.

"I'm sorry," he said, and meant it.

"Zachary," said the Devil, pouring himself another Scotch.

"Yes," said Fish, wrapping his hand in a sixty-dollar dish towel. "Yes, Zachary. Of course. You know, if you give that finger back, they can sew it back on, if it hasn't been too long."

The Devil chewed the finger, and swallowed.

"Zachary *will* change the world. Just not the way he thinks."

"Zachary," said Fish. "All right. Hurts. Okay."

TWO AFTERNOONS LATER, the Devil and the CEO of Assurance Mutual stood across from a jumbled workbench.

"Fish has some money to invest," prompted the Devil.

Zachary looked doubtful.

He also looked like what you'd expect from a twenty-six-year-old Indian still living at home. His hair was longer than ever; he wore a Black Sabbath concert T-shirt and dirty jeans. But his eyes were keen, and he seemed glad to have company. He seemed less likely to taper off into sleep, or to drool on himself.

"I need fourteen thousand BTUs in a fifth of a second," said Zachary.

"That's a lot of energy," said Fish. "What for?"

"To freeze something so fast that the freezing doesn't kill it."

"Something?" asked the Devil.

"A dog."

The Devil frowned. He liked dogs. "Where the hell do you plan to get—?"

"Leave that to me. It'll be okay."

Zachary's mother walked in just then, through the utility room door. She set a plate of cookies and orange punch down on a stack of used tires, and left them alone.

"If the dog works out," said Zachary, "we freeze a person. Then we try again to get people to register and pay for tanks."

"And we get rich," said Fish.

"More importantly, we keep people's lives from ending for stupid reasons, when they still ought to have good years left. We create a world where people don't have to be afraid of death, because we can hold death off until we're ready."

"You want a world of immortals?"

"You wouldn't *get* a world of immortals. You'd get a world where little kids don't die because a cure is a year away, or people don't die because the liver they need is on the other side of the country."

"Well," said Fish, "that's good, because it's a small world. We need for people to die, and make room. Besides—"

"Shut up, Fish," said Zachary and the Devil at the same time.

Fish shut up, and forked over two hundred thousand dollars.

"Give me a week," said Zachary.

SO FISH AND THE DEVIL went fishing in the Superstition Mountains, and when they returned, Zachary's mother let them shower and shave, and brought them sandwiches.

Zachary waited in the garage, still poorly groomed, still wearing his Black Sabbath T-shirt. He looked up as they entered the garage, and met their eyes over the top of something like a miniature ice-cream truck married to a jet engine.

"Catch anything?" he asked.

Shaking his head, the Devil pointed at the machine and said, "Well?"

Zachary showed them his mother's punch bowl, filled with ordinary tap water. And, like a magician instructing a crowd, showed them the inside of the ice-cream-truck machine, large enough to contain a massage table.

Nothing in his pockets, nothing up his sleeve.

He placed the punch bowl on the massage table. Then he closed what would have been the big side door of the ice-cream truck, and cranked a knob.

There was something like an explosion inside the machine. Air shot out, here and there—freezing, winter, January air—and tossed their hair back.

And then there was quiet.

Zachary opened the machine. Vapor unfurled in a foggy waterfall and covered the floor. From this artificial weather he gingerly removed the punch bowl and set it down on the stack of used tires. "Voilà."

The water in the bowl was frozen solid. Not only that, but it had not swollen or bulged or broken the bowl.

"That *was* fast," admitted Fish, admiring. "Where's the dog?"

THE DOG BELONGED to Zachary's neighbors, old friends. Zachary had explained his work to the family, and when their dog began to die of old age, *they* had come to *him*.

"Is there room in your experiments for Dooley?" asked Mark, their fifteen-year-old boy, and Zachary had to admit that there was.

"If I can freeze Dooley," Zachary had explained, "and then thaw him again, I'll refreeze and store him for you for free. Maybe veterinarians can figure out a way to give him a few more years, and when they do, we'll thaw him for good."

Dooley and his masters had nothing to lose.

After the punch-bowl demonstration, Zachary excused himself and walked next door. He returned an hour later with an arthritic, half-blind Airedale on a leash. Fifteen-year-old Mark came with him, petting the dog and looking red around the eyes.

"I'll bring him back over when we're done," Zachary told him.

"It won't hurt, will it?" asked Mark.

Zachary forced himself to be truthful.

"I'm eighty-five percent sure it won't."

Good enough. Mark walked away, and Fish shut the garage door behind him.

IT WENT BEAUTIFULLY.

Dooley lay down on the massage table without a whimper. Zachary closed the door gently, and turned the knob without hesitation.

The machine BOOMed and blew.

Zachary opened the door and shooed the mist away, and there lay Dooley just as if he were sleeping, solid as a rock.

The Devil wondered for the first time if maybe he was wrong; maybe this *was* how Zachary was meant to make the world better. But he was riding a half dose of Turkish smack, and inclined to have nice feelings about things.

They waited together on lawn chairs. Dooley, defrosting, began to drip. Now and then, Zachary got up to hook the dog up to something, or inject him with things.

"An Airedale," said Fish, "is a complicated organism."

"Yeah," said Zachary, applying electrical current to Dooley's chest.

"I'm just saying. It'll be one hell of an accomplishment. That's all I'm saying."

Dooley the pioneer dog whimpered and stirred.

"Heads up," said the Devil.

Zachary lifted the dog down. Dooley staggered a bit—the freezing didn't seem to have helped his arthritis any—then wagged his tail. Once. Blinking, he took one step toward the garage door. Then another.

Zachary could hardly contain himself.

"Mark won't believe it!" he said. "Can you imagine what it's going to be like when, you know, people—"

He was on the verge of opening the door when the dog gave an unearthly shriek.

The Devil's hair rose.

Fish ran and hid among the used tires.

The dog melted.

Not like ice melts, but like flesh that has suffered a billion tiny explosions all over. He slid apart right in front of them; his scream became a low, sick gagging, and then there was too little of him left to suffer.

Outside, running steps, and Mark's voice.

"Hey!" called the boy. "Hey, Dooley?"

"Lie to him!" advised the Devil.

"Yes," breathed Zachary, drooling a little.

He opened the garage door just enough to roll outside in his own private cloud bank, and for a while they listened, Fish and the Devil, to raised voices. Then lower voices.

Zachary came back in. His eyes were red.

"I need a million dollars," he told Fish. "At least."

Fish stared at him.

The Devil raised his eyebrows.

"On one condition," said Fish, slowly.

20.

Taco Restaurant Detox

San Francisco, 1975

NO MATTER HOW HARD she tried, Memory couldn't feel good about the disco album.

It might sell. Nothing wrong with that.

She sighed.

And it might be seen as a desperate last stab by a washed-up, drug-addled former star.

That was it.

Clap, clap!

"Open your eyes," said a soothing male voice.

Memory opened her eyes. She sat facing a man with eyes like a wounded puppy. All around them, other pairs of strangers sat facing each other.

They were the clients of the beloved Bay Area therapist Raymond Utrecht, aka "the Bay Area Buddha." Raymond Utrecht loved getting his clients together in large groups. The groups were called "Encounter Sessions."

Memory had started seeing Dr. Ray because he thought he could help her kick heroin. But she was mostly here because Dr. Ray also thought he might be able to cure her amnesia. She didn't really *want* to kick heroin, but Dr. Ray didn't need to know that. She kind of *did* want her memory back.

"Talk to each other," urged Raymond Utrecht softly. He walked among them in his socks, sometimes touching them on the head.

He touched Memory on the head.

"It doesn't matter what you say," said the Buddha. "Just talk. Discover each other."

"I know," said the wounded-puppy guy, "Dr. Ray said we were supposed to try and ignore that you're this big celebrity, but I feel it actually adds to the experience. I also feel like it has to be talked about, or at least acknowledged, before we can discover anything new."

The group was spread out all over some kind of rented minigym.

Dr. Ray made everyone take their shoes off. The minigym smelled like Ben-Gay and sock feet.

"You're probably here because of drugs, right?" said Wounded Puppy.

Memory focused on his eyes. Tried to be mature.

"That's not really fair. Are you making assumptions just because I was in a band? Maybe being famous is a *disadvantage* to me in this situation. Think about it. What are you here for?"

"It's not a prison sentence," said Wounded Puppy. "We're not being punished. But since you ask, I'm here because my kid frustrates me and I'm afraid I'll beat him."

"You'd better not!"

Dr. Ray was there, touching their heads.

"Anger is okay," he said. "Everything's okay. This is a safe place."

"I'll bet this asshole already beats his kid. '*Might* beat my kid,' my ass."

"You're trying too hard to control things," soothed Dr. Ray. "That's the addiction talking."

"I'm an addict because I point out this fucker is an abusive coward?"

"She's right," whispered Wounded Puppy. "But I'm here to talk about it, aren't I?"

Dr. Ray said something about Responsibility, but Memory was on her feet.

She tried hard not to storm out. The tabloids loved to write articles when famous people stormed out of places.

She stormed out.

As the alley door closed behind her, she felt broken concrete through her socks, and realized she'd forgotten her shoes.

Fuck!

No way was she going back. Not this week.

MEMORY WAS HAVING a year full of shitty moods.

A week before, she had read an article in a music-industry magazine. The writer had marveled at how fast Memory Jones had aged, after the collapse of Purple Airplane. She wasn't like a grandma, yet, said the writer, but a far cry from the willowy space child she had been just five years ago.

"She's more like one of those barmaids with five kids you run into all the time," the article said. "That's the kind of 'old' she is."

Memory missed being treated with respect. She wanted to storm out again, but she was already out. She was home.

She took some pills.

THE BAY AREA Buddha had contacted Memory through her old L.A. studio, after reading about her amnesia. It had taken the studio a month to deliver the message.

"No promises," he told her, "but I might be able to help. I've had some success with that kind of thing."

Sometimes, since the end of Purple Airplane and the beginning of the unforgiving magazine articles, Memory felt like a model of something or a picture of something, rather than a person. Dr. Ray saw beyond the Story of the Willowy Space Child, and for that she was willing to trust him for five minutes at a time.

On her first visit, Dr. Ray had her lie on her back and kick the hell out of an old, heavy gymnastics mat.

"Harder!" he urged, until her pelvis heaved and she tossed her head violently from side to side, screaming. After a minute of this, he said, "Now stop. Quick, say the first thing that comes to mind! Now! Don't think, just do it!"

"Cracker desert Jesus drain!" she blurted.

"Again!"

"Furk!"

Which, while it was all very advanced and spontaneous, yielded nothing in the way of results.

Then, the seventh time they tried this, something had broken open in her. She had a momentary visual, like an acid flash or a dream, of being in a long hall or even an alleyway, with people crowding one another to hear her play music on an instrument, or to sing. It was like a dream, unclear.

And gone. It zipped itself up and she couldn't get it back. But they kept trying, and she kept kicking the mat until Dr. Ray finally said "Huh," and put the mat away for good.

She had been going back for a month, now, trying one strategy or another. In the meantime, Memory's agent had convinced the studio to gamble on disco.

Why not?

AFTER THE PILLS, she found some healed territory between her gum and her bottom lip, and gave herself a long, slow dose of something they were calling "King George."

Heroin was like fashion. It changed. It had names.

She fell asleep standing up in her kitchen. She awakened when she fell and hit the floor hard. The glass in her hand rolled away without shattering.

She stayed on the floor and slept there until it was time to get up and go do the disco album.

That would be a kind of therapy, too, she imagined.

AFTER A WEEK, the master tapes were ready for the final mix.

A drunk Andy Gibb had told her at a party six months ago: *"You can make a disco song out of anything. Anything."*

She had laughed her new whiskey-voiced laugh, and he sang "Ring Around the Rosie" in a falsetto voice, and damned if it didn't make her want to dance.

She had written what was more or less an album of surreal folk songs. Listening to them in the studio, overproduced, bursting with techno-noise, they sounded like robot anthems.

"It's good," she remarked to the producers. "It's not going to change the world or anything, but hey."

"You can dance to it," the producers said.

"Yeah, but is that all?"

"What else do you need?" they asked, looking at her as if she had two heads.

MEXICO. All of a sudden everything was about Mexico.

The studio heavies knew about a party in Mexico that had been going on since 1870. Always, there were new people floating in and out. Always, somehow, there was beer and wine and solid gold everything you could want. There were girls and boys of all persuasions. There was a talking dog named Fidel.

"If you wanna be somebody again," the producers told Memory, "you gotta be seen there."

And Memory thought, Fuck you, but what she said was "Fine."

The producers, Memory, and an entourage of studio dancers climbed aboard a company jet, flew south across the Sea of Cortés, and landed at midnight in the backyard of the ancient party.

Memory wore sunglasses and a wide-brimmed hat, the armor from her Purple Airplane days. And for a while, the party throbbed around her like the parties of the old times. It was nice, because her armor worked, and she wasn't mobbed or surrounded.

Until it became plain that either no one recognized her or no one really cared.

She dug out her kit and shot up.

In the old days, the drug had made parties more intense. Now she used it like coffee: just to get her started, get her through.

Wandering the party's many corridors, she encountered the talking dog, Fidel.

He stared up at her with eyes as deep and black as the sea.

"Why do dogs always look like they have really, really old souls?" she rasped.

Fidel blinked. He said nothing.

Memory sat down beside him on the shaggiest carpet she'd ever seen. The dog lay down beside her, and when he laid his massive head on her knee, she almost cried. She stroked the back of his neck.

"I'm not really famous anymore," she told him. "You know? I mean, I'm famous, but not *famous* famous, like before."

Fidel heaved a sigh. Memory's dress puffed out like a balloon.

"I think it's supposed to happen like that. I mean, it's supposed to be okay, when they stop screaming for you and it all sort of falls apart, you know? You know? But guess what?"

"What?" asked Fidel in a smooth, oily baritone, but Memory wasn't paying attention, and was high, and missed it.

"It's *not* okay. They scream and dance and follow you around because they need you, they need something you have, right, until they make you need them, too. And then they bail on you. That's cold. That's a cold thing to do. If one person did something that cold, people would let them know how uncool it was. But if a million people turn their back on you, it's anonymous; it's supposed to be okay. I used to think if a zillion people listened to me sing, it would make up for not remembering most of my life."

The thing was, it had. While it lasted. But nothing lasted. Which would be fine, except the human mind seemed geared to miss what it no longer had, miss it so much that memories, if you really thought about it, mostly *hurt*.

She imagined what the dog must be thinking. Aw shit, he must be thinking. Another whining, washed-up, spoiled loser with a pile of money in the bank crying the blues in her heroin. Wouldn't know a real problem if it bit her leg off.

At least the dog was a good listener.

Fidel rose to his feet, drenched Memory with a sloppy kiss, and loped away.

Memory's head crystallized for a second, and her brow furrowed.

"Hey, man!" she shouted after Fidel. "Did you fucking *say* something?"

AS SHE WAS COMING BACK through customs at the San Diego airport, the drug dog sniffed out her drugs and equipment, and they arrested her.

They frog-marched her as gently as possible between rows of flashing cameras, and stashed her in a federal marshal's cruiser.

She was a little high, still. She barked like a dog at the marshal.

"You barked at me," he observed.

Like the talking dog, Memory had little to say.

The marshal drove her downtown to jail.

JAIL WAS EVERYTHING the party had not been. It was the nicest twenty hours she had spent in a long time.

The women recognized her, and it made a difference. They paid her respect, the same way they paid respect to the rough bull dykes who ran the jail. Later, they could say they were in jail with Memory Jones. Extra upside-down cake came her way at mealtime. They brought a hose and a spike and a spoon for a cooker, and got her high. The stuff they got her high with was so bad, it left her mouth tasting like rusty copper, and just put her to sleep. But it was good to be treated that way. She slept without dreaming.

THE NEXT DAY, the Devil bailed her out.

He, himself, didn't look so hot. He was pale, but with red sores here and there. He looked as if he might cry.

"Where have you been hiding?" Memory asked.

The Devil offered a sad, thin smile, and didn't answer.

Memory was allowed to shower, and allowed to change into a

wildflower sundress the Devil had brought. The sundress came with a plastic top hat.

The Devil, sniffling in a T-shirt and a Chargers ball cap, spirited her away in the Kennedy limo.

"The court's going to want to put you in rehab," he told her. "Can I give you some advice?"

"What?"

"Kick *before* you go in. It'll be ten times harder if you actually go through withdrawal their way."

"How do you know?"

The Devil fidgeted, looking out the window. "I'm fifteen billion years old," he said. "I know things."

Memory's eyes narrowed. She gave the Devil a hard stare.

He watched the road go by. They passed out of San Diego, past mountains of cracked boulders, and turned right, into Arizona.

"I'll do it if you will," the Devil said.

"All right," she said, nodding. The plastic hat had a giant plastic daisy glued to the rim. The daisy bobbed up and down whenever her head moved.

Miles passed in great leaps beneath them.

Before she stopped expecting the Devil to say something else, or maybe take her hand, or just look at her, fifty miles had gone by.

Arizona was like that.

THE PLACE HE PICKED OUT for them to detox was a dusty hotel with a fiberglass horse rearing on top of the office. Across the highway was a general store and a taco restaurant shaped like a huge sombrero.

When you hunkered down and tried to work heroin out of your system, the Devil insisted, you needed orange juice.

As the heroin leaves your body, it leaves all kinds of hungry places behind. Orange juice helps fill in some of those hunger holes with vitamins and other nice things.

For the first five hours, they sat on the double bed together watching TV, and just when Memory thought it was going to be easy, it started.

Shivers and sweats. She didn't make it to the bathroom to puke up the orange juice. The Devil cleaned up after her, looking a little shaky himself.

"Wh-why are you d-doing this?" She shuddered.

"Doing what?"

"Helping m-me."

"Maybe you're h-helping me. Ever think of th-that?"

She considered. She fought back a dry heave.

"Why would you need my help?" she said.

"'Need' is a strong w-word," he answered, wrapping his arms around his belly, rocking back and forth, shivering.

Memory crawled up to him. She put her hands on his knees, partly to keep from falling over. She gave him a long, jittery stare, and he had no choice but to stare back. There was nothing else to look at.

"Why me?" she asked.

He looked as if he were trying to find words. How strange it was, watching him struggle. Memory turned, leaning back against his legs, giving him some privacy.

At length, his crooked hand found her head, and stroked her hair. She felt his knees shake.

"There's m-more than one kind of addiction," he whispered.

Memory reached over her shoulder, took his hand, and pressed it against her cheek.

The Devil lurched sideways, and vomited on the cheap carpet.

At least he'd made sure not to hit her.

Acts of love come in many different forms.

THE DEVIL GOT it much worse than Memory.

"It's that shit you've been using," he rasped from the bathroom, beginning his third battle with diarrhea.

"Shut the door," she croaked.

"Bad shit is easy to kick. You've probably been shooting sawdust."

"Shut the door. Jeez. You *stink*."

"I've been using the b-best."

"But you're . . . you're—"

"The Devil. I know. Maybe being the Devil isn't all it used to be."

Memory coughed up phlegm.

She drank some milk and managed to keep it down.

"Shut the door," she demanded again.

The Devil shut the door.

THEY SWEATED their way through two whole sets of bedsheets.

If they took hot showers, they felt too hot afterward. If they took cold showers, they felt too cold.

"I just want to be comfortable," Memory sobbed.

They both felt like skeletons. Sometimes they lay abed, holding each other. But there was nothing particularly intimate about it. Their bodies and minds were alien, somehow. Their nerves were contradictory signals, telegraphed from the moon. Sometimes the Devil's touch warmed her. Other times it felt like spiders.

Their skin was clammy and goose-bumped all over.

"Like a turkey before you cook it," said the Devil. "That's where they got the expression 'Quit Cold Turkey.'"

"Knock-knock."

"Who's there?"

"Why don't you ever shut up? That's who."

WHEN THEY RAN OUT of milk and orange juice, the Devil said it was time to try to eat something. So they dressed up in all the clothes they owned, sunglasses, hats, including the hat with the plastic daisy, and shuffled down the highway to the little general store. They bought chips and hard-boiled eggs.

Feeling brave, they shuffled into the fiberglass sombrero, where their shivers turned to hot flashes at the same time. They stripped down to shorts and T-shirts, and ordered fried ice cream.

The fried ice cream stayed down.

Afterward, they shuffled out from under the sombrero's brim, shuffled back when they realized they'd left the groceries behind, shuffled out again, and looked up into the Arizona sun together.

"Comfortable," said Memory. "Almost comfortable."

Then they threw up their fried ice cream together and went back into hiding.

THE DEVIL FELT at home around Memory. That was how he explained it to himself.

Memory felt more solid, somehow. She had a quality of permanence he didn't understand, and didn't try to, that set her apart from her fellow mortals. Maybe it was the singing they had in common. He'd been a singer, once, after all. Sometimes he almost reached for her in a certain way, but always drew back. She scared him. Partly, she scared him because *he* didn't scare *her*, not that he could see. Mostly, though, she scared him because of what he *couldn't* see, or feel. As if the woman he saw before him, with the dreaming eyes and disappointed mouth, were just the tip of the iceberg, as if the rest of her might be lurking around a corner or caged in a basement somewhere, dangerous and waiting.

They went their own ways, when they felt strong enough. There was a certain awkwardness in it, as if, without the jitters and the sweats, they had lost the means to talk to each other. So certain things didn't get said.

As they hugged and left each other, Memory on a Greyhound bus and the Devil in the death car, she found herself almost wishing they could be sick again.

Funny, the things that hold people together.

DR. RAY WELCOMED her back with his soft touch, his warm voice.

"You look good," he told her.

"I'm clean," she said.

He gave her a suspicious look. Therapists always give you a suspicious look when you tell them you're clean.

He clapped his hands at the rest of his clients, all sitting around in groups of three, telling one another what each thought the others needed to hear.

"Pillow fight!" cried the Bay Area Buddha, spinning away like a child among children in a childish age.

He spun back their way, amid flying pillows.

He touched Memory on the head, then clobbered her with a pillow hard enough to knock her eyes out of focus.

"Symmetrical aardvark!" she rasped.

"That's the spirit!" he said.

21.
April
Michael

Apache Junction, 1976

ZACHARY WAS DOUBLE-CHECKING his equipment. His equipment? Or Assurance Mutual's equipment?

Fish had loaned him a million bucks, but it came with strings.

Fifty percent of the profit, but that wasn't the big one. Zachary, Fish insisted, had to quit trying to find a way to thaw his customers.

It wasn't about people, obviously, from Fish's point of view.

That was fine. He would work with what he had, and have faith that in the future, there would be others like himself. Those others would have to finish what he had started. If you couldn't trust the future, he told himself, this whole thing was pointless, anyhow.

Zachary had crowded his parents' garage with ten hot-water heaters, each specially modified to hold a kind of cocoon made of aluminum foil, and thirty gallons of liquid nitrogen.

He was testing the thermometer on the first water heater when the side door opened up and the Devil hurried in. He carried something in a cardboard box, and seemed excited.

"Don't touch anything," Zachary warned. "What's that?"

The Devil cut the box open, and carefully extracted . . . another box. A more complicated box, made of metal. It had a row of switches on one side, and some lights. It looked like something you'd use to operate electric trains.

"That's a computer," announced the Devil. He stood proudly beside the workbench in a tan leather jacket with straps around the waist, paisley bell-bottoms, hair and beard like a streetwise TV detective.

"What's it do?"

"It, you know, computes things."

"We're back to that again, are we?"

Zachary turned his back, and tinkered in silence with the thermometer. The problem, so far, was that liquid nitro destroyed the sensor end of all his thermometers. As the Devil watched, he dipped a foil-wrapped sensor in the nitro, and tapped it against the metal tool rack.

The sensor shattered. Shit.

"I'll have to measure the air temp," he said, "and calibrate how that relates to the temperature of the nitro itself."

"Or maybe," said the Devil, "it's something you could use this computer for."

"Computers are the size of rooms," said Zachary.

The Devil turned red and made a funny noise, as if he were putting a lot of effort into not doing or not saying something.

Something buzzed and made noises in Zachary's pocket.

His beeper.

"I have to get to the hospital," he said.

"Your first customer?"

"First one to actually die," said Zachary, hurriedly covering the liquid nitro. "Norm Reasoner. Skin cancer. He signed on last week. Paid in full, too, which ought to make Fish happy. If I don't start cooling him down in like ten minutes . . ."

He was gone.

"I'll wait here," said the Devil. "Shall I?"

ZACHARY RUSHED IN as the doctor was signing Norm Reasoner's chart, dragging a plastic tub the size of a coffin filled with twenty-seven bags of party ice behind him.

It took twenty minutes to get Reasoner packed out the front door and into a rented hearse (you can rent hearses!).

"Too slow," Zachary muttered, running a stop sign.

At home, in the garage, he began the process of getting his client "canned." Reasoner couldn't go into the flash-freezer or the nitrogen cocoon until there was something in his tissue to stop ice from forming, and Zachary couldn't put the antifreeze in until his blood was out.

"Party ice?" remarked the Devil, appearing at his elbow.

"Either help or get out of the way."

Dumping blood in the storm gutter was probably not strictly legal, Zachary thought as he rigged up a mortuary needle and a garden hose. Sometimes it was a good thing he had the Devil on his side.

"But really, you're telling me, with a straight face," said the Devil, moving aside, "you think this is the future? *These* people, living forever?"

"You got a better idea, white man?"

The Devil frowned. "I'm not white. I'm one of those swarthy colors, like Puerto Rican."

"Puerto Rican isn't a color," snapped Zachary, "and I'm *not* having this conversation with you."

FOR TWO HOURS, Zachary pumped Reasoner's chest like he was performing CPR, squeezing the heart until he forced the final gurgle of blood out down the drain. "Okay," he said. "He's ready for the antifreeze stuff."

"This kind of thing presents me with a problem," said the Devil, handing Zachary a plastic jug. "I mean, is he dead or not? What's the status of his soul?"

"You can't go to Heaven," said Zachary, "if your soul's on hold, I wouldn't think."

The Devil grinned. "That's true!" he said.

× × ×

AFTER A WHILE, bored, and realizing he wasn't going to get Zachary to look at the computer, the Devil went out for steak and ice cream.

By midnight, Zachary got Reasoner leaning upright inside the first hot-water heater, pulled on a specially treated face mask, and started adding liquid nitrogen.

He kept falling asleep, which frightened him. He imagined splashing liquid nitro on himself. It would be like getting burned. Liquid nitrogen was deep space in a jar.

He awoke one time to discover his father standing in the utility room door, looking out over the phalanx of water heaters in what had once been his garage.

Proud Henry looked baffled. He had looked that way a lot, the last year or so. A stroke had paralyzed half of his face, and his left shoulder slumped, too. His gray plaid bathrobe hung loose, on its way to falling open. He wasn't tying it with both hands, Zachary figured, the way the therapists had taught him. If he got in the habit of being lazy, they'd been warned, Proud Henry would lose coordination all over.

Zachary was too tired, tonight, to lecture his father.

"What happens to your soul," slurred Proud Henry, "when you . . . ice . . . like this?"

His language, like his body, sometimes lost direction.

"We were just wondering that same exact thing," said Zachary.

"I mean," said the old man, "what if you get up to Heaven, and you're happy perfectly up there for a hundred years, then all of a sudden you get sent back down to Earth because your body has been . . . has got . . . defrosted?"

"I don't know," was all Zachary could say.

Proud Henry stood and watched for another minute or so. He was a client, too.

Then he said, "Good night."

"Night, Pop," answered Zachary.

× × ×

AND HE DID BURN HIMSELF with the liquid nitro, before it was all over. But he got Reasoner canned, minus a working thermometer, and went to bed, where he dreamed about trying to stay awake.

Dreams can be cruel.

AS IF NORM REASONER were some kind of death spark, business picked up. More people signed on, and died off regularly. The fresh income allowed Zachary to start advertising the newly named enterprise "Horizon Cryonics" and to spend money on specially coated thermometer sensors. He was left with the difficulty of having to open the capsules in order to get a reading, which caused the temperature to spike, but he forced himself to stop worrying about things he couldn't yet change. Things were looking up, one solution at a time.

Soon, Zachary found himself struggling to keep up with the demands of canning, freezing, maintaining the water heaters, and continuing his desperate search for better technology.

The Devil offered to lend a hand, but only if Zachary agreed to give the computer a try.

Zachary had no choice; he couldn't afford paid help.

The fact was, Zachary had been afraid of the computer. Being able to crunch numbers in his head wasn't the same as being able to master a machine designed to mimic the human brain. What if it was beyond him?

It wasn't.

Once he sat down and actually looked at the neglected box, it made sense. It worked like an electronic flowchart, and processed information in ways he could grasp. The trouble was, there was no way to tell it what he wanted it to do, and no way for it to tell him what it had done.

"It needs a language," he told the Devil.

"Teach it Spanish," suggested the Devil, busy lining the inside of water heater number six. "Spanish is spicy."

Zachary focused every watt of his electrocuted brain on the problem. His posture suffered, and his drooling made a comeback—Mrs. Bull Horse worried that Proud Henry's stroke had proved contagious—but after two weeks, he managed to succeed where a lot of the early computer wizards were failing. On spools of tape, in hole-punch patterns, he had written a language the computer could read, and which he could use to write instructions.

He put the computer to work.

The next morning, Zachary was standing by the workbench when the Devil arrived (late) for work, materializing out of the floor. The computer picked that same moment to spit out three feet of tape.

"What's it doing?" asked the Devil, eating orange chicken out of a Chinese take-out container. Cheating, with a fork.

"Oh, you'll be proud. It's telling me how fast the nitro is boiling off in capsules two and three."

"How fast is it boiling off? Too fast?"

"I don't know. I have to write another program to read the ribbon."

The Devil finished his chicken. He left the empty container on the workbench, and knocked on the second water heater.

"Don't do that," said Zachary.

"How are our people-sicles doing, anyway?"

"Fine."

"Aw! I thought you'd say they were 'cool' or something. Wouldn't you piss yourself if she knocked back?"

WITHIN WEEKS, ZACHARY had four clients in water heaters.

Now, when the computer belched ribbon, he fed the ribbon into a box of his own invention, made of rubber wheels and magnets.

The box communicated with a small black-and-white television set by means of a Gordian knot of labeled wires.

Numbers appeared on the screen.

"Everything is stable," Zachary told the Devil, feeling a little like a mad, but very successful, scientist. He found that he felt, more than ever before, a warm and fatherly affection for his frozen people.

Then his mouth tightened.

"Except for four," he said, "which is bleeding off faster than I'd like."

"Shit!" cried the Devil.

"No, it's okay. That's Mrs. Yu. She's still cooling, so the temperature exchange is faster, for now."

"Ah," said the Devil. "It's strange, isn't it, the way something so morbid and sick can sound like it makes perfect sense?"

"Oh, yeah."

EXCEPT MRS. YU kept boiling her nitro away.

Three days after canning, when she and her capsule were the same temperature, the nitro was still disappearing.

Zachary opened the tank and had a look.

The readings were right.

"What's wrong?" asked the Devil, climbing up beside him.

"The tank is bleeding. Or it's not sealed right. Or this stuff boils off faster depending on outside heat and humidity. I don't know."

"What about the other tanks?"

"I was going to check them."

The other tanks had problems, too. All registered low.

Especially Norm Reasoner.

Alarmed, Zachary broke the seal on Norm's water heater. Even through his face mask he could smell it.

"Oh, no," he said.

The fog cleared away, and there was Norm, hardly more than a skeleton, flesh sagging like rotten blue-green leather.

"Mrs. Reasoner's gonna want a refund," said the Devil.

Zachary stared into space for a long time. His face became the face of a man trying to accept a difficult and agonizing reality. He looked at the garage full of water heaters with sad, knowing eyes. Then he sank into a lawn chair with an expression he had never worn before. It was the expression of a man who is giving up on something.

"They're *all* going to want refunds," he said.

SHUTTING DOWN HORIZON didn't happen without a degree of turmoil. It wasn't that people wanted their money back. It was about *hope.* These people wanted to come back from the dead in some shiny future, and that future had folded like a bad land deal.

As for three remaining clients who were already dead, there was no good way to do it. The clients had known it might not work. They had signed carefully crafted legal work saying they knew it. Now their relatives would have to pay morticians to come and get their shrunken blue-green loved ones, and do something *final* with them.

Zachary mailed notices saying no more payments would be accepted. Any Horizon funds not already spent would be refunded. This came to sixty-three dollars and ten cents, which came to twenty-one dollars and three cents per customer.

He mailed the money.

Three nights later, someone threw a rock through the front window.

That was the extent of the turmoil. Zachary figured he'd gotten off easy.

THE EVENING AFTER the rock, Zachary was staring into space some more, drooling and pretending to watch TV with his father, when the doorbell rang. Zachary ignored it. So did Proud Henry.

Mrs. Bull Horse answered the door, then presented herself in the living room, standing in front of the TV. "There's a man here to see you," she told Zachary. "Stop feeling sorry for yourself and go talk to him."

Her voice had a new edge to it, Zachary thought. Frowning, wiping his chin, he got up and shuffled down the hall, where he found a thickset man with a buzz cut waiting in the foyer, twisting a ball cap in his hands.

"Hello," said Zachary, reminding himself to shake hands.

"Mr. Bull Horse," said the man, "I'm Clifton Michael. I've come to see you about Horizon."

Of course he had.

"Mr. Michael," he said, "I appreciate your interest, but Horizon has failed. I don't know what you've heard—"

"I've heard," said Clifton Michael. "But I had to talk to you anyway. I hope you'll hear me out."

Zachary did not want to hear Clifton Michael, but the man's voice had an edge similar to what Zachary had just heard from his mother. Determined, and compelling. Mrs. Bull Horse stepped up and offered lemonade. Clifton Michael accepted, and they wound up sitting in the living room. Proud Henry abandoned the couch to give them some privacy.

"I'm listening," said Zachary.

"I'll come to the point," said Clifton. "See, three years ago, I lost my wife to hepatitis. She needed a liver transplant, and could have used a service like what you did with your company. But your company wasn't around then."

"It's not around now," Zachary interjected. "I'm sorry about your wife."

"She left behind our one-year-old," said Clifton, as if Zachary hadn't spoken. "April. She's four now. And she has leukemia."

Aw, shit, thought Zachary, seeing where this was going.

"I'm sorry," he said. "But, Mr. Michael—"

"I've done all right in road construction," said Clifton, becoming urgent. "I have the kind of money you'd need to activate one of your . . . freezing units, whatever you call them. I've read your advertising, and—"

Zachary let Clifton talk. Here was a man who was losing his family. First the wife, and now his child. It wouldn't hurt to let him say what he'd come to say. Talking helped. Zachary had learned this much, at least, from doing business with the dying.

Except Clifton Michael didn't want therapy. He wanted a new chance for his little one, however slim that chance appeared.

"The water heaters don't work," Zachary finally said. "That's all they are. Did you know that? Water heaters filled with nitrogen."

"There's more to it than that, Mr. Bull Horse," said Clifton. "You don't strike me as a con man or a dilettante."

Clifton let his eyes do the talking, after that. His sad, iron-willed eyes.

Zachary didn't want to do it, for a lot of reasons. For one, he was out of the business. For another, he liked for his clients to make their decisions with clear, well-informed minds, and April wasn't old enough for that. Zachary worried that Clifton Michael was acting, and willing to throw away a lot of money, out of desperation.

Desperation was bad business, bad science, and a bad reason for anything.

Zachary met the father's huge, wet, not-quite-crying eyes, and saw the right thing to do.

He told Clifton Michael "No."

And went to bed hating himself.

CLIFTON MICHAEL PLAYED a dirty trick. He came back the next day, with April.

Aw, shit, Zachary thought, again.

April had wide, wondering eyes, and a way of falling in love very quickly with people—*all people*—in the way dogs have. She could shriek and laugh, but most often she spoke softly.

Clifton Michael knew enough to sit back, shut up, and let his baby do all the work.

April and Zachary talked about cats. Zachary amused her by pressing two bottle caps over his eyelids.

She shrieked. Then she vanished down the hall.

Zachary and Clifton talked about road construction.

April returned with other things for Zachary to stick in his eyes: a toothbrush. A bar of soap. A Dixie cup.

When a child that young, especially one you know is going to die, falls in love with you, you can't help falling in love in return.

And when her father stops talking about road construction and asks one last time if you'll accept his check and please just try, that's all he's asking, you say "Yes."

IT HAPPENS FASTER than you are ready for. April goes in the hospital once, and comes home, and goes back, and does *not* come home. By the time you get there with your plastic casket full of party ice, her father, shell-shocked, has already got a pile of ice from the cafeteria, and you pack her away together. Of course it reminds you of your sister in her iron lung fifteen years ago, and you realize she would be twenty-five now.

You advise Clifton Michael not to come with you to the house. You tell him he wouldn't want to see the liquid nitrogen process. You tell him, "That's not how you want to remember your daughter."

He believes you. He trusts you. You and the crazy shit in your parents' garage are all this man has left.

You go home and can the little dead girl in the unit you have prepared.

You advise Clifton Michael to go ahead and have a funeral. He refuses.

"I'm not going to think of it that way," he insists. "She's been put under, just as if she had appendicitis, and they'll wake her up when they can. It's just a medical procedure."

And you leave him with that queer, haunted hope, flipping channels in the empty hospital room.

THE NEXT DAY, everything changes.

With April Michael's water heater humming steadily in the corner, you are sitting at what you have finally come to think of as your computer. You are putting in numbers like when April Michael was born, and how much she weighed, and how old she was when she got sick. You put these numbers into a program you have written.

You add other numbers. Numbers that tell about research, and money, and leukemia, and cells and ice and history. And you run these numbers through the computer and make a tape, and you run the tape through the reader and new numbers come up on the monitor, and they tell you that it will be one hundred years before people know all the things they'll need to know before they can pop the cork on April Michael and make her live again, and make her well.

And you look at the numbers, but it's not the numbers you see. You look at this machine you have made, with its tapes and TV and switches and wires, and you realize the Devil, this wonderful friend of yours, is standing behind you—you can see him reflected like ectoplasm in the monitor—and you say, "This machine can make things happen faster. It's like a little electric God. If everyone had one of these in their office, on their desk, even at home, think how much faster things could happen. Things that *need* to happen."

You think about how you and your sister and old Walter Bull Horse used to meditate and play bass guitar, and it was as if you shared the same flash of life and soul in those hours, and you think computers could be like that, too. They could talk to one another. All over the world. And you see it in the future, not far away, but right there, this year, and next year. This is how you will change the world.

The Devil leans forward and looks at the screen and says, "How do you know these numbers are even right?"

And you say, "Because I'm a fucking genius, that's how."

EVERYTHING TO DO with computers was happening in San Francisco.

So Zachary got ready to move to San Francisco. Mrs. Bull Horse said it was going to be a tough nut looking after his dad by herself.

Proud Henry, lost in time, looked up from the TV to tell Zachary he had met someone and would be getting married, if she'd have him.

"He means me," said Zachary's mom.

"Oh," said Zachary. "Well, good."

× × ×

ZACHARY DIDN'T DRIVE to San Francisco alone, of course. He took a passenger.

April Michael.

April Michael, age four until further notice, made the trip strapped to a boat trailer behind an old station wagon filled with everything Zachary owned. She neither boiled nor drained, carefully checked every two hundred miles. Zachary wondered what he would say if he got pulled over.

He didn't get pulled over.

He did, however, look in the rearview mirror somewhere in the Big Empty, to find the Devil grinning at him.

He almost drove off the road, but steadied himself and drove on, heart beating a little faster.

"Sorry," said the Devil. "It's just that . . . well, here you are on your way to the big computer brouhaha in California, finally, and I can reasonably be expected to say, 'I told you so.'"

"And I can reasonably be expected to ignore you."

"I told you so."

Zachary ignored him until the Devil stuck out a wooden index finger and held it just a millimeter from his right ear.

"Stop that," said Zachary, remembering that this was the kind of crap he and Nita had done to each other in the family car as young kids.

"I'm not touching yooooooooooou." The Devil giggled.

It was a long trip.

22.

Daughterry and the Devil Make a Bet

Maryland, 1863

A DEAD SOLDIER LAY FOLDED over a fence gate. He might have been reaching for something on the ground. Plucking a wildflower, maybe. His uniform was blue turning to gray, and gold-braided. His boots had been taken.

Others lay twisted in the grass along the fence, between the fence and a piece of country road. The smell of them made the air itself feel rotten.

Eggert G. Daughterry stopped to take a picture. The Devil helped him set up his tripod. They had learned the trick of breathing through their mouths.

It was wartime. Not on a transatlantic battleground, but right here in Maryland.

In Mississippi, too, and Tennessee. Places that had been imaginary, for Daughterry, before the war. Places he knew, now. Places he had photographed. He made his way through this universe of horror in a sort of miniature house on wheels, painted white, drawn by mismatched horses, advertising EGGERT G. DAUGHTERRY, PHOTOGRAPHIC ARTIST on both sides.

“People need to know what a horror show war is!” Daughterry often said.

It was why the Devil traveled with him.

He agreed, war was a horror show. He believed if people weren’t used to it, they would resist it, and that would mean trouble, in decades to come, when the horror shows would be much worse. People, thought the Devil, needed to *see* war. To learn to see it without feeling sick, or being paralyzed by remorse. Because civilization was going to need war for a while longer, yet. Like an enema or a transfusion, war purged the old and forced in the new. Maybe one day humans would find a better way to advance, but that day hadn’t come.

One time, early on, the Devil had found a Confederate corpse, half skeleton, missing its lower jaw. He had replaced the jaw with a tin coffee cup and arranged the whole body on his knee like a talking doll. Daughterry had ordered him to sit still until he’d made his picture. Then they’d traded places, and the Devil photographed Daughterry.

It was the kind of thing you did in your free time, rolling in the wake of monster armies, through the quiet countrysides of the dead.

“Such nasty business,” said the Devil, “you’d think they’d get it done with.”

Daughterry stepped around beside the camera, gave the sun a glance, and removed the lens cap.

“Maybe,” he said, “it’s not as easy as you think.” His voice had a buzz to it, like a bee’s, and he was in fact shaped strangely like a bee, bottom heavy and always leaning forward.

The Devil thought.

“I didn’t say it was easy,” he said. “I just think Lincoln and his fine, educated fellows ought to be able to see a way to get the better of these slaveholding inbreeds—”

“Watch your tongue. This isn’t exactly loyal country,” advised Daughterry.

“They don’t scare me,” said the Devil. “You know that.”

“That,” said Daughterry, “is because you’re the Devil. Care to fold this thing up and stash it in the wagon? We’re done here.”

THE DEVIL OWNED Daughterry’s soul.

He’d promised the photographer his pictures would live for centuries, provided that he focused his attention on the dead. Daughterry had given his soul—a bumblebee—on the condition that if the Devil were going to travel with him, he’d pull his share of the load.

It was more than he felt equal to, some days. Daughterry the taskmaster helped keep him mindful that the war was about slavery.

“What’s being the Devil got to do with it?” he asked the photographer, breaking down the tripod. “I’ve been in battle. I strode the plains of Assyria. My sword was heavy with blood.”

“It’s not the same for you. It’s not as if you were going to die.”

“It’s not my fault I’m immortal,” argued the Devil.

They climbed up onto the bench before the miniature house. The Devil took up the reins, and whispered at the horses which way to go.

“I said it’s not my fault—”

“I heard you,” said Daughterry, settling back for a nap. He exchanged his top hat for a straw cap, which he planted over his face. Nothing more about it was said for two whole weeks.

Good thing the Devil had the horses for company. They talked about apples. Fern, the elder, preferred apples fresh from the tree. Millie, the younger, liked them better when they’d lain on the ground a while, and had a chance to ferment. The Devil brokered a compromise by casting his vote for cider.

THEY FOLLOWED THE SHORES of the Chesapeake north, trying to guess where the war might break out next.

You developed a sense for it, if the madness went on long enough. One night in Pennsylvania, having left the Chesapeake behind, they stopped earlier than usual, largely because their senses had picked up a strange rumor. Depending on whom you asked,

General Lee had magically transported himself up north. He might be around the next corner, parked in the woods, or camped out in some hollow.

Whether or not they liked to admit it, all Yankees were scared of General Lee. He had a reputation for pouncing out of the night or pouring out of the woods miles from where he was supposed to be. Usually outnumbered, he could, like Jesus multiplying loaves and fishes, make a thousand men fight like ten thousand. The Devil often wondered if Lee had a fallen angel somewhere in his family tree; his reputation seemed clearly more than human.

Whatever General Lee was, the idea of stumbling into Confederate pickets in the Pennsylvania dark made Daughterry and the Devil uncomfortable, so they stopped for the night, and rose the next day at midmorning, ready to pick their way forward in the relative safety of daylight.

They fixed beans and corn bread for breakfast, surrounded by an army of crickets, lulled by the heavy smell of mown hay and a light breeze in the woods nearby.

"The trouble with you being immortal," said Daughterry, picking up the conversation from before, "isn't whether it's your fault or not. It's a matter of *understanding* people. How can you understand what moves people when you don't understand that the meaning of life is death?"

The Devil chewed his beans. He waved his fork in a circle that meant "Go on."

"Well," continued Daughterry, "it's not complicated. It's not even philosophy, really. Just a hard fact. When you are doomed to die, that becomes the main force behind your life. You do what you do because you want to be remembered a certain way, or because it is or isn't healthy. You do what you do because you are running out of time. You do what you do because you're twenty years old and that's what twenty-year-olds do, or because you're fifty, and that's what fifty-year-olds do. It's the reason you're careful about what you say when you're forty, because you have to live with consequences, and it's the reason old people say whatever the hell they want. It's the reason people get married and have kids; we have to replace ourselves."

Daughterry took a sip of coffee.

"It's what makes us happy or sad or mad about things. Because it's all so damn wonderful and so terrible, and it's going to be taken away. And, of course, there's the fact that it's so scary. How does it not drive us mad with panic, every moment, knowing that we are going to end? How strangely nonchalant, how divinely resilient we are! Being mortal means being bedmates with horror."

"You'd be amazed," said the Devil, "how boring time can get. You'd go crazy living to be much more than a hundred, let alone a thousand. A life is like a day. Night comes. You get tired. You sleep. You *want* to sleep."

"Horse balls. That's just the kind of thing an immortal would say. It changes a thing, when you're afraid of it."

The Devil swished some beans and corn bread around in his mouth. He added coffee, and swallowed.

"So you think I'd be more sympathetic if I were mortal."

"I know you would. But that's just part of it. You'd . . . understand more."

The Devil gave Daughterry a sideways look.

"You think there are things you understand better than I?"

"Yep."

"Like what?"

"What it's like to be small. Or sick. Or not as smart as you used to think you were."

"You think I'd find that useful?"

Daughterry picked a stick from the fire, and used the hot end to light a cigar.

"Yep. You've got some awfully big ideas about how people should live. You might understand better why we don't find it easy to be great all the time, if you knew what it felt like to know there was a chance you might not be here a week from now, and to know for certain you weren't going to be here in fifty years."

Daughterry leaned forward.

"A lot of the things we do, John Scratch, we do for people who'll come along after we're gone."

"I do *everything* with the future in mind," said the Devil.

"You work for the future because you have to live in it. If you were going to die, you'd do everything for different reasons. Mere mortals, friend, understand things you aren't equipped to grasp."

The Devil cracked his knuckles. Despite the warmth of the summer evening, he felt a passing chill. Suddenly the night seemed haunted by more than the specter of Robert E. Lee. The travelers were silent.

Then Daughterry said, "I'll make you a bet you can't stand being mortal for three days without going half crazy."

"What do you mean, 'being mortal'?"

Daughterry looked at him in a hot, challenging way that meant "You know what I mean."

"You mean . . . like I would shed my immortality for three days?"

"Yessir."

"And you bet I couldn't hack it as well as any human rag picker, king, or carpenter?"

"Nope."

"Three days. I could do *anything* for three days."

"So it's possible, then? You could, as you say, shed your immortality?"

"And lock it away somewhere? Sure. In fact, I'll go you one better."

"How's that?"

The Devil got to his feet, fetched a beer bottle from a crate inside the traveling laboratory, pulled the stopper with his sharp teeth, and drained it in one swallow. Then he fussed with his trousers, loosed a rugged blue-veined dick, urinated into the bottle, recorked it good and tight, and handed it, softly glowing, to Daughterry.

"You keep it," he said, buttoning up.

Daughterry's eyes bulged.

He wrapped the bottle in a cocoon of shop towels and dirty laundry, and secured it within the lab, beneath the tool rack.

When he turned back, it seemed to him that the Devil looked smaller.

It had always seemed that there was something extra about the Devil, something hard to focus on, as if there were more of him there than what you could see and touch. As if a desert or an ocean or a starry night had dressed up and grown a beard. You got used to it, traveling with him, but there it was, just the same.

Until now.

"Three ordinary days," said the Devil, shrugging shoulders that seemed suddenly fragile and temporary.

He already looked a little nervous, thought Daughterry.

He was considering whether to dig out the beer bottle and call off the wager when a column of Confederate soldiers came walking out of the woods.

Daughterry's mouth went dry. In three years, they'd rarely laid eyes on living troops in the field. Feeling his own mortality a bit more keenly than he cared for, he called the Devil's attention to the advancing rebels.

"Let's toss everything on board and get out of the way," he suggested, trying to sound like an experienced human. "We can sort out the dishes later."

Down the road, a whistle, a yell, and the sound of galloping hooves. Union troops rose up out of nowhere, and pointed muskets at the rebels.

A cloud of blue-gray smoke appeared in silence about the soldiers. A moment later, the thunder of gunfire reached Daughterry's ears.

A wave of minié balls tore through the air.

Ziiiiiiiiiiip! Ziiip-zip! Ziiiiip!

One bullet smashed through the rolling laboratory.

Fern caught a minié ball and fell dead as a doornail.

The rebels came on, unlimbering their own weapons.

"Goddamn," muttered Daughterry, looking over at poor, dead Fern. Millie had spooked and vanished into a shallow valley beyond a snake-rail fence. If they were going to get out of harm's way, they'd have to do it on foot.

Daughterry looked around and found himself alone.

He spied the Devil flying down the road, legs and arms a blur, toward a little town whose steeples poked above the treetops a mile or two away.

Daughterry followed at a trot, keeping low, one hand securing his top hat, the other waving a white handkerchief. He aimed to the left of the Union troops, who, having greeted the enemy, seemed to be backing away.

The town was called Gettysburg, he thought, if he remembered their maps correctly.

USUALLY, THE DEVIL thought a lot about how he looked, and what kind of impression he was making. He thought about Heaven and Earth, and what it meant to be a beast or what it meant to be a man. He thought about what he was going to say next and how it would be received. He wondered what people were saying *about* him.

These things, along with every other kind of thought, had been shoved into a closet of some kind. The Devil's life had been pared down to a single hot purpose: not to be hit by any of the bullets that were slicing through the air.

He ran around the Union troops, flew across a road, through some woods and past some houses, until he came to a garden concealed in a rectangle of picket fence posts. Part of the garden was a field of sunflowers.

The Devil dove in among the sunflowers, buried his face between his knees, and said "Oh, no!" over and over and over.

IT TOOK SOME DOING, but Daughterry found him there, shaking and bug-eyed. The photographer, a wise mortal, had fought down his urge to run mindlessly, and concentrated on following the Devil's trail, one step at a time. He had followed raw, churned earth to the edge of the garden, and parted the sunflower stems.

"There you are!" cried Daughterry, at which the Devil promptly jumped up and out of the sunflowers, and vanished underground through a nearby cellar door.

Daughterry followed him patiently, driven by a sense of culpability. The fact that he couldn't have known that the Blue and the Gray would come smashing together just then, right on top of them, didn't really change anything. And while there were those who would have said, had they known, that a chance to kill the Devil with a simple minié ball or cannon shell was a blessing, Daughterry had been with the Devil long enough to know that divine justice probably wasn't that simple.

He wasn't evil, it seemed to Daughterry, although he sometimes did evil things.

He wasn't good, the Lord knew, although he sometimes did good things.

If anything, the Devil seemed to think that the world should do what came naturally, that everything natural was just fine, and that questions of Good and Evil were silly. He did what he did to help a better future come faster. Daughterry respected that, whether the Devil's reasons were selfish or not.

He sat down at the bottom of the cellar stairs and whispered "Hey."

Nothing. Maybe some mice tiptoeing around, leaving little turds behind.

Then, just as faintly, a small voice.

"We're going to die," said the voice.

"Maybe," said Daughterry. "Maybe not."

Whimpering.

Far away, dull thuds, heard on the air and felt through the earth. Cannon.

"I didn't know it was going to be like this," whispered the Devil. "Whoever invented the part of the brain that makes you afraid, they should be shot. It's useless, but I swear it's going to fucking kill me."

"You've had feelings before. You know how strong feelings can be."

The Devil's brow furrowed. Pocahontas had complained about that very thing: the intensity of feeling that came with being human.

It was the only kind of thought that could distract him from his terror. It didn't distract him for long.

"How come *you're* not afraid?" he asked Daughterry.

"I am! I pissed my pants!" (He had indeed.)

Thud. Thud! Like an approaching giant, the artillery walked closer.

"I didn't," said the Devil.

"Brave fellow!"

"Really?"

"Well, no."

The cannonade gave the earth a good shaking just then, so that streams of dirt rained down from the ceiling, and the Devil curled up (Daughterry's eyes had adjusted; that *was* the Devil over there, wasn't it, wrapped around a sharpening stone? It was either the Devil or an old coat) and made noises like a sick kitten.

Daughterry wondered when the owners of the house would appear. Sooner or later, wanting shelter, they'd throw open the garden door and come sliding pell-mell down the stairs.

The battle seemed to be drifting into town. The cellar shook again.

The owner and his family never came.

THE SHAKING GOT worse and worse.

Above, glass broke.

Pop! Crack! Musket fire.

The Devil sat partway up (it *was* him, wound about the grindstone), and said, "There is nothing, nothing at all, keeping one of those cannon shells from punching through upstairs and exploding down here, right in our faces."

"That's true," said Daughterry.

The Devil did not handle this thought well at all.

Daughterry was a good man and a good friend, and never described to anyone, even his diary, that he had seen the Devil suck his thumb.

THE POUNDING AND SHAKING and popping and yelling drifted out of town, it seemed, receding like a flood, and there came a time when Daughterry felt that he should talk to the Devil about one or two things.

"Hey," he stage-whispered across the cellar.

The Devil said, "Yes?"

"I hate to bring it up."

"Bring what up?"

"The wagon. Our wagon."

"What about it?"

"They took it."

Silence.

The ground shook.

"Someone took our wagon," said the Devil. "The wagon with the laboratory and the glass plates and our food and clothes."

The Devil seemed to have raised himself to a crouch. His eyes glowed.

"The wagon," he continued, "with my immortality aboard, wedged under the tool rack?"

Daughterry nodded. "The Federals have it," he said.

"Get it back."

"Now, see here—"

The Devil pounced, and would have bitten off one of Daughterry's little fingers, except that Daughterry objected, and shoved the Devil away.

The Devil seemed surprised. Then he seemed to remember that he was mortal. He seemed defeated. His shoulders slumped, and he slouched off to the farthest corner.

"Get it back," he croaked. "Please."

Daughterry replied that he would try, and they did their best to sleep.

THE NEXT MORNING, Daughterry crept upstairs.

Before long, he crept back down.

"Bad news," he announced to the dark cellar.

"You didn't get the wagon," said the Devil. He was feeling braver than before. He could hardly feel less brave, after all.

"The Federals seem to be using the wagon for a traveling pharmacy."

"Then one can reason with these Federals. Pay them something, if necessary—"

"The wagon," Daughterry explained, "is in a place where I am not welcome. You don't cross Union lines if you're not a Union soldier."

The Devil nodded. He looked very serious.

"I am willing to face down my fear," he said, "and go up there and talk to whoever needs talking to, if all it needs is a Federal uniform."

He closed his eyes, and drew both hands down through the air, as if putting on a rain poncho. Then he stood still. He looked puzzled.

"Were you," asked Daughterry, "by some chance, trying to 'magic' a uniform out of thin air?"

"No," lied the Devil.

The floor shook.

Dust rained down.

"They've started again," observed Daughterry.

The Devil's eyes widened. He shook visibly. His hands twitched.

Then his eyes narrowed. He still shook a little, but his hands, rolled into fists, were steady.

"I could just be somebody from the town," he said.

"What?"

Cannon fire, close by. The Devil twitched.

"Who's to say I'm not just plain John Scratch from Gettysburg?"

he said, making his way up the cellar stairs. "A plain old fellow from plain old town can ask questions about a medicine wagon, can't he? Maybe even poke around under the tool rack—"

"No!"

"Yes!"

"But—!"

But the Devil was gone.

THE DEVIL EMERGED to find the garden just as he'd left it, with some of the sunflowers a bit sat upon. In the street beyond the gate, he found a barricade thrown up by retreating Federals. Furniture, firewood, oxcarts, and wagon wheels, it had been shot up and blown apart. Here and there, houses themselves bore wounds.

One second, the street was deserted. The next second, a train of horses and wagons and mounted swivel guns came charging along. It was a Confederate train, guarded by Confederate soldiers in homespun clothes, long-haired and dusty from top to bottom.

Several officers rode alongside this train, and one of them rode up to the Devil, drew his sword, and poked him in the throat.

"What're you about?" demanded the officer, a mountain of hair in an ancient leather coat and straw hat.

"I am John Scratch," said the Devil, "a local photographer. I am going up the lines to see about—"

"You ain't in uniform," the officer observed. "Hazard!" he bellowed. "Scatlock!"

Two Confederate guards left the train and galloped over.

"A man out of uniform," said the officer, "out and about and having a look at General Lee's supply trains, seems an awful lot like a spy to me."

"Here, now!" exclaimed the Devil, but the officer spurred his horse and rode off, calling back over his shoulder that the spy was to be held behind Confederate lines until sundown, when he should be hanged without ceremony.

Hazard jumped down off his horse and approached the Devil with a set of heavy chains. The Devil squared off to hit him and wrestle him to the ground, but the other soldier, Scatlock, kicked his horse forward and knocked him off balance.

That wouldn't have happened, thought the Devil, on any other three days.

He caught his balance just in time for Hazard to swing the armload of chains at him.

HE WOKE UP secured to a young maple tree, alone in the middle of some woods.

One whole side of his head felt lumpy and smashed.

He remembered that he was to be hanged, and laughed. Then he remembered that he was not invulnerable, and stopped laughing.

The ground shook. Great cracklings, like popcorn, tore the air from horizon to horizon.

He thought, at first, that he had been left alone and unobserved in whatever portion of the universe this was, but then he glimpsed a couple of ragtag Confederates leaning against a tree in the middle distance. They looked his way and spat.

The shadows on the ground lengthened quickly.

This couldn't really be happening.

After thousands—millions?—of years, he was going to be hung like a horse thief by a squad of rednecks. He, who had conquered Sumeria. He, who had helped raise the pyramids, and walked in the surf at Troy.

"I walked the surf at Troy!" he screamed in frustration.

One of the guards wove a stout hemp noose.

The Devil gritted his teeth. He sighed. He who . . . with Pocahontas . . .

Far away, the shaking and booming and crackle of musket fire reached a crescendo, and began to fall off some.

"I rode with Nat Turner, you bastards," he roared, "when he burned down your granny's house and chopped her up with—"

That got their attention. These were Virginia men. They said a word or two about its being close enough to sundown, and came his way with the noose.

Oh, no.

One of them whirled the hanging rope around his head. When he loosed it, damned if it didn't fall right over the Devil's head like a lasso.

The guard tugged hard, and the noose tightened. The Devil struggled against his chains. He would fight, goddammit! If he had to head-butt every single one of these—

A horse and rider interposed. The officer from town.

"Leave off, dog-fuckers!" he snapped, slicing the rope with his sword. "Sentence is rescinded. Command says we might need every man jack tomorrow, including prisoners."

The guards vanished into the darkening woods.

"We're marching tomorrow," the officer told the Devil. "And you're marching with us. Somebody'll be by with supper."

THE CONFEDERATES HAD WON the first day. They had driven the Federals into the hills. The second day, they tried to push them out of the hills and destroy them, but the Federals pushed them back. So General Lee was going to gather his soldiers together in one humongous mile-long wave, and roll over the Federals like an ocean.

His soldiers would have to run a mile over open fields, with cannonballs falling on them the whole way. Some of General Lee's staff thought this was a dumb idea.

"It's a long mile," they argued.

General Lee didn't care. He was mad.

General Pickett's division would lead the charge. It would be called "Pickett's Charge'" even though it wasn't his idea and he would watch most of it through spyglasses.

THE OFFICER WHO had captured the Devil came to fetch him, and half drag him through the woods. There had been no supper and no breakfast, and he was feeling weak. He was not familiar with feeling weak. He wondered if it was part of the terror, part of his mortality, which he felt in abundance.

The officer chained him to a tree with several other prisoners. Spies? Deserters?

The officer explained to the prisoners that they were being given a rare chance to escape sentence and prove themselves.

"You will take part in the charge this afternoon," he said. And he talked about what an honor it was, and how they were dog-fuckers who didn't deserve it. He explained that they would not be given muskets, or even knives. They would not be permitted to carry a flag of any kind. The soldiers behind them would have orders to shoot them in the back if they did anything other than march forward and happily fight the enemy with their bare hands. If they survived, they would not be hanged. If they behaved bravely, they would go free.

The prisoners seemed grateful.

Then the officer explained the wave, and they seemed less grateful.

"Might as well be hanged," one of them was dumb enough to mutter.

"Done," barked the officer, and had the man hauled off and hanged.

The Devil thought about the wave.

He almost said something about organizing the Boston Tea Party, but the officer looked at him with a fierce yellow eye, and he shut up.

THERE WAS A LOT of ground shaking before the wave moved.

The two armies stood and fired cannonballs at each other all day . . . one army strung out in a line of trees, the other atop a gentle slope, crouched behind a stone wall. Between them, a mile of summer haze, with blackbirds and white moths. Overhead, a sky too hot to be blue, with clouds painted on.

Sitting on the grass or waiting in the woods, the men did not move when the cannonballs came. Their officers had told them they were either going to get hit or they weren't, and there wasn't anything they could do about it, so they might as well hold still.

It was like holding still and trying to keep from flinching while someone hit you in the face, but they did it. And they paid the price. A cannonball would come screaming in, and sometimes, if your eye moved just right, you might actually see it, like a crow flying at unholy speed. Some said you could tell by the scream, somehow, if it was going to hit you, or near you. Others said, "You never hear the one that gets you," and things like that. There were a thousand things said, all to assure yourself that you were safe, that you were going to be fine. And then here it came, and exploded close by, and you saw incredible sights, like one half of a man go spinning like a top thirty feet in the air, and great trees cut off in the middle, twisting and falling. Men blinded by splinters, staggering with hands over their eyes. Arms and legs that ended too suddenly, and blood like red fountains. Men standing mere yards apart were divided by a grotesque contrast: in one place, horror and explosive slaughter, while five steps away others stood waiting quietly, eyes forward, as if inhabiting a separate world.

Like many of the soldiers up and down General Lee's tree line, the Devil had pissed himself without noticing. Most of the southern soldiers had an empty, hollow sort of gaze, but not the Devil. He was looking at something in particular, and he hardly blinked.

Across the deadly mile, atop the gentle slope of the ridge, behind some cannon and a low stone wall, was a white wagon. It bore huge black letters, and if you had the Devil's stillness and focus that afternoon, you could almost read EGGERT G. DAUGHTERRY, PHOTOGRAPHIC ARTIST upon the side.

It might have taken a bullet or two. It might have a bite taken out of it. Hard to tell at this distance. The Devil's fingers curled and uncurled on his knees as he remembered things like immortality and the sands of Troy, and felt the smallness of just being a man. The soldiers around him felt this smallness, too, and were alone with it, each in their way, behind the blankness of their eyes.

When the generals rode out into the still July grass and called to them (*"Up, men, and to your posts!"*), they rose from the ground and shook themselves alert and quit leaning on trees, and marched out in rows.

How they did it, the Devil didn't know. Then he did it, too, and he realized that sometimes there is no How. There is only what you do or do not do, and he did it. He was so damn proud of himself! When they called a cheer for Jeff Davis and the Confederacy and the Honor of Old Virginia, he roared as loud as the best of them, and waved his hat, too.

It was a form of insanity. It was wonderful! Being in church was probably like this, he thought. They were like one whole creature. That was how they were able to move, he realized, even while some of them died.

Then the wave started rolling across that long mile. He didn't think he could stop if he tried. What genius!

AS FOR THE SOLDIERS behind him, he forgot all about them until they were gone. A cannonball dropped in behind the prisoners and took out eight or nine of the row behind them.

There was a moment when the world tore right in two, and the Devil found himself in the air, perhaps on fire, arms pinwheeling. Then he hit the ground and got up fast, just to prove to himself that he could, and the thing was, it didn't make him any more scared than he'd been before, putting one foot before the other.

Spare weapons littered the ground. He grabbed a musket, checked to see that it was charged and loaded, and pushed on.

The grass and ground were uneven beneath his boots. He had never noticed, before, how terribly uneven the earth was.

A minié ball tossed his hair just above the collar. Lifted his hat just a little.

Here and there, he heard the *thud* of bullets hitting targets.

The enemy, leaning over their stone wall, grew nearer.

The prisoner beside the Devil gave a moan. Just a moan, and fell. Two steps later, he was invisible in the grass.

What a strange and unbearable feeling, that you might not experience the next second because you might be dead.

Now. Now. Now. Now . . .

Each second began to seem impossible. But the soldiers pushed on, drawn, the Devil recognized, by something that eclipsed them all. Even him.

The seconds passed. The mile was behind them, and the enemy was there.

THERE WAS THE ENEMY, all lined up, all white smoke and fire and bullets whistling.

Ziiiiiip! Ziiip! Zip-Zip! Ziiiiiip! Thud! Thud! Thud thud thud thud!

Screams.

Not far away, a cannon fired straight into the Confederate line, and blew men down like wheat.

One great shout from the rebel throats. The Devil's, too, as if the many throats were one throat, and he was over the wall. Right away, he killed a man.

The Federal soldier looked scared. Looked as if he couldn't believe the ratty, trashy-looking rebels had gotten this far, and then the Devil stuck his musket in the soldier's side and pulled the trigger.

The musket bucked. Gun smoke huffed. The Federal went down with his side torn open, and the Devil stepped over him.

He could not shoot again; a musket needed loading between rounds. So he gripped the muzzle and made it a war club, and waded through surging, howling chaos toward the white wagon, now visible, now invisible beyond the struggle, the smoke. He was beginning to believe he might make it when someone speared him in the leg.

It hurt, but he found himself more offended than frightened. He looked down, saw the bayonet flash through his own flesh, then disappear—that *hurt*!—as it was yanked free.

Wild with rage, the Devil spun on his heel, almost lost his balance in blood-soaked grass, but steadied himself and found his attacker. One swing with the musket knocked the Federal down. One punch with the stock should have burst his head like a melon. No. Two punches. Just a broken nose.

Third punch. A demonic shriek of frustration, and finally the soldier's face caved in.

On toward the wagon, hobbling. Losing blood.

Most of the battle fell behind him.

One more soldier. The Devil picked a stone off the ground, a stone the size of a baby, and smashed the Federal's shoulder.

He was ten feet away with nothing in between when a rebel cannonball—you *do* hear the one that gets you, of course. Why wouldn't you?—screamed out of the sky and tore him up like a dog toy.

He spun through the air, and came down on the other side of the wagon.

The Devil smelled himself cooking. Felt broken bones, and flesh hanging in rags.

He croaked like a frog, and darkness swallowed him.

HE DIDN'T WAKE UP until General Lee's wave had been pushed back.

A Federal soldier knelt over him, blocking the sun. The sun made him appear to glow, and to shoot solar rays.

"Don't try to move," said the Federal in a kind voice. The Devil cleared his throat, which seemed to be all there.

"Listen," he said, and promptly coughed up a bucket of blood.

"Don't try to talk."

"Listen!" And he did his best to describe the bottle in the white wagon, which had been chewed up and knocked over by the same explosion that had eaten the Devil.

"This wagon?" The soldier gestured.

"Yes."

The soldier looked puzzled, and the Devil found himself in strange circumstances. He had never begged for anything before, not even from God, not in all of time and history. Suddenly he found himself begging.

He blacked out again.

Then he felt his head lifted, tilted back. Felt something warm and heavy slide down his throat.

It tasted like piss, and he fought the urge to spit it out. Instead, he lay patiently as the bottle emptied.

HIS BODY FILLED like one of the great observation balloons, capturing hot air.

He felt himself coming together. Swelling and hardening like an erection. Filling again with the thing that made him bigger on the inside than the man he was on the outside. The golden and forever thing.

It happened slowly. Too slowly.

He tried to get up.

"Don't," said the kind soldier.

The Devil went dizzy, and fell. Frustrated, he collapsed on the grass.

After a while, the soldier summoned stretcher bearers, who scooped him up and bore him off to a hospital tent.

SOME DAYS LATER, he went marching over this hill and that, until he came upon Daughterry roasting sausages over a small fire. Nearby sat the wagon, more or less repaired. Millie, recovered, stood hitched in the traces, apparently pulling double duty in memory of poor Fern.

The Devil held a kerchief over his face. Gettysburg, after the battle, was an open, stinking grave. When Daughterry half turned and caught sight of him, his face was tied up in a red sheet the size of a tablecloth.

The dead blanketed the ground, draped over rocks and stones, festering and bloating in creeks, in the sun. Pigs chewed them. The bodies swelled, popping buttons. Sometimes the bodies themselves popped. Clouds of blowflies drifted low. Black birds of all sizes crowded the air.

Daughterry offered him a sausage and said, "Well?"

"You were right," said the Devil. "It's harder than it looks."

Daughterry gave a satisfied sort of nod and snort.

"All the more reason," continued the Devil, "to press the matter and get it done with." His eyes fell on the body of a young soldier. A southern soldier. He might have been fourteen. The Devil hoisted the dead boy like a puppet.

"To be ordered into a deadly fight and walk straight into your own death. Knowing that you might be made a monster—disfigured, torn apart, or burned. The horror is unconscionable. The horror itself is a wound."

"Yet—"

"UNCONSCIONABLE!" the Devil roared, eyes bleeding, shaking the dead soldier. "Men should think about these things before they send soldiers to fight in terror for years, because their leaders are too cowardly to really *fight,* decide the issue and get it over with. Any animal could teach our leaders how to war!" He paused to spit fire. "Any animal has more respect for its young."

He flung the dead boy away.

"War is necessary," he said, bringing himself under control. "But it doesn't have to go on and on! A thrust here, a charge there, for years and years, eating up boys like dog food. If we're going to have wars, and we are, then they need to be quick and terrible. A war shouldn't chew like a kitten. It should pounce and devour like a tiger! Do its job and get back in its cage."

Daughterry nodded, surveying the battlefield with a keen sadness he hadn't felt before.

"And people need to see pictures of it, not so they can get used to it, and not care if it goes on and on. But so they can be sickened by it, and want to do it right, and get it done with. Maybe the day will come when they won't want to do it at all. But today isn't that day, and men learn slowly."

After a time, the sadness passed, and something else crossed his mind. The corners of his mouth twitched, almost but not quite forming a smile.

"So," he said to the Devil. "You were wrong."

The Devil still looked sad. He looked far, far away. He said, "What's that?"

"You just admitted that you were wrong. It surprises me. That's all."

The Devil looked ever farther away. His voice on the air sounded as if it were crossing oceans and years.

"I get everything wrong," he said. "Maybe that's my job."

The sun sat in the sky as if nailed there, dulled by smoke. Daughterry and the Devil stared at it for a time.

Then the Devil seemed to shake himself awake. He rubbed his eyes and turned away. He made himself busy around the fire.

A soft wind blew. A summer breeze that would have been pretty, except that it stank.

23.
Jenna's Live Multimedia Near Suicide

Dayton, Ohio, 2005

JOHN SCRATCH THE TV STAR was in surgery again. This time, though, he was too mad to fall asleep at all. The anesthesiologist finally gave up and went away, leaving the doctors to operate under their patient's very direct, very burning gaze.

The Devil hadn't found a silver lining to getting shot, so far.

How come his wounds didn't just slam shut, like in the old days? He wished Arden would come to him. Didn't she know what was happening? She should be here. Why wasn't she?

He coughed blood, and closed his eyes.

"That's better," said the surgeon.

Gloved and gowned behind the lead surgeon, the insurance agent grinned beneath his mask.

"Lucky break on the anesthetic," he said. "I'll bet more people could forgo that, if they gave it the old college try."

As he fell asleep at last, the Devil decided that when he recovered, he was going to eat that guy's soul like a corn dog.

× × ×

"THEY FOUND HER!" cried the Devil's nurse, almost tumbling into his hospital room. "They found her! They found her! They found her!"

The Devil opened one fiery eye.

"Jenna," gulped the nurse. "Miss Steele. They found her."

"The police?"

She shook her head. "The phone people traced her down. She kept sending multimedia to her fan clubs, and the phone company was like 'She's on Third Street!' She's on TV, right now."

The Devil found the TV remote.

Jenna Steele filled the screen from several perspectives, in three separate interactive boxes. One was a police camera, filming from behind as they chased her up a flight of parking garage stairs. Another was a feed from the parking garage surveillance cameras, and the other was Jenna's own cell phone, in which her face—sweaty, desperate, but perfectly made up—appeared; she was breathing hard, and crying.

"I love you, Johnny!" she bawled.

"Stop!" yelled the police.

BANG! She threw herself against an exit door and ran onto the parking garage roof.

"She loves you," sighed the nurse, enraptured.

On the screen, Jenna Steele hopped up on the wall, and teetered at the edge of a five-story drop. An online poll asked subscribers if she should jump.

"The bitch shot me," the Devil reminded the nurse.

The online poll came back split: 51 percent Jump, 49 percent Don't.

On the TV, on five million phone screens, Jenna jumped.

"Johnnnnnnnnnnnnnnnnny!" she screamed, all the way down.

She landed on a Dumpster, smashed through the plastic lids into a half ton of medical waste.

Would she live? Polls were 57 percent in favor.

JENNA SURVIVED her fall.

The Devil awakened to hear them moving her in down the hall, crowded round by press and police.

"I love you, Johnny!" he heard her cry.

A herd of minicams came to see the Devil.

This had to be more celebrity drama, mused the Devil, than Ohio had ever seen.

"Whaddya say, Johnny?" gushed the webcasters, pushing doctors, nurses, and insurance thugs out of the way. "Seventy percent want to see what your baby would look like."

"The bitch *shot* me!" he said.

"Yeah . . ." The press seemed bewildered. "But *seventy percent*!"

The Devil's eyes glowed. His teeth sharpened. The skin over his forehead began to part, revealing—

Something snapped in his chest.

"Get someone," he tried to tell them, but he couldn't get his breath.

Fifty-eight percent of subscribers texted that Johnny didn't look so hot.

So they went to get someone.

24. Some Kind of Cult Rip-Off

Apache Junction, 1979

IN JULY, Zachary's dad died.

Just died. Proud Henry was having something like a normal day, watching TV. Mom brought him some things, like a sandwich and a crossword-puzzle book, and they talked about the cracked tile on the front walk. He took a nap after lunch, and Mom came in and found him dead.

Just like that (finger snap).

IT WASN'T EASY for Zachary to get away for the funeral.

He had a computer company up and running, for one thing. Bullhorse Technologies. Bullhorse had been featured in every tech publication in the world, and had made the cover of *Time* magazine (a photo of a home-computer monitor, under the title slug "The Face of the Future"). The company consisted of himself, an accountant, fifteen technicians, and a kick-ass patent lawyer, and it was like a child he'd never left home alone before. Speaking of children, he also had a dead, frozen, illegally interred four-year-old in a hot-water heater in his extra bedroom, sucking up secrecy and electricity.

So he left the technicians in charge of themselves, the accountant in charge of the lawyer, the lawyer in charge of securing the rights to whatever the technicians did, and went home to Apache Junction.

PROUD HENRY'S FUNERAL was well attended. Zachary and his mother were pleased to discover that they had been forgiven, by and large, for the Horizon debacle. It had taken a couple of years to get his clients buried, but buried they were, and time had passed. No one offered any but kind words at the graveside.

April Michael's father came to the picnic, afterward, at the Bull Horse home. He had lost weight, and seemed afraid to ask Zachary about anything but the article in *Time*.

"I still have her," Zachary assured him. "That's not going to change."

"What about money?"

"I have money," said Zachary. "As long as I've got money, she's paid up."

April Michael, by God, was going to make it to the future.

BEFORE HE LEFT, Zachary asked his mom if she felt like moving to San Francisco, and she said, "Not yet."

He drove his rental car out to the cemetery and stood over Proud Henry's new grave. It didn't seem fair; Dad had put up with dead future-people stuffed in his garage, and had never complained. Now that it was his turn, into the ground he went, and straight to the afterlife to take his chances.

"Do you want to know?" someone asked, just behind him.

The Devil. Dressed in black. Standing there holding a single white rose.

"Know?"

"What's next. Heaven, Hell, nothing. I'll tell you."

"No, I don't want to know."

"Sorry about your dad," said the Devil, handing him the rose. "*Riders of the Purple Sage* is a classic."

"Thanks."

He took the rose, smelled it, and laid on the grave.

Back at his very large Frisco home, Zachary stopped in April Michael's room. He stood in the dark before the softly humming capsule.

"Your dad says hi," he told her.

LESS THAN A MONTH after the funeral, Zachary's mother moved out of Apache Junction without bothering to sell the house.

"I'm in New England," she told him, over the phone. "There's this nice community out here, kind of like a farm. Everybody does some of the work, and most of the money they make goes back into the farm. I like it. And the people are nice. They do everything for themselves."

"I don't like it," Zachary told his mother. "Sounds like some kind of cult rip-off."

And she told him, "Zachary, honey, I wasn't really asking what you thought. After ten years of picking up after you and Henry, it's nice to be someplace where people pull their own weight. I love you. Maybe I can get out there at Christmas."

Zachary sat staring at the phone for fifteen whole minutes.

25.

Showbiz in the Time of the Black Death

Dayton, Ohio, 2005

THE DEVIL LAY in his hospital bed, dreaming of low times. His dreams and memories took him to Spain, in the time of the Black Death.

HE COULDN'T REALLY complain about the Black Death. It was his idea.

There were too many people, and not enough land. So they fought like animals over the land, until the Devil got sick of it and loosed the plague on them.

He rode a funny little donkey from village to village, saddlebags teeming with fleas, marking his progress by columns of smoke as villagers burned their dead behind him.

It was grim work, even for the Devil. He drank more than usual. One week in Salamanca, it was almost the end of him.

He hit the city gates at noon on a Friday, after a particularly macabre week in the provinces. Brushing ash from his jacket, he tied up his donkey, and stepped into a public house for a sack of ale. Out on the street, he fell to drinking with the thespians of a penniless traveling circus. He bought the acrobats and magicians bread and beer all around. In return, they entertained him.

They tumbled. They recited poems and balanced things on their noses. There was no hint of trouble until one of the magicians made his hat disappear (tumblers had eaten his rabbit), and the Devil, feeling competitive in his cups, made the magician disappear into thin air. The fellow popped unharmed out of a nearby hay wagon, but the harm was done.

Tricks were one thing. Serious black magic was another.

The circus folk averted their eyes and backed away.

Soldiers of the Inquisition invaded the Devil's room before dawn, and by lunchtime he was sentenced to burn for witchcraft.

His head hurt. He wasn't in the mood. Besides, metaphysical science was still at sea on the subject of whether or not he could be killed, so when they strapped him to the pyre and lit him up, he changed himself into a flock of carrion birds and fluttered away. Left his ropes hanging empty, the executioner minus his fee, and a crowd trying to figure out if they'd witnessed a miracle or more witchcraft, and marveling, out of priestly earshot, at how hard it was to tell the difference.

He rematerialized in an alley behind the cobbler's shed with a sparkling-clear head, wrapped himself in physician's robes, and collected his donkey.

The Inquisitors had eased his conscience about the Black Death. No matter what he did or what age he did it in, he could always count on the Church to try to top it.

At the gate, there was an awkward moment when the Devil and the traveling circus blew town at the same time. He smiled and winked. They pretended not to see him.

Cheeky bastards. He tossed some fleas their way, and nudged his donkey toward the next town.

26.

People Don't Have to Take Your Shit If You Don't Have Any Money

Chicago, 1984

FISH WAS DRUNK at the Chicago Four Seasons when his in-room movie was interrupted by a knock at the door.

He opened the door to find three men in dark suits.

One of them presented a badge and said, "Mr. Fish, I'm Special Agent Zimmerman, with the FBI. These are agents Early and Dunn. May we come in?"

There were smart choices and dumb choices at moments like this, and Fish had no idea which was which.

"Do I need my lawyer?" he asked.

"We just want to ask some questions," said Zimmerman.

He let them in.

Made them wait while he changed out of his hotel bathrobe, and put on something he hoped implied dark powers.

Then he joined them in the outer room. They had all removed their jackets, and were sitting or standing around in a way that made the room feel like *their* room, not his.

"Have you ever met Congressman Buzz Joplin?" asked Zimmerman.

"Indiana," said Dunn. "Fourth District."

Sure he had. Buzz Joplin was one of the congressmen he bribed each month. Buzz Joplin had made it illegal not to have life insurance.

"I would like to contact my attorney," Fish told them.

WHEN HE CALLED the Devil, Fish hoped he would pick up and say, "Don't worry about it."

He didn't pick up.

"You could call another attorney," said Special Agent Zimmerman.

"I want that one," snarled Fish. "He's the Devil himself."

"Impressive!" said Zimmerman, pretending to look impressed. He looked around at Early and Dunn to see if they were impressed. They were.

"I'm sorry I can't assist you any further today," Fish told them. "Maybe I could call your Chicago field office after I contact my attorney. Don't know what's keeping him."

"We're not from the field office, Mr. Fish," said Zimmerman. "If you can't help us out with Congressman Joplin, maybe you can tell us how you know—" and Zimmerman, without notes, rattled off a list of maybe fifty people and organizations Fish and Assurance Mutual had bribed, defrauded, extorted, or blackmailed.

He tried to call his attorney again. This time, the number didn't even ring through. The number was no longer in service.

Fish stood.

Time to retake control. He did his best to radiate dark powers. He reminded himself that he had killed a man with an ashtray at the Helen of Troy in Troy, Ohio. At least they hadn't asked about that.

"I can't talk to *you* until I get hold of *him,*" he said. "So whether we talk about Buzz Joplin or the moon, it's going to have to be another day. So unless you have an arrest warrant hidden up your ass, I bid you gentlemen Good Day."

This last was a bluff. Maybe they had a ton of evidence and a warrant, and maybe not. He bet not.

He bet right, this time.

"Thank you for your assistance, Mr. Fish," said Zimmerman as they gathered their jackets. "We'll be in touch."

Fish ran for the toilet the second the door clicked. He grabbed the phone on the way, hoping the line would reach. The line did reach. Fish called his accountant.

"There's trouble," he told his accountant.

The accountant was supposed to be really, really good. The Devil had recommended him. The guy had sold his soul, according to the Devil, to be a very good accountant.

"Yeah?" said the accountant.

Fish knew this game. The accountant didn't want to say anything on an unsecured line. Fish would have to do the talking.

"The FBI just came to see me," he said. "I need to get hold of—"

"I don't think that's going to be possible, Fish."

Fish? What had happened to *Mister* Fish?

"Listen," he commanded. "Meet me at four this afternoon."

"Where?"

"You know where."

"*You* listen, Fish. I got a lot going on, and there's no way in hell I can make it to—"

"You'll make it," said Fish, and hung up.

IN THE END, it was Fish who had trouble getting there.

He called the airport and told them to get his plane ready to go to Mexico.

"We can't do that, Mr. Fish," said the airport.

"Listen," he said. "You call George Kaplan at the FAA, and ask *him* if you can or cannot—"

George Kaplan at the FAA was paid good money to keep Assurance Mutual flying without a lot of regulatory red tape.

"Mr. Kaplan," said the airport, "has been placed on leave by the FAA so that he can assist a congressional fact-finding panel with certain inquiries. I have been asked to give you contact information for a Special Agent Zimmerman, sir, if—"

Fish hung up.

He frowned out the window, massaging his neck.

He paid a freelance pilot to zip him across the country, across the border, to an airstrip outside the world's longest-running party.

He charged up the stairs to the swimming pool, anticipating the usual backdrop of music and shouting, zoo animals, cocaine, half-naked billionaires, and a talking dog. It was the backdrop against which he had learned to do business (when he *had* to do business). But the pool area was only populated by the pool guy and his long-handled brush.

"Where is everyone?" asked Fish.

The pool guy said he was just there to clean the pool.

Inside, a crew in white jumpsuits shampooed or replaced carpets, cleaned bathrooms, washed or replaced walls, yelling back and forth in Spanish. As Fish made his way through the house, he felt they were yelling about him. After he had gone by, they laughed.

Just as he was sure his accountant had been and gone, if he had come at all, he met him by the pool.

"You waited," said Fish. "That's good."

The accountant nodded at him.

They faced each other without shaking hands.

"Now," growled Fish, "there's no fucking phone line for you to worry about, so I want some answers. I want to know why the FBI is asking me questions about very private arrangements. Arrangements *you* made—"

The accountant punched him very hard in the face and told him to shut the fuck up.

Fish fell, clutching his face, but got back up again. He weaved, almost slipping into the pool, and decided not to hit the accountant back.

"You will recall," said the accountant, "that I warned you against a number of those arrangements, and you would not listen. I told you that there were arrangements that could be protected, and others that could not. But you know everything. Now listen to this, and know this: I don't work for you. I only came down here to see the look on your face when I broke your nose. Do not call me again."

The accountant walked off and disappeared down the stairs.

Fish sat down beside the pool. He let his feet and legs soak, although he was fully dressed. Shoes and all. It felt good.

Water sprayed him.

Fish looked up to see the pool guy regarding him with distaste.

"You're in my way," he said.

PAYING FOR THE PRIVATE FLIGHT to Mexico and back used up Fish's ready cash. In Chicago, walking down the street to his building, he stopped at one of the new automatic bank-teller machines that were starting to pop up all over the place.

The machine said that it was unable to complete his transaction, and that it was sorry.

Upstairs in his living room, with the dark of Lake Michigan reflecting his broken nose and swollen face, he called a special, privileged number. It was the number the bank gave you when you had enough money to cause trouble if you took it out all at once. A tired-sounding voice picked up.

He told the bank who he was, and before he could ask about the ATM, the voice told him his accounts had been frozen and seized.

"Which?" asked Fish, confused and in pain. "Frozen or seized?"

"Both. Some have been frozen; the others have been confiscated and are no longer considered, you know, yours."

Some of Fish's accounts were in banks overseas. Some were American.

"It's mostly the overseas accounts that are frozen," the voice informed him.

Fish launched a screaming fit that might have lasted half an hour if the voice hadn't hung up on him.

People don't have to take your shit if you don't have any money.

× × ×

THE NEXT DAY, Fish went to his office at the top of the Assurance Mutual office building, the twenty-fifth tallest building in the world.

"Did you know that forty percent of the world's tallest buildings are owned by insurance companies?" the architect had asked him, back when it was still just a blueprint.

"Wow," Fish had answered. "No."

The offices were quiet. The halls were dark. The doors were all closed.

A note waited on his desk. It said that everyone's Friday paycheck had bounced sky-high, and the comptroller had advised everyone not to clock in again until they could be sure things were going to change. Under the comptroller's signature, a PS informed him that his own check, Fish's, had bounced like a refrigerated SuperBall.

He picked up his desk phone.

It sounded dead, at first. Then it rang in his hand.

"Hello?" he said.

"Mr. Fish?" asked a voice, somewhat familiar.

"Who is this?"

"Zimmerman, Mr. Fish. FBI. Are you in your office?"

"I am."

"I'd like to ask you to remain there, Mr. Fish, until—"

Fish didn't remain. He laid the phone down on his desk blotter, and ran for one of the three separate elevator banks installed by his friend the architect.

It was a long ride down. Long enough for him to devote serious thought to whether or not the FBI had provided enough agents for Zimmerman to cover all the ins and outs of the Assurance Tower.

The doors hissed open on an empty lobby. No. The FBI had not.

"Underresourced chimps," he muttered, and ran like a fugitive.

HE CALLED THE airport and tried to speak with any of a number of freelance pilots. Whenever anyone asked who he was, even if he lied, they asked him to hold.

He called the car-rental place near the bus station.

They were not on Zimmerman's call list, apparently. They said for him to come right down there and they'd fix him up.

He drove south toward Texas.

Sometimes, by daylight, he thought cars were following him. When he pulled over to get gas, they zoomed on. Or sometimes they didn't. Sometimes they pulled off and looked like they were watching him.

He stopped only once for a bite to eat. He walked into a Carl's Jr., but everyone was watching him, so he left.

SOUTH OF BROWNSVILLE, he parked, got out, and left the door open. He took nothing with him.

The fence at the border was much taller than he'd thought it would be. But it was unlit, and this portion seemed unwatched.

It was almost a relief, the idea of starting over. The little money in his Mexican accounts would count for something, down here. After a time, who knew?

He climbed the fence. Every second, his back crawled, waiting for Border Patrol bullets, or the glare of spotlights.

Over the top. Halfway down, he let go and landed on his feet.

Catlike, he thought.

He was free. Not rich, but free.

Free was better.

Who would have thought it? He almost wept.

Nearby, across the street from the fence, an open bar with wide screens for windows. He could see the bartender inside, a big, sad-looking Mexican man.

He had enough pocket money for a beer or two, then he'd have to find a bench until the banks opened.

He ordered a beer, but when he went to pay for it, somcone said, "I got this," and handed the bartender a brand-new American five.

The Devil.

The bartender brought them both beers, and they took a first sip together.

"You sure this is what you want?" asked the Devil.

"What I want," gasped Fish, "is for you to return my phone calls when I'm in a hotel room full of feds. You promised—"

"I promised you'd have money. You had it."

"We set up companies and organizations! That's not just money. Those things are meant to last!"

"They do, if you treat them right."

"You promised!"

"No, I didn't. Anyhow, given what you've got left, which is this bar and that fence, are you sure this is what you want? Because . . . well, let me tell you something about that fence—"

"I don't want to hear it," sighed Fish. "If that's all you have for me is some advice about the border, you can shove it up your ass. I want my money back. I want what you promised me."

The Devil looked disappointed, but not surprised.

A second later, FBI agents from the Brownsville field office burst through the door and performed a felony takedown on Fish. His beer bottle went flying. His broken nose radiated agony. His face pressed the barroom floor.

"You can't!" he cried, struggling to raise his head, to make himself understood. "This is Mexico, you retards!" He spit out a bloody tooth.

"This is Brownsville, numbnuts," answered the agent responsible for cuffing him. "That's the farm-league baseball park fence you climbed. Way to go. The border's half a block down, still."

Fish laughed. A little, at first. Then more. He got it under control as they walked him to their unmarked car, but a curious, eerie glow ignited in his eye—not unlike swamp gas or Saint Elmo's fire—and never went out again until the day he died.

27.

We'll Always Have Rome

Dayton, Ohio, 2005

THE DEVIL, BORED STIFF with being in the hospital, started sleeping more than was normal for him.

He dreamed about the second time he'd won Arden back, long ago, in Rome.

A SPRING EVENING, near the beginning of the empire. The Devil crossed the forum in late afternoon, crisp paving stones under his sandals, the smells of the city in his nose. Smoke, food, garbage. Horseshit. Sweat.

Rome reminded him of Egypt, with its bigness: giant temples, giant columns, giant armies. A suitable challenge to Heaven.

Maybe it would be good enough for Arden. Maybe she'd come back.

He was watching a street show when the idea struck him.

The show featured a monkey who pretended to find a coin in his ear.

He had to laugh. Great civilizations boasted the weirdest entertainment. This was and always would be true.

The monkey was a good sign.

× × ×

AT HOME THAT NIGHT, the Devil stood in the courtyard, looking up.

"Arden," he said, "you've got to see Rome. God would have made Rome Himself, if He had an imagination."

The wind blew. The sky was cloudless, like a sea.

He went inside, and read poetry by firelight until it began to rain, and then he went to bed.

WHEN HE WOKE UP in the morning, she was there beside him.

The Devil roared with joy and crushed her to him.

Her eyes glowed. She cried his name over and over.

They didn't leave the bed for three days, and when they did, it was just to buy a new bed.

IT BEGAN like Egypt.

They had a house with a courtyard, at the crest of a hill.

At dawn and dusk, the sun touched the marble city with fire, and they watched from their windows, admiring. This time, they decided, they would not try to push things. He would not teach them astronomy. She would not play angel music for mortals.

They were in Rome. They would be Romans.

For now, they would learn about each other. A thousand years had got between them.

But one day at the local market, when they were shopping for their supper, a clay tile slipped loose from a restaurant rooftop, tumbled two stories through the air, and shattered over Arden's head.

She ducked—too late—and dropped her purchases to hold her head in her hands. But there wasn't much blood, and she didn't even feel dizzy.

The Devil held her to him, shocked and terrified.

"I'm all right," she said.

So they bought for a second time all the things she had dropped, and went home to supper. And the sun set, and the city, as always, appeared to burn. Then the lights of candles and braziers and the lanterns of boats on the Tiber made Rome a jewel in the dark, the center of Heaven and Earth.

IN THE MORNING Arden did not wake up.

The Devil was half mad, at first. He screamed and shook her, and would have run through the city in monstrous forms if a storm hadn't broken, bringing him to his senses with lightning and sharp thunder. So he calmed himself, and hired some street urchins to go and bring him a physician.

"What physician?" asked one of the boys, nearly naked and streaked with filth.

"Any physician!" cried the Devil. "All of them!"

And he returned to her and tried again to wake her. What knowledge he knew and what strengths he had, he used. But something in him was no longer able, or allowed, to heal an angel. She was beyond him.

So he had to trust the doctors.

The doctors came and failed, one by one.

"She will awaken or she will not," they told him.

The first one who told him this, he ate. After that, he was a better listener.

WHEN SOME DAYS had gone by, he dressed their bed like an altar, and covered her in white silks. When he fed her, she swallowed, like a cleverly made automaton. And the Devil realized that she might lie like this forever. It was so cruel it made him spit laughter, that they would be together, finally . . . but like this.

He fed and bathed her. He did not feed himself, or bathe.

He stared out windows, at home, or stumbled aimlessly in the streets. He went out less and less often, until a familiar sleepiness began to steal over him. But he knew the dangers of that sleep, and shook it off.

"No," he said. He stood, and walked to Arden's bedside. He took her hand.

Action was needed.

Inspiration bloomed in him like a bursting sun.

Not just any action, but the sort of action that had brought them together to begin with.

His heart thumped in his chest. His pulse quickened. Slowly, with impossible tenderness, he drew back the bedclothes. Even more slowly, as if handling crystal, he undressed Arden until her sleeping form lay naked on the mattress.

His eyes drank in her pale skin. The sheer bareness and simplicity of her whispered to his blood, which ran faster, until his jaw slackened and his breath became a lumbering, heavy thing. Trembling, he stripped away his own clothes and lay down beside her. Pressed against her and kissed her still lips until sadness and desire became a single thing inside him.

He rose to his knees, gasping because the weight of desire was almost too much. Shaking, he parted her legs, and it was all he could do not to just let himself fall over her.

He stroked her thigh with an unsteady hand. Stroked the softness of her lower belly.

His blood and breath heaved like a hundred work gangs, but he forced himself to concentrate, to move softly. He coiled his arms around her legs, lowered his open mouth between her thighs, and kissed her there with a sad, yawning hunger until night fell dark around them.

But she didn't awaken, and she didn't move.

At dawn she lay still against him, and didn't move, and when the pulsing and heaving crested inside him and surged and flooded the bedsheets, he lifted his head at last and screamed a silent scream. In the red light of morning, he fell exhausted against her and slept without dreaming.

× × ×

THAT EVENING, shuffling in rags past the open baths, he found himself, by chance, in one of Rome's quiet places. It was a pleasant slope of manicured lawn, peppered here and there with white stones, low shrubs, and stands of umbrella pine.

The place had a serene quality that worked on him, and within minutes, if he could not be said to have quite returned to himself, he at least felt less as if something were devouring him. His senses cleared, and he became aware of several voices, nearby, in earnest conversation.

One of the voices was familiar.

No . . . it wasn't the voice. It was a sense of presence, like a trembling on the air, as if someone had just strummed a harp.

"It can't be," said the Devil to himself.

The last time—the *only* time—he had sensed this presence, had been twenty years ago on a hill over Bethlehem, in Judah. He and two astronomers from the East had followed the light of an exploding supernova, and stumbled across a Jewish family caring for a baby in a cowshed. The woman had given birth to a boy, and the boy lay in a feeding trough with this supernatural soul music playing all around him.

The astronomers, like everyone else, were silly with religion. They immediately connected the child with the exploding star, and fell to worshipping. Everyone seemed to expect the Devil to do the same, so he fetched from his camel a curiosity he'd picked up in Babylon, a wooden puzzle box containing frankincense, and presented it to the father.

The Devil assumed the baby was descended from some long-dead fallen angel, although he had never seen the supersoul effect to quite this degree before.

"This little guy is turned all the way up," he remembered thinking, that night in Bethlehem. "We'll be seeing more of him, someday."

And there he sat, in a grove of pines, amid other youths: olive-skinned, with long hair and shocking, multicolored eyes. He toyed with the grass between his knees, looking troubled.

"What's happening?" asked the Devil, ducking into the grove.

"Micah dared Jesus to shave off his beard," said the roundest of them.

"And he did," said a redhead with one eye.

"And now," said the round one, "he's mad."

"Not mad," said Jesus. "Just not sure it was the thing to do, after all."

"See?" said another of the youths. "There's the Uncertainty Constant. I told you we couldn't predict how he'd feel about it later."

"My parents," said Jesus, looking up at the Devil, "never did get that puzzle box open."

"Who's this?" someone asked.

"A friend," said Jesus.

The Devil, having traveled in Judah and knowing how Jewish men felt about their beards, appreciated that Jesus might have regrets.

"Why'd you do it?" asked the Devil.

"He told Berlios," said One-Eye, before Jesus could answer for himself, "that the mysteries of the heart were stronger than the Law, and Berlios said, 'Even Jewish Law?' and Jesus said, 'Of course,' so Berlios dared him to defy Jewish Law by shaving off his beard, and Jesus said, 'It's not so much a law as part of the *spirit* of the Law,' and Berlios said that was even better, and . . . so. There we are."

"Took him three days to make up his mind," observed a dark-eyed youth. "It's not like I pushed him into it."

Jesus stood, gathering up a burlap shoulder sack.

"Tomorrow?" he asked his friends, looking from face to face.

They all nodded. They almost seemed to bow, and the Devil realized that despite the jokes and bantering, this circle of young men had a respect for Jesus akin to wonder and dread.

The Devil bowed goodbye and followed Jesus out of the glade. They hiked together uphill in gathering dusk.

"I missed some kind of argument," said the Devil.

"A debate," said Jesus. "I'm teaching them how to explore ideas through argument, the way we study the Torah in Judea. And they're teaching me Skeptical philosophy."

"Skeptical—?"

"It's a method of inquiry. Teaches you to ask questions, that there are always more questions, that nothing is ever known completely, or for certain."

"What's in it for you?" asked the Devil.

"Let's just say I'm sharpening myself."

"To practice law?"

"Beyond law. Law, we have. Nature has law. Scripture gives us Law. Rome gives us law. What I want to find is our *heart.* Man's heart. I wonder if people can't learn to be good and fair to each other out of love, not just because the law compels them."

The Devil considered.

"You'd meet resistance," he said. "They'd have to take responsibility for their own actions, and thoughts and words and feelings, instead of laying it all on some faceless authority."

"That's the trouble," Jesus replied, pausing to pick a rock out of his sandal, grasping the Devil's shoulder for balance. "People always want to bring God into it. They might not want to hear that they, themselves, are in control. Who do you use for a crutch, when you're in control? Who do you blame things on?"

"Dangerous work," said the Devil, "telling people new things."

As they reached the fringes of the hillside garden, the Devil's belly rumbled, and he realized he hadn't eaten since his last supper with Arden.

"Want to get something to eat somewhere?" he asked Jesus. "You hungry?"

They found a dive in the bath district, and ordered lamb.

WHAT HAPPENED afterward was simple, and it was not simple.

Because of course the Devil told Jesus about Arden, and of course Jesus came home with him right away, and laid hands on her.

The Devil didn't see why the healing mojo should work for Jesus, and not for him. Even if he had fifty or a hundred extra souls all smashed together inside him, he was still a human. He would never be an angel, or be able to heal or harm an angel, if he lived to be a thousand.

But then Arden's eyes fluttered open, she sat up in bed, then fell right back down again, moaning, "My head!" and the Devil forgot all about that.

He held her hand. He brought her whatever she needed, which was mostly water, and didn't notice until after midnight that Jesus had slipped out the door.

"Thank you," said the Devil to the door.

Returning to Arden, he found her asleep. Panic rose in him for a moment, until he saw that her sleep was the sleep of ordinary rest. Healthy, and full of the little movements that signal good dreams.

HE LAY DOWN with her without undressing, and didn't know when he fell asleep. But he awakened after midnight to discover her face hovering close above him, her breath on his lips and eyelashes in the dark. What little light the window admitted made silver moons of her eyes.

She silenced him with a finger before he could speak. "I felt you," she whispered, "while I was asleep."

The Devil knew immediately what she meant. He felt something like regret. The regret quickly became shame.

Shame was a new and devastating experience. He opened his mouth with a wild croak, but she kissed him, hushing him.

And quietly she told him how she had known she was not awake, how she couldn't feel her body and had walked strange, dreamy corridors and floated on strange seas of time and space, unable to find her way out for what seemed like an age.

"And then I felt you," she said, brushing his hair back, caressing his forehead. And she told him how a slow fire had risen inside her until she seemed to return to her body entirely, feeling the mattress beneath her, the breezes from the window against her naked skin, and feeling *him*, feeling him touch her. More, unbelievably, she felt the desire course through her motionless limbs. Still, she couldn't break free.

But he had awakened her. Awakened her enough that she didn't fade, was still there to be brought out of it when the mysterious young healer had come.

She thanked him, and kissed him and called him "my love" over and over. They moved together like two halves of the same storm until the mattress was reduced to a haystack, small cracks appeared where the walls were weak, and the next-door neighbors hid their children.

THE NEXT DAY—bathed and whole—the Devil found Jesus in the grove again, among the Skeptics, and thanked him.

He meant well, he really did.

He bowed, and tossed Jesus a glass ball, and Jesus looked into it.

When he put the ball down in the grass, Jesus looked older. He looked like a man who has lived a whole sad life in the space of five minutes. As if he had seen two thousand years of people doing hateful, ignorant things and saying it was all *his* idea.

"Maybe people aren't ready to take charge of their own hearts. Maybe the time isn't right, yet," Jesus said, looking at the Devil.

It wouldn't matter, the Devil knew. Whatever he said, now or years from now, they'd make a religion out of it, and the religion, like all religions, would go mad.

Jesus rose, stepped carefully around the Skeptics, passed between the pines, and vanished from public life for ten more years.

WHEN THE DEVIL got home, Arden was gone.

Again? Why?

She had left a note, with lovely swooping letters that burned without consuming a sheet of expensive papyrus.

It wasn't complicated. She was scared, that's all.

What kind of world was this, where even an angel could be struck comatose by a piece of clay? She might have spent ten thousand years in that limbo, and he knew it.

Maybe she would be back when Earth was less earthy. Or when she was braver. Maybe it was her fault. Yes, probably. She was sorry.

THE DEVIL RODE FAR into the country, where he kept an olive farm, and sat brooding at an upstairs window with a view of the highway and an aqueduct a hundred feet high.

Egypt had fallen short.

Rome, too, would fail.

The thought of it broke his heart. It broke the heart of everyone who knew Rome.

The years passed, and his hair grew, and the house crumbled around him.

Sometimes news reached him. He heard about it when Jesus resurfaced, back home in Judea, and died of free speech.

Three hundred years passed, and grass grew over the road. Trees grew in the aqueduct.

People forgot.

Like cavemen, they built cook fires in the shadow of the aqueduct, puzzled by the ruins, and wondered what gods had built them, what purpose they had served. They pulled stones loose, and used them to build little houses roofed with sod, and little stone churches.

Trees grew up around the Devil, and he slept.

28.

The Car Wreck Song

Los Angeles, 1984

JUST AS SHE WAS GETTING really good and mad at the Devil for wasting her life, Memory became famous again.

Funny thing about not being greased up on heroin: Normal life didn't bug her as much. She was getting along okay without headlong, everyday superstardom. She had learned to ignore the voice in her head that insisted there was supposed to be more.

It charmed her that people still bought Purple Airplane albums. That she was talked about and admired. Sometimes she got a check in the mail—a *big* check—along with a report saying how many more records and tapes had been sold. But it was just numbers.

She wasn't that person anymore, anyway. The haunted, doe-eyed sorceress on those records wasn't the same woman she saw in the mirror now. The woman in the mirror had memories. She had frown lines and gray hair.

She had a job, clerking at a library. The job was the routine and rhythm that kept her from the bottomless pit of shooting up.

THEN ONE DAY she got a phone call from a producer named Dennis Hogg, with Jupiter Productions.

"Kind of part of Universal," he said. "How you doing?"

He practically shone, right through the phone.

"Fine," she said.

"Great," said Dennis Hogg. "Super. Listen, to start with, I'm a big fan of your music—who isn't?—but let me save us both some time and cut to the chase, as it were. You listening?"

She was listening.

"We've been working on a pilot down here. Not much, we don't even have our own soundstage. Anyway, there was an article about you in *Parade,* and everyone in the cast was like 'I didn't know she lived right here in L.A.! I thought she was a San Francisco gal!'"

"I moved," said Memory. "San Francisco's expensive when you're not working."

"Well," said Dennis Hogg, "we all said, 'Wouldn't it be cool if she were involved with the show?'"

Dennis Hogg shut up, and was waiting for her to say something.

"What's it about?" asked Memory. "The show."

"Would it be possible . . . I mean, it would be a lot easier to just show you. I could come and get you tomorrow. We're shooting in . . . I can't remember where, some burb somewhere."

Memory was stunned. It sounded like a fly-by-night kind of deal, but . . . they wanted her! They loved her!

"Please?" said Dennis Hogg.

"All right," she said, playing it cool. "Why not?"

MEMORY STOPPED HATING Dennis Hogg the second she opened her door. It was like meeting someone you've listened to on the radio, thinking they look like a preacher, and they turn out to have dreadlocks and a lazy eye.

That was Dennis Hogg, with the hair and the eye. Her first thought was that she was glad he wasn't one of those shiny West Coast people. Her second thought was that there was no way a freak like this was ever going to get a TV show off the ground.

They got coffee at a drive-through on the way.

"I've been on TV," said Memory, "but I've never *worked* in TV, you know?"

"I *love* TV," gushed Dennis Hogg. "Can I just tell you? Love it, love it, love it, love it!

"Oh, wow," said Memory.

THEY WERE FILMING at an ice-cream shop when Dennis Hogg arrived with Memory.

Not the usual kind of ice-cream shop. The eighties were a kitschy, fun little decade, with new twists on the usual things. The good old-fashioned ice-cream parlor was now a frozen yogurt place. Yogurt was supposed to be healthier because it had a live bacteria culture in it. People were also wearing their hair big.

The second Memory walked in, there was screaming and excitement, because they were her biggest fans. They lounged around the tables eating frozen yogurt and asking questions. First, the cast and crew asked Memory about being her famous self. Then she asked them about themselves and their show.

There were six of them. It was kind of like a band.

Jenny was loud and friendly and sort of pretty.

Rob, a tall, pale, quiet man, was the male star.

Katie, a short girl with long black hair, had a way of being astonished by everything in a way that was contagious. You could say, "My frozen yogurt is becoming unfrozen," and Katie would go, "No *way*!" in a way that made you look at your frozen yogurt with a real sense of betrayal.

SHE SAT OUT of the way with Dennis Hogg while they filmed.

It was the strangest show she'd ever seen.

There was a plot, kind of. Rob and Jenny were trying to think of someone for Katie to go out with. They kept suggesting different fictional people, and sometimes people in the yogurt place, and Katie would say, "No way!"

The frozen yogurt store remained open and went about its business. That was part of the show. Dennis Hogg liked having a little reality in his TV.

"You know you wouldn't get paid," Dennis Hogg told Memory, "until, you know, unless the pilot gets picked up by a studio. A *big* studio."

Most pilots didn't get picked up.

"It's okay," said Memory.

MEMORY AGREED TO be the show's narrator. Every show would begin with her sitting to one side with a guitar, opening with a question or a casual observation. That first day, in the yogurt shop, she told the camera: "Secrets are usually dumb. You know what I mean? Most secrets are secret because nobody wants to know them. Take Jenny, for example."

Then, for the opening theme, she improvised a soft but psychedelic tune while the camera drifted over to find Jenny and Rob. And the secret, the "core" of the show, as Dennis Hogg called it, was that Jenny was naked under her not very long overcoat, because she'd locked herself out of somewhere (the scripts, all agreed, lacked clarity).

At the end of the show, Memory would make up another song. It was okay if the song was stupid.

They went ahead and recorded music for the end of the pilot, too. The song she made up at the very end went like this:

Na na-na na, nanana na
Na na-na na, nanana na
Out on the street, on the other side of this huge
Yogurt-store window, a car just hit another car
Not hard enough to hurt anybody, just like a tap
I can't think of anything else to sing about
You'd think it would be easier, but hey
That's why I'm singing about the car
That hit the other car

The words weren't bouncy, but she sang them in a bouncy way:

Now the guy in the car that got hit
Is getting out of his car
He looks all mad
Why? It was an accident
It doesn't even look expensive
There's all kinds of serious shit out there
To get mad about, but
People only get mad about petty shit anymore
You'll probably have to cut out the parts where I said "Shit"
And that last part, too

Na-na naaaaah, na-na!
Nanna-nunt nunt muumuu nunna na-na . . .

The song made Dennis Hogg cry, and they all hugged. They were like a little family.

The show was called *Random Planet.*

"We're the *Random Planet* family!" Dennis bawled.

THAT NIGHT, feeling pretty good and looking forward to the next *Random Planet* shoot, Memory left the bathroom with a toothbrush sticking out of her mouth, and the Devil was sitting on her sofa in the dark.

"Nanna-nunt nunt muumuu nunna na-na!" sang the Devil.

"Shut up," she said, sitting down at the other end of the couch, still brushing.

The Devil looked at her without saying anything. His eyes, which could be warm when he wasn't being full of himself, or menacing, or an asshole, were suddenly the oldest safe place she knew.

Before she quite knew it was happening, they had come together in the middle of the couch, and she was kissing him.

HE BRUSHED HER HAIR back and cupped her head and drew her to him. What she liked best about it was she could tell he had never kissed any other woman (or angel, or cow) in quite this way, because this was how she and she alone needed to be kissed.

She pulled back. Her robe had come undone. Realizing this, she was suddenly self-conscious.

"If we're going to start doing that kind of thing," she said, "and if I'm going to be famous again, I want to get some work done first."

THE *RANDOM PLANET* family met seven more times at different public places, finishing up the pilot episode. Then someone took the unedited footage to Universal, where it vanished into a time warp and they didn't hear anything for a long time.

Memory used the time warp to get a face-lift. Afterward, it was as if the doctor had gone in with a scalpel and removed twenty years of smack and wine and resentment and disappointment. She looked her age. That was fine.

She rented a black-and-white movie where everyone in it was either really old or dead, and went home to watch it by herself.

UNIVERSAL BOUGHT *Random Planet.*

Dennis Hogg called everyone and screamed in their ears.

"Aiiiiiiiiiiiiiiiiiiiiiiiiigh!" he screamed. "I can't believe it. They're going to pay us to do that shit. Are you excited? I'm peeing my pants. Are you *peeing*? I am."

SO THEY HAD A BUDGET now, and could have used a soundstage. But they decided to keep filming out in what Dennis called the quasi-real world.

"You had something done," said Katie, taking her aside the first time they filmed on the Universal budget. "You had your hair straightened."

They were setting up in a shopping mall.

"No," said Memory. "Well, yeah." She had. "And a face-lift."

"No way! You look great."

"Thanks."

"You look almost like in some of the old pictures."

Younger people talked about the sixties like they were Roman times.

"It was fourteen years ago," she told Katie.

"Yeah," said the girl, and you could tell she was thinking, Roman times.

THE NIGHT THE PILOT AIRED, Memory came home from the library and found the Devil cooking gumbo in the kitchen.

"You're famous again!" he said, twirling a ladle, splattering sauce everywhere.

Memory shrugged and tried to play it off, but couldn't. She was excited, and it showed.

He'd been cooking for hours. *Everything* went into the Devil's gumbo. All over the counter and floor lay lobster shells and clamshells and oyster shells and signs that sausage had been ground fresh. A murder-scene spray of cocktail sauce coated the wallpaper.

He made her taste some. Like the best cooking, it was a thousand flavors, and it was one mighty flavor alone.

When she opened her eyes, he was holding a tiny green ear of corn over the kettle. It was somehow reflective . . . Hmm.

It was a marijuana bud so drenched in crystals it might have been a disco ball.

"Don't you dare."

The Devil dropped it in the gumbo.

And they watched the pilot together, giggling more and more, until they were laughing at the commercials, too. And when it was over—

He pounced like a tiger, flattening her against the wall, driving his jaws against her throat. Nightmare fingers gripped her legs. Clothes shredded like clouds in a hurricane.

She pulled his hair, forcing him closer. Their foreheads met. They glared at each other, point-blank, then thundered to the floor.

29. Like Having a Psychic Heart

San Francisco, 1985

THEY CALLED HIM Big Zach.

The nine hundred people at Bullhorse Technologies dominated the home-computer market. Had practically *invented* the home-computer market.

Being called "Big Zach" was inevitable, especially now that Zachary had put on some weight. The effect was imposing.

A hush fell over the offices of Bullhorse Technologies when he came towering through, usually accompanied by engineers from senior staff. The hush lasted after he was out of sight, too.

That's what happens when you change the world. People hush when you go by.

THE DEVIL FOLLOWED HIM to work three days in a row, and wandered around touching things and asking dumb questions until Zachary finally asked, "What do you want?"

The Devil loped over, spun around twice in an ergonomic swivel chair, and said, "Games."

Zachary tapped his teeth with a pencil.

"We've got games."

"They're stupid."

Zachary argued that games had come a long way. That they had started out with games like video tennis and video hockey, where you doinked around a little white square. There were better games, with spaceships and asteroids and racetracks—

"You have to go to an arcade to play them. What if you could play them at home?"

"On your computer?"

"Bingo! This market will eat you, Zach-O, if you don't stay ahead of the curve."

When had it quit being history and started being a market?

"Games." Zachary tried the idea out on his tongue, before letting it play in his brain.

HE TRIED TO think about things that were fun. Things that would make a good game. He couldn't think of any. So he drove to Golden Gate Park, where he sat watching the bay change colors.

It occurred to him that he was lonely.

Being unmarried, very busy, and a little shy about his extra weight, he sometimes passed a year between dates. Women, more and more, felt like a part of his life that was getting away from him. Still, he had always believed that he was destined to fall in love. Since he was a little kid, he'd had a premonition that he would meet a girl, the love of his life, and she would ask him if he rode horses.

He would stammer, and reply, "Sometimes. Not real well or anything," and when he said that, she would realize who he was, because she'd had the dream, too, and they would rush into each other's arms and be together.

It was like having a psychic heart whose prediction hadn't come true yet.

He was a little old for this kind of fantasy, surely. He was a man of eminent practicality. Wasn't he?

And instead of his heart starting to ache the way another man's would, Zachary's electrocuted brain kicked on.

Being lonely, said his brain, really meant that he wanted to be in love. Right?

Love, suggested his brain, was a game.

Zachary almost stopped breathing.

"That's it!" he whispered to the park and the bay and the setting sun.

He got a speeding ticket on the way back to the lab, and when he got there he put all his single young nerds on a new project.

Two weeks later, City Park Pickup, complete with graphics that barely made it past the censors, generated white-hot sales in the first forty minutes of its release.

"You've got it!" cheered the Devil. "You're like the pimp of technology. This is the kind of thing that will bring people to computers. Not just lots of people. I mean *everybody,* man. You hear me? This is what it's all about."

And Zachary agreed with him for a while, until the day he fell in love for real.

THE BULLHORSE TECHIES built something called a "game system."

It was a bunch of hardware you could use to play different kinds of games, including competitors' games. It was a masterstroke of market domination. Zachary threw a Fourth of July costume party to celebrate, and met his wife right smack in the middle of it.

She worked for him, as a chemical engineer in hardware, designing the parts of computers where something made of plastic had to fit something made of rubber, or where rubber had to be attached to metal. She had a master's from Caltech, her name was Clara, and she came to the party as Abigail Adams.

Zachary was Benjamin Franklin. He stuck himself with the task of roasting the pig, which meant he couldn't wander around much. Clara brought him a beer, asked how the pig was coming along, and three hours later they were still talking (Clara did not experience the Hush in his presence).

She was single. She had always been single. She had no children. She had a dog named Jake who would rip your balls off.

"If what?" asked Zachary.

"If he feels like it. Is it true you used to freeze people? You know, like—"

"I know what you mean. Yes, it's true."

"Did you ever think it would really work?"

"Yes," he answered. "It tore me up when they started failing."

She looked at him long and hard. Then she said, "I was going to get another drink. Come with me?"

"Of course," he said, and pointed a ladies-first finger at the shipping dock, temporarily serving as a bar.

"Not here," she said. "I was going somewhere else."

Oh.

"I can't really leave . . ."

"You're the boss."

He *was* the boss.

He left.

They went to his house and played City Park Pickup on his game system, and when their characters kissed on-screen, Zachary leaned over and kissed Clara for real.

In his bedroom, they both undressed completely, and folded their clothes before facing each other, before coming together.

AFTER, HE SAID, "Ask me if I ride horses."

"Do you?"

"No, I mean, I want you to say—"

"Why?"

"It doesn't matter."

And it didn't.

× × ×

PILLOW TALK seemed to be where their best selves came out, even if they were just being silly, their postorgasmic brains floating in oxytocin.

"Knock-knock." Zachary's brain, for some reason, gravitated to jokes.

"Who's there?"

"Interrupting cow."

"Interrup—"

"MOO!"

Even after Zachary noticed that telling knock-knock jokes in bed seemed to make continued lovemaking statistically unlikely, he still did it. He couldn't help it.

SOMETIMES THEIR PILLOW talk was more personal.

"How come you waited," Clara asked, half straddling him, her cheek pressed against his sternum, "until I was, you know, almost forty before you showed up in my life?"

"It's like our hearts waited until we were old enough and wise enough for each other. They waited until practice was over."

The personal pillow talk was usually pretty cheesy, but it was great, too.

"I wouldn't have been ready for you when I was younger," he added.

"I would've liked to have gone to Woodstock with you," she whispered.

"I would've liked to have gone to Caltech with you. Besides, I got electrocuted at Woodstock. I drooled a lot, after that."

Clara considered.

"Maybe it is best that we came along later. You know, for each other."

Then she licked his chest.

Zachary noticed that the personal kind of pillow talk was statistically much more likely to lead to further lovemaking.

× × ×

ONE NIGHT, the pillow talk started before the lovemaking was over.

It was Zachary's fault. It took them both by surprise.

Clara was on top, slowly grinding in circles with her hips. This always drove him crazy, so when he suddenly bellowed, "Holy *God*!" she didn't think anything of it, at first.

But then his big hands tightened around her buttocks and he said, "What if you could get a computer file on one system to talk directly to a file on another system?"

Clara stopped grinding.

Work thoughts sometimes popped into Clara's head, too, when they were making love. She'd just always felt it wise to keep them to herself. So even though she was a little miffed, she understood.

"Go on," she said.

"There are internets all over the place, right?" he said. "The military has them. Different companies have them, and colleges and so on. But they all run on different languages and protocols, so we can't get one internet to talk to another internet. Right?"

"Duh."

"What if I had suddenly figured out a way to design a digital 'package' that would travel between systems and . . . *ignore* . . . the system boundaries and go straight from one file to another? If the package could establish a link between the documents, it could build a web between systems, and systems could talk to each other even if they were programmed with different languages. We could build an internet that could be used by regular people, all over the world."

"You make it sound easy," said Clara.

Zachary moved his hips a little. He was still hard.

"Not easy," he said. "But possible. I'm sure it's possible. I'm going to put the whole lab on it tomorrow."

"Good. Are you finished?"

Zachary nodded. He moved his hips again, and the grinding picked up where it left off. Work thoughts jumped like popcorn in both of their heads, but they kept quiet about it.

× × ×

THAT NIGHT BORE two earthshaking fruits.

One was the World Wide Web, which would take five years to build and propagate, and would land Zachary's face on the cover of *Time,* over the words "Connecting the World."

The other was a child. A boy, Seth, who came along within months.

Zachary, gloved and gowned, pretended to help with the delivery, the way they let men do.

They let him hold the baby for a couple of minutes. Those two minutes became the center of his life.

He had to admit the baby was hardly a movie star. Like most babies, he had a frightening, undercooked look about him. Most of him was wrapped up and hidden in a blue cocoon anyhow, but all it took was the soft scrap of weight against Zachary's forearm, the tiny roundness of the head in his palm, and Zachary was lost.

Seth didn't cry. He never would, much. He lay there with his two moon-pool eyes unblinking, and it seemed to Zachary that his whole life and his whole world vanished into those eyes and was multiplied, as if he had magically become ten times the Zachary he'd ever been before. He understood why Clifton Michael had been so desperate, and seemed so small compared to his daughter. He understood why people with families had an easier time dying than people without. He understood why almost everything that ever happened to him, no matter how wonderful it was, felt secretly hollow compared to this.

This was how you changed the world.

He understood this without thinking it, without thinking anything at all, really, because his nerves chose that moment to have one of their electronic hiccups, and the nurses took the baby away before his father could drool on him.

STILL GLOVED AND GOWNED, honorably bloody, Zachary was walking in a daze down a long, bright, hospital-smelling corridor

when he found the Devil crouched on the floor with his arm halfway up inside a snack machine.

"Hey," said Zachary.

"Congratulations," grunted the Devil.

"What's up?"

"Goddamn bag of pretzels didn't drop. A dollar for a bag of pretzels with maybe nine pretzels in it."

"Move your arm. Get your arm out of there."

The Devil extricated himself and hopped to his feet. He watched expectantly as Zachary's giant hand gripped the top corner of the machine, wobbled it once, and let go.

The pretzels fell. The Devil retrieved them.

"I mean," said Zachary, "what are you doing *here*?"

"Looking out for things."

Zachary didn't know what that answer meant, and he didn't like having the Devil in the same building as his son. Things were different now.

"What are the chances," he asked, "of getting my soul back?"

The Devil had eaten all nine pretzels already, and was cleaning up the loose salt with a long, thrashing tongue.

"None," he replied, licking his lips.

Zachary pursed his lips. Struggled not to say anything more. Now wasn't the time. He felt dirty. Now that his son was here, now that Clara was here, he wanted a new past to go with his new future. Knowing that wasn't possible, he resolved that the new future would at least be complete, and be clean.

The Devil walked away.

Zachary let him go.

The Devil might be the Devil, but *he* was Big Zach, the man who was going to connect everybody in the world.

He tore off his scrubs as if changing into Superman.

30. Fish in Prison

Tall Timbers Minimum Security Correctional Facility for Men, 1987

FOUR YEARS DRAGGED OUT in court. Four years of sleepless nights and throwing up and almost shooting himself, all for nothing. He was convicted and packed off to the kind of prison they pack naughty businessmen off to.

It wasn't so bad.

"It's not so bad," Fish whispered in the night to his cellmate, Charles, on the lower bunk, a former vice-president of the Coca-Cola Corporation.

"That's because it's not real prison," said Charles.

Charles was a Harvard man. This seemed to be a prison for Harvard men. Yale guys went someplace else. If you were a self-made man like Fish, and had not completed college, you rubbed shoulders with the Ivy League felons, but they didn't have to talk to you or pretend you had the right to be there among them.

"If it's not a real prison," said Fish, "then walk out and go home after roll call tomorrow. I dare you."

Silence.

You can't dare a Harvard man unless you're a Harvard man yourself.

× × ×

YOU COULD WORK, if you wanted to, at Tall Timbers. Most inmates wanted to. It passed the time and earned them money.

Fish lucked into a job in the prison library. The library was a nice assignment, because you had a lot of outside contact. Interlibrary loans, requests for articles, ordering new material, dealing with new technology.

For a week, Fish shelved books, and pushed a magazine cart around the various cells and dayrooms. The jobs no one else wanted to do. The other library clerks were mostly guys in their fifties. They winked at him and made "new guy" jokes.'

His second week, though, he decided enough was enough. Time for these old sacks to learn some respect. He might be a new guy, but he was still Mark Fish, goddammit. He had taken insurance to a whole new level! He was friends with the Devil!

So on Monday morning, he sat himself down at the front desk, and started stamping returned books.

Fish was on his tenth book when someone gave him a poke from behind and said, "My spot there, son."

Fish cast an irritated eye over his shoulder.

"Huh?"

There stood Harry Truman, or someone who looked a lot like him, in a prison jumpsuit accented with a massive gold Rolex.

"You're in my spot," said Truman.

Fish told Harry to blow it out his ass, and went back to stamping.

The day came and went. Nothing more was said.

Fish thought, Somebody must have told him who I am.

THE PEOPLE WHO CAME and got him in the middle of the night did not wake him up. They just yanked his mattress off the top bunk, spilling him against the wall.

He struggled to his knees, but was kicked down by flying wingtip shoes, and held motionless by invisible fat hands, some with gold rings.

He blinked, trying to clear his eyes, trying to see who held him, but all he could discern were jumpsuits and leather shoes and a few strong but manicured hands. How many, he couldn't tell. But they laughed together, a low, collective rumble. The sort of fraternal laugh you hear over the tinkling of ice in Scotch glasses. Mostly, they were just shadows. Strong shadows, faceless judges, and their contempt for him needed no words.

The shadows shuffled and parted, and a separate shadow, shorter and bespectacled, entered the cell with its hands in its pockets, and looked down its nose at Fish.

"Harry Truman," coughed Fish, speaking aloud before he could get a grip on things.

"Sure," said Truman, softly.

A wingtip lashed out and stabbed at Fish's kidney. He threw up a little, in his mouth, but didn't scream.

Truman crouched down and looked Fish in the eye, and told him who he was. He wasn't Harry Truman, of course. But he had been famous once, and Fish finally recognized him. His name didn't matter, really. Fish continued to think of him as Truman, in his head. What mattered was that the guy was scary, now. He was the kind of guy who, in another time and place, might have been a famous Nazi. In this time and place, he was a certain kind of businessman.

"I'll tell you the same thing I told Nixon," said Truman.

"You disrespected me publicly, so you're going to be punished publicly."

Fish, Truman said, would have to apologize at breakfast, in front of the entire general population. He would buy Truman subscriptions to the *Robb Report* and the *Wall Street Journal*. He would clean Truman's cell and do his laundry for a year—

"A *year*?" coughed Fish.

A flurry of wingtips wrecked his solar plexus. This time he screamed.

He would have to carry Truman's tray in the cafeteria, the voice continued, and find a way to download stock apps on the library computers. And if there was anything else Truman wanted, anything at all . . .

The low, rumbling laugh made another round.

The dim corridor light made eyeless disks of Truman's glasses, but behind the lenses, one eyebrow moved, and Fish understood that Truman had winked at him.

Bracing himself against another wingtip attack, Fish cleared his throat and spat in Truman's face.

Tried to, anyhow. He missed.

They didn't kick him. They didn't laugh.

"Slow learner," pronounced Truman, rising.

Something gritty was shoved into Fish's mouth. He gagged, and avoided vomiting by plain force of will. His hands and ankles were tied, and they—whoever they were—dragged him down the hall, downstairs, down something like a steam tunnel until it seemed they couldn't possibly still be on prison property, and then they tossed him up on a steel table and wrapped him in a clean, white sheet. Wrapped him tight. He could breathe fine, except for the gag in his mouth.

Then, as they flipped and turned him, wrapping him up, he glimpsed a dead man, half blue, cut open on the next table.

A morgue, he thought.

He tried not to scream.

He was going to have to control himself. He tried some of the crazy breathing tricks he'd heard about through the years, trying to calm himself. Didn't they want to talk to him? If they would only unstrap the gag.

They never said a word to him, and that was almost the scariest part. What really got his attention was the open square in a wall of what looked like minifridge doors, and a metal drawer extended.

More screaming. More gagging. They slid him in headfirst, slid the drawer into the wall, and shut the fridge door down by his feet, and left him there for a long time.

× × ×

FISH DISCOVERED CLAUSTROPHOBIA.

If he could only go mad or die.

But he could not stand this confinement. For the first time in his life, he understood and felt sorry for people who said they were claustrophobic. He longed to move his arms, to sit up. To run and move freely, and being trapped like this was like being trapped beneath the earth itself.

At first, he squirmed and shrieked, knocking his feet against the door, hoping to attract someone's attention.

That made him hot and feverish. He lay still, and was faced with rivers of warm saliva and mucus trying to run down his throat, down his windpipe.

His mind was a cruel accomplice. Every time they opened the fridge door down there and pulled him into the cool air, it was a dream, and he snapped awake in darkness, in the stifling air.

Then, one time, it wasn't a dream. They yanked him out by his feet, cleaned him up with rough hands, and made him choke down something like oatmeal. Before he could get his eyes to focus or his mouth to form words, they shut him up in the drawer again. Did it matter if it was a dream or not? The cruelty staggered him. He tried to scream, but only produced a dull rattle.

Days passed. Not imaginary, hallucinatory days. Actual, whole days. He could tell. He fouled himself, but only a little. His dehydrated body stopped making urine.

They seemed to know exactly how long he could last without water and food. His days became long tunnels of dark between sudden, violent washings and feedings.

Every now and then, they thought up new horrors.

One day they shoved an actual corpse in there with him, on top of him like a lover, and closed the drawer again. The weight made it almost impossible to breathe. In the dark, the dead nose touched his.

Horror and panic broke fresh.

He tried to die.

Tried to horror himself to death, think himself into a coma.

Couldn't.

He tried to go mad.

Maybe he could pass into a kind of wonderful insanity, an escape to an imaginary personal universe where he lived in a cabin in the middle of a wildflower meadow, but the second he got a grip on what that might look like, the dead man on top of him began to jerk. He knew, he had heard stories, that dead people were apt to do all kinds of strange things as their systems died. They might belch or pass gas, or even sit up or open their eyes.

The dead man jerked and shuddered. His chin dug into Fish's shoulder.

The dead man began to leak. Something dripped on Fish's face, and stung.

Clarity like a searchlight in the rain.

He saw the face of Harry Truman at the sawmill, and the faces of the other thousand grandfatherly paper shufflers in the white-collar prison, and understood that even these venal, greedy little fuckers were ten times the man he was, because they were smart or talented or aggressive, and things like this, this drawer, were what happened to men who inconvenienced them.

Money was meant for that sort of person. Not for little turds like him who thought it would be neat to be rich. Little turds like him who didn't understand just how real the real world was.

It was a tiny, useless realization in his bed of rot and horror.

And whatever the dead man was dripping on him must be something really caustic, because it was burning his face, dripping and running.

And one day there was a blur of light and a momentary coolness, and the dead man was removed.

Fish heard someone gag.

Then they slid him back into darkness.

Sometimes, in the dark and silence, he would hear or feel something of the outside world. A muffled voice, or a vibration in the walls as other drawers slid open, slid closed. The intrusions scraped at his senses, and he screamed for them to Be silent and Go away!

When they finally took him back to his cell, he didn't know it was real for almost a week. He sat on the floor shitting himself, tugging at his beard, and it took a while for him to know his dreamworld from the real.

When he returned to the general routine, to the cafeteria and the exercise yard, he was not the same. How could he be? He was not visited again by Truman and his wingtipped gang. He served them best now as a cautionary tale. He saw them sometimes pointing him out to new inmates.

His beard had grown in straight, long and gray, except where embalming fluid had bleached a river down the side of his face, and his eyes had grown deep without growing wise. He was thin, now. His walk had a bounce, as if he walked to a strange music.

He sat by himself and read by himself and kept his thoughts to himself, and every day for the rest of his life was a struggle not to feel dead.

31.

Cutters for Jenna

Dayton, Ohio, 2005

THE DEVIL WAS JUST starting to run out of interesting crap to watch on TV when Presto! Jenna Steele made a televised speech from her hospital bed. Still bruised, still in a double arm cast and neck brace from her Dumpster jump, she nevertheless looked stunning.

"Johnny," she was saying, speaking directly to the camera, "if you'll take me back, I've got a list of things I promise."

There was a pause, and you could barely hear her hissing to someone off camera: "Hold the list up, dumbshit."

The list, read aloud by Jenna, went like this:

"I promise to always wear that magenta lipstick you like so, so much, that I never wore enough because of that allergic thing.

"I promise to try and like clams, which I don't like, but I'll try to like them.

"I will go to this psychic woman I know who does previous-life charts, and find out for sure if we were lovers back in history, because I swear to God we were, Johnny. I can feel it.

"I promise I will let us get a dog, if we move in together."

("How about promise not to shoot me," said the Devil, "you self-absorbed, bipolar cunt?")

"I promise," she was saying, "not to shoot you again, no matter what."

Then she said, "This is just for you," and somehow, with both arms in casts, lifted her hospital gown to expose her breasts.

The TV cut away a moment too late.

God, she had nice ones, he thought. He couldn't help it.

ONE OF THE NURSES woke the Devil with a snap of the blinds, bright daylight. He squinted, raised one arm to cover his face, and said, "Man!"

"This is your fault," the nurse whispered, flicking on the TV and dropping the remote in the middle of his wound pattern.

The TV told him—and showed him—how Jenna's nurse had entered her room that morning to find that the megastar had cut herself. Not to death, not even badly. Just a ladder of tiny slices, inflicted with the sharp-edged lid of a disposable coffee cup.

Jenna was a cutter.

"Who'da thunk it?" said the Devil.

But the celebrity news snippet wasn't over.

It went on to tell how thousands of teenage girls all over the world were cutting themselves in exactly the same ladder pattern, to show support for Jenna, and to protest against Johnny Scratch for not forgiving her.

The nurse who brought the Devil lunch paused after setting the tray down, pulled up the cuff of her uniform pants, and showed him a ladder of tiny slash marks. Neatly healing, but still red, and smeared with antibacterial gel.

He had to get out of Dayton. The place made people crazy.

"We're *everywhere,*" the nurse whispered at him, glaring.

THE DOCTOR was taken aback that afternoon when he walked in and caught the Devil cutting himself with a plastic cafeteria knife.

It was unpleasantly difficult, the Devil had discovered, with plasticware. There was no way for it to be sharp enough, so you had to saw. So far, his little ladder only had three rungs in it. He would stop at four. After all, he was just curious.

"This isn't what it looks like," the Devil told the doctor.

"It's a cry for help," said the doctor, trying to soothe him.

"If you try to help me," barked the Devil, "I swear to *God*—!"

"Are you *crying*?"

The Devil pulled the sheets over his head and said, "I *hate* you people! I hate you *all*!"

32.
Revelation Ninja

San Francisco, 1997

THE DEVIL PICKED FISH UP in the JFK limo the day he got out of prison. Stepping out through a double set of postern gates, Fish wore loose, white clothing, sandals, and really long hair. It was a little thin on top, but long in the back. A chemical burn scarred his face from scalp to jawline.

They were going to drive out to San Francisco, but halfway across Missouri Fish almost leaped from the car, screaming, "Stop! Far out! Stop!"

The limo ground to a halt outside an impressive, diamond-shaped building. It was a church, but not like any church Fish had ever seen. It might have held an army. From a duck pond by the parking lot rose a fifty-foot fiberglass Jesus.

"Wonderful!" cried Fish, flying from the car and racing across the empty parking lot.

The Devil parked the limo, muttering under his breath.

"Fucksticks," he said. Churches, predictably, annoyed him. People fell into religion because they were drawn by the company and approval of others. It was the oldest drug on the market. People who said they had found Jesus had really found Jesus people.

He caught up with Fish inside.

Fish wandered, gaping, across an open lobby an acre wide, with couches and chairs arranged in groups beneath soaring steel rafters and enormous skylights. On the far side, he found three sets of heavy double doors, flung the middle pair wide, and there he stopped.

The Devil caught up with him, and together they looked out over a landscape of ten thousand theater chairs, all facing a raised dais, way far away down there, with two lecterns, a piano, and enough musical instruments for a whole rock festival. Television sets gazed from every wall, mounted in banks ten screens wide.

"Do you think it's fair to say," asked Fish, a little breathless, "that these people are *addicted*?"

The Devil nodded. "It's called a Megachurch," he explained. "They have TV stations and everything."

"I can work with these people," said Fish.

"It's a crock," said the Devil, who remembered the real Jesus, and felt he owed it to Him to say something.

"It's money waiting to happen," said Fish, "is what it is."

FISH TALKED THE DEVIL into staying for worship service that evening. The Megachurch had services every single night, it turned out.

"Because the Devil never rests!" boomed a preacher, one of four.

"Blow me," whispered the Devil, slumped in a chair along the back wall. Fish sat on the Devil's right, trembling with excitement.

The preacher seemed to fly above his congregation on all sides, on a hundred screens, floating and smiling, his hair a Missouri buzz cut, his eyes football-coach bright.

It was hard not to get swept up in the service. The cavernous church, thundering with electric guitars and underscored by a choir on high reverb, literally rocked. The air itself seemed charged with adrenaline. Here and there, individuals rose, lifted their hands, then fell back as if shot.

And then Fish was running down the aisle, white prison-issue pimp suit fluttering behind him, beard like a worn-out flag, shower shoes flapping.

The Living Water technical crew were savvy dudes. Before Fish was halfway to the dais, spotlights caught him in a blaze of white soul-light. He looked gauzy, like a special effect, and seemed to waft onto the dais, where the preacher, who knew a money moment when he saw one, surrendered the microphone without greeting or preamble.

FISH TOLD THEM how he had awakened to a new life, in prison.

They loved him. The volume rose. Here and there, shouts of encouragement.

"Everyone talks about the cross," echoed Fish, expertly turning, giving equal time to all sides. "The cross this, and the cross that. But until hard times come down on you, sometimes it's easy to forget what the cross means. That the cross means hard choices. That sometimes you have to break something before it can be made whole. I think how the cross was the instrument of our Lord's agony, and I think of all the terrible things He has forgiven me for and all the terrible things that are done and waiting to be done, and I think of all the forgiving that's needed out there in that bad world. Forgiving that can't start until some confessing gets done and some changes get made!"

They were stomping now. Ten thousand people.

"I'm sick and tired of this great nation pretending that every change is a good change, and every new thing is a good thing! Some things are good because they're simple, like what makes a marriage, what makes a person a person whether they've been born yet or not, and what makes truth! Can you dig Jesus? Can you TAKE Jesus? Are YOU READY TO DISH HIM OUT?"

It was Thunderdome.

Fish floated on-screen, high above, arms outstretched, beard flying.

The Devil found himself on his feet, hands raised high, feeling the spirit.

Embarrassed, he collected himself and went out to wait in the car.

× × ×

LATER, AFTER MIDNIGHT, the Devil left town alone. Fish stayed behind to take over duties as Projected Revenue Accountant for Living Water Ministries, Inc., which maintained nonprofit status despite owning interest in a publishing house, a profitable summer camp, and a chain of family-friendly video stores.

The Devil headed for L.A., where Memory answered her door in a slinky warm-up outfit. Nearing fifty, she looked great. She kept on getting her body tightened and firmed and vacuumed, which the Devil liked. Her sitcom had tanked, after two okay seasons, but she still worked in commercials and the occasional miniseries.

They made love, and then watched TV by candlelight.

"Fish is out of prison," he told her.

"I know."

"He found Jesus."

"I *doubt* it!"

"He found a church that wanted an accountant. And he's actually not a bad preacher. You start to believe if you spend enough time around those people. They're like soccer fans."

Memory said nothing.

"Zachary's company is doing all right," said the Devil.

"Duh. Everybody knows that."

"I bring it up," said the Devil, "because it might be nice if you guys worked together again, after all this time."

"What, like the band? No way, José."

He shook his head.

"No," said. "Not like the band."

The Devil wanted them to take over the Internet.

"Not in a rule-the-world kind of way. I just think it could be more useful. It could be doing more with information. Information is good. When information moves, people improve."

"Groovy jingle," said Memory.

"Oh, shut up. I mean it. The Internet is the whole architecture of the future. We need to make it better."

"And you're talking to me about this because . . . ?"

"The Internet needs a face. A wise face. A pretty face. And a voice."

So they got in the JFK car and drove off to visit Zachary in San Francisco.

Memory started making up a song, out loud, with just the words "When information moves, people improve."

"Stop it," said the Devil, but she wouldn't.

THEY FOUND ZACHARY in the lunchroom at Bullhorse Technologies.

He practically launched himself at Memory, picking her up and spinning her around. She kissed him on both cheeks, and then once, really hard, on the lips.

After a half hour of catching up, the Devil asked Zachary, "How come the Internet is so fucking slow?"

"It's still getting off the ground," answered Zachary, sounding hurt.

"No shit. I mean, everyone's *heard* of it. But hardly anyone is actually plugged in. Everyone *knows* about e-mail and shit, but they don't know how to get it and use it."

"I'll see what I can do," Zachary said.

"Cool beans," said the Devil.

ZACHARY AND THE BULLHORSE techs designed what they called a "snowball." It was like a glob of information that shot out over the Internet, and found similar information. The new information became part of the snowball, which was then able to move faster and gather more information. By the time it returned to the Bullhorse mainframe, it was a planetary ball of categorical data, containing links to documents all over the world.

The snowball allowed Bullhorse Technologies to map and index the Web.

When they made the new search technology available to the public, information all over the world accelerated overnight.

The Devil looked up some pictures from the Hubble Space Telescope, and they loaded within a minute. They were pictures of huge columns of gas, light-years across, where new stars were being born.

"God's still busy," observed the Devil.

Then he called Memory and said, "Time to move back to San Francisco, kid."

"Don't call me 'kid,'" she said, but she moved.

ZACHARY PRODUCED A new line of computers specially designed for the Internet.

Memory filmed a series of TV ads for these computers. The ads showed her flowing in and out of fiber-optic cables. She also became the spokeswoman for a new line of computer games. You could have these games piped right into your computer. You didn't even have to go to the store.

Overnight, Memory was the psychedelic face of the future, recognized everywhere. She appeared on the cover of *Electronics* magazine twice in three months.

She became friends with Zachary, again, and with his wife, Clara. She got to know their kid, Seth. A nice kid, with a crossed wire or two. Like his grandmother, who lived in some kind of planned community in Massachusetts, he liked to bring people things. He might bring you a glass of water or a crayon, or something belonging to Mom or Dad that had to be put back.

Memory couldn't help recalling the early days, with Dan Paul on Haight-Ashbury.

"San Francisco," Memory told Clara one day, shoe-shopping downtown, "is one of the first places I remember."

And now, having returned, she felt at home for the first time . . . when? Ever?

Memory did some calculations. If her guess was correct, and she had been about twenty years old when her memory kicked in on that long-ago gravel road, she was forty-eight now. And, for the first time in a while, she felt at home. Not just in San Francisco, with good friends and a fun job, but with herself and with the whole world.

She didn't wish she were a music sensation again. She didn't wish she were high. She didn't wish anything. It all fit, and felt good. Even time didn't seem to be able to get a grip on her, somehow. She flowed with it. She changed. It didn't hurt that she had been artificially zipped and lifted and injected until she looked eternally thirty-one (she also, in the wrong kind of light, looked vaguely shrink-wrapped, but she avoided that kind of light). Even her amnesia seemed to have mellowed away. Everyone's past did that, didn't it?

She finally felt at home in her own life.

SOMETIMES MEMORY and the Devil went to the Bull Horses' as a couple.

Seth always brought the Devil a tissue and said, "You look sad," and the Devil always said, "Thanks, little dude."

When Fish moved out there and started hanging around, too, Seth looked at him as if he were a kind of creature he'd never seen before. He liked to bring Fish cookies and hors d'oeuvres, like feeding an animal at the zoo.

"See if you can get Seth to bring him arsenic," Memory muttered to Clara one night when they all gathered to drink wine and play trivia games.

"Be nice," said the Devil, who overheard.

"Maybe we can get him to bring you some, too," she said, but she smiled when she said it, and draped her arm around him.

FISH MOVED to San Francisco because, like lots of people, he hated Missouri after living there for a while.

He convinced Living Water Ministries to move their corporate offices west, for tax purposes. Once there, the church branched out into five new locations and a cable network.

"I'm finally doing what I should have been doing all along," said Fish, drinking orange juice poolside with the Devil at the Logan Beach Tabernacle branch. "I'm not selling something that doesn't exist. I'm *doing* something. You know what else?"

No, thought the Devil.

"I think I *believe.* I think it's gotten into my heart, man."

The Devil chuckled.

"What?"

"Fish, man, I knew Jesus. He's dead."

Fish stared at him from behind designer shades and said, "This is the new model I'm talking about."

THE NEXT DAY, Fish showed up unannounced at Bullhorse Technologies. He strolled past the receptionist, found his way without difficulty through the sea of cubicles to Zachary's office, and let himself in without knocking.

"Bless you," he said to Zachary, who was concentrating on something.

"Mmm," said Zachary.

"Got a business idea for you," said Fish, seating himself, lacing his fingers behind his head. "It's a game."

Zachary looked up—annoyed but curious.

"Faith-based computer games!" said Fish, arms spread in rapture. "They'll be really, really violent. Sell a million of 'em."

The Devil materialized at Zachary's shoulder.

"You'd sell a lot of computers to people who aren't normally fans of scientific advancement," he suggested.

"A whole new market," said Zachary, the business side of his brain seeing the potential, like a sleeping pile of dynamite.

Fish leaned forward. "This is how people communicate, now," he said. "No one listens or reads anymore. But they *will* play games! With games, you can sell computers and I can missionary the world. We might even convert all the pagans and heathens and wild Indians, still!"

"Shut up about the Indians," hissed the Devil. "You don't know dick about Indians."

"Whatever. It's all part of God's business plan."

ZACHARY'S DESIGNERS worked on a crash schedule. Zachary watched over their shoulders as basic character templates moved through a field program for a game called Revelation Ninja. Shots didn't look like shots yet and blood didn't look like blood, but when this particular game was finished, the templates would be Christians left behind by the Rapture defending themselves against soldiers of the gay, married, double Antichrist. The Christians would know kung fu.

Other games would follow, including the Christmas debut of Abortion Clinic Assassin, projected to be the first digital game to sell more than five million units.

"This is making me kind of sick to my stomach," Zachary told his money guys.

"We're talking a lot of money," said the money guys.

SOMEONE HAD ASSIGNED Fish an office of his own.

When Zachary found out who it was, he planned to give them a disapproving look. It was getting away from him. The whole thing.

At his desk, three weeks into the Revelation Ninja crash program, Fish was all eyes and thumbs, testing the product at his desk.

Zachary hovered in the doorway. Part of him didn't want to enter Fish's office. Didn't want to admit Fish *had* an office.

"What if the player character dies?" asked Zachary. "Does he go to Heaven?"

"Fuck yeah."

"You want effects for that, right?"

"Affirmative. Those other guys go to Hell. The ones in the Gay Antichrist armor. We need effects for that, too."

× × ×

SOMETIMES ZACHARY WENT to April Michael's room, checked the nitro and the pressure levels, and told her, "You'd be thirty-two years old this year."

It made him sad to say it.

"You're not missing anything," he told her.

ZACHARY BUSIED HIMSELF with other ideas, other games.

Rock-star games were his favorite. He paid real pop musicians to come in and be filmed against a green screen backdrop. Later, their images would appear on consumer TV screens and computer monitors, as if they were right there in the room. It made the Bullhorse crew feel sort of cool to find themselves rubbing shoulders with the stars. Some of them started reporting for work in sunglasses and leather jackets.

Even the Devil got caught up in the buzz. He wore sunglasses and a black cowboy hat on the coolest day of all, the day Jenna Steele came in, complete with entourage, paparazzi in tow, to film six minutes of digital video for next season's showpiece, Atomic Top 40.

EVERY COUPLE HAS A STORY about the first time they met. Jenna Steele and the Devil met in front of a green-screen.

Jenna Steele.

Jenna Steele had been a child star. Then she had skyrocketed to even greater fame as a grown-up, writing and singing her own songs. She was wholesome. She was blond, with huge eyes and a million-dollar smile, and a body that made men feel bad for looking at it, considering she'd been a child star.

As the day wore on (green-screen shoots took a long time, and were really boring), it became increasingly obvious that Jenna was not as nice or as wholesome as her people wanted the world to believe. Despite the fact that a dressing room had been provided for her by Bullhorse Technologies, Jenna went right ahead and changed her costumes when and where she felt like it. She wandered around topless for ten solid minutes between singing her hit "Cream Cheese" and doing the action sequence for "Night Krush."

The Devil went over and talked to her. A lot of cameras flashed.

These first pictures showed two great-looking people having a conversation.

The cameras flashed some more. This time, Jenna and the dark stranger were touching. Just a hand on an elbow, here. His hand on her leg, there, and her pretending not to notice.

Jenna's bodyguards didn't like it. These days, there were scripts for things like that, and this dark stranger was definitely off script. Later, after the shoot, a big mook in a jogging suit pushed up against the Devil outside the washroom and suggested he enjoy the memory of the day and not think about calling Miss Steele or bothering her.

The Devil turned the mook into something like a scorpion on the bottom of the ocean, a pair of ragged claws that lived for a split second before the pressure got it.

Goddamn if anyone was going to tell him who he could call. And he definitely wanted to call.

SHE CALLED *HIM,* as it happened. She asked him out on a date, and he said "Yes."

The press followed them on motorcycles.

"Assholes," rumbled the Devil. Maybe he'd raise a fog, and lose them.

"Oh, just let 'em," said Jenna, squeezing his arm. "It's free advertising."

Jenna loved the press. She texted her fan club in the middle of dinner just so they could update her Web site and tell everyone she was having étouffée. And to maybe post a picture of this smoldering older man across the table from her.

The press was waiting for them outside the restaurant. They flashed and mooned over *her,* and were less worshipful with *him.*

"Who are *you,* buddy?" they called.

FLASH.

"I'm the fucking president of France," he answered.

Jenna, playing along, acted blind and said she was fucking Helen Keller.

She was having fun. She liked him.

He decided not to tell her he was the Devil. Maybe later. Not yet. Maybe not.

MEMORY WAS HAVING a quiet night at home, watching TV and thinking about getting her belly tucked, when she saw the Devil on TV with Jenna Steele.

Jenna Steele, she thought, sneering. These artificial-sweetener dance bands today wouldn't know an honest rock-'n'-roll feeling if it stabbed them.

Was that jealousy?

What did it mean, she wondered, when you felt sorry for yourself, not to mention surprised, that the Devil had let you down?

They weren't married, after all.

If she could get to sleep before she cried, she decided, it wouldn't count.

33.

The Coma Channel

New York City, 2001

"DON'T WORRY. Breece is a closer."

"We'll have it wrapped before lunchtime."

"Guy's a monster. M-O-N-*ster*."

"Maybe by ten, if we keep 'em on track and skip small talk."

Memory was having breakfast in lower Manhattan with two tall, thin lawyers. They were helping her buy Dingo Studios, which was going out of business.

Woo-hoo.

It was the kind of law firm the Devil recommended if you went to him and said, "I need lawyers."

"Guns and cocaine lawyers?" he had asked. "Or—?"

"I want to buy something."

"Gotteshalk, Hammer, Breece, and Pei," he told her, and rattled off the phone number. "What do you have in mind?"

She had hung up without answering. It was either that or explain that she couldn't stay on the West Coast and watch him make an ass of himself with Jenna. That she wanted to be as far from him as the U.S. map allowed.

So why had she called him? He wasn't the only jerk who knew about lawyers.

The subconscious is a tricky bastard.

Gotteshalk, Hammer, Breece, and Pei had a catered breakfast brought in for their meeting with Memory. They treated her like a star, which said something about her. These lawyers didn't give their attention to just any old thing.

So when someone said, "Goddamn. Look at that!" in a certain tone of voice, some of them looked and some didn't.

Some looked out the window and saw the commercial jet come diving for them, and some did not. It was like an optical illusion, so fast it grew and filled the window.

THE DEVIL SAW IT on TV, like everyone else. He was in line at a San Francisco coffee shop when the news broke on three wide screens behind the pickup counter.

On-screen, a tall building was on fire.

An airplane had hit the tower, the TV explained.

Then, right there live on TV, a second airplane ripped through a second building. Millions of people gasped as if gut-punched.

The Devil bared his teeth and cried hot tears in the coffee shop. Like everyone else, he kept watching, frozen.

The two towers burned like smudge sticks against a perfect September sky.

MEMORY FELT HEAT like the sun.

Then it was all smoke, and the floor tilting crazily under her.

Over here, sparks. Over there, an elevator.

Smoke, rushing across the floor. She pulled her jacket over her head, and started crawling . . . where?

Then the entire world shook, as if a freight train were cannonballing straight down out of the sky. Closer and louder.

Sparks. Smoke.

Then a sense of being expelled, of being shot through walls into cool air, surrounded by clouds of printer paper and dust, and falling.

× × ×

FIREMEN BROUGHT HER on a stretcher into a tent, and paramedics rifled through her clothes, looking for wounds, finding only scratches.

"Some guy said she fell," said one of the medics. "Like, came down with the building."

"No."

"I'm just telling you what the guy said."

"She won't wake up."

They sent her way uptown, where she lay in bed and didn't move unless they moved her.

THERE WAS A WAR, of course.

It had been a while since they'd had a good war.

War, the Devil reminded himself, was like ex-lax for money and new ideas. War cleansed the national pipes.

But something funny happened this time. It turned out people didn't like war so much when they could watch it live on TV or stream it in real time on their computers. Every time an American got killed, they went pale. They grumbled. By the time ten Americans had died, the grumbling had gotten ten times louder. What country could fight a war like that?

The Devil, slouching in a chair at Memory's bedside, stormed quietly to himself.

"Whatever happened," he seethed, "to the days when you could wipe out five thousand soldiers and people would suck it up and talk about 'duty'? We'll never get any momentum going, at this rate!"

He called Fish.

"Distract them," he said.

LIVING WATER MINISTRIES put seventeen new televangelists on cable, led by Fish.

"Trust Jesus!" cried the televangelists. "God has a plan! God has a *war* plan!"

Every fifteen minutes, flashy commercials offered new and exciting things God had provided for you to buy. There was a sponge-thing on a handle that would finally make it easier to clean the inside of your windshield! There was a chemical you could spray inside your shower, and it would fight mildew without any scrubbing! Many of the commercials were concerned about your health. There was a GPS unit that broadcast a distress signal if it detected that your heart had stopped. There was a pill that made it perfectly okay to have an erection lasting all night long. There was a fast-acting sinus medicine, and a sinus medicine that lasted up to twenty-four hours. It was usually expensive as hell, but now there was a special offer if you called within ten minutes.

Eventually, Living Water Ministries just set up a full-time Pill Channel, and people watched it like a Saturday-morning cartoon.

Good, thought the Devil. As long as they weren't watching the news.

MOST OF A YEAR went by.

The Devil found himself very busy.

The war was scary and expensive. You had to work hard to keep it going, especially when it obviously wasn't accomplishing anything.

There was television, and Jenna. Three years he had been dating America's favorite bad girl. Three very public years. One time they had even been filmed—badly, at night—making love in a Malibu swimming pool. Jenna's CD sales exploded. John Scratch remained a mystery. He kept claiming to be the president of France. Fans blogged that he probably looked great naked. His popularity grew. So did the popularity of the actual president of France.

WHENEVER POSSIBLE, the Devil found himself in New York, at Memory's bedside.

At first, he thought she might wake up. When she didn't, he remained at her bedside anyway, and didn't allow himself to wonder why.

Was it guilt? Was it love? He didn't dare think about it. Didn't dare think about her voice, or her eyes. He didn't dare think about the simple satisfaction of holding her on the couch in front of the TV, and the odd human feeling that she was *his*.

He wasn't the only one watching over her.

Right after the towers fell, television had taken a renewed interest. Memory Jones! Faded rock star, TV star, Internet sensation, forever young, forever Woodstock, one of several famous names in the World Trade Center that day. Their interest faded quickly, but now, after a year, they were back.

A celebrity in a coma was one thing.

A celebrity in a coma that went on and on was a story that went on and on.

Purple Airplane CD sales went through the roof. Her picture began to appear on T-shirts, with a dreamy psychedelic halo and *X*s over her eyes. She became a cult icon. Young people with confused lifestyles and nothing better to do traveled to New York and tried to sneak up to her room.

Eventually, both TV and the Internet started a full-time Coma Channel, streaming a live camera feed from Memory's bedside. They kept a running clock in the lower right-hand corner of the screen, ticking off the months and days and hours and minutes and seconds Memory Jones had been under.

Fine, thought the Devil, half asleep, just off camera. Whatever distracted them.

MONTHS PASSED, AND a whole new war started.

A war there was no good reason for at all, based on shadows and lies, and nobody even protested very much.

They had a whole new kind of satellite TV by then, with so many channels people could hardly see straight. A war was just one of the choices on television.

Cooking shows were big that year, too.

34.

"It's That President-of-France Guy Again!"

Los Angeles, Spring 2003

THE ALL-CELEBRITY NEWS CHANNEL was the Devil's idea.

If the TV people were obsessed with Memory in her coma, he reasoned, they'd be even more obsessed with celebrities who were awake.

"People perk up when the news is about celebrities," he whispered into a studio exec's ear.

"Yeah?" said the executive.

"They're not threatening, see, because *they don't actually affect people*! Celebrities can get arrested, start charities, beat up paparazzi, get drunk and naked in public, and it won't change your life."

"Fuck yeah!" cried the executive.

And so the All-Celebrity News Channel was born.

ONE OF THE first items on the All-Celebrity News Channel turned out to be John Scratch.

"Look!" viewers said. "It's that President-of-France-guy again. Jenna Steele's boy toy."

"He's not really the president of France," more alert viewers argued. "That's just some shit he tells people."

"Who is he, then?"

No one knew.

Viewers were tired of not knowing who, exactly, John Scratch was. They wanted answers.

Jenna's studio people knew that if viewers wanted to know something, you could turn that into *money.* So three executives in shiny, fashionable shirts came to Jenna's condo one night and offered John Scratch his own television show.

The Devil was a little fuzzy-headed. He and Jenna had fallen asleep watching the Foreclosure Channel, and the doorbell awakened them.

"My own TV show about what?" asked the Devil.

"Doesn't matter," they told him.

"You'll think of something, baby," sighed Jenna, still curled up on the white leather couch.

He thought of something.

"I WANT YOU to sponsor my show," said the Devil to Fish.

They were batting a beach ball around in a hot tub at the Neverending Mexican Party.

Fish was an official preacher now, with a degree straight off the Internet. "What's your show about?" he asked.

"Doesn't matter," said the Devil. "There's some new miracle pill I keep hearing about. I saw it on your morning show."

"The White Pill," said Fish, nodding. "It's like white noise for your neurochemicals. Makes you feel content. Not high or anything. Just content."

"It's a lobotomy in a prescription bottle," said the Devil.

"I should get out of here," said Fish. "Seriously. This is no place for a preacher." He got up.

"Sit down."

Fish sat down.

"I want the White Pill to sponsor my show," said the Devil.

Fish nodded. "*Think It Over.* That's what you're calling your show?"

"Uh-huh."

"I'll have to pray on it," said Fish. "But it should work fine, I think—"

The Devil tuned Fish out.

He imagined jumping up and down on Fish until Fish came apart. He pretended to listen, with a weird little smile on his face.

35. Fish Is Raptured or Something

San Francisco, 2003

WHAT HAPPENED TO FISH, when it happened, happened fast.

It started with a tornado in Faribault, Minnesota. A bad motherfucker straight out of *The Wizard of Oz,* it ripped through the biggest neighborhood, killing two hundred people. Whole families were buried.

The Devil, when he saw it on TV, up late at night with a bowl of ice cream, a joint, and a pack of Rolaids, had to put down the ice cream and sit with his hands to his mouth, eyes filling. Those poor people, those families (Jesus, he was getting soft).

He changed the channel, and there was Fish, preaching.

The Devil picked up his ice cream, but didn't take a bite just yet.

He listened, and couldn't believe what he heard.

"There's victims," Fish preached. "Sure there are. There's crime victims and disease victims and mad cow disease victims and just all kinds of victims. But you got to have eyes to see God's will! Sometimes being a victim is God's way of bringing a message. God's way of saying you have strayed. God's way of saying: 'Danger, you poor, blind sinful worm!'"

The Devil put down the ice cream and hit the joint.

"Now, we bleed for those families out in Minnesota. But we've got to look with hard eyes and say, 'Why?' It's that age-old question, 'Why does God let bad things happen to good people?' And the answer is as plain as day, plain as *Judgment Day*: Maybe they ain't good people."

"Fish," sighed the Devil. Could anyone possibly be such an asshole?

"Lest we forget, it was Minnesota that said a teacher *had* to teach evolution, even though he knew it was a crock. Tonight, Minnesota has reaped the whirlwind. Mourn the dead in Faribault, but know they only got what they deserved. Amen."

It wasn't the first time an evangelist had said mean things in the name of God.

There were preachers who said that the people who died in the World Trade Center deserved what they got because America tolerated fags. He thought about preachers who said people deserved tragedy because they got pregnant or went broke, and it made him want to vomit.

The Devil decided the world had put up with Mark fucking Fish long enough.

He clenched his fist, and on the screen, Fish went up in a ball of blue fire. The TV audience just barely had time to see his hair turn to smoke before the flames swallowed him up.

The Devil sat there for a while. He didn't finish his ice cream.

Fish, he thought. You poor, stupid asshole.

He felt like crying, but he didn't. He sat, tired but sleepless, watching infomercials instead. He ordered an egg slicer and a pinkie ring.

FISH, THE TELEVANGELIST community decided, had been Raptured.

Chosen early, and taken up. Everyone had seen it. Fish had gone to Heaven right there on TV. Amen.

Zachary hadn't been watching the "Rapture" broadcast, but he'd seen it replayed on the Web.

If it could happen to Fish, it could happen to him.

And in the back of his mind, he thought, Maybe the best defense is a good offense, but he tried to pretend he hadn't thought it, or hadn't heard himself think it.

36.

Rising and Vanishing Almost Politely

Hiroshima, Japan, 1945

THE WARS ON TV reminded the Devil of other wars he had seen. Bigger wars. Not long ago, in Europe. He started dreaming about them, more and more.

The Devil had been a busy fellow during the Big One.

The world had needed a good convulsion, and boy, did he deliver.

He was everywhere.

On all sides, he had commanded and followed. He had crouched in the bellies of submarines. He had wooed sweethearts left behind. He had grown Victory gardens. He had watched from the London streets at night as the bombers bombed and made the great city a rubble pile. And he had ridden with Patton, and dreamed with Patton of the great conquerors and ancient times. He had stood with Patton amid ruins he remembered when they were built new. He liked Patton.

Half of the world had been smashed to rubble, and still the war wouldn't end. It kept rolling and eating, until the only thing left to do was build a weapon as horrible as the war itself.

One final atrocity. Something they would look back on and call monstrous.

Thing was, it was going to be beautiful, too, and damned if he was going to miss it.

HE DID NOT FLY with the bomb across the sea. He did not want to meet the men who dropped it, or know their names.

On the day they dropped the bomb, he was a Japanese man on a Japanese bridge near a Japanese church by a Japanese river when the warplane appeared in the sky.

There had been one air-raid alarm already that morning, and with the all clear sounded, the people of the city were reluctant to race back inside. They were reticent. Many of them looked up at the bomber once, and did not see it anymore, or wish to.

The Devil thought perhaps he might see the device fall, see it leave the belly of the flying machine, but he didn't, and it took him by surprise like everyone else.

A FLASH like nine Heavens.

He saw a man seated in a doorway disintegrate and fly away in a cloud of ash or vapor. He saw many such, many instant ghosts, and he saw how the light photographed them on walls, on the sides of a passing—now burning—trolley.

This was what the end of the most terrible war looked like. A sunny day left out in the sun until it brightened beyond meaning.

People were the worst of gods and the worst of animals combined.

Perhaps this kind of violence was the only message they would ever really understand. Something so terrible they would never want to see it happen again. Maybe they would be less warlike now, because they had finally become frightened of themselves.

It would be so human of them, wouldn't it? To be thrust into goodness by something vast and evil.

Did he feel guilt? A little. Mostly he just hoped it would work, that this would be the turning point the world needed. He burned with it, black-eyed and howling, urging it on: the mighty flash, the shock wave, the firestorm, and the burning river.

Half of the city stopped and was gone. A great crowd of the dead, rising and vanishing almost politely.

37. Those Games Are About Jesus

San Francisco, 2003

ONE DAY, ZACHARY BULL HORSE had chauffeur duty. It was his turn in the evening to pick up the neighborhood kids from one particular house, and drop them all off at home.

When he arrived to pick the kids up, he stood in the hallway just off the playroom, and watched while three boys and two girls, all jacked into one Bullhorse Tech game box, finished playing Revelation Ninja 4. Then they all held hands in a circle and prayed. The game told players that once you got past the third level, Jesus might grant you a wish.

Feeling queasy, Zachary cleared his throat and said, “Let’s go, gang.”

He had to say it three times.

“WHAT DID YOU WISH FOR?” he asked Seth, when all the other kids were dropped off.

“More wishes,” said Seth.

× × ×

THE FOLLOWING MORNING, Zachary walked into the lair of the money guys, and said, "How big a hit will we take if we ditch the faith-based assassin games?"

The money guys were eating donuts. One of them almost choked.

"Too big," the money guys answered. "Jesus, Big Zach, what—"

"HOW big?"

"They're our largest single inventory," said the department head. "If we don't sell them—"

"Stop selling them," said Zachary. "I'm telling you."

The money chief gulped. "We'll have to take that to the board," he said.

Zachary made a farting noise and said, "Do it."

THE BOARD MEETING was a satellite extravaganza, with members and their cell phones scattered all over various golf courses. It took five minutes.

Hell, no, said the board, they weren't going to eat that much inventory! Besides, the games were about Jesus. What would it look like if they canceled a bunch of Jesus games?

"You text those assholes back," Zachary told the money guys. "And tell them to be here—actually here, in the boardroom at Bullhorse Technologies, in the real world—tomorrow by noon."

Twenty-six hours later, a very pissed-off board was seated around a heavily waxed, artificially stressed table.

They offered no reverential hush when Big Zach walked in.

"What's this about, Bull Horse?" barked a cowboy type wearing a turquoise tie ring.

"Shut up," Big Zach barked back.

And he stood there glaring at them.

"I'm sorry, Zach," someone said. "It's just too much money."

A long silence.

"I quit," said Zachary.

The silence lived on.

Then there was an explosion, naturally.

"But you're the brains of the operation!"

"But you personally own thirty percent of the stock!"

"Besides," said the cowboy type. "It won't change anything. Those games will still be sold."

"Probably," said Zachary. "But they will be sold without my further participation."

"You can't," they all said.

"I can," he said. Then he turned and walked out the door with his head high and a big fat smile on his face.

DRIVING HOME, Zachary listened to the radio news.

The star of a popular TV show was spotted on the beach without makeup.

A former president's daughter had sustained a spider bite, and was coping.

At home, Zachary went straight to April Michael's room. He pressed his forehead against the tank. It felt cool. It felt nice.

Then he made his way upstairs to Seth's room.

Zachary had been happy when he left the boardroom, but now his eyes clouded again.

It wasn't enough. Things would have to change all over.

He stared at the San Francisco 49ers helmet printed on Seth's bedspread. He stared until the helmet didn't look like a helmet anymore, the way things do when you stare at them.

One small step at a time, he thought, and he fell asleep like that, with his eyes open.

38.

An Already Pretty Embarrassing Life

Los Angeles, Fall 2003

THINK IT OVER would be filmed live, when possible.

It began with a knock on a door.

The door was opened by Scott Newill, an average-looking man who happened to be out of work. He was married to an average-looking woman he'd met in college. They were both forty years old.

Scott Newill gaped at the cameras and the Devil, and said, "You're that Scratch guy."

And Scratch, looking impossibly cool in a designer suit and wraparound shades, said, "That's right, Scott. Can we come in and have a word with you?"

And Scott Newill said "Yes," and they all went in and sat around the living room and had a talk.

It went like this:

Scratch showed Scott Newill a photograph, an elementary school photograph over thirty years old (the TV audience also got a look at the photograph, at Scott Newill when he was a wimpy little seven-year-old, and they laughed in their two million living rooms).

"Do you recognize *this* guy?" Scratch asked, showing him a second photograph.

Newill hesitated.

For the first time he looked like he wished Johnny Scratch and his people, including the two million, had gone somewhere else.

"That's Phil Hilbert," said Scratch, "isn't it? The bully who used to beat you up every day, I mean *every single day,* when you were in second grade?"

"He beat up a lot of kids," said Newill, embarrassed.

"Yeah, but mostly you. Wouldn't you like to get some payback, Scott?"

Then they cut to a commercial for something called the White Pill, a new drug that made you feel nice inside.

When they came back, Scratch offered Newill five thousand dollars to go beat up Phil Hilbert.

"He lives eight blocks from here," said Scratch. "We can be there by the end of the next break. All you have to do is knock on his door, and when he answers, punch that asshole in the face."

Newill said it was a ridiculous thing to ask a grown man to do. His wife, off camera, remarked that it wouldn't be the first childish thing he'd ever done, and the TV audience got the impression that Mrs. Newill was thinking about how much they could use the five thousand dollars. They also got the sense that if Newill didn't step up to this particular live-TV challenge, he was going to get made fun of for the rest of his already pretty embarrassing life.

When they came back from the second White Pill break, Newill was knocking at the door of a small, run-down bungalow with one boarded-up window.

The door opened, and there was Phil Hilbert.

He had been a large child. He had grown into a large adult, but something had happened.

He was a sick, shrunken man with all the signs of a bad cancer fight.

Newill looked over his shoulder at Scratch, who gazed back, expressionless.

The TV audience froze. People held their breath, Cheetos halfway to their mouth.

Newill punched him.

Coast to coast, people gasped.

It wasn't a good punch. But it was enough to seal the five thousand. Newill turned away, wearing a complicated look. The cameras zeroed in.

Phil Hilbert, a tough bastard, cancer or not, grabbed Newill by the shoulder, and hit him in the neck hard enough to drop him. Newill got up and took another swing, but Hilbert, coughing, kicked him down and stomped on his wrist.

Then he went back in his house and shut the door. Newill lay on the concrete walk, obviously trying not to cry. The cameras filmed a check for five grand placed gently over his left ear, and then the credits rolled.

THE DEVIL DROPPED BY Memory's room the next day.

"We debuted at number one in the ratings," he told her, kneeling by her bed. "That's eight hundred places ahead of your Coma Channel. You might even say it makes your ratings look a little *sleepy*."

Only the Devil sinks low enough to fuck with people when they're in a coma.

Memory's hands had curled into fists. Sometimes the nurses straightened her fingers, in order to trim her nails, to keep her nails from growing right through her palms.

"Well," said the Devil, in a high-pitched voice, pretending to be Memory, "congratulations on your hugely successful TV show."

"Thank you, baby," he answered, in his own voice, standing to go. He kissed her on the forehead.

Then he flew out west to Jenna's, and she screamed "Johnnyyyyyyyyyyyyyyy!" and made him give her a pony ride before they went out and got drunk and got ice cream, and got photographed a lot, celebrating.

39.

His Big Season Opener

Los Angeles, 2003

FOR A WEEK AFTER his big season opener, the Devil got mixed reactions in public.

Driving around in the Kennedy limo, top down, John Scratch was easily recognized. People shouted at him and took pictures with their phones.

Others watched him pass in an uncomfortable silence.

He kept wondering what Memory would think. About the show, and other things. The weather. Lightbulbs. Medical billing. Ostriches. She had become his compass, he admitted. He needed her.

Pulling up to a stop sign, the Devil waved to fans. Girls hooted at him. Some boys pumped their fists in the air.

Needed? He was getting soft.

He was getting soft because the *world* was getting soft.

"Humans have such small souls these days," he growled. "We live in small times. Otherwise people would talk about stuff that really happened, not what they saw on TV last night.

"Who are you pissed at?" he asked, as if in reply. "What's the *real* problem here?"

He realized he was sitting at a stoplight, hyperventilating and talking to himself.

Some girls on the opposite corner took his picture.

LIKE A SNAPPING TURTLE, he hardened on the outside. His eyes were charismatic lances; his TV smile shone like a mouthful of combat knives. He tried not to think about what was happening on the *inside.* He didn't look there anymore.

There were more shows to film, of course, now that they knew *Think It Over* was solid TV gold.

They filmed a show in a school, where he dared a teacher to tell the parents of his students what they really needed to hear. So the guy told a group of parents, at Open House, what everyone knew but wouldn't say: that kids in America were getting dumber by the minute because parents, at home, didn't challenge them to read or behave themselves. The parents got indignant. The teacher got fired, but he walked to his car with a big smile on his face.

They filmed a show where anonymous and respectable people, pillars of communities, were offered five hundred dollars to walk around the parking lot of a Babies "R" Us letting the air out of pregnant women's tires. Most of them wouldn't do it. It was a surprising episode. They came back the next week and offered a thousand, and it was a whole different story.

Their ratings went up and up.

Then they did a show with a woman whose husband beat her and threatened to kill her if she left, and she had been going around saying she was going to kill him, first.

This show became known as "The Mistake."

John Scratch showed up and dared the woman to put her money where her mouth was. The producers assumed that she wouldn't be able to do it, and the point would be that saying something like that and doing it were two different things. The night of the show, she let the cameras in the house an hour before the abusive jerk got home from work. When he walked through the door, she opened a cabinet, pulled out a sword—a *sword!*—and ran him straight through the gut.

The camera crew, and Scratch himself, came diving out of the next room and pulled her off, but the jerk died on the way to the hospital.

His wife went off to prison with her head high.

The Devil had better lawyers, so he got out on bail for a while before his trial started. Right away, he fled south to the Never-ending Mexican Party.

People brought him drinks and pills, and showed him new dances. He began to feel almost free, but the lawyers found him and brought him back to reality.

"Don't get your hopes up," they cautioned. "You're going up the river unless you know some kind of magic spell, ha-ha."

Ha-ha. Assholes.

He was drinking alone in a third-floor bedroom when the Great Dane, Fidel, appeared before him.

"Listen," said Fidel. "You're going to learn something in prison. Something hard, but very important."

"Far out," belched the Devil.

Fidel turned to go, but stopped at the door.

"Just so you know," he said, "the thing you're going to learn? It's something dogs have known for a long time."

Then he lifted his leg, drowned a basket of geraniums, and disappeared around the corner.

40.

The Devil Goes to Prison

San Quentin, Spring 2004

THE COURT GAVE THE Devil three years, and locked him away.

He could have escaped with a snap of his fingers, of course. But the idea of going to prison intrigued him, and he decided to serve out his sentence.

He learned more than he bargained for.

The first day he was there, a skinhead gang dragged a black inmate into the shower, held him up to one of the nozzles, and forced water into him until he drowned. The Devil, with a lot of other men, stood back and watched.

You had to admire their inventiveness, he thought.

He accepted a job mopping floors, and that's what he was doing when the Aryan Brotherhood sent a kid named Ernie to talk to him.

"Hey, white brother," said Ernie. You'd think an Aryan recruiter would be a huge corn-fed dude with swastika ink, but not Ernie. Ernie had boobs, as if his hormones didn't know he was male. Ernie must have run to the Aryan Brotherhood to keep worse things from happening to him.

I'm not *white,* dammit! thought the Devil, gritting his teeth.

"No thanks," he told Ernie.

"Got a problem with the Aryan Brotherhood?" asked Ernie.

The Devil nodded.

Ernie's brow furrowed. He was out of things to say.

The next day, another Aryan showed up, and this second recruiter was everything Ernie had not been. He was corn-fed. He had swastikas tattooed on both sides of his neck.

He took the Devil's mop, placed it in the bucket, and whispered, "We seen your show on TV. Good show. They do reruns, since you been in here."

"I didn't know that," said the Devil. He reached for his mop, but the corn-fed Aryan slapped his hand away.

"Ernie says you got a big mouth."

The Devil didn't answer, so the Aryan hit him. The Devil staggered against the wall. The dayroom regulars, black and white and Puerto Rican and Mexican, started wandering over.

The Aryan looked like he was about to hit the Devil again, but something happened. What happened, exactly, depended on who you asked.

Some said the Devil forked his fingers at his big white enemy. Some swore they heard him say *"Je vous corse!"* Others said the Devil said nothing, but flashed his eyes like the flash on a camera. Others said he just stood there and looked sort of annoyed.

What all agreed on was that the Aryan's penis fell off, tumbled down the inside of his left jumpsuit leg, and rolled onto the floor. The Aryan went out of his mind, screaming, and guards poured in. They were going to haul the Devil off to solitary until they saw what had happened, and were told the Devil hadn't lifted a finger.

Prison docs fumbled the reattachment, and that was the last the Devil heard from the Aryan Brotherhood.

JENNA STEELE CAME to visit when he'd been in prison for a year.

"You abandoned me," she snapped into the visitors' phone, tapping the window with a long, black nail.

"I've been in here," he pointed out.

"How selfish is that?" she cried, and stomped away, forgetting her purse, coming back for it, and stomping away again.

AN UNHOLY REPUTATION began to hover and whisper about the Devil. His fellow inmates made efforts to gain his approval.

They showed him things, sometimes. Things calculated to impress in the only way they knew how.

The leader of the Vietnamese gang showed him a collection of human scalps.

The oldest inmate, a ninety-year-old man-rapist who worked in the cafeteria, showed him a hole in his leg big enough to lower a dead rat through.

Someone left him a freshly cut human ear, like a Secret Santa gift.

Even the guards wanted to impress him. He woke up one night and found three of them in his cell, peering at him over the edge of his top-bunk mattress.

"Come with us," said one.

"Come with us," echoed the other two.

They stepped back and let him climb down, and then led him through the double doors leading to the next block, through the darkened cafeteria and the weight room, to a stairway leading down, down, down, to the special dungeon cells every prison has but doesn't talk about. There, they locked him in a cell with another prisoner, saying, "We thought you might find this interesting."

The Devil was puzzled. Then his eyes adjusted, and he got a look at his cellmate.

His cellmate was a skeleton.

A human approximation, anyway. He breathed, he had eyes that looked here and there. But his hair was gone, and so were his teeth.

"How long have you been in here, bro?" asked the Devil.

The prisoner made a gagging noise. The Devil realized that this was the man's attempt at language. His mind was peanut butter.

The Devil tried to get his cellmate to count to five, to say his name, to say how old he was or what year he thought it was. But all he could ever get was the gagging.

At mealtimes, the man moved. He crawled, moaning, to the slot near the floor, ate from his tray right where it appeared, and pushed it listlessly back into the corridor. Then he crawled back and sat down again.

When the guards let the Devil out, they let him know that this man had been in solitary for fifteen years. He was their prize, their cautionary tale.

The guards had to be worse than the prisoners, explained the guards.

It made sense.

AFTER THE GUARDS showed him their pet, the Devil found prison more disturbing than before. These were *people*? This was the species he'd thought could challenge God?

He almost let himself out. But staying had become an exercise in discipline and pain management, like a kung fu master holding his palm over a burning candle.

He tried to stop thinking about the creature in the dungeon, but couldn't. And when you couldn't stop thinking about something, the Devil knew, your subconscious was trying to get your attention.

Hiroshima and Auschwitz should have clued him in, he thought. A thousand things should have clued him in, but they hadn't grabbed his attention the way this single, mangled human had finally done.

He had raised humanity as if they were his child. Like any parent, he believed his child's mistakes were just growing pains. What if you had a kid, and like all kids, he wasn't perfect, but you had high hopes for him, and sometimes he was bright and showed promise. Sometimes he even amazed you. When he was mean to other kids, you tried to teach him better. You tried not to notice when he pulled wings off flies. He would grow out of these things, you thought. But what do you do the day you find out he's been killing people and burying them in the vegetable garden?

That wasn't being a proud rebel. That was just being a sick-ass motherfucker.

The Devil came smashing out of prison like a comic-book demon.

HE WAS BONES and flames on a flying motorcycle, screaming east like a meteor, to New York, where he burned to a stop beside Memory's bed. He locked the door and switched the Coma Channel to play reruns.

"Wake up," he commanded. His voice cracked.

She lay still.

He burned himself naked. He froze himself hard.

He missed her, *wanted her,* so badly. He was sick with the crazy tide that comes with panic and not knowing what to think or do.

He gathered her in his arms, his anguish and frustration and rage boiling though him. But he wasn't soothed—his tongue uncoiled like a dragon's. He fought himself, but the engine of want began to churn out the hope that love and need and desire this strong might bring her back, the way it had Arden—and that loneliness fed the engine, too, until it was all he could do to be tender. It almost made him scream, but he curled his fists until his knuckles burst and went slowly—and waited until he felt her loosen around him somewhat, before thrusting, once, twice—and erupted with a roar.

He pulled free, shivering over her like a rag doll propped on its haunches. Head hanging, hair hanging, horns gleaming.

Memory lay still.

The Devil crouched there breathing, simply breathing, for some time, before he admitted to himself that she was not going to wake up. He gently smoothed her hair back into place, tidied her bed, and kissed her goodbye.

He fled the dawn across the sky and shrank at last back into his cell.

He didn't know what to think. Of what he had done. Of himself. Of people. Of anything.

So he didn't think at all. He just sat there, smelling like smoke.

TIME PASSED like a long, dry fart.

When fourteen months had gone by, they came and got him and let him out.

Just like any other prisoner, he looked older, and was smaller in some ways, and haunted.

When they gave him back his cell phone, there were nine thousand calls stacked up, mostly from the TV studio.

He dialed.

"Hello?" said the phone.

"John Scratch," he said.

And the phone got all excited and told him they had decided to pick up *Think It Over* right where they'd left off, minus the felony programming.

He should say "No," he knew.

And just like that, right there at the prison bus stop, the Devil understood the thing he'd been trying not to understand.

People were nothing special, after all. They were just animals. Humanity was just a fiction he had created to help himself believe he had a chance to get Arden back. Evolution hadn't produced humans yet, just a Frankenstein monster that kind of *looked* human.

Maybe he had known this, even before prison. He had always wanted to think that one day they'd shake off the spell, stand up, and say, "Enough is enough! We've become addicted to stupidity! Leapin' lizards, we're better than this!"

That's what humans would do. They would break the addiction.

Except it wasn't an addiction. Stupidity was their natural state. Their shiny civilizations were nothing more than a cheap coat of paint, the work of a few bright people, stolen and perverted by a world of village idiots.

Egypt. Rome. Smoke.

Camelot. America. Mirrors.

The realization became bright and clear, as if his brain were a sun made of glass.

The Devil threw up down the front of his cheap, complimentary getting-out-of-prison suit, and people at the prison bus stop moved away and pretended nothing was wrong.

"JOHNNY?" SAID HIS CELL PHONE. "We want to restart the show as soon as possible. John?"

Think It Over wasn't going to jar people awake, the Devil knew. It was animal cruelty, pure and simple, like playing mean tricks on puppies.

So what? Who was he, Mother Teresa? No, he was the fucking Devil, so watch out.

"Soon as possible," he told the phone, snarling. "Great. I'll be there."

The phone gave a cheer and asked if he needed any money or drugs or pussy or anything.

THE DEVIL PUT HIS PHONE in his pocket, rode a bus to L.A., got the death limo out of mothballs, and drove east, straight to Memory's bedside.

He curled up on the windowsill, thinking, Wake up, wake up.

Even though she was one of them, he still felt alone without her.

The Devil. Really, what was that? The people-animals ran laps around him when it came to darkness, to being able to live in sickness and thrive on death. For the first time in his life, he realized that what he was maybe wasn't so much. Just built to last, was all.

He tried to shake it off, but it was like a fly that kept buzzing back.

41. Pocahontas

The New World, 1608

THE DEVIL FELT TIRED in a way he'd never felt before.

Kneeling beside Memory's bed, both hands wrapped around her fists, he fell asleep and dreamed of the one thing he always tried so hard not to remember. He had lost the strength to protect himself from pain.

The memory took him back four hundred years, into the woods, when the woods were deep and dark. He had come across the sea, to the new world behind the sunset, where he hunted with his hands and slept on raw earth.

THE PEOPLE WHO LIVED THERE called themselves the Falling Water People and they were afraid of him. They drew lots to see who would try to kill him.

A young hunter named Wahsinatawah—"Great Big Head"—chanced to be elected, and he approached the Devil without fear.

Great Big Head was well named. His enormous head nearly creaked atop his shoulders, which had grown muscular in order to support it. Unfortunately for Wahsinatawah, girls found his great head repulsive. He had given up all hope of ever getting one of them to become his wife, and turned all his strength and all his heart to the hunt. He made himself a peerless hunter. Now he hunted the strange, terrible creature.

Three days into the woods, Wahsinatawah spied a great buck deer leaping through the trees. Instinctively, he nocked an arrow and took aim, muttering a prayer—

Thud! Something slammed into his left leg.

An arrow! He'd been *shot*!

Something zipped through the brush over his head, and the buck was shot, too. It tumbled across a thicket, pierced through the heart.

The Devil appeared up the trail. He held a bow in one hand, and a bone knife in his teeth. He approached Wahsinatawah, smoking a bluebird in a long clay pipe.

"You shot me," Watsinatawah said to the Devil.

"You were about to shoot my deer. I chased him all the way from the river."

The Devil gave Wahsinatawah a narrow-eyed look, marveling at the size of his head.

"Tell you what," he said, pointing with the stem of his pipe at Wahsinatawah's bleeding leg. "Either I can pull that loose and heal it for you, or you can draw an arrow of your own and shoot me through the heart. Only be warned: Choose to shoot me and miss, and it will be my turn."

Wahsinatawah chewed his lip. The hunter in him was hypnotized by the thought of shooting the Devil and carrying him back to his village. It was the only thing that might get him a wife.

"I'll shoot," he decided.

"It is a good day to die," said the Devil, backing off a little distance and closing his eyes.

Watsinatawah nocked an arrow, took aim, and let fly.

There came a hard *thunk* as if the arrow had gone astray and lodged in a tree, but it hadn't. It quivered right on target, stuck in the Devil's chest as if he were made of wood.

"Oh, fuck," said Wahsinatawah as the Devil nocked an arrow of his own. He tried to think of something wise and clever, something lifesaving, to say.

The Devil loosed his arrow—

—and missed. The arrow slashed off into the woods.

Something had distracted the Devil. Watsinatawah turned to see a girl in a buckskin dress, with wild, burning eyes, kneeling beside the dying buck. She waved her hands over the deer, then fell forward as if embracing it.

The Devil walked toward her. The girl whipped upright, staring.

Her eyes were uncertain, but not fearful. The Devil opened his mouth to say something to her, but she whirled and shot away through the woods before he could manage a sound.

The Devil was a streak, right behind her.

Wahsinatawah drew his knife, and was torn between whether to cut the arrow from his leg or dress out the deer.

He did the deer first. Then his leg. Then he passed out.

"STOP, GIRL!" the Devil commanded.

"Why?" she called out. "So you can drag me home to eat?"

"I'm not a monster," he said.

"You're the Devil, aren't you?"

The Devil leaped forward, scooped her up, and came to a stop with her in his arms.

"Being the Devil and being a monster are not the same thing," he explained.

She wrapped her arms around his neck, lifted her head, and looked into his eyes. She must have liked what she saw.

"Take me swimming," she said.

WAHSINATAWAH WOKE UP in the weeds, with the dead buck hanging nearby, and felt a touch of fever behind his eyes. He knew he would have to get home and let the healer rub snake piss on the wound, or it would kill him. Cutting down the deer, he packed up the best meat and limped off through the forest.

If he hadn't been distracted with fever, things might have gone better for him.

Certainly he would have heard voices, or maybe even smelled something out of place. As it happened, though, he came stumbling into a clearing where five men sat around a smoky campfire. They wore shining helmets, and had great, horrible beards and bad eyes and pale skin, like dead men.

They stared at him, astonished by his sudden appearance and his enormous head, but they got over it quickly, and clubbed him unconscious.

AT THE RIVER, the Devil was surprised when the girl stepped out of her dress without hesitation, and plunged into the water.

He followed.

They didn't play games with each other. There were no coy words, no hard to get. Just a certain looking and knowing and wanting. In minutes, they had fallen in love. It happens that way sometimes.

They came together in the water like one fish. She rubbed against him, gasping, and although the Devil's desire was quickly obvious, she stopped short of taking him inside her. The Devil ground his teeth, but didn't press her.

They curled up together amid cypress roots, and she told him she was called Pocahontas, that her father was a chief and her brothers were hunters, and that they were likely to come looking for her if she didn't return home in a day or two.

He would take her back to her father and brothers, and they would be married. He didn't say so, but he didn't have to. And she didn't agree, not in so many words, but she didn't have to either.

THE DEVIL couldn't sleep.

He was troubled with love.

Not for the first time. He had taken wives, from time to time. Always, though, he reserved the very core of his heart for Arden. Until now.

Was it ridiculous to compare a thousand hundred years with the sport of a single afternoon?

But it wasn't a trial of arithmetic. He was in love, that was all, and for the first time he thought perhaps it was time to settle for what he could have and grasp here on Earth. Pocahontas was who she was, and he wanted to dive into it like a river, run in it like a forest, and hunt there, and sleep under its stars.

He said her name, once, quietly, and finally fell asleep.

IN THE MORNING, he awoke to find that she had captured fish with her bare hands, and cooked them, wrapped in leaves. They ate, and they swam again, and after a while they dressed and turned toward her village.

They were holding hands, lost in separate thoughts, when they made exactly the same mistake poor Wahsinatawah had made. They walked into a broad, open field, and there on the other side were white men in silver helmets keeping watch outside a crude fort.

The Devil dropped out of sight in the tall weeds, pulling Pocahontas down with him, cursing.

"Who—?" she whispered, curious about the white men just as she seemed curious about everything.

He had to pull her down again, shushing her.

He had come a long way to get away from white men. No good could come of them crossing the ocean. He would have to convince her of this. Just as he was about to explain it to her, something happened to silence him.

Five white men emerged from the woods not too far away, dragging Wahsinatawah between them.

"Your friend," whispered Pocahontas.

"He's not—"

"You have to help him. Or else I will."

"Fine," sighed the Devil. He was her slave. He wondered if she knew it.

THAT NIGHT, the Devil slipped over the stockade wall, and found a shadow to hide in.

A lot of pale men sat around various cook fires, talking in low tones, sometimes pausing to eye the treetops swaying above and beyond their fort, as if they feared the night and the land itself.

Following his nose from shadow to shadow, the Devil found Wahsinatawah writhing on a wooden table, held down by white men stripped to the waist. They were digging in his wounds with red-hot knives. The Devil understood that these men were trying to help the young hunter. To heal him. Maybe to slaughter and eat him later, who knew?

The Devil stepped up to this assembly, nine feet tall, breathing fire. They scattered to hide in barrels and sheds, and the Devil picked up Wahsinatawah like a dead turkey and leaped with him over the wall.

Into the meadow, Pocahontas had lashed together a rough sled of saplings and green branches, upon which Wahsinatawah could be pulled through the woods.

The young hunter had fallen unconscious immediately upon his rescue. He now woke up to say "Thank you," and stayed awake just long enough to have a peek up Pocahontas's skirt.

THE DEVIL WASN'T too surprised when he sniffed the air, just before dawn broke, and listened to the wind, and discovered that they had been followed.

Goddammit! All he wanted to do was hold Pocahontas and sing songs to her and put his knobby wooden cock in her and be happy, and these white men were fucking it all up.

He put down his side of the travois, ran deerlike through the woods, over moss-fat stones and dead trees, until he nearly stumbled over what looked like a knight.

The Devil remembered knights. This one wore chest armor, and had stopped to refresh himself at a stream. He had dipped his helmet in the cool water and appeared quite relaxed, but the moment the Devil came flying out of the woods, he hopped to his feet and drew a long, bright sword.

The Devil allowed the sword to break off in his side, and bashed the knight unconscious with his fist. The man went down hard in the creek, and would have drowned if the Devil hadn't pulled him onto the sand.

As he was performing this act of mercy, three very serious-looking hunters—Falling Water men—came jogging up the creek bed, hallooing and waving.

It took a minimum of conversation to make it plain that these fellows were looking for their sister. The Devil introduced himself with discretion, and, with the armored man slung over his considerable shoulder, led them back to where Pocahontas sat doing her best to keep poor Wahsinatawah's wounds clean, and humming a prayer-song to herself.

She leaped up when she saw her brothers, who hugged her and fussed over her and scolded her some. Then this strange party struck out together for home, arriving just in time for lunch.

"Just in time for lunch!" cried the village children, leaping about Pocahontas.

Pocahontas beamed, hoisting a tiny girl on one hip, and placing a boy on the Devil's shoulders. The remainder of the children boiled around them as they walked, clutching at her dress, reaching for her hands, and singing her name.

Children, the Devil, saw, loved Pocahontas the way animals loved him.

LUNCH, SERVED IN THE VILLAGE longhouse, took a while. There were speeches.

There was a speech from each of Pocahontas's brothers, welcoming the Devil to their village and hearth, wondering aloud what his intentions were and what he'd already tried. Their father, a thick, strong man of middle years, wondered more about the white man in the damaged armor. The Devil had left him propped up outside the door, and every once in a while they heard a metallic *ding!* as the village children threw rocks at him.

It was decided that they would lay the white man on a stone and smash his head. "Then we'll go kill the rest of them, too," said the chief.

The three brothers stripped the woozy, terrified knight to his pantaloons, dragged him to a big rock in the middle of the village, and forced him to rest his head on it. The eldest brother was swinging a war club around his head when Pocahontas came storming through the crowd and threw herself over the knight in a thoroughly inappropriate way.

"Get *off* of him!" commanded her father.

She did get off, but she stood over him like a mother lynx, tense and hissing.

"This is senseless!" she spat.

No one met her eyes.

"They will come here," answered her eldest brother. "More and more of them. It's true, and you know it."

She didn't answer him. She looked at the Devil, who stepped forward. They parted for him, and he carried the white man away from the stone and out of the village, with Pocahontas beside him, still angry, still glaring.

"Fools," she hissed.

She banged on the white man's armor. "Him and his kind, too."

They passed over streams and open meadows until they came to the edge of the land's broadest river.

There was a different look in her eyes when she said she wanted to stop there, a look like a clear sky or clear water. She reached between his leggings, took hold of him in a way she hadn't before, and made him gasp. Her dress came apart like spidersilk in his fingers, and then they were in the water.

The Devil had seen Pocahontas run like a doe and swim like a fish, but this did nothing to presage the animal she now became. His erection wobbled between them, and she drove herself upon it with a scream, convulsing in every part, tightening around him like a snake. They slipped underwater, twisting until their lungs burst and they surfaced, shrouded in her hair, gulping air. She made love to him as if she meant to devour him, opening her legs until her hip joints popped, until their eyes locked and stayed locked, and they were tender with each other the way lions must be tender.

When they had exhausted each other, Pocahontas and the Devil sprawled naked on the sand. The Devil reached for her, afraid she'd be cold, but she pulled away.

What?

"I can't," she said.

"Can't what?"

"I can't . . . how can I say it? I can't *be* this." And she gestured in frustration, indicating herself, her body.

Couldn't be what? Flesh? Human?

"It's too much," she said. "It's like lightning! It's like having a storm inside me!"

He held her face in his hands, and looked deep, and there she was.

"Arden," he gasped.

"Yes."

They held each other's eyes for a long time. Long enough for shadows to shift around them. For the tide to turn in the river, and fall back toward the ocean, and for gulls to begin their evening cries.

SHE EXPLAINED THAT the body she wore, this nut-colored girl-goddess, was not hers. She had chosen to share a body already human, already grown, because she thought maybe this way she wouldn't be shocked by the world and its flesh.

"But it's too much."

"You can—" he began, desperate.

"I *can't*!" she wailed, beating at his chest. "You don't understand! It's like taking a creature bred in a cave and plunging it into the sun! It's like being on *fire*!"

"Yes!" he crowed. "Wonderful, glorious *fire*!"

"I hate it!" she screamed, and, like a slippery fish, squirmed loose. She ran, and he gave chase.

It was like before, except without joy or the thrill of play. It seemed to the Devil that he was trying to catch everything he thought he'd given up, and the thing he'd given it up for. Without her, there was nothing.

With a wild leap, he bore her to the sand, turned her over, and struggled for words.

But she was gone.

The girl in his arms was a magnificent woman-child, but she was only that.

He gathered his pride. He still had that. He spoke to the girl, wanting to make her feel safe, but this proved unnecessary. She knew nothing of the angel who had possessed her. Instead, she remembered everything that had happened as if she had done it herself. She was proud of her words at the killing stone. She was glad about what they had done in the river. She did not quite remember the things that had been said afterward, or why she had run from him, but shrugged it off the way young people do, blaming youth and passion.

She resolved upon taking the white man to his fortress town, and maybe they would all become friends. Maybe they could keep fear from turning into fighting.

Even without Arden inside her, thought the Devil, this girl had some fallen-angel blood in her family, way back sometime.

Walking naked beside him as they returned down the beach, she was not self-conscious. Indeed, she held up her head and seemed to appreciate the wind in her hair and on her skin, even to appreciate the wind in *his* hair, and the woodenness and smoothness of *his* skin, taking his arm as they walked.

He nearly choked, thinking of Arden, but remembered that he was proud.

HE SPENT THE NEXT YEAR grasping at shadows.

They lived together in a lodge of green branches and buckskin, between the forest and a slow, deep stream. He built wickets and caught fish, and they hunted together and sang hunting songs together, and when they made love they looked deep inside each other with a sadness neither spoke of.

He knew he should leave her, but he couldn't.

She allowed each day, as it came, to be enough. She loved the man-demon who was sometimes able to love her back. She felt the Earth turning beneath her feet, and let that be enough, too, and was thankful.

They lived together that way for four seasons.

The Devil had conquered Assyria and ruled Egypt and driven Sumeria to its knees, but he wasn't strong enough to walk out on Pocahontas.

REALLY, WHEN HE LOOKED BACK on it, *she* left *him*.

Winter came, and with it a long, heavy snow, until branches creaked and the forest sighed as if turning in its sleep.

Pocahontas worried about the white men, in the fortress they were calling Jamestown. The Devil awakened one night to find her sitting up. She had let the deerskin blankets slip aside, and was shivering.

"They'll starve," she said.

"Yes," he answered.

It was true. He had watched them from the trees, eating their leather shoes and belts. Eating their dead. Eyeing one another like hungry rats.

He almost said, "Let them starve," and she almost said, "Who will we become if we allow such a thing?"

THEY BROUGHT GAME to the stockade gates, and roasted corn. They brought blankets. They told the white men what trees to cut for wood that would burn hot and burn slowly, and where the sturgeon swam in the winter, and could be caught with nets, sleeping.

The white man they had saved came forward. He was grateful, and treated them with respect. Now that he was not lost in the woods or about to be killed, he had a good and intelligent light in his eyes, a rare light. The Devil saw that he was a complicated man who wanted complicated things.

The man wanted Pocahontas to stay. She could be of such value to them.

She shook her head, smiling, and touched the white man's cheek. Then they left together, she and the Devil, and returned to their strange, lonely home.

HER BROTHERS VISITED, painted for war, and told Pocahontas and the Devil how their father had decided that the whites and their fortress must be pushed into the river. They must be stopped before their numbers were too many.

Pocahontas told them "No!"

But they didn't listen. They warned her, warned the Devil, to leave their lodge, because soon it would not be safe there.

"Come back to the village with us," they said, but they knew their sister's answer without having to hear it.

"Make yourself a spear and come with us," they told the Devil, who filled his pipe and ignored them.

The brothers left, and that night Pocahontas slipped away to the fortress and warned the white men there.

She stayed with them, then. She had no choice, nowhere else to go.

Pain lanced the Devil's heart.

He coughed and gasped, but it wasn't his heart, really. It was his whole self feeling his love being torn from him. Or worse, getting up and walking away.

He felt the weight of his years, which was a weight too vast even for an immortal soul. The only thing that could bear such weight was the Earth itself.

So the Devil returned to the Earth for a time. As he had after Egypt, and after Rome. He walked with a bleak stare into the mightiest, deepest, most unknown forest, among great trees and ancient stones, and there he crouched and closed his eyes and let the snow cover him, let the ice harden on him until he, too, was like a stone. And he stayed that way across five summers or more, until one day two hunters, Corn People, traveling afar, came upon him and remarked how this stone was so like a man. Not just a man, but a man who had been saddened beyond endurance. They poked him with their spears, just as you might stir coals in a fire or dry leaves with your foot, and cried out in surprise when the stone stood, cracking and creaking and shedding ice, gave them a sleepy, irritated look, and stumbled away, yawning.

The hunters looked at one another in disbelief, and looked off after the Devil until he was out of sight, walking north.

Then they continued hunting. The deep woods were probably the same everywhere in the world, they thought. Strange things happened there and abided there, and if you wandered there, you got what you deserved.

42.

A Silence Encompassing a Thousand Hundred Years

New York, 2005

LEAVING THE DREAM was like leaving the woods at night.

The dark of the woods became the dark of the hospital room, where the Devil had fallen half out of his chair, and sprawled across Memory's legs. His throat ached from snoring, and drool soaked his cheek.

He drew himself up straight.

Then he jumped in the chair, startled.

Memory's eyes were open. She was looking at him.

MEMORY TRIED TO SPEAK, but couldn't.

Her jaw creaked. Muscles and tendons were shrunken tight.

Her throat pulsed, but not in a useful way.

There were plenty of things Memory would have liked to talk about, now that the Devil was awake.

Her amnesia was gone, for one thing.

The memories that flooded in were hard to grasp, at first. But she had been awake for an hour now, and was dealing with it.

It's not easy, waking up and remembering that you are an angel.

It's not easy remembering that you gave yourself amnesia because you knew if you forgot you were an angel, you might be able to get used to life as an animal.

Which you wanted very badly, because your boyfriend, the Devil, lived down here. The Devil, who had been your boyfriend for a shockingly long time.

Your boyfriend, the Devil, who had been asleep across your legs, and who now sat up in his chair, looking at you.

You would have liked to say something, you really would. But you couldn't.

He had figured it out, too.

"Arden," he said.

Memory nodded.

A single tear fell from the Devil's right eye.

He wanted to ask if she planned to stay this time, but wasn't sure he could handle the answer. So they sat like that in a silence encompassing all the years they had been apart, and Memory kept on remembering things, *knowing* things.

She felt her body around her, pinched and dry, shrunken like a mummy. But she felt and knew something else, too.

She was pregnant.

Pregnant?

"How—?" she tried to say, but only croaked.

The Devil sat there looking at her, with that one tear falling down his face.

How, indeed!

"Oo ASTARD!" she screamed through locked teeth.

"What?" he said, his eyes worried. He leaned closer.

Good thing for him that her muscles were out of tune. He had no idea that she was straining to beat the hell out of him. As it happened, all she could do was sit there and give him an intense stare.

She tired quickly, and calmed down.

She remembered the strange night in Rome, across a universe of time, when he had held her with such love that it made him shake, trying to bring her back to him. He had tried it again, only this time there wasn't enough left of him to do it right. What was happening to him? Maybe angels, on Earth, waxed and waned like the moon. Maybe they grew old, at last, and died. Maybe they fell asleep . . . what was the difference?

She wouldn't allow it. She would protect him from time itself, if necessary. From *himself,* if necessary.

There was no way she would let him just wink out or fade, not now when, finally—

She lay still, feeling the odd warmth below her belly, the tiny pulse.

Did he know?

She wouldn't tell him. Not yet. Serve him right.

He took her hand. Another tear left his eye.

He quietly cried himself to sleep in his chair, almost four years of waiting finally catching up with him.

He snored horrible snores, beastly and snaggletoothed.

"Astard," Memory croaked at him.

She commanded her arm to work, and gently stroked his hair.

SHE MADE AN EFFORT to stretch her arms and legs. To crack her neck and roll her head around. To work her jaw until it opened and shut. To breathe in and out, and swallow and think and be awake.

Around midafternoon, some guys from the Coma Channel burst in, having caught her awakening on the live feed, from the hidden camera in the ceiling.

"We'll do a special!" they crowed.

One of them shook her hand, which hurt.

"We'll do a miniseries!" cried another.

Her exercises paid off. First she threw a water pitcher at them, then the cup, and both pillows. Mostly it was the look in her eyes, which seemed superhuman, somehow, and pissed off. When she threatened to rip down the hidden camera and feed it to them, they scuttled out of the room sideways, afraid to turn their backs on her.

The Devil slept through it all.

43.

The Shining Moment

Washington, 1962

THE DEVIL HAD FALLEN ASLEEP thinking how good things could be now, and from now on, if they didn't screw it up.

Things had been good before, after all, and then gone south.

He dreamed of a time when he'd almost thought they had it made, down here on Earth, just a few decades back, when America had a nifty new president called JFK.

JFK HAD BEEN HANDSOME. He was a war hero. He had a million-dollar smile and a million-dollar wife and a million dollars. People loved him whether they meant to or not, and everything he did just installed him deeper in the department stores of their hearts.

Trouble was, it was a dangerous time, too. America and Russia each had thousands of hydrogen bombs, and any day they might blow up the planet. Just when there were so many new consumer products to buy, and department stores in which to buy them.

It would be just like people, thought the Devil, to commit a whole planet full of suicide just when things were going so well. JFK might be a swell guy, but the Devil doubted he, or any other human, no matter how handsome, could stop the Unthinkable once it got rolling.

Which was why the Devil took a jet airplane flight to Washington, caught a taxi to Pennsylvania Avenue, slipped past the White House guards and up to the second-floor residence, where he found JFK eating breakfast alone, reading the first of several newspapers.

The Devil flew in through his ear and curled up in his brain and looked out through the president's eyes.

Time to go to work. Just as soon as he finished the president's breakfast.

JFK's wife wafted into the room just then, wearing a robe of loose-fitting silk.

The Devil's eyebrows shot up.

Breakfast and work could both wait a little while, he decided.

SOME THINGS CHANGED around the White House, in those first few weeks. For one thing, JFK suddenly paid a lot more attention to his wife. The poor gal didn't know what hit her.

"What's got *into* you?" she gasped once, after the fifth time during one Tuesday morning.

JFK had a brother named RFK, whom he had made attorney general. He didn't listen to him enough. That also changed, which was good, because RFK was smart, and he could be mean. The Devil sent RFK to be mean to people who weren't worried enough about hydrogen bombs.

THERE WERE OTHER problems besides the bombs.

Some people from the NAACP came to see JFK. They were black leaders from communities in the South, where black people didn't have the same rights as white people. They explained to the president that not everybody was inclined to be so damn happy about all the new consumer products, because they were worried about getting lynched.

The Devil knew about it already, of course. In recent years, though, black people had started doing something very interesting and impressive. They began boycotting things white people needed them to spend money on.

Even rednecks are smart enough to hate losing money.

The black leaders had new plans, too. They told JFK they were going to ride into Alabama on Trailways buses and do things black people weren't supposed, in Alabama, to do. Like eat at white lunch counters in the bus stations, and wait in white waiting rooms.

And the Devil thought: At last! They were rising up again, and this time they would strike hard enough to end slavery for real. Sometimes, the Devil knew, it took a little violence to get the ball of Justice rolling.

"We are committed to nonviolence," added the leaders.

If he had been listening closely, that would have caught the Devil's attention. But he was too busy congratulating himself for bringing America to this moment.

The Freedom Riders were going to need help. He picked up the phone and said, "Miss Lincoln, uh, get me RFK."

IT WAS SO, so, so terrible.

People thought the Freedom Rides were just about people going places they had been told not to go, but it was also about people getting beaten half to death while cops looked the other way.

Which was what happened in Alabama.

Klansmen set one of the Trailways buses on fire with half the people still in it. Those people got out, some badly burned, and the Devil couldn't believe it when they didn't fight back. He sank into his desk chair, and winced. JFK had a bad back. He took pills for it.

He picked up the phone.

"RFK," he said.

RFK didn't answer the phone. He came over to the White House in person.

He showed up in a limo with a famous black preacher called MLK. And the three of them went for a walk together around the south lawn of the White House, and MLK told JFK, "Love your enemies, Jack."

His voice was big and hot. He was not a tall man, but everyone who met him came away thinking he was.

It was a mild day on the south lawn. Two yellow birds spiraled by, chasing each other.

JFK said, "'Love your enemies' doesn't, ah, make sense, Martin. It's something only preachers can afford to believe in."

MLK told JFK, "You can't build a house with fire."

MLK took his time, in his long, slow, Sunday-morning way, telling JFK that how you made a thing was as important as the thing itself. And if you made a thing with violence, then that thing would be a violent thing. What a tragedy, then, if black people tried to make freedom out of violence, and enslaved themselves again with a violent freedom.

"I'd say, uh," said JFK, "a violent freedom is what you have now."

And MLK drilled him with hot prophet's eyes and said, "Exactly. It's not enough."

"Love can be a weapon, Jack," said RFK. He wasn't always mean.

"A tool," corrected MLK, turning to make his way back to the limo. RFK followed.

When they were gone, the Devil turned to look at the great white fang of the Washington Monument out on the Mall.

Was it possible? Had he underestimated people? Could they improve in ways beyond his own comprehension? The idea was exciting.

Sitting on a bench to keep his back from spasming, he only had a hunch that this nonviolence thing was as naturally a part of America as Gettysburg. That the hall of earthly fame would value nonviolence as much, if not more, than a man on the moon.

Weird.

A man on the moon, though. *There* was an idea he could understand.

He hurried back to make some notes, make some calls, and locate that sexy wife of his.

× × ×

WHEN KHRUSHCHEV MADE HIS MOVE and tried to set up rockets down in Cuba, JFK knew what was going on, and knew how to stop it.

Which was not the way his generals advised him.

"Hydrogen bombs on rockets!" they thundered. "Ninety miles off of Florida! There's no choice but to attack! Attack, attack!"

"And, uh, then what?" he asked them.

Then, the generals explained, one thing would lead to another, and Russia and America would launch hydrogen bombs at each other. But it was either that or be a big pussy.

JFK didn't take the bait. "We'll, ah, reconvene this afternoon," he said, "after we've examined, ah, some more options."

In the end, the problem was solved by a lot of quiet conversation instead of a war. It was one of the most reasonable moments in history.

The Devil was beside himself! This was America's Shining Moment! This was the combination of power and progress he had always wanted for the world. *His* world!

He meant to let JFK have his wife and his job and his body back after that, he really did. But it was too much fun to take the ball and run with it. Who could blame him?

He got up in front of Congress and dared the country to put a man on the moon. (Challenging God on His own high-and-mighty turf. See how He liked that!)

Then he took JFK's wife on a working vacation to Dallas, and was drop-kicked out of the president's head by a bullet.

For years, the Devil read that JFK's last words went something like this:

The first lady of Texas had just turned around in her seat, supposedly, and said, "You can't say Dallas doesn't love you, Mr. President!" to which he had replied, "No, you sure can't."

The Devil knew, although he kept it to himself, that in fact he had just turned to his own first lady and said, "Gee, Jackie, this sure is a swell car."

Then POW! The shining moment was over.

WHEN THE DEVIL WOKE UP again in the hospital room, Memory had fallen back asleep.

This alarmed him, at first. But her breathing was the breath of a woman taking a nap. The twitch of her eyes beneath her eyelids was lively.

She'd wake up again, soon enough.

But . . . Aw, hell, he wouldn't be here. Today was a workday. They were broadcasting the comeback episode of *Think It Over,* somewhere in Ohio.

He stood. Found his jacket. Ran his fingers over stubbled cheeks.

He'd be back that night. That would have to be soon enough.

Kissing Memory's forehead, he felt happiness and frustration at war inside him.

Memory was awake! Memory was Arden!

The thought of going to work made him feel mean as a snake.

A lot of people probably feel that way on days they're going to get shot.

44.

The World Without a Rebel Angel

Dayton, Ohio, 2005

THE DEVIL FLEW TO OHIO, where he met his TV crew at the Dayton airport. His heart and mind stayed behind with Memory. He saw her face on every woman-animal who walked by, even the trolls.

Then he saw something that sort of focused him.

Jenna Steele.

"Oh, fuck," said the Devil. *Please, not her, not right now!*

Jenna cracked her gum and stood on tiptoe to kiss him.

"Baby," she cooed at him, head buried against his tie. "Welcome back from jail!"

He didn't have the energy, he found, to turn her away. He was still so tired. So he turned and led the march out of the airport, and she came with, popping her gum.

What if she got on camera—she always got on camera—and Memory saw?

Shit shit shit, he thought, stalking past the ticket counters, out the revolving doors, into a waiting limo. What could he do about it, with everyone watching? He didn't want to be filmed with her, but he couldn't afford to make a scene either.

Jenna piled in beside him.

The crew was probably already filming. Those guys were *always* filming.

LATER, DURING PRIME TIME, a record-breaking audience watched John Scratch offer a loving couple a million dollars to split up. It was a terrible thing to do. He wasn't sure if he cared. He wanted to feel better about people, with Memory awake. With *Arden* back. But *did* he? Not yet. Maybe.

The woman took the money and broke her husband's heart.

It made people all over the world wonder if their wives and husbands loved them a million dollars' worth. The show caused a lot of arguments even before the second White Pill commercial was over.

Memory, watching, sitting up in bed, reached for the remote and turned the TV off.

"Asshole," she said.

HE HOPED THE ZOMBIES out in TV land at least learned a lot of hard, new truths, and he hoped they hurt. He was going to sit in his limo and smoke a bag of weed and think of all the reasons he had to be happy, and that was what the Devil was thinking when he saw Zachary Bull Horse step out of the crowd.

Zachary sort of bulldozed his way through. He sent a cameraman and an onlooker sprawling, and the Devil saw how strange and pale he looked.

"Big Zach," the Devil started to say.

Something was wrong.

The Devil saw the gun.

The gun flashed and banged six times, and he felt every bullet tear through him.

Good thing the limo was right there. He kind of fell into it.

He didn't see Zachary tangle with the bodyguards, but he sensed, as he lost consciousness and felt the limo peel out for the hospital, that the big genius had gotten away. And he was glad. He wanted that fucker for himself.

He coughed blood.

He hurt so bad.

He had never been the same, really, since Gettysburg.

Everything went dark.

THEN EVERYTHING GOT LIGHT again, and then dark again.

They kept having to explain to him that he'd been shot.

Dark again. Light again. Surgery. Dark again.

And in the twilight spaces between the light and dark, he knew he was dying. One of those slow, critical-condition deaths, with complications, where doctors said, "He's a fighter!" But every day you were weaker. You were losing blood, but from where?

And you weren't the tough old Devil you used to be, that much was certain. You were tired. When had you started getting tired? Was it just time? All that time? Was it knowing that you'd been wrong about practically everything for all that time?

Poor judgment became a theme, sleeping and waking. He had an attack of courage one day, and woke up and broke up with Jenna Steele, who shot him.

Great.

Dark again. Light again.

Was he tired because of Love? Loving thousands? Loving lots of women like Jenna Steele, but mostly loving someone who wasn't there?

SPEAKING OF LOVING SOMEONE who wasn't there, where was she?

Surely Memory had been released from her own hospital by now. Why wasn't she here?

He asked the nurses about her.

"Jenna?" asked the nurses.

"Not Jenna," said the Devil. "Memory Jones."

The nurses didn't like it when the Devil asked about Memory.

"Don't know," they said.

"Well"—he coughed—"could you find out?"

Grudgingly, they called the hospital in New York.

"She checked out," they told him. That was all they knew. She didn't seem to be on TV, or in the news.

Then some of the nurses texted their friends and told them Johnny Scratch had been asking about Memory. The All-Celebrity News Channel got wind of it and sent reporters.

"Call me!" the Devil bellowed at the cameras.

"Who?" asked the reporters, never looking away from their viewfinders. "Memory Jones or Jenna Steele?"

The Devil made a cruel face and said, "Jenna *who*?"

Wow! The meaner the better! They couldn't get that streaming fast enough.

"Jenna *who*?" flashed out on Web, cable, and satellite within the minute. Flashed all the way down the hall, where Jenna Steele lay lightly sedated in chemical restraints.

"Baby," she whispered, crying softly. "Oh, Johnny."

Jenna Steele was both smarter and sicker than a lot of people gave her credit for. That night, focusing through a blue-edged drug haze, she leaned out of her bed and reached, straining for her IV. With every ounce of strength and will available to her, she turned up the drip on her chemical restraint, and collapsed back into bed.

Black sleep came at her with an open throttle. She barely had time to arrange herself and make herself look good before it softly ran her down.

Bells rang and alarms buzzed, and nurses came. Doctors followed.

They poked and prodded and shined lights, and announced that Jenna Steele was alive, but would probably never wake up again.

The announcement flashed out. Millions mourned.

The Coma Channel staff, recently unemployed, found themselves employed again. They rushed across Manhattan to the hospital, charging batteries and dusting off hidden cameras.

Jenna Steele was way deep asleep, but by God she'd still be on-screen 24/7. Millions sighed with relief.

And was it just their imagination, or did they detect, in the on-screen stillness of their sleeping beauty, the dreamy hint of a smile?

THE DEVIL THOUGHT about Zachary, too.

Why? Why had he done it? Was he just protecting himself? Old-fashioned fear? A newfound sense of right and wrong? Didn't matter. You don't shoot the Devil, man. Why didn't people know that?

The Devil imagined eating Zachary, bones and all.

It made him feel better. At the same time, it brought the dark closer.

THE REAL DARK, when it finally came for him, wasn't dark at all.

It was light.

A *tunnel* of light, just like in the movies.

You've got to be shitting me, thought the Devil.

He felt himself racing up. Racing forward.

And there was a Light in the middle of the light, the brightest light of all, and it was holding out its bright hands, beaming at him with its eternal, smug-ass face.

NO WORDS WERE NECESSARY here. Never had been.

The Light reached inside him, and healed him. Took all his tiredness and uncertainty and petulance, and drained them like used oil.

Peace flooded him like an April breeze.

The Devil wept openly.

Was he forgiven? Could he come back?

He was forgiven. He could come back.

Oh God, he thought.

Behind him, all that horror and pettiness and savagery. So human, so animal.

Fun while it lasted.

The Great Light reached for him.

WHEN THE DEVIL'S MONITOR FLATLINED, the data went out to the nurses' station, and to each nurse's beeper. It went to the beepers and cell phones of at least four separate doctors, two life insurance heavies, and a stringer for the All-Celebrity News Channel.

Even before anyone got the news, the world was a little different. It happened the way subconscious things happen, down deep, showing up later in the way things look or the way things happen.

The world without its rebel angel would be a world where rebellion had run out of juice. It was a better world in some ways, and in some ways not.

It was a world that felt less connected to the things that make rebels in the first place, like appreciating things of quiet value. Like seeing the aurora borealis, flying over mountains, or remembering what it was like to be three. It took self-belief to be a rebel. From now on, that belief would be hard to find.

It was a world where people felt hollow. Where they watched TV more, then slept more in front of the TV. Where they worried less, which sounds nice until you consider that the dead don't worry. The dead don't blush or embarrass themselves. They don't eat things they shouldn't or refuse to go to bed on time. They don't call in sick when they're not. They aren't fascinated by firecrackers. They don't celebrate, because they don't accomplish anything.

The world without the Devil was a world without certain kinds of fun. The kind you keep to yourself, like if women's shoes excite you or you like to eat dirt. It would be a world where the urges were shallow and sleepy, where you wanted to go to Mars less, wanted to get in shape less, wanted to do it doggie-style less.

Left behind were the Devil's mistakes and the mess he'd made of things, here and there. Things like always being in a hurry. Things like living with a broken heart until the broken heart felt normal. His absence spread over them like a plague, everywhere over the whole Earth.

It would be a world with less shouting, less pushing back. Less pushing all the elevator buttons just because you could. It would be the kind of world where people didn't build pyramids or Empire State Buildings or cars that ran on old french fries.

It would be like a stagnant pond. The big fish would work themselves to death eating the little fish. It would be a world where the best you could hope was that maybe, just maybe, being eaten wouldn't hurt very much. It was a shitty kind of hope, the kind that made hope feel like a joke. But in a world without rebels, it would suffice, just because no one had the balls to imagine anything better.

HEAVEN, FOR THE DEVIL, was like walking into an old photo album.

Above, the exploding stars.

(*Let there be light!*)

Below, ankle-deep, the waters.

All around, circling, choir upon choir of divine music.

And he turned to the brightest of lights, walking beside him.

And he spoke with more peace and kindness in his voice than ever before.

He said, "No."

HIS HEART CRACKED like a hot rock when he said it, but he meant it.

Leave his Earth behind?

Even if it was stupid and hopeless and doomed to rut in its own blood, it was ten times better than *this*.

Heaven was the only conceivable thing *worse* than doom and stupidity.

It was peaceful, but it was the kind of peace that came with nothing ever changing.

The Light pulsed. It looked sort of disgusted, and turned away with its nose in the air.

The tunnel came and sucked the Devil up like a vacuum cleaner, sent him burning like a meteor back to Earth, back to his hospital bed in Ohio.

Beep, said the machine by his bed. *Beep. Beep.*

"Memory?" he rasped.

Silence.

45.

The Colony

Ohio, and then someplace deep in the woods, 2005

WHEN HE FELT STRONG ENOUGH, they let him go.

They wanted him to ride out in a wheelchair. He refused.

Two insurance thugs materialized, and explained that he could either ride in the chair like a good dog or they could strap him in with duct tape.

He wasn't feeling *that* strong, so he rode.

When he got to the door, he sniffed the air.

Hunting.

What he was hunting was a long way away. It took a while to catch the scent. Longer than it should have. He felt supernaturally limited. He also drew stares.

The Devil didn't usually like quick fixes, but he was in a hurry, and frustrated, so he waved his hand and made his limo appear at the curb before him.

Except it didn't.

He tried again. It was like turning the ignition on a dead battery.

What had happened to the strange, dark powers that came with being the Devil? They weren't gone, exactly, but they were faded. Was this the price of God's healing touch? Of falling back to Earth again? Was it like the electricity going out, and would it come back on?

He caught a bus north, out of town. North and east, until the concrete gave way to grass and fields, and then woods on either side.

From time to time he sniffed the air, making sure he still had the trail.

Either the trail was growing fainter, as trails do, or his sniffer was dying.

Maybe both.

IN A SMALL TOWN not far from the Massachusetts coast, he followed his nose off the bus. He sniffed the autumn air, which bit, the way New England autumn air does. The cold bothered him more than it should have, so he bought a toboggan cap at a thrift store before letting the trail take him out of town and into the woods.

It was Memory's trail, he realized. A smell like burning light and eternity. If he could find her, he would sleep in her arms until he was himself again, and they would live here together until the Earth itself was swallowed by the sun.

It was Zachary's trail, too.

Both trails made him tremble with anticipation. But why were they together?

Zachary's trail made sense. It went into hiding, into the woods.

Why did Memory have a trail at all? Why wasn't she with him now?

It felt better to concentrate on Zachary.

HE DID NOT hurry.

At sundown, he made a fire amid the roots of an old dead hickory, and watched an open spot between the branches, watched stars pass by.

Let there be light.

Lying there with his shirt open, scratching at his chest, he encountered bullet scars. Smooth and bowl-shaped, like moon craters.

He would cook Zachary Cajun-style, the Devil decided.

IN THE MORNING, he awoke to find an old woman standing over him. She had long gray hair and bright eyes, and leaned on a tall wooden cane.

"Morning, Devil," said the old woman.

He knew her, he realized.

It was Zachary's mother.

"Mrs. Bull Horse?" he said, clearing his throat, removing his hat. Something in her bearing commanded respect. Something about her was new, since she'd lived in Arizona with her crippled husband, her son, and a garage full of frozen dead people.

"Don't you 'Mrs. Bull Horse' me," she snapped. "I know why you're here, and you and I are going to make a deal before you walk another step. Or I can crack your head with this big goddamn stick, if you prefer."

The Devil might have been tired, and his Devil-batteries might have been dead, sometimes, but he still had his pride. He stood, and tried to tower.

"I've come for your son," he said, "And Memory Jones, too."

"All right," said Mrs. Bull Horse. "So you've come for them. It didn't take a genius to know you'd come for them."

"Are they with you? Take me to them."

Mrs. Bull Horse raised the mighty cane.

"Manners," she warned.

The Devil almost tore his hat in two.

"Please," he said. "Please take me to them."

"Maybe I will," she said. "It's not like you don't have reason to see them; it's not my place to say. We mind our own business here. They've agreed to see you, but you have to do something for us, first."

The hat came apart. "Who is 'we'?" asked the Devil. "And what do you mean, 'do something'?"

"'We' is the people I live with. 'Do something' is like singing for your supper. If you want something from us, you give something. It's an exchange. It's how things work."

The Devil tried to mash his hat back together, to grow it back into a hat, but it refused.

"I'll do it," he said. "What is it?"

"Dig a grave," said Mrs. Bull Horse, and for the first time he observed that her walking stick was not a walking stick at all, as such, but a sturdy shovel of hand-turned wood and hammered steel.

She tossed it to him.

He caught it, and followed her through the woods a ways, into a village right out of a fairy tale.

A WIDE, GRASSY ROAD passed between rows of stone houses. The village seemed to be built over the ruins of an older village, the Devil saw. Here and there, ruins broke through the earth like stone milk teeth.

The Devil, even at the worst of times, had a big mouth, and he talked about what he saw.

"Sure is quiet," he said. "Everyone must be at work."

"They are where they are," said Mrs. Bull Horse. "About their business, I suppose."

They passed the ancient remains of a church, with a cherry tree rooted amid the walls. They passed over a creek, where at last the Devil saw more people. Two men and two women with hand tools were rebuilding a fallen stone bridge.

"Devil," they said, and nodded.

"You don't have electricity," observed the Devil.

"We have it where it's needed."

They passed through trees again, and when the woods thinned out, they stood atop a hill. Weathered gravestones surfaced here and there, overgrown with tall grass and clinging weeds. The Devil saw the sea itself, cold and gray beyond the edge of a rocky cliff. He smelled the rankness of dead things washed up on stone and sand, the familiar funk which the land-bound say is the smell of the sea, but which sailors know is the smell of the shore.

And Mrs. Bull Horse, pulling her shawl tight with one hand, pointed at the ground with the other, and said, "Here."

The Devil let the shovel fall. The hand-forged blade bit weeds and dirt.

"Who is the grave for?" he asked.

"You don't need to know. You just need to dig."

And off she went, back downhill, among the trees.

THE DEVIL DUG.

Started to, anyhow.

It took exactly four times driving the shovel into the ground, driving it down with his boot heel, lifting it up and throwing the earth aside, for him to get awfully tired.

Four shovels of earth isn't much of a dent, he observed, taking a break.

A little later, he hit his first root. The root had to be chopped through, which took time and caused blisters.

Four shovels after that, he struck an old, submerged headstone, and had to start over, a few steps away.

That's how he spent the first hour.

This, he mused, feeling sorry for himself, was going to be a bitch. Digging holes wasn't easy to begin with, and graves were pretty big holes. Six feet down, three feet across, and they had to be nice and square, didn't they?

Devil paused, grabbing another dose of the ocean breeze, and scanning the land around him. On the inland side, beyond the village and the narrow wood, a pasture fell away toward the true forest. The grass was dotted, far away, with black-and-white cows.

The cows looked his way. They seemed glad to see him, and began to move uphill toward the cemetery.

It was good to know some things never changed, thought the Devil, and while he was thinking this, a large black cow interposed, causing the others to stop.

Not a cow. An enormous bull, shining like obsidian, hump like Mount Rushmore, neck like a tower, head like a Viking palace.

The bull snorted. The cows began grazing their way east again.

"That's Palestine," someone said.

The Devil turned to find Mrs. Bull Horse behind him, carrying a pitcher of water and a glass. "You'll want to keep an eye on him; he'll gore you to death quick as look at you. If he gets close, you want to get up a tree or down a hole. Speaking of which, it doesn't look as if there's much digging been done."

The Devil eyed the water pitcher, licking dry lips.

"Maybe it's too much for you," suggested Mrs. Bull Horse. "Maybe you need help."

Proud disdain flooded the Devil's features.

"Fair enough," said Mrs. Bull Horse. She left the pitcher sitting in the grass, and walked off through the trees.

The bull, the Devil noticed, downing the whole pitcher at one swallow, had come the slightest bit closer in the meantime. Hadn't he?

The thought lent him new strength as he addressed himself again to the grave.

HE SHOVELED for twenty minutes without stopping, just to see if he could.

New blood made the shovel handle sticky and brown. Blisters formed and burst—and didn't *that* hurt like a bastard—but he didn't stop until the grass had risen waist-deep around him, and he was about to lean on his shovel and see if maybe he couldn't raise enough magic to fill the water pitcher, and maybe some cheese and Oreos, when a rustling in the grass behind made him turn with a muffled cry—

Dread Palestine!

—but it wasn't Palestine, it was Memory, carrying water and some apples.

"Oh," he said.

He tried to lean on the shovel in a handsome, workman kind of way.

She looked better, considering the last time he'd seen her, she had just come out of a long coma. Her long, flaxen hair looked healthy again. So did her mystical eyes. She wore the simplest of homespun dresses, with a shawl, and some kind of wooden pendant on a leather string around her neck.

"You haven't gotten very far," she said, bending to hand him the water and apples. The Devil took a long swallow and ate half an apple with one bite. Then he turned and got back to work, saying, "Interesting place."

"I suppose it is," she answered, sitting down cross-legged at the edge of the grave.

"You like it?"

"I do."

"How come?"

She was quiet for a long time. He threw out nine loads of earth, waiting, careful not to hit her.

"They're doing what you've been trying to get people to do for five thousand years, baby. They're building a place where people can live together."

"I've done that. I've gotten people to do it."

"That's fine, but these people are doing it on their own, so far. They're not trying to build Rome or anything. They're just trying to build this one small place. The place where they live. And that's all."

The ocean breeze came on a little stronger. Maybe a little colder, a late-afternoon chill.

"I feel at home here," she said, standing and turning to go.

But she stopped.

With her back to him, she asked: "What do you want with Zachary?"

He kept digging.

"Why?" he asked. "Are you protecting him?"

"I was. I brought him here. After he shot you, I was afraid for him."

He stopped shoveling.

"And now?"

She still faced away from him.

She said, "You can't really protect another person. Not forever. You can help people, but in the end they have to take up for themselves." Her voice shook. "You have to trust people to stand on their own, and hope for the best."

"So," he said, "now—"

"Now it's up to you."

HE WORKED IN A TRANCE, after that. Conserved his water. Stopped now and then to stretch and eat an apple.

The sun reddened. The grave made its own shadow, which leaned on him as he gouged out the last foot of earth, bled and broke the fifth generation of blisters on his numb hands, and finally came to rest after using the blade to square off the edges all around, and even stamp the bottom flat, make the raw earth as tidy as raw earth could be.

And damned if he wasn't proud of it.

Pride again, but this time, well, dammit, he had a right, didn't he? It wasn't the first time he'd made something with his hands, but it was the hardest he'd ever worked, outside of battle or the bedroom. It was a fine grave he'd dug, if he said so himself.

He took a deep breath, and as he did, he heard footsteps above. A rustling in the grass. His pride surged again, and he sat up, eager to show off his work.

Except the figure that appeared at the lip of the grave bore a head as proud as the Devil's. Palestine.

He blotted out the dusk, darkening the hole. He snorted a great snort, which caused its own weather, was deafening, and moistened the Devil to an uncomfortable degree.

The Devil sat there, trying to magic Palestine back to the bottom of the hill, back among the cows. But the bull remained, and so the Devil remained, and remained seated.

Maybe he could scare the bull away.

It was just a bull, after all. And he was still the Devil, wasn't he?

So he jumped up and screamed a satanic scream, which only galvanized Palestine and made him lurch around the perimeter of the grave, roaring and scooping around murderously with his horns. Before the bull settled down, it was a little darker, and the Devil had bull drool in his hair.

× × ×

WAS HE GONE?

"Palestine?" said the Devil, after some time had passed.

Maybe he'd gone away.

But no . . . here was a snort, and a sound of bull flesh rising to its feet, and momentarily the awesome head appeared high above, actively salivating.

"Who's a nice bull?" said the Devil, trying a different tack. "Who's a nice, good bull?"

You wouldn't believe how much madder this made the bull. He bellowed with rage, and started looking for a way to climb down into the grave.

The Devil's pride fled.

"HELP!" screamed the Devil.

He wasn't supernaturally loud, but he hoped it might be enough. Enough to reach downhill, through the trees to the village.

Palestine got down on his forelegs and hooked his left horn—the nastier, sharper, more jagged of the two—deep into the earth an inch above the Devil's head.

The Devil's next scream sounded much more like a little girl. Even Palestine paused for a second, before resuming his attack, madder, as always, than before.

The sun balanced on the horizon. Red light tinged the bull's horns.

Then Palestine raised his Viking head as if something had caught his attention.

The Devil heard something. Didn't he?

Was it voices?

"Help!" he called, with urgency, but with dignity, too, this time. Not pride. Dignity. There's a difference.

And voices answered. There was a sort of general murmur and hustle, as of voices talking and bodies climbing uphill between trees, snapping twigs and moving branches aside.

Flash beams played about Palestine's head.

The bull seemed to consider things and weigh choices, and then he withdrew, head high, dignified, downhill.

Rising, as it were, from his grave, the Devil noted that some of the cows remained at the foot of the pasture, while others had wandered off along the cliff's edge around the village perimeter. They grazed there, silhouetted against an explosive sunset.

Hoisting himself onto grass, the Devil found himself half surrounded by people in work clothes. All sorts of people. People with beards. Women. Kids. People with hats. Black people. People with bright eyes. Suspicious-looking people. White people. People with jewelry on. People with tattoos. Even people with cell phones, which surprised him.

Front and center, three men and three women carried a hot-water heater.

The hot-water heater was familiar. So was one of the men carrying it.

Zachary.

Zachary didn't look at the Devil. His face was strained and busy. "To the right a bit," he grunted. "Little bit more, gang. Watch your step."

Ropes were stretched across the grave. Someone told the Devil, "You're gonna wanna scoot, fella," and he backpedaled, hands in his pockets.

The pallbearers lowered the water heater onto the ropes, and the ropes were slackened an inch at a time until it rested on the bottom.

One by one, then, they all began to come forward and drop a shovel of earth into the grave.

Someone touched the Devil's arm.

Memory.

"Nice grave," she said.

"Thanks," said the Devil. But even though she was there, and he liked the way she wrapped both of her arms around his and huddled close, his mind was elsewhere.

For the moment, his mind was on the figures around him, visible by the last of the bloody sun, by flashlight here or lantern light there. Doing what needed to be done, bit by bit. Without words. Without pettiness. And he realized that these were, in fact, humans. Not animals, so much.

It seemed there were, in fact, some animals who had taken the next evolutionary step. If they were here, they were elsewhere, too.

He discovered Zachary looking at him over the half-filled grave.

And Zachary said, "I'm sorry."

The Devil thought about self-control. Thought about saying it was all right, it was a hard world and sometimes you got shot, but he didn't.

"You fucking *should* be sorry!" he barked. "I almost died!"

"I was scared."

"You should *still* be scared!"

He was. You could tell. But he stood there, his whole enormous frame shaking, waiting to see what the Devil would do. He didn't run.

The Devil looked down into his nice, neat grave, where the last of the water heater had vanished beneath the parade of falling earth. Even now, with danger and rage in the air, the villagers came forward one by one and did what needed doing.

The one exception was Mrs. Bull Horse, who stood quietly, almost out of sight, at the edge of the trees, waiting.

Pointing down into the earth, the Devil said, "April Michael?"

Zachary quietly said, "Yes. She would have been thirty-three next week."

"Or still four," said Memory, "depending how you look at it."

"What about her dad?" asked the Devil.

"Gone," said Zachary. "Last year. Stroke."

"I'm sorry," said the Devil, indicating the grave.

Zachary shook his head.

"It's the way it should have been in the first place," he said. "Things run their course, and then they end. Other things start. Some things aren't complicated. Birth and death aren't complicated."

"You had a deal with her father," said the Devil, a little harshly. "You promised him."

"And a deal or a promise is only good as long as it's really useful, don't you think?"

"Is that a dig?"

"If it is, you deserve it."

"Okay," said the Devil. If it was going to be about who deserved what, then so be it. And he leaped over April Michael's grave, grabbed Zachary's arm, and bit him good and deep before anyone knew what was happening.

EVEN THEN, they didn't interfere.

Except Zachary's mom, who grabbed the shovel and poked at the Devil until he turned her son loose, which, momentarily, he did.

The Devil, spitting blood and looking grim, managed to offer her a respectful bow.

He would have winked, too, just to be the Devil, but she wouldn't have appreciated it, and she still had the shovel.

Zachary sat on the grass, fighting tears and pain, cradling his forearm.

"Happy?" he asked the Devil.

"Happi-*er,*" the Devil answered.

"What *was* that? You *bit* me! What's that supposed to accomplish?"

"Maybe nothing," said the Devil. "Maybe a lot. When's the next full moon?"

He walked away, and they left it at that.

HE FELT STRONGER, maybe.

Did he? It was hard to tell. He walked alone to the edge of the cliff, and stood there looking out over the sea, the great night sea, the most mysterious thing in the world.

He breathed in.

Maybe it was the sea air, the night air. He *did* feel stronger. For now.

Maybe later he'd try to make it rain.

He breathed out.

Memory slipped up beside him again, and handed him a mug of steaming coffee. She had thrown on a cable-knit sweater big enough for Palestine the bull, and some kind of shapeless New England hat.

In one hand, she held her own mug. Her free hand hooked around his elbow.

"Thanks," he said.

And his free arm slipped around her waist.

His hand crept inside the great sweater, to the slightest of swellings below her belly.

She let his hand rest there.

And he knew.

She knew he knew.

Below them, the sea roared its dark roar.

Behind them, in a hundred windows, candles appeared. A bonfire blazed and figures crowded around. There were smaller fires, too, with smaller crowds, or couples.

Humans.

The Devil thought about moon rockets and Rome and the hat he'd torn in two that afternoon.

He had lost control of it all, for sure.

Maybe he'd just let these humans have it. Let it happen.

"Let *them* happen," he said, aloud.

And the great thing about Memory and having her there was that she knew exactly what the Hell he was talking about.

Behind them in the dark, suddenly, great shadows moved.

Five of them. Heavy, ponderous shapes. They moved closer.

Memory's hand tightened on his elbow.

"It's just cows," said the Devil.

The cows approached with an old, familiar look in their eye, and he wondered if things were going to become awkward.

"Cows love me," he explained.

ACKNOWLEDGMENTS

This book wouldn't have happened if three extremely smart and adventurous women had not gotten behind it and pushed hard: Huge thanks to my wife and friend, writer Janine Harrison, for her support, patience, and famous red pen. To my agent, Michelle Brower, at Folio and my editor at Ecco, Abigail Holstein. Michelle sold Abby on the story. Abby brought Ecco on board, and then helped me turn a stack of insanity into a book. Thanks, Janine, Michelle, Abby. I bow to you.

My thanks to Mark Mirsky and Andrew Lieb at *Fiction* for publishing "The Fires of Krypton," the experimental short story which served, partly, as the genesis of this book. My thanks to Dad for the enthusiasm he has always, *always* shown, and for taking me up to the Superstitions, some years ago, to explore and hunt for stories and to stay in the room where Elvis slept. To Barbara and to Cavell, who have been energetic supporters. To my stepdaughter, Jianna, a boundless source of energy and wonder. Thanks to Mindy, Todd, Missy, Meri, Steve, Shannon, Britt, Logan, Reagan, Jack, and Charlie. Thanks, as always, to Mom and Bill, without whom . . . And to Steven. Wish you were here. To John Gibbons, who taught my first creative writing class, and to Marlene Hannah at Troy High, who made it clear that history was both real and, at the same time, a story. And to Nancy Yarger, who encouraged my writing despite the fact that I did it to the exclusion of my math homework. Thanks to my friend, poet James Hill, for his support and good eye for the best part of twenty years. The same to writer Rachel Mork, my tireless cheerleader, and to Michael and Cynthia Passafiume. Thanks to my friend and collaborator, science fiction writer Ted Kosmatka, for his support and energy, and for getting us started on "Blood Dauber" (he wrote all the smart stuff). Thanks to the Highland Writers' Group, Indiana Writers' Consortium, and other Indiana writers, particularly Kenneth Alexander, Kara Dokupil, Cynthia Echterling, Karen Eldred, Dorothy Emry, Katherine Page Camp, Larry Ginensky, Sharon Ginensky, Michael Gonzalez, Holly Granzow, Scott Guffy, Chad Hunter, Zach Heridia, Jack Kus, Jeff Manes, Rachel Miller, Catherine Osborne, Joshua Perz, Angella Pierce, Harry Pierce, Sunila Samuel, Maureen Smith, Gordon Stamper, Heather Stamper, Micah Urban, and Mary Tina Vrehas. Thanks, and a bottle of Vietnamese cobra wine, to Daniel Wallace, for his support and good humor. Thanks to Amanda LaFleur, coordinator of Cajun Studies at Louisiana State University, for her excellent translation assistance at the eleventh hour. Special thanks to the Mean Group: Ted, MT, and Josh. Big time thanks to all my McKinley family, especially Merielene, Ayanna, Angel, Casey, Anitra, Carlos, and Michelle, for their enthusiasm and support. Best wishes and thanks to everybody at Borders: Shaun Victor, Elaine, Jessica, Nikky, and Jimmy, for always sometimes sort of making sure my table was available. Not at all least, my thanks to Jake, Reggie, Buzz, Samantha, China, and Baloo. It's a poor writer who isn't grateful to his dogs.